THE CROSSING

'Two teenage boys cross from the south-west of America into
Mexico, on horseback. In so doing they cross a temporal frontier
and find themselves in the world of the vanished American West
where blood, violence and dying are conditions of living . . . Once
again he sets off on those vista sentences that warp and shimmer
and acknowledge no grammatical horizon other than their own
eventual resolution . . . What *The Crossing* demonstrates most
powerfully is the long reach of human kindness . . . McCarthy
must remain a self-elected outcast or, as an old man in the book
says, a "*huerfano*" (literally, orphan); "He said that . . . he contained
within him a largeness of spirit which men could see and that men
would wish to know him and that the world would need him as he
needed the world for they were one." Yes' – Geoff Dyer, *Guardian*

'To readers who get caught in McCarthy's spell, his sonorous
passages become part of the storm system – dark, brooding clouds
. . . What makes Cormac McCarthy an undismissable writer is the
authority he brings to the best stretches of *All the Pretty Horses* and
The Crossing . . . He doesn't indulge in irony or trickery or self-
referential striptease; he has an old-fashioned calling of the writer
as truth-bearer . . . McCarthy's determination to go his own way
deserves admiration, and his descriptive firepower commands
awe. He can make the death of a horse as vivid an agony as any
painting by Goya. As in Goya's canvases, McCarthy's victims
contort as if they're drowning in air' – James Wolcott, *Observer*

'There are great moments and wonderful descriptions that quite
startle you . . . It's a sad book, really recording the vastness of
a world that will never be the same' – Henry Sutton, *European*

'The best writers create their own landscapes. Cormac McCarthy's turf is the unforgiving range of hardscrabble mountains and desolate prairie on either side of the Mexican/United States' border . . . Billy, the elder brother at sixteen, traps a she-wolf that has been plundering local cattle . . . His description of the wolf may be the best piece of animal writing since Jack London . . . McCarthy is the master of imagery that can be at once beautiful and harrowing . . . characterized by individual moments of genius' – Stephen Amidon, *Literary Review*

'How does a writer like Cormac McCarthy – if there is any writer like Cormac McCarthy – follow up on the immense critical and popular success of his novel *All The Pretty Horses*? . . . The answer is that he writes an even better book . . . *The Crossing* is a miracle in prose, it deserves to sit on the same shelf certainly as *Beloved* and *As I Lay Dying* . . . McCarthy is a great and inventive storyteller, and he writes brilliantly and knowledgeably about animals and landscapes – but finally the power and delight of the book derive from the fact that he seems incapable of writing a boring sentence . . . *The Crossing* [is] a masterwork. And most interesting of all, Mr McCarthy is not through yet. We can await the conclusion of the Border Trilogy' – Robert Hass, *New York Times Book Review*

'In the wind-blown wastes of the desert prairie, Cormac McCarthy is on an endless quest for the great American novel and refrains his *All the Pretty Horses* with a fresh literary bout of horseback journeyings by the last cowboys. Not an easy read, but intellectually rewarding for its haunting inner and outer landscape' – *Daily Mail*

'It's a book full of quick dialogue and sparse description, but its austere informality can be beautiful, and the pace is compelling' – *Elle*

'[*The Crossing*] is the book everyone will be talking about . . . It does for the lupine what its precursor [*All the Pretty Horses*] did for the equine. The former made you want to saddle up and head for the hills, and this makes you long to dance with wolves. A brilliant and painful book' – *Tatler*

'Whether writing of the minutiae of the setting of a trap, evoking a landscape, or intimating characters' feelings, McCarthy achieves a sense of realism and universality with an almost mythical resonance . . . The prose here is bare-boned but lyric, reflecting the world it is employed to evoke entirely vindicating comparisons with Joyce, and especially William Faulkner' – *Impact*

CORMAC McCARTHY lives in El Paso, Texas. *The Crossing* is his seventh novel and the second book in The Border Trilogy. His earlier novels, *The Orchard Keeper, Outer Dark, Child of God, Suttree, Blood Meridian* and *All the Pretty Horses*, are all available in Picador.

THE
CROSSING

Cormac McCarthy

Volume Two
The Border Trilogy

PICADOR

First published 1994 as a Borzoi Book by Alfred A. Knopf, Inc., New York,
and simultaneously in Canada by Random House of Canada Ltd., Toronto

First published in Great Britain 1994 by Picador

This edition published 1995 by Picador
an imprint of Macmillan General Books
Cavaye Place London SW10 9PG
and Basingstoke

Associated companies throughout the world

ISBN 0 330 34121 9

1 3 5 7 9 8 6 4 2

A CIP catalogue record for this book is available from
the British Library.

Printed and bound in Great Britain by
Cox & Wyman Ltd, Reading, Berkshire

I

WHEN THEY CAME SOUTH out of Grant County Boyd was not much more than a baby and the newly formed county they'd named Hidalgo was itself little older than the child. In the country they'd quit lay the bones of a sister and the bones of his maternal grandmother. The new country was rich and wild. You could ride clear to Mexico and not strike a crossfence. He carried Boyd before him in the bow of the saddle and named to him features of the landscape and birds and animals in both spanish and english. In the new house they slept in the room off the kitchen and he would lie awake at night and listen to his brother's breathing in the dark and he would whisper half aloud to him as he slept his plans for them and the life they would have.

On a winter's night in that first year he woke to hear wolves in the low hills to the west of the house and he knew that they would be coming out onto the plain in the new snow to run the antelope in the moonlight. He pulled his breeches off the footboard of the bed and got his shirt and his blanketlined duckingcoat and got his boots from under the bed and went out to the kitchen and dressed in the dark by the faint warmth of the stove and held the boots to the windowlight to pair them left and right and pulled them on and rose and went to the kitchen door and stepped out and closed the door behind him.

When he passed the barn the horses whimpered softly to him in the cold. The snow creaked under his boots and his breath smoked in the bluish light. An hour later he was crouched in the snow in the dry creekbed where he knew the wolves had been using by their tracks in the sand of the washes, by their tracks in the snow.

They were already out on the plain and when he crossed the gravel fan where the creek ran south into the valley he could see where they'd crossed before him. He went forward on knees and elbows with his hands pulled back into his sleeves to keep them out of the snow and when he reached the last of the small dark juniper trees where the broad valley ran under the Animas Peaks he crouched quietly to steady his breath and then raised himself slowly and looked out.

They were running on the plain harrying the antelope and the antelope moved like phantoms in the snow and circled and wheeled and the dry powder blew about them in the cold moonlight and their breath smoked palely in the cold as if they burned with some inner fire and the wolves twisted and turned and leapt in a silence such that they seemed of another world entire. They moved down the valley and turned and moved far out on the plain until they were the smallest of figures in that dim whiteness and then they disappeared.

He was very cold. He waited. It was very still. He could see by his breath how the wind lay and he watched his breath appear and vanish and appear and vanish constantly before him in the cold and he waited a long time. Then he saw them coming. Loping and twisting. Dancing. Tunneling their noses in the snow. Loping and running and rising by twos in a standing dance and running on again.

There were seven of them and they passed within twenty feet of where he lay. He could see their almond eyes in the moonlight. He could hear their breath. He could feel the presence of their knowing that was electric in the air. They bunched and nuzzled and licked one another. Then they stopped. They stood with their ears cocked. Some with one forefoot raised to their chest. They were looking at him. He did not breathe. They did not breathe. They stood. Then they turned and quietly trotted

on. When he got back to the house Boyd was awake but he
didnt tell him where he'd been nor what he'd seen. He never
told anybody.

The winter that Boyd turned fourteen the trees inhabiting
the dry river bed were bare from early on and the sky was gray
day after day and the trees were pale against it. A cold wind
had come down from the north with the earth running under
bare poles toward a reckoning whose ledgers would be drawn
up and dated only long after all due claims had passed, such is
this history. Among the pale cottonwoods with their limbs like
bones and their trunks sloughing off the pale or green or darker
bark clustered in the outer bend of the river bed below the house
stood trees so massive that in the stand across the river was a
sawed stump upon which in winters past herders had pitched a
four by six foot canvas supply tent for the wooden floor it gave.
Riding out for wood he watched his shadow and the shadow of
the horse and travois cross those palings tree by tree. Boyd rode
in the travois holding the axe as if he'd keep guard over the wood
they'd gathered and he watched to the west with squinted eyes
where the sun simmered in a dry red lake under the barren
mountains and the antelope stepped and nodded among the
cattle in silhouette upon the foreland plain.

They crossed through the dried leaves in the river bed and
rode till they came to a tank or pothole in the river and he
dismounted and watered the horse while Boyd walked the shore
looking for muskrat sign. The indian Boyd passed crouching on
his heels did not even raise his eyes so that when he sensed him
there and turned the indian was looking at his belt and did not
lift his eyes even then until he'd stopped altogether. He could
have reached and touched him. The indian squatting under a
thin stand of carrizo cane and not even hidden and yet Boyd
had not seen him. He was holding across his knees an old
singleshot 32 rimfire rifle and he had been waiting in the dusk
for something to come to water for him to kill. He looked into
the eyes of the boy. The boy into his. Eyes so dark they seemed

all pupil. Eyes in which the sun was setting. In which the child stood beside the sun.

He had not known that you could see yourself in others' eyes nor see therein such things as suns. He stood twinned in those dark wells with hair so pale, so thin and strange, the selfsame child. As if it were some cognate child to him that had been lost who now stood windowed away in another world where the red sun sank eternally. As if it were a maze where these orphans of his heart had miswandered in their journey in life and so arrived at last beyond the wall of that antique gaze from whence there could be no way back forever.

From where he stood he could not see his brother or the horse. He could see the slow rings moving out over the water where the horse stood drinking beyond the stand of cane and he could see the slight flex of the muscle beneath the skin of the indian's lean and hairless jaw.

The indian turned and looked at the tank. The only sound was the dripping of water from the horse's raised muzzle. He looked at the boy.

You little son of a bitch, he said.

I aint done nothin.

Who's that with you?

My brother.

How old's he?

Sixteen.

The indian stood up. He stood immediately and without effort and looked across the tank where Billy stood holding the horse and then he looked at Boyd again. He wore an old tattered blanketcoat and an old greasy Stetson with the crown belled out and his boots were mended with wire.

What are you all doin out here?

Gettin wood.

You got anything to eat?

No.

Where you live at?

The boy hesitated.

I asked you where you lived at.

He gestured downriver.

How far?

I dont know.

You little son of a bitch.

He put the rifle over his shoulder and walked out down the shore of the tank and stood looking across at the horse and at Billy.

Howdy, said Billy.

The indian spat. Spooked everthing in the country, aint you? he said.

We didnt know there was anybody here.

You aint got nothin to eat?

No sir.

Where you live at?

About two miles down the river.

You got anything to eat at your house?

Yessir.

I come down there you goin to bring me somethin out?

You can come to the house. Mama'll feed you.

I dont want to come to the house. I want you to bring me somethin out.

All right.

You goin to bring me somethin out?

Yes.

All right then.

The boy stood holding the horse. The horse hadnt taken its eyes from the indian. Boyd, he said. Come on.

You got dogs down there?

Just one.

You goin to put him up?

All right. I'll put him up.

You put him up inside somewheres where he wont be barkin.

All right.

I aint comin down there to get shot.

I'll put him up.

All right then.

Boyd. Come on. Let's go.

Boyd stood on the far side of the tank looking at him.

Come on. It'll be dark here in just a little bit.

Go on and do like your brother says, said the indian.

We wasnt botherin you.

Come on, Boyd. Let's go.

He crossed the gravel bar and climbed into the travois.

Get up here, said Billy.

He climbed out of the pile of limbs they'd gathered and looked back at the indian and then reached and took the hand that Billy held down and swung up behind him onto the horse.

How will we find you? said Billy.

The indian was standing with the rifle across his shoulders, his hands hanging over it. You come out you walk towards the moon, he said.

What if it aint up yet?

The indian spat. You think I'd tell you to walk towards a moon that wasnt there? Go on now.

The boy booted the horse forward and they rode out through the trees. The travois poles dragging up small wind-rows of dead leaves with a dry whisper. The sun low in the west. The indian watched them go. The younger boy rode with one arm around his brother's waist, his face red in the sun, his near-white hair pink in the sun. His brother must have told him not to look back because he didnt look back. By the time they'd crossed through the dry bed of the river and ridden up onto the plain the sun was already behind the peaks of the Peloncillo Mountains to the west and the western sky was a deep red under the reefs of cloud. They set out south along the dry river breaks and when Billy looked back the indian was coming along a half mile behind them in the dusk carrying the rifle loosely in one hand.

How come you're lookin back? said Boyd.

I just am.

Are we goin to carry him some supper?

Yes. We can do that I reckon.

Everthing you can do it dont mean it's a good idea, said Boyd.

I know it.

HE WATCHED the night sky through the front room window. The earliest stars coined out of the dark coping to the south hanging in the dead wickerwork of the trees along the river. The light of the unrisen moon lying in a sulphur haze over the valley to the east. He watched while the light ran out along the edges of the desert prairie and the dome of the moon rose out of the ground white and fat and membranous. Then he climbed down from the chair where he'd been kneeling and went to get his brother.

Billy had steak and biscuits and a tin cup of beans wrapped in a cloth and hidden behind the crocks on the pantry shelf by the kitchen door. He sent Boyd first and stood listening and then followed him out. The dog whined and scratched at the smokehouse door when they passed it and he told the dog to hush and it did. They went on at a low crouch along the fence and then made their way down to the trees. When they reached the river the moon was well up and the indian was standing there with the rifle yokewise across his neck again. They could see his breath in the cold. He turned and they followed him out across the gravel wash and took the cattletrail on the far side downriver along the edge of the pasture. There was woodsmoke in the air. A quarter mile below the house they reached his campfire among the cottonwoods and he stood the rifle against the bole of one of the trees and turned and looked at them.

Bring it here, he said.

Billy crossed to the fire and took the bundle from the crook of his arm and handed it up. The indian took it and squatted before the fire with that same marionette's effortlessness and set the cloth on the ground before him and opened it and lifted out the beans and set the cup by the coals to warm and then took up one of the biscuits and steak and bit into it.

You'll black that cup, Billy said. I got to take it back to the house.

The indian chewed, his dark eyes half closed in the firelight. Aint you got no coffee at your house, he said.

It aint ground.

You cant grind some?

Not without somebody hearin it I caint.

The indian put the second half of the biscuit in his mouth and leaned slightly forward and produced a beltknife from somewhere about his person and reached and stirred the beans in the cup with it and then looked up at Billy and ran the blade along his tongue one side and then the other in a slow stropping motion and jammed the knife in the end of the log against which the fire was laid.

How long you live here, he said.

Ten years.

Ten years. Your family own this place?

No.

He reached and picked up the second biscuit and severed it with his square white teeth and sat chewing.

Where are you from? said Billy.

From all over.

Where you headed?

The indian leaned and took the knife from the log and stirred the beans again and licked the blade again and then slipped the knife through the handle and lifted the blackened cup from the fire and set it on the ground in front of him and began to eat the beans with the knife.

What else you got in the house?

Sir?

I said what else you got in the house.

He raised his head and regarded them standing there in the firelight, chewing slowly, his eyes half closed.

Such as what?

Such as anything. Somethin maybe I can sell.

We aint got nothin.

You aint got nothin.

No sir.

He chewed.

You live in a empty house?

No.

Then you got somethin.

There's furniture and stuff. Kitchen stuff.

You got any rifleshells?

Yessir. Some.

What caliber?

They wont fit your rifle.

What caliber.

Forty-four forty.

Why dont you bring me some of them.

The boy nodded toward the rifle standing against the tree.
That aint a forty-four caliber.

Dont make no difference. I can trade em.

I caint bring you no rifleshells. The old man'd miss em.

Then what'd you say anything about em for?

We better go, said Boyd.

We got to take the cup back.

What else you got? said the indian.

We aint got nothin, said Boyd.

I wasnt askin you. What else you got?

I dont know. I'll see what I can find.

The indian put the other half of the second biscuit in his
mouth. He reached down and tested the cup with his fingers
and picked it up and drained the remaining beans into his open
mouth and ran one finger around the inside of the cup and licked
his finger clean and set the cup on the ground again.

Bring me some of that coffee, he said.

I caint grind it they'll hear it.

Just bring it. I'll bust it with a rock.

All right.

Let him stay here.

What for?

Keep me company.

Keep you company.

Yeah.

He dont need to stay here.

I aint goin to hurt him.

I know you aint. Cause he aint stayin.

The indian sucked his teeth. You got any traps?

We aint got no traps.

He looked up at them. He sucked his teeth with a hissing sound. Go on then, he said. Bring me some sugar.

All right. Let me have the cup.

You can get it when you come back.

When they reached the cattlepath Billy looked back at Boyd and he looked back at the firelight among the trees. Out on the plain the moon was so bright you could count the cattle by it.

We aint takin him no coffee are we? said Boyd.

No.

What are we goin to do about the cup?

Nothin.

What if Mama asks about it?

Just tell her the truth. Tell her I give it to a indian. Tell her a indian come to the house and I give it to him.

All right.

I can be in trouble along with you.

And I can be in more trouble.

Tell her I done it.

I aim to.

They crossed the open ground toward the fence and the lights from the house.

We ought not to of gone out there to start with, Boyd said.

Billy didnt answer.

Ought we.

No.

Why did we?

I dont know.

It was still dark in the morning when their father came into their room.

Billy, he said.

The boy sat upright in the bed and looked at his father standing framed in the light from the kitchen.

What is the dog doin locked in the smokehouse?

I forgot to let him out.

You forgot to let him out?

Yessir.

What was he doin in there in the first place?

He swung out of the bed onto the cold floor and reached for his clothes. I'll let him out, he said.

His father stood in the door a moment and then went back out through the kitchen and down the hall. In the light from the open door Billy could see Boyd crumpled asleep in the other bed. He pulled on his trousers and picked up his boots off the floor and went out.

By the time he'd fed and watered it was daylight and he saddled Bird and mounted up and rode out of the barn bay and down to the river to look for the indian or to see if he was still there. The dog followed at the horse's heels. They crossed the pasture and rode downriver and crossed through the trees. He pulled up and he sat the horse. The dog stood beside him testing the air with quick lifting motions of its muzzle, sorting and assembling some picture of the prior night's events. The boy put the horse forward again.

When he rode into the indian's camp the fire was cold and black. The horse shifted and stepped nervously and the dog circled the dead ashes with its nose to the ground and the hackles standing along its back.

When he got back to the house his mother had breakfast ready and he hung his hat and pulled up a chair and began to spoon eggs onto his plate. Boyd was already eating.

Where's Pap? he said.

Dont you even breathe the steam and you aint said grace, his mother said.

Yes mam.

He lowered his head and said the words to himself and then reached for a biscuit.

Where's Pap.

He's in the bed. He's done ate.

What time did he get in.

About two hours ago. He rode all night.

How come?

I reckon cause he wanted to get home.

How long is he goin to sleep?

Well I guess till he wakes up. You ask more questions than Boyd.

I aint asked the first one, Boyd said.

They went out to the barn after breakfast. Where do you reckon he's got to? said Boyd.

He's moved on.

Where do you reckon he come from?

I dont know. Them was mexican boots he was wearin. What was left of em. He's just a drifter.

You dont know what a indian's liable to do, said Boyd.

What do you know about indians, said Billy.

Well you dont.

You dont know what anybody's liable to do.

Boyd took an old worn screwdriver from a bucket of tools and brushes hanging from the barn post and he took a rope halter off the hitchrail and opened the stall door where he kept his horse and went in and haltered the horse and led it out. He halfhitched the rope to the rail and ran his hand down the animal's foreleg for it to offer its hoof and he cleaned out the frog of the hoof and examined it and then let it back down.

Let me look at it, said Billy.

There aint nothin wrong with it.

Let me look at it then.

Go ahead then.

Billy pulled the horse's hoof up and cupped it between his knees and studied it. I guess it looks all right, he said.

I said it did.

Walk him around.

Boyd unhitched the rope and led the horse down the barn bay and back.

You goin to get your saddle? said Billy.

Well I guess I will if that's all right with you.

He brought the saddle from the saddleroom and threw the blanket over the horse and labored up with the saddle and rocked it into place and pulled up the latigo and fastened the backcinch and stood waiting.

You've let him get in the habit of that, said Billy. Why dont you just punch the air out of him.

He dont knock the air out of me, I dont knock it out of him, Boyd said.

Billy spat into the dry chaff in the floor of the bay. They waited. The horse breathed out. Boyd pulled the strap and buckled it.

They rode the Ibañez pasture all morning studying the cows. The cows stood their distance and studied them back, a leggy and brocklefaced lot, part mexican, some longhorn, every color. At dinnertime they came back to the house stringing along a yearling heifer on a rope and they put her up in the pole corral above the barn for their father to look at and went in and washed up. Their father was already seated at the table. Boys, he said.

You all set down, their mother said. She set a platter of fried steaks on the table. A bowl of beans. When they'd said grace she handed the platter to their father and he forked one of the steaks onto his plate and passed it on to Billy.

Pap says there's a wolf on the range, she said.

Billy sat holding the platter, his knife aloft.

A wolf? Boyd said.

His father nodded. She pulled down a pretty good sized veal calf up at the head of Foster Draw.

When? said Billy.

Been a week or more probably. The youngest Oliver boy tracked her all up through the mountains. She come up out of Mexico. Crossed through the San Luis Pass and come up along the western slope of the Animas and hit in along about the head of Taylor's Draw and then dropped down and crossed the valley and come up into the Peloncillos. Come all the way up into the snow. There was two inches of snow on the ground where she killed the calf at.

How do you know it was a she? said Boyd.

Well how do you think he knows? said Billy.

You could see where she had done her business, said his father.

Oh, said Boyd.

What do you aim to do? said Billy.

Well, I reckon we better catch her. Dont you?

Yessir.

If old man Echols was here he'd catch her, said Boyd.

Mr Echols.

If Mr Echols was here he'd catch her.

Yes he would. But he aint.

THEY RODE after dinner the three of them the nine miles to the SK Bar ranch and sat their horses and halloed the house. Mr Sanders' granddaughter looked out and went to get the old man and they all sat on the porch while their father told Mr Sanders about the wolf. Mr Sanders sat with his elbows on his knees and looked hard at the porch floorboards between his boots and nodded and from time to time with his little finger tipped the ash from the end of his cigarette. When their father was done he looked up. His eyes were very blue and very beautiful half hid away in the leathery seams of his face. As if there were something there that the hardness of the country had not been able to touch.

Echols' traps and stuff is still up at the cabin, he said. I dont reckon he'd care for you to use whatever you needed.

He flipped the stub of the cigarette out into the yard and smiled at the two boys and put his hands on his knees and rose.

Let me go get the keys, he said.

The cabin when they opened it was dark and musty and had about it a waxy smell like freshkilled meat. Their father stood in the door a moment and then entered. In the front room was an old sofa, a bed, a desk. They went through the kitchen and then on through to the mudroom at the back of the house. There in the dusty light from the one small window on shelves of roughsawed pine stood a collection of fruitjars and bottles with ground glass stoppers and old apothecary jars all bearing antique octagon labels edged in red upon which in Echols' neat script were listed contents and dates. In the jars dark liquids. Dried viscera. Liver, gall, kidneys. The inward parts of the beast who dreams of man and has so dreamt in running dreams a hundred thousand years and more. Dreams of that malignant lesser god come pale and naked and alien to slaughter all his clan and kin and rout them from their house. A god insatiable whom no ceding could appease nor any measure of blood. The jars stood webbed in dust and the light among them made of the little room with its chemic glass a strange basilica dedicated to a practice as soon to be extinct among the trades of men as the beast to whom it owed its being. Their father took down one of the jars and turned it in his hand and set it back again precisely in its round track of dust. On a lower shelf stood a wooden ammunition box with dovetailed corners and in the box a dozen or so small bottles or vials with no labels to them. Written in red crayon across the top board of the box were the words No. 7 Matrix. Their father held one of the vials to the light and shook it and twisted out the cork and passed the open bottle under his nose.

Good God, he whispered.

Let me smell it, Boyd said.

No, said his father. He put the vial in his pocket and they

went on to search for the traps but they couldnt find them. They looked through the rest of the house and out on the porch and in the smokehouse. They found some old number three longspring coyote traps hanging on the smokehouse wall but those were all the traps they found.

They're here somewheres, said their father.

They began again. After a while Boyd came from the kitchen. I got em, he said.

They were in two wooden crates and the crates had been piled over with stovewood. They were greased with something that may have been lard and they were packed in the crates like herrings.

What caused you to look in under there? said his father.

You said they was somewheres.

He spread some old newspapers on the linoleum of the kitchen floor and began to lift out the traps. They had the springs turned in to make them more compact and the chains were wrapped around them. He straightened one out. The greaseclogged chain rattled woodenly. It was forked with a ring and had a heavy snap on one end and a drag on the other. They squatted there looking at it. It looked enormous. That thing looks like a bear-trap, Billy said.

It's a wolftrap. Number four and a half Newhouse.

He set out eight of them on the floor and wiped the grease from his hands with newspaper. They put the lid back on the crate and piled the stovewood back over the boxes the way Boyd had found them and their father went back out to the mudroom and returned with a small wooden box with a wirescreen bottom and a paper sack of logwood chips and a packbasket to put the traps in. Then they went out and fastened back the padlock on the front door and untied their horses and mounted up and rode back down to the house.

Mr Sanders came out on the porch but they didnt dismount.

Just stay to supper, he said.

We better get back. I thank you.

Well.

I've got eight of the traps.

All right.

We'll see how it goes.

Well. You probably got your work cut out for you. She aint been in the country long enough to have no regular habits.

Echols said there wasnt none of em did anymore.

He would know. He's about half wolf hisself.

Their father nodded. He turned slightly in the saddle and looked out downcountry. He looked at the old man again.

You ever smell any of that stuff he baits with?

Yessir. I have.

Their father nodded. He raised one hand and turned the horse and they rode out into the road.

After supper they set the galvanized washtub on top of the stove and hand filled it with buckets and poured in a scoop of lye and set the traps to boil. They fed the fire until bedtime and then changed the water and put the traps back with the logwood chips and chunked the stove full and left it. Boyd woke once in the night and lay listening to the silence in the house and in the darkness and the stove ticking or the house creaking in the wind off the plain. When he looked over at Billy's bed it was empty and after a while he got up and walked out to the kitchen. Billy was sitting at the window in one of the kitchen chairs turned backwards. He had his arms crossed over the chairback and he was watching the moon over the river and the river trees and the mountains to the south. He turned and looked at Boyd standing in the door.

What are you doin? said Boyd.

I got up to mend the fire.

What are you lookin at?

Aint lookin at nothin. There aint nothin to look at.

What are you settin there for.

Billy didnt answer. After a while he said: Go on back to bed. I'll be in there directly.

Boyd came on into the kitchen. He stood at the table. Billy turned and looked at him.

What woke you up? he said.
You did.
I didnt make a sound.
I know it.

WHEN BILLY got up the next morning his father was sitting at the kitchen table with a leather apron in his lap and he was wearing a pair of old deerhide gloves and rubbing beeswax into the steel of one of the traps. The other traps were laid out on a calfskin on the floor and they were a deep blueblack in color. He looked up and then took off the gloves and put them in the apron with the trap and set the apron on the calfhide in the floor.

Help me with the washtub, he said. Then you can finish waxin these.

He did. He waxed them carefully, working the wax into the pan and the lettering in the pan and into the slots that the jaws were hinged into and into each link in the heavy fivefoot chains and into the heavy twopronged drag at the end of the chain. Then his father hung them outside in the cold where the house odors would not infect them. The morning following when his father entered their room and called him it was still dark.

Billy.
Yessir.
Breakfast be on the table in five minutes.
Yessir.

When they rode out of the lot it was breaking day, clear and cold. The traps were packed in the splitwillow basket that his father wore with the shoulderstraps loosed so that the bottom of the basket carried on the cantle of the saddle behind him. They rode due south. Above them Black Point was shining with new snow in a sun that had not yet risen over the valley floor. By the time they crossed the old road to Fitzpatrick Wells the sun was up there also and they crossed to the head of the pasture in the sun and began to climb into the Peloncillos.

Midmorning they were sitting their horses at the edge of the upland vega where the calf lay dead. Where they'd come up through the trees there was snow in the tracks his father's horse had made three days ago and under the shadow of the trees where the dead calf lay there were patches of snow that had not yet melted and the snow was bloody and trampled and crossed and recrossed with the tracks of coyotes and the calf was pulled apart and pieces scattered over the bloody snow and over the ground beyond. His father had taken off his gloves to roll a cigarette and he sat smoking with the gloves in one hand resting on the pommel of his saddle.

Dont get down, he said. See if you can see her track.

They rode over the ground. The horses were uneasy at the blood and the riders spoke to them in a sort of scoffing way as if they'd make the horses ashamed. He could see no traces of the wolf.

His father stood down from his horse. Come here, he said.

You aint goin to make a set here?

No. You can get down.

He got down. His father had slipped the packbasket straps and stood the basket in the snow and he knelt and blew the fresh snow out of the crystal print the wolf had made five nights ago.

Is that her?

That's her.

That's her front foot.

Yes.

It's big, aint it?

Yes.

She wont come back here?

No. She wont come back here.

The boy stood up. He looked off up the meadow. There were two ravens sitting in a barren tree. They must have flown as they were riding up. Other than that there was nothing.

Where do you reckon the rest of the cattle have got to?

I dont know.

If they's a cow dead in a pasture will the rest of the cattle stay there?

Depends on what it died of. They wont stay in a pasture with a wolf.

You think she's made another kill somewheres by now?

His father rose from where he'd squatted by the track and picked up the basket. There's a good chance of it, he said. You ready?

Yessir.

They mounted up and crossed the vega and entered the woods on the far side and followed the cattletrail up along the edge of the draw. The boy watched the ravens. After a while they dropped down out of the tree and flew silently back to the dead calf.

His father made the first set below the gap of the mountain where they knew the wolf had crossed. The boy sat his horse and watched while he threw down the calfhide hairside down and stepped down onto it and set down the packbasket.

He took the deerhide gloves out of the basket and pulled them on and with a trowel he dug a hole in the ground and put the drag in the hole and piled the chain in after it and covered it up again. Then he excavated a shallow place in the ground the shape of the trap springs and all. He tried the trap in it and then dug some more. He put the dirt in the screenbox as he dug and then he laid the trowel by and took a pair of c-clamps from the basket and with them screwed down the springs until the jaws fell open. He held the trap up and eyed the notch in the pan while he backed off one screw and adjusted the trigger. Crouched in the broken shadow with the sun at his back and holding the trap at eyelevel against the morning sky he looked to be truing some older, some subtler instrument. Astrolabe or sextant. Like a man bent at fixing himself someway in the world. Bent on trying by arc or chord the space between his being and the world that was. If there be such space. If it be knowable. He put his hand under the open jaws and tilted the pan slightly with his thumb.

You dont want it to where a squirrel can trip it, he said. But damn near.

Then he removed the clamps and set the trap in the hole.

He covered the jaws and pan of the trap with a square of paper soaked in melted beeswax and with the screenbox he carefully sifted the dirt back over it and with the trowel sprinkled humus and wood debris over the dirt and squatted there on his haunches looking at the set. It looked like nothing at all. Lastly he took the bottle of Echols' potion from his coatpocket and pulled the cork and dipped a twig into the bottle and stuck the twig into the ground a foot from the trap and then put the cork back in the bottle and the bottle in his pocket.

He rose and handed up the packbasket to the boy and he bent and folded the calfskin with the dirt in it and then stood into the stirrup of the standing horse and mounted up and pulled the hide up into the bow of the saddle with him and backed the horse away from the set.

You think you can make one? he said.

Yessir. I think so.

His father nodded. Echols used to pull the shoes off his horse. Then he got to where he'd tie these cowhide slippers he'd made over the horse's hooves. Oliver told me he'd make sets and never get down. Set the traps from horseback.

How did he do it?

I dont know.

The boy sat holding the packbasket on his knee.

Put that on, his father said. You'll need it if you're goin to make this next set.

Yessir, he said.

By noon they'd made three more sets and they took their dinner in a grove of blackjack oaktrees at the head of Cloverdale Creek. They reclined on their elbows and ate their sandwiches and looked out across the valley toward the Guadalupes and southeast across the spur of the mountains where they could see the shadows of clouds moving up the broad Animas Valley and beyond in the blue distances the mountains of Mexico.

You think we can catch her? the boy said.

I wouldnt be up here if I didnt.

What if she's been caught before or been around traps before or somethin like that?

Then she'll be hard to catch.

There aint no more wolves but what they come up out of Mexico, I reckon. Are they?

Probably not.

They ate. When his father had finished he folded the paper bag the sandwiches had come in and put it in his pocket.

You ready? he said.

Yessir.

When they rode back through the lot and into the barn they'd been gone thirteen hours and they were bone tired. They'd come the last two hours through the dark and the house was dark save for the kitchen light.

Go on to the house and get your supper, his father said.

I'm all right.

Go on. I'll put the horses up.

THE WOLF had crossed the international boundary line at about the point where it intersected the thirtieth minute of the one hundred and eighth meridian and she had crossed the old Nations road a mile north of the boundary and followed Whitewater Creek west up into the San Luis Mountains and crossed through the gap north to the Animas range and then crossed the Animas Valley and on into the Peloncillos as told. She carried a scabbedover wound on her hip where her mate had bitten her two weeks before somewhere in the mountains of Sonora. He'd bitten her because she would not leave him. Standing with one forefoot in the jaws of a steeltrap and snarling at her to drive her off where she lay just beyond the reach of the chain. She'd flattened her ears and whined and she would not leave. In the morning they came on horses. She watched from a slope a hundred yards away as he stood up to meet them.

She wandered the eastern slopes of the Sierra de la Madera for a week. Her ancestors had hunted camels and primitive toy horses on these grounds. She found little to eat. Most of the game was slaughtered out of the country. Most of the forest cut to feed the boilers of the stampmills at the mines. The wolves in that country had been killing cattle for a long time but the ignorance of the animals was a puzzle to them. The cows bellowing and bleeding and stumbling through the mountain meadows with their shovel feet and their confusion, bawling and floundering through the fences and dragging posts and wires behind. The ranchers said they brutalized the cattle in a way they did not the wild game. As if the cows evoked in them some anger. As if they were offended by some violation of an old order. Old ceremonies. Old protocols.

She crossed the Bavispe River and moved north. She was carrying her first litter and she had no way to know the trouble she was in. She was moving out of the country not because the game was gone but because the wolves were and she needed them. When she pulled down the veal calf in the snow at the head of Foster Draw in the Peloncillo Mountains of New Mexico she had eaten little but carrion for two weeks and she wore a haunted look and she'd found no trace of wolves at all. She ate and rested and ate again. She ate till her belly dragged and she did not go back. She would not return to a kill. She would not cross a road or a rail line in daylight. She would not cross under a wire fence twice in the same place. These were the new protocols. Strictures that had not existed before. Now they did.

She ranged west into Cochise County in the state of Arizona, across the south fork of Skeleton Creek and west to the head of Starvation Canyon and south to Hog Canyon Springs. Then east again to the high country between Clanton and Foster draws. At night she would go down onto the Animas Plains and drive the wild antelope, watching them flow and turn in the dust of their own passage where it rose like smoke off the basin floor, watching the precisely indexed articulation of their limbs and the rocking movements of their heads and the slow bunching and the slow extension of their running, looking for anything at all among them that would name to her her quarry.

At this season the does were already carrying calves and as they commonly aborted long before term the one least favored so twice she found these pale unborn still warm and gawking on the ground, milkblue and near translucent in the dawn like beings miscarried from another world entire. She ate even their bones where they lay blind and dying in the snow. Before sunrise she was off the plain and she would raise her muzzle where she stood on some low promontory or rock overlooking the valley and howl and howl again into that terrible silence. She might have left the country altogether if she had not come upon the scent of a wolf just below the high pass west of Black Point. She stopped as if she'd walked into a wall.

She circled the set for the better part of an hour sorting and indexing the varied scents and ordering their sequences in an effort to reconstruct the events that had taken place here. When she left she went down through the pass south following the tracks of the horses now thirty-six hours old.

By evening she'd found all eight of the sets and she was back at the gap of the mountain again where she circled the trap whining. Then she began to dig. She dug a hole alongside the trap until the caving dirt fell away to reveal the trap's jaw. She stood looking at it. She dug again. When she left the set the trap was sitting naked on the ground with only a handful of dirt over the waxed paper covering the pan and when the boy and his father rode through the gap the following morning that was what they found.

His father stood down from the horse onto the calfhide and surveyed the set while the boy sat watching. He remade the set and rose and shook his head doubtfully. They rode the rest of the line and when they returned the following morning the first set was uncovered again and so were four more. They took up three of the sets and used the traps to make blind sets in the trail.

What's to keep a cow from walkin in em? the boy said.

Not a thing in the world, said his father.

Three days later they found another calf dead. Five days later one of the blind sets in the trail had been dug out and the trap overturned and sprung.

They rode in the evening down to the SK Bar and called on Sanders again. They sat in the kitchen and told the old man all that had occurred and the old man nodded his head.

Echols one time told me that tryin to get the best of a wolf is like tryin to get the best of a kid. It aint that they're smarter. It's just that they aint got all that much else to think about. I went with him a time or two. He'd put down a trap someplace and there wouldnt be the first sign of anything usin there and I'd ask him why he was makin a set there and half the time he couldnt answer it. Couldnt answer it.

They went up to the cabin and got six more of the traps and took them home and boiled them. In the morning when their mother came into the kitchen to fix breakfast Boyd was sitting in the floor waxing the traps.

You think that will get you out of the doghouse? she said.

No.

How long do you intend to stay sulled up?

I aint the one that's sulled up.

He can be just as stubborn as you can.

Then I reckon we're in for it, aint we?

She stood at the stove watching him bent at his work. Then she turned and took the iron skillet from the rack and set it on the stove. She opened the firebox door to put in wood but he'd already done it.

When they'd done eating breakfast his father wiped his mouth and put his napkin on the table and pushed back his chair.

Where's the traps at?

Hangin from the clothesline, said Boyd.

He rose and left the room. Billy drained his cup and set it on the table in front of him.

You want me to say somethin to him?

No.

All right. I wont then. Probably wouldnt do no good noway.

When his father came back from the barn ten minutes later

Boyd was at the woodpile in his shirtsleeves splitting stove chunks.

You want to go with us? his father said.

That's all right, said Boyd.

His father went on in the house. After a while Billy came out.

What the hell's wrong with you? he said.

Aint nothin wrong with me. What's wrong with you?

Dont be a ass. Get your coat and let's go.

It had snowed in the night in the mountains and the snow in the pass to the west of Black Point was a foot deep. Their father led his horse afoot through the snow tracking the wolf and they followed her all morning through the high country until she ran out of snow just above the Cloverdale Creek road. He got down and stood looking out over the open country where she'd gone and then he remounted and they turned and rode back up to check the sets on the other side of the pass.

She's carryin pups, he said.

He made four more blind sets in the trail and then they went in. Boyd was shivering in the saddle and his lips were blue. His father fell back alongside him and took off his coat and handed it to him.

I aint cold, Boyd said.

I didnt ask you if you were cold. Put it on.

Two days later when Billy and his father ran the line again one of the blind sets in the trail below the snowline was pulled out. A hundred feet down the trail was a place where the mud had washed out in the snowmelt and in the mud was the track of a cow. A little further on they found the trap. The prongs of the drag had caught and she'd pulled loose leaving a swag of bloodied hide accordioned up on the underside of the trapjaws.

They spent the rest of the morning looking through the pastures for the lame cow but they couldnt find her.

Be a good job for you and Boyd tomorrow, his father said.

Yessir.

I dont want him leavin the house half naked like he done the other day.

Yessir.

He and Boyd found the cow in the early afternoon of the day following. She was standing at the edge of the cedars watching them. The rest of the cattle were drifting along the lower edge of the vega. She was an old dry cow and she'd probably been alone when she walked in the set up on the mountain. They turned into the woods above her to head her out into the open but when she saw what they were about she turned and went back into the cedars. Boyd booted his horse through the trees and cut her off and got a loop on her and dallied and when she hit the end of the rope the girthstrap broke and the saddle was snatched from under him and disappeared down the slope behind the cow whacking and banging off of the trunks of the trees.

He'd done a somersault backwards off the horse and he sat on the ground and watched the cow racketing down through the cedars and out of sight. When Billy rode up he'd already mounted again bareback and they set off after the cow.

They started finding pieces of the saddle almost immediately and after a while they found the saddle itself or what was left of it, just the wooden tree with pieces of leather hanging off of it. Boyd started to get down.

Hell, just leave it lay, Billy said.

Boyd slid down off the horse. It aint that, he said. I got to come out of some of these clothes. I'm damn near afire.

They brought the cow limping in at the end of a rope and put her up and their father came out and doctored the leg with Corona Salve and then they all went in to get their supper.

She tore up Boyd's saddle, Billy said.

Can it be fixed?

There wasnt nothin left to fix.

The latigo busted?

Yessir.

When was the last time you looked at it?

That old hull never was any account, Boyd said.

That old hull was all the hull you had, said their father.

The next day Billy ran the line by himself. Another of the sets had been walked in but the cow left nothing in the trap save some peels and scrapings of hoof. In the night it snowed.

Them traps are under two feet of snow, said his father. What is the use in goin up there?

I want to see where she's usin.

You might see where she's been. I doubt it will tell you where she's goin to be tomorrow or the next day.

It's got to tell you somethin.

His father sat contemplating his coffee cup. All right, he said. Dont wear your horse out. You can hurt a horse in the snow. You can hurt a horse in the mountains in the snow.

Yessir.

His mother gave him his lunch at the kitchen door.

You be careful, she said.

Yes mam.

You be in by dark.

Yes mam. I'll try.

You try real hard and you wont have any problems.

Yes mam.

As he rode Bird out of the barn his father was coming from the house in his shirtsleeves with the rifle and saddlescabbard. He handed them up.

If by any chance at all she should be in a trap you come and get me. Unless her leg is broke. If her leg is broke shoot her. Otherwise she'll twist out.

Yessir.

And dont be gone late worryin your mama neither.

Yessir. I wont.

He turned the horse and went out through the stockgate and into the road south. The dog had come to the gate and stood looking after him. He rode out a little way on the road and then stopped and dismounted and strapped the scabbard alongside the saddle and levered the breech of the rifle partly open to see that there was shell in the chamber and then slid the rifle into the scabbard and buckled it and mounted up and rode on again. Before him the mountains were blinding white in the sun. They looked new born out of the hand of some improvident god who'd perhaps not even puzzled out a use for them. That kind of new. The rider rode with his heart outsized in his chest and the horse who was also young tossed its head and took a sidestep in the road and shot out one hind heel and then they went on.

The snow in the pass was half way to the horse's belly and the horse trod down the drifts in high elegance and swung its smoking muzzle over the white and crystal reefs and looked out down through the dark mountain woods or cocked its ears at the sudden flight of small winter birds before them. There were no tracks in the pass and there were neither cattle nor tracks of cattle in the upper pasture beyond the pass. It was very cold. A mile south of the pass they crossed a running branch so black in the snow it caused the horse to balk just for any slight movement of the water to tell that it was no bottomless crevice that had split the mountain in the night. A hundred yards farther the track of the wolf entered the trail and went down the mountain before them.

He stood down into the snow and dropped the reins and squatted and thumbed back the brim of his hat. In the floors of the little wells she'd stoven in the snow lay her perfect prints. The broad forefoot. The narrow hind. The sometime dragmark of her dugs or the place where she'd put her nose. He closed his eyes and tried to see her. Her and others of her kind, wolves and ghosts of wolves running in the whiteness of that high world as perfect to their use as if their counsel had been sought in the devising of it. He rose and walked back to where the horse stood waiting. He looked out across the mountain the way she'd come and then mounted and rode on.

A mile further she'd left the trail and gone down through the juniper parklands at a run. He dismounted and led the horse by the bridlereins. She was making ten feet at a jump. At the edge of the woods she turned and continued along the upper edge of the vega at a trot. He mounted up again and rode out down the pasture and he rode up and back but he could see no sign of what it was she'd run after. He picked up her track again and followed it across the open country and down along the southfacing slope and onto the benchland above Cloverdale Draw and here she'd routed a small band of cattle yarded up in the junipers and run them off the bench all crazed and sliding and falling enormously in the snow and here she'd killed a two year old heifer at the edge of the trees.

It was lying on its side in the shadow of the woods with its eyes glazed over and its tongue out and she had begun to feed on it between its rear legs and eaten the liver and dragged the intestines over the snow and eaten several pounds of meat from the inside of the thighs. The heifer was not quite stiff, not quite cold. Where it lay it had melted the snow to the ground in a dark silhouette about it.

The horse wanted no part of it. He arched his neck and rolled his eyes and the bores of his nose smoked like fumaroles. The boy patted his neck and spoke to him and then dismounted and tied the bridlereins to a branch and walked around the dead animal studying it. The one eye that looked up was blue and cast and there was no reflection in it and no world. There were no ravens or any other birds about. All was cold and silence. He walked back to the horse and slid the rifle from the scabbard and checked the chamber again. The action was stiff with the cold. He let the hammer down with his thumb and untied the reins and mounted up and turned the horse down along the edge of the woods, riding with the rifle across his lap.

He followed her all day. He never saw her. Once he rode her up out of a bed in a windbreak thicket on the south slope where she'd slept in the sun. Or thought he rode her up. He knelt and placed his hand in the pressed grass to see if it was warm and he sat watching to see if any blade or stem of grass would right itself but none did and whether the bed was warm from her or from the sun he was in no way sure. He mounted up and rode on. Twice he lost her track in the Cloverdale Creek pasture where the snow had melted and both times picked it up again in the circle he cut for sign. On the far side of the Cloverdale road he saw smoke and rode down and came upon three vaqueros from Pendleton's taking their dinner. They did not know that there was a wolf about. They seemed doubtful. They looked at one another.

They asked him to get down and he did and they gave him a cup of coffee and he took his lunch from his shirt and offered what he had. They were eating beans and tortillas and sucking at some sparelooking goatbones and as there was no fourth plate nor any way to divide what any had with any other they passed through a pantomime of offer and refusal and continued to eat as before. They talked of cattle and of the weather and as they were all workscouts for kin in Mexico they asked if his father needed any hands. They said that the tracks he'd followed were probably of a large dog and even though the tracks could be seen less than a quarter mile from where they were eating they showed no inclination to go and examine them. He didnt tell them about the dead heifer.

When they'd done eating they scraped their plates off into the ashes of the fire and wiped them clean with pieces of tortilla and ate the tortillas and packed the plates away in their mochilas. Then they tightened the latigos on their horses and mounted up. He shook out the grounds from the cup and wiped it out with his shirt and handed it up to the rider who'd given it to him.

Adiós compadrito, they said. Hasta la vista. They touched their hats and turned their horses and rode out and when they were gone he got his horse and mounted up and took the trail back west the way the wolf had gone.

By evening she was back in the mountains. He followed afoot leading the horse. He studied places where she had dug but he could not tell what it was she was digging for. He measured the remaining day with his hand at arm's length under the sun and finally he stood up into the saddle and turned the horse up through the wet snow toward the pass and home.

Because it was already dark he rode the horse past the kitchen window and leaned and tapped at the glass without stopping and then went on to the barn. At the dinner table he told them what he had seen. He told them about the heifer dead on the mountain.

Where she crossed back goin towards Hog Canyon, said his father. Was that a cattletrail?

No sir. It was not much of a trail of no kind.

Could you make a set in it?

Yessir. I would of had it not been gettin on late like it was.

Did you pick up any of the sets?

No sir.

You want to go back up there tomorrow?

Yessir. I'd like to.

All right. Take up a couple of traps and make blind sets with em and I'll run the line with you on Sunday.

I dont know how you think the Lord is goin to bless your efforts and you dont keep the Sabbath, their mother said.

Well Mama we aint got a ox in the ditch but we sure got some heifers in one.

I think it's a poor example for the boys.

His father sat looking at his cup. He looked at the boy. We'll run it on Monday, he said.

Lying in the cold dark of their bedroom they listened to the squalls of coyotes out in the pasture to the west of the house.

You think you can catch her? said Boyd.

I dont know.

What are you goin to do with her if you do?

What do you mean?

I mean what will you do with her.

Collect the bounty, I reckon.

They lay in the dark. The coyotes yammered. After a while Boyd said: I meant how will you kill her.

I guess you shoot em. I dont know no other way.

I'd like to see her alive.

Maybe Pap will bring you with him.

What am I goin to ride?

You could ride bareback.

Yeah, Boyd said. I could ride bareback.

They lay in the dark.

He's goin to give you my saddle, Billy said.

What are you goin to ride?

He's gettin me one from Martel's.

A new one?

No. Hell, not a new one.

Outside the dog had been barking and their father went out to the kitchen door and called the dog's name and it hushed instantly. The coyotes went on yapping.

Billy?

What.

Did Pap write Mr Echols?

Yeah.

He never heard nothin though. Did he?

Not yet he aint.

Billy?

What.

I had this dream.

What dream.

I had it twice.

Well what was it.

There was this big fire out on the dry lake.

There aint nothin to burn on a dry lake.

I know it.

What happened.

These people were burnin. The lake was on fire and they was burnin up.

It's probably somethin you ate.

I had the same dream twice.

Maybe you ate the same thing twice.

I dont think so.

It aint nothin. It's just a bad dream. Go to sleep.

It was real as day. I could see it.

People have dreams all the time. It dont mean nothin.

Then what do they have em for?

I dont know. Go to sleep.

Billy?

What.

I had this feelin that somethin bad was goin to happen.

There aint nothin bad goin to happen. You just had a bad dream is all. It dont mean somethin bad is goin to happen.

What does it mean?

It dont mean nothin. Go to sleep.

IN THE WOODS on the southfacing slopes the snow was partly melted from the prior day's sun and it had frozen back in the night so that there was a thin crust on top. The crust was just hard enough for birds to walk on. Mice. In the trail he saw where the cows had come down. The traps in the mountains lay all undisturbed beneath the snow with their jaws agape like steel trolls silent and mindless and blind. He took up three of the sets, holding the cocked traps in his gloved hands and reaching under the jaw and tripping the pan with his thumb. The traps leapt mightily. The iron clang of the jaws slamming shut echoed in the cold. You could see nothing of their movement. Now the jaws were open. Now they were closed.

He rode with the traps packed under the calfhide in the floor of the packbasket where they would not fall out as he rolled sideways in the saddle to duck low branches. When he came to the fork in the trail he followed the track she'd taken the evening before going west toward Hog Canyon. He made the sets in the trail and cut and placed stepping sticks and returned along a route of his own devising a mile to the south and continued down to the Cloverdale road to visit the last two sets on the line.

There was still snow in the upper stretches of the road and there were tiretracks in the road and horsetracks and the tracks of deer. When he reached the spring he left the road and crossed through the pasture and dismounted and watered his horse. It was near noon by the sun and he intended to ride the four miles into Cloverdale and go back by way of the road.

While the horse was drinking an old man in a Model A pickup truck pulled up out at the fence. Billy pulled the horse's head up and mounted and went back out to the road and sat the horse alongside the truck. The man leaned out the window and looked up at him. He looked at the packbasket.

What are you trappin? he said.

He was a rancher from the lower valley along the border and Billy knew him but didnt say his name. He knew the old man wanted to hear that he was trapping coyotes and he wouldnt lie, or wouldnt exactly lie.

Well, he said. I seen a lot of coyote sign down here.

I aint surprised, the old man said. They done everthing down at our place but come in and set at the table.

He scanned the country with his pale eyes. As if the little jackal wolves might be afoot on the plain in broadest day. He took out a pack of readymade cigarettes and shucked one up and took it in his mouth and held up the pack.

Smoke?

No sir. Thank you.

He put the pack away and took from his pocket a brass lighter that looked like something for soldering pipe, burning off paint. He struck it and a bluish ball of flame whooshed up. He lit the cigarette and snapped the lighter shut but it continued to burn anyway. He blew it out and dandled it in one hand to cool it. He looked at the boy.

I had to quit usin the hightest, he said.

Yessir.

You married?

No sir. I aint but sixteen.

Dont get married. Women are crazy.

Yessir.

You'll think you've found one that aint but guess what?

What?

She will be too.

Yessir.

You got any big traps in there?

Like how big?

Number four, say.

No sir. Truth to tell, I dont have none with me of no kind.

What did you ask me how big for then?

Sir?

The old man nodded at the road. There was a mountain lion crossed about a mile down here yesterday evenin.

They're around, the boy said.

My nephew's got some dogs. Got some blueticks out of the Lee Brothers' line. Pretty good dogs. He dont want em walkin in no steeltraps though.

I'm back up here towards Hog Canyon, the boy said. And up towards Black Point.

The old man smoked. The horse turned its head and sniffed at the truck and looked away again.

You hear about the Texas lion and the New Mexico lion? the old man said.

No sir. I dont believe so.

There was this Texas lion and this New Mexico lion. They split up on the divide and went off to hunt. Agreed to meet up in the spring and see how they'd done and all and whenever they done it why the old lion been over in Texas looked just awful. Lion from New Mexico he looked at him and he said Lord son you look awful. Said what's happened to you. Lion been over in Texas said I dont know. Said I'm about starved out. Other old lion said well, said tell me what all you been doin. Said you might be doin somethin wrong.

Well the Texas lion said I just been usin the old tried and true methods. Said I get up on a limb overlookin the trail and then whenever one of the Texans rides underneath it why I holler real big and then I jump out on top of him. And that's what I been a doin.

Well, the old New Mexico lion looked at him and he said it's a wonder you aint dead. Said that's all wrong for your Texans and I dont see how you got through the winter atall. Said look here. First of all when you holler thataway it scares the shit out of em. Then when you jump on top of em thataway it knocks the wind out of em. Hell, son. You aint got nothin left but buckles and boots.

The old man fell across the steering wheel wheezing. After a while he began to cough. He looked up and wiped his watery eyes with one finger and shook his head and looked up at the boy.

You see the point? he said. Texans?

Billy smiled. Yessir, he said.

You aint from Texas are you?

No sir.

I didnt allow you was. Well. I better get on. You want to catch coyotes you come down to my place.

All right.

He didnt say where his place was. He put the truck in gear and pulled the sparklever down and pulled away down the road.

WHEN THEY RAN the traps on Monday the snow had melted off everywhere save in the northfacing rincons or in the deeper woods below the north slope of the pass. She'd pulled out all the sets save for the ones in the Hog Canyon trail and she had taken to turning the traps over and springing them.

They took the traps up and his father made two new sets with double traps, burying one trap under the other and the bottom trap upside down. Then he made blind sets in the perimeter about. He laid these two new sets and they returned home and when they ran the traps the next morning there was a coyote dead in the first set. They pulled this set entirely and Billy tied the coyote on behind the cantle of his saddle and they went on. The coyote's bladder leaked down the horse's flank and it smelled peculiar.

What did the coyote die of? he said.

I dont know, said his father. Sometimes things just die.

The second set was dug out and all five traps sprung. His father sat looking at it for a long time.

There was no word from Echols. He and Boyd rode the outlying pastures and began bringing the cattle in. They found two more calves dead. Then another heifer.

Dont say nothin about this less he asks, Billy said.

Why not?

They sat their horses side by side, Boyd sitting Billy's old saddle and Billy in the mexican saddle his father had traded for. They studied the carnage in the woods. I wouldnt of thought about her pullin down a heifer that big, Billy said.

Why not say nothin? said Boyd.

What would be the use in worryin him over it?

They turned to go.

He might want to know about it anyways, Boyd said.

When's the last time you heard bad news you were glad to get?

What if he finds it himself?

Then he'll find it.

What are you goin to tell him then? That you didnt want to worry him?

Damn. You're worse than Mama. I'm sorry I raised the question.

He was left to run the traps on his own. He rode up to the SK Bar and got the key from Mr Sanders and went to Echols' cabin and studied the shelves in the little mudroom pharmacy. He found some more bottles in a crate in the floor. Dusty bottles with greasestained labels that said Lion, that said Cat. There were other bottles with curled and yellowed labels that bore only numbers and there were bottles made of purple glass dark near to blackness that had no label at all.

He put some of the nameless bottles in his pocket and went back to the front room of the cabin and looked through Echols' little packingcrate library. He took down a book called *Trapping North American Furbearers* by S Stanley Hawbaker and sat in the floor studying it but Hawbaker was from Pennsylvania and he didnt have all that much to say about wolves. When he ran the traps the next day they were dug out as before.

HE LEFT the next morning on the road to Animas and he was on the road seven hours getting there. He nooned at a spring in a glade of huge old cottonwoods and ate cold steak and biscuits and made a paper boat of the bag his lunch had come in and left it turning and darkening and sinking in the clear still of the spring.

The house was on the plain south of the town and no road to it. There had been a track at one time and you could see where it ran like the trace of an old wagonroad and that was where he rode till he came to the cornerpost of the fence. He tied the horse and walked up to the door and knocked and stood looking out over the plains toward the mountains to the west. Four horses were walking along the final rise out there and they stopped and turned and looked his way. As if they'd heard his rapping at the door two miles distant. He turned to rap again but as he did the door opened and a woman stood looking at him. She was eating an apple but she didnt speak. He took off his hat.

Buenas tardes, he said. El señor está?

She bit crisply into the apple with her big white teeth. She looked at him. El señor? she said.

Don Arnulfo.

She looked past him toward the horse tied to the fencepost and she looked at him again. She chewed. She watched him with her black eyes.

Él está? he said.

I'm thinking it over.

What's there to think about? He's either here or he aint.

Maybe.

I aint got no money.

She bit into the apple again. It made a loud cracking noise. He dont want your money, she said.

He stood holding his hat in his hands. He looked out to where he'd seen the horses but they had disappeared over the rise.

All right, she said.

He looked at her.

He's been sick. Maybe he wont say nothin to you.

Well. He will or he wont.

Maybe you like to come back some other time.

I aint got some other time.

She shrugged. Bueno, she said. Pásale.

She held open the door and he stepped past into the low mud house. Gracias, he said.

She gestured with her chin. Atrás, she said.

Gracias.

The old man was in a dark cell of a room at the back of the house. The room smelled of woodsmoke and kerosene and sour bedding. The boy stood in the doorway and tried to make him out. He turned and looked back but the woman had gone on to the kitchen. He stepped down into the room. There was an iron bedstead in the corner. A figure small and dark prone upon it. The room smelled as well of dust or clay. As if it might be that which the old man smelled of. But then even the floor of the room was mud.

He said the old man's name and the old man shifted in his bedding. Adelante, he wheezed.

He stepped forward, still holding his hat. He passed like an apparition through the banded rhomboid light from the small window in the western wall. The routed dustmotes reeled. It was cold in the room and he could see the pale wisps of the old man's breath rise and vanish in the cold. He could see the black eyes in a weathered face where the old man lay on the bare ticking of his pillow.

Güero, he said. Habla español?

Sí señor.

The old man's hand rose slightly on the bed and fell again. Tell me what you want, he said.

I come to ask you about trappin wolves.

Wolves.

Yessir.

Wolves, the old man said. Help me.

Sir?

Help me.

He was holding up one hand. It hung trembling in the partial light, disembodied, a hand common to all or none. The boy reached and took it. It was cold and hard and bloodless. A thing of leather and bone. The old man struggled up.

La almohada, he wheezed.

The boy almost put his hat on the bed but he caught himself. The old man's grip suddenly tightened and the black eyes hardened but he said nothing. The boy put the hat on and reached behind the old man and got hold of the limp and greasy pillow and stood it against the iron bars of the bedstead and the old man clutched his other hand as well and then leaned back fearfully until he came to rest against the pillow. He looked up at the boy. He'd a strong grip for all his frailty and he seemed loath to release the boy's hands until he'd searched out his eyes.

Gracias, he wheezed.

Por nada.

Bueno, the old man said. Bueno. He slacked his grip and Billy freed one hand and took off his hat again and held it by the brim.

Siéntate, the old man said.

He sat gingerly on the edge of the thin pad that covered the springs of the bed. The old man did not turn loose of his hand.

What is your name?

Parham. Billy Parham.

The old man said the name in silence to himself. Te conozco?

No señor. Estamos a las Charcas.

La Charca.

Sí.

Hay una historia allá.

Historia?

Sí, said the old man. He lay holding the boy's hand and

staring up at the kindlingwood latillas of the ceiling. Una historia desgraciada. De obras desalmadas.

The boy said that he did not know this history and that he would like to hear it but the old man said that it was as well he did not for out of some certain things no good could come and he thought this was one of them. His raspy breath had faded and the sound of it had faded and the faint whiteness of it also that had been briefly visible in the cold of the room. His grip on the boy's hand remained as before.

Mr Sanders said you might have some scent I could buy off of you. He said I ought to ask.

The old man didnt answer.

He give me some that Mr Echols had but the wolf's took to diggin out the traps and springin em.

Dónde está el señor Echols?

No sé. Se fué.

Él murió?

No sir. Not that I've heard.

The old man closed his eyes and opened them again. He lay against the ticking of the pillow with his neck slightly awry. He looked as if he'd been thrown there. In the failing light the eyes betrayed nothing. He seemed to be studying the shadows in the room.

Conocemos por lo largo de las sombras que tardío es el día, he said. He said that men took this to mean that the omens of such an hour were thereby greatly exaggerated but that this was in no way so.

I got one bottle that says Number Seven Matrix, the boy said. And another that dont say nothin.

La matríz, the old man said.

He waited for the old man to continue but the old man did not continue. After a while he asked him what was in the matrix but the old man only pursed his thin mouth in doubt. He continued to hold the boy's hand and they sat that way for some time. The boy was about to put some further query to the old

man when the old man spoke again. He said that the matrix was
not so easily defined. Each hunter must have his own formula.
He said that things were rightly named its attributes which
could in no way be counted back into its substance. He said
that in his opinion only shewolves in their season were a proper
source. The boy said that the wolf of which he spoke was in
fact herself a shewolf and he asked if that fact should figure in
his strategies against her but the old man only said that there
were no more wolves.

Ella vino de Mexico, the boy said.

He seemed not to hear. He said that Echols had caught all
the wolves.

El señor Sanders me dice que el señor Echols es medio lobo
el mismo. Me dice que él conoce lo que sabe el lobo antes de
que lo sepa el lobo. But the old man said that no man knew
what the wolf knew.

The sun was low in the west and the shape of the light from
the window lay suspended across the room wall to wall. As if
something electric had been cored out of that space. Finally the
old man repeated his words. El lobo es una cosa incognoscible,
he said. Lo que se tiene en la trampa no es mas que dientes y
forro. El lobo propio no se puede conocer. Lobo o lo que sabe
el lobo. Tan como preguntar lo que saben las piedras. Los
arboles. El mundo.

His breath had gone wheezy from his exertions. He coughed
quietly and lay still. After a while he spoke again.

Es cazador, el lobo, he said. Cazador. Me entiendes?

The boy didnt know if he understood or not. The old man
went on to say that the hunter was a different thing than men
supposed. He said that men believe the blood of the slain to be
of no consequence but that the wolf knows better. He said that
the wolf is a being of great order and that it knows what men
do not: that there is no order in the world save that which death
has put there. Finally he said that if men drink the blood of God
yet they do not understand the seriousness of what they do. He

said that men wish to be serious but they do not understand how to be so. Between their acts and their ceremonies lies the world and in this world the storms blow and the trees twist in the wind and all the animals that God has made go to and fro yet this world men do not see. They see the acts of their own hands or they see that which they name and call out to one another but the world between is invisible to them.

You want to catch this wolf, the old man said. Maybe you want the skin so you can get some money. Maybe you can buy some boots or something like that. You can do that. But where is the wolf? The wolf is like the copo de nieve.

Snowflake.

Snowflake. You catch the snowflake but when you look in your hand you dont have it no more. Maybe you see this dechado. But before you can see it it is gone. If you want to see it you have to see it on its own ground. If you catch it you lose it. And where it goes there is no coming back from. Not even God can bring it back.

The boy looked down at the thin and ropy claws that held his hand. The light from the high window had paled, the sun had set.

Escúchame, joven, the old man wheezed. If you could breathe a breath so strong you could blow out the wolf. Like you blow out the copo. Like you blow out the fire from the candela. The wolf is made the way the world is made. You cannot touch the world. You cannot hold it in your hand for it is made of breath only.

He had pulled himself slightly erect in order to utter these proclamations and now he subsided against the ticking and his eyes seemed to study only the roofpoles overhead. He eased his thin cold grip. Where is the sun? he said.

Se fué.

Ay. Ándale, joven. Ándale pues.

The boy withdrew his hand and he rose. He put on his hat and touched the brim.

Vaya con Dios.

Y tú, joven.

Yet before he reached the door the old man called to him again.

He turned and stood.

Cuántos años tienes? the old man said.

Dieciseis.

The old man lay quietly in the dark. The boy waited.

Escúchame, joven, he said. Yo no sé nada. Esto es la verdad.

Está bien.

The matríz will not help you, the old man said. He said that the boy should find that place where acts of God and those of man are of a piece. Where they cannot be distinguished.

Y qué clase de lugar es éste? the boy said.

Lugares donde el fierro ya está en la tierra, the old man said. Lugares donde ha quemado el fuego.

Y cómo se encuentra?

The old man said that it was not a question of finding such a place but rather of knowing it when it presented itself. He said that it was at such places that God sits and conspires in the destruction of that which he has been at such pains to create.

Y por eso soy hereje, he said. Por eso y nada más.

It was dark in the room. He thanked the old man again but the old man did not answer or if he did he didnt hear him. He turned and went out.

The woman was leaning against the kitchen door. She was silhouetted against the yellow light and he could see her figure through the thin dress she wore. She did not seem troubled that the old man lay alone in the dark at the rear of the house. She asked the boy if the old man had told him how to catch the wolf and he said that he had not.

She touched her temple. He dont remember so good sometimes, she said. He is old.

Yes mam.

No one comes to see him. That's too bad, hey?

Yes mam.

Not even the priest. He came one time maybe two but he dont come no more.

How come?

She shrugged. People say he is brujo. You know what is brujo?

Yes mam.

They say he is brujo. They say God has abandoned this man. He has the sin of Satanás. The sin of orgullo. You know what is orgullo?

Yes mam.

He thinks he knows better than the priest. He thinks he knows better than God.

He told me he didnt know nothin.

Ha, she said. Ha. You believe that? You see this old man? You know what a terrible thing it is to die without God? To be the one that God has cast aside? Think it over.

Yes mam. I got to go.

He touched the brim of his hat and stepped past her to the door and walked out into the evening dark. The lights of the town strewn across the prairie lay in that blue vale like a jeweled serpent incandescing in the evening cool. When he looked back at the house she was standing in the doorway.

Thank you mam, he said.

He is nothing to me, she called. No hay parentesco. You know what is parentesco?

Yes mam.

There is no parentesco. He was tío of the dead wife of my dead husband. What is that? You see? And yet I have him here. Who else would take this man? You see? No one cares.

Yes mam.

Think it over.

He unlooped the bridlereins from the post and untied them. All right, he said. I will.

It could happen to you.

Yes mam.

He mounted up and turned the horse and raised one hand. The mountains to the south stood blackly against a violet sky. The snow on the north slopes so pale. Like spaces left for messages.

La fe, she called. La fe es toda.

He turned the horse out along the rutted track and rode on. When he looked back she was still standing in the open door. Standing in the cold. He looked back one last time and the door was still open but she was not there and he thought perhaps the old man had called her. But then he thought probably that old man didnt call anybody.

TWO DAYS LATER riding down the Cloverdale road he turned off for no reason at all and rode out to where the vaqueros had nooned and sat his horse looking down at the dead black fire. Something had been digging in the ashes.

He dismounted and got a stick and poked through the fire. He mounted up again and walked the horse about the perimeter of the encampment. There was no reason to think that the scavenger had been anything other than a coyote but he rode anyway. He rode slowly and turned the horse nicely. Like a show rider at a judging. On his second circling a little farther from the fire he stopped. In the windshadow of a rock where the sand had drifted lay the perfect print of her forefoot.

He dismounted and knelt holding the reins behind his back and he blew at the loose dirt in the track and pushed at the delicate edges of the track with his thumb. Then he mounted up and went back out to the road and home.

The following day when he ran the traps that he'd reset with the new scent they were pulled out and sprung as before. He set them again and made two blind sets but his heart was not in it. When he rode down through the pass at noon and looked out over the Cloverdale Valley the first thing he saw was the thin spire of smoke in the distance from the vaqueros' cookfire.

He sat the horse a long time. He put his hand on the cantle

and looked back toward the pass and he looked out over the valley again. Then he turned and rode back up the mountain.

By the time he'd pulled the traps and packed them in the basket and ridden down into the valley and crossed the road it was early evening. Once more he checked the sun by the width of his hand on the horizon. He had little more than an hour of daylight.

He dismounted at the fire and took the trowel from the packbasket and squatted and began to clear a space among the ashes and charcoal and fresh bones. At the heart of the fire there were live coals yet and he raked them aside to cool and dug a hole in the ground beneath the fire and then got a trap from the basket. He didnt even bother to put on the deerskin gloves.

He screwed down the springs with the clamps and opened the jaws and set the trigger in the notch and eyed the clearance while he backed off the clampscrew. Then he removed both clamps and dropped the draghook and chain into the hole and set the trap in the fire.

He placed one of the squares of oiled paper over the jaws that no coals lodge under the pan to keep it from tripping and he drifted ash over the trap with the screenbox and scattered back the charcoal and the charred bits of wood and he put back the bones and rinds of blackened skin and drifted more ashes over the set and then rose and stepped away and stood looking at the cold fire and wiping the trowel on the side of his jeans. Lastly he smoothed a place in the sand before the fire, digging out small clumps of grass and buckbrush, and there he wrote a letter to the vaqueros, etching it deep that the wind not take it. Cuidado, he wrote. Hay una trampa de lobos enterrado en el fuego. Then he flung away the stick and dropped the trowel back into the basket and shouldered the basket and mounted up.

He rode out across the pasture toward the road and in the cold blue twilight he turned and looked a last time toward the set. He leaned and spat. You read my sign, he said. If you can. Then he turned the horse toward home.

It was two hours past dark when he walked into the kitchen.

His mother was at the stove. His father was still sitting at the table drinking coffee. The worn blue ledgerbook in which they kept accounts lay on the table to one side.

Where you been? his father said.

He sat down and his father heard him out and when he was done he nodded.

All my life, he said, I been witness to people showin up where they was supposed to be at various times after they'd said they'd be there. I never heard one yet that didnt have a reason for it.

Yessir.

But there aint but one reason.

Yessir.

You know what it is?

No sir.

It's that their word's no good. That's the only reason there ever was or ever will be.

Yessir.

His mother had got his supper from the warmer over the stove and she set it down in front of him and laid down the silver.

Eat your supper, she said.

She left the room. His father sat watching him eat. After a while he rose and took his cup to the sink and rinsed it out and set it upside down on the sideboard. I'll call you in the mornin, he said. You need to get over there fore you catch you one of them Mexicans.

Yessir.

We never would hear the end of it.

Yessir.

Aint no guarantee that a one of em can read.

Yessir.

He finished his supper and went to bed. Boyd was already asleep. He lay awake a long time thinking about the wolf. He tried to see the world the wolf saw. He tried to think about it running in the mountains at night. He wondered if the wolf were so unknowable as the old man said. He wondered at the world it smelled or what it tasted. He wondered had the living blood with which it slaked its throat a different taste to the thick iron tincture of his own. Or to the blood of God. In the morning he was out before daylight saddling the horse in the cold dark of the barn. He rode out the gate before his father was even up and he never saw him again.

Riding along the road south he could smell the cattle out in the fields in the dark beyond the bar ditch and the running fence. When he rode through Cloverdale it was just gray light. He turned up the Cloverdale Creek road and rode on. Behind him the sun was rising in the San Luis Pass and his new shadow riding before him lay long and thin upon the road. He rode past the old dance platform in the woods and two hours later when he left the road and crossed the pasture to the vaqueros' noon fire the wolf stood up to meet him.

The horse stopped and backed and stamped. He held the animal and patted it and spoke to it and watched the wolf. His heart was slamming inside his chest like something that wanted out. She was caught by the right forefoot. The drag had caught in a cholla less than a hundred feet from the fire and there she stood. He patted the horse and spoke to it and reached down and unfastened the buckle on the saddlescabbard and slid the rifle free and stepped down and dropped the reins. The wolf crouched slightly. As if she'd try to hide. Then she stood again and looked at him and looked off toward the mountains.

When he approached she bared her teeth but she did not growl and she kept her yellow eyes from off his person. White bone showed in the bloody wound between the jaws of the trap. He could see her teats through the thin fur of her underbelly and she kept her tail tucked and pulled at the trap and stood.

He walked around her. She turned and backed. The sun was well up and in the sun her fur was a grayish dun with paler tips at the ruff and a black stripe along the back and she turned and backed to the length of the chain and her flanks sucked in and out with the motion of her breathing. He squatted on the ground and stood the rifle before him and held it by the forestock and he squatted there for a long time.

He was in no way prepared for what he beheld. Among other things he'd not considered simply whether he could ride to the ranch and be back with his father before the vaqueros arrived at noon if they would so arrive. He tried to remember what his father had said. If her leg were broke or she were caught by the paw. He looked at the height of the sun and he looked back out toward the road. When he looked at the wolf again she was lying down but when his eyes fell upon her she stood again. The standing horse tossed its head and the bridlebit clinked but she paid no attention to the horse at all. He rose and walked back and scabbarded the rifle and took up the reins and mounted up and turned the horse and headed out to the road. Half way he stopped again and turned and looked back. The wolf was watching him as before. He sat the horse a long time. The sun warm on his back. The world waiting. Then he rode back to the wolf.

She rose and stood with her sides caving in and out. She carried her head low and her tongue hung trembling between the long incisors of her lower jaw. He undid the string from his catchrope and slung it over his shoulder and stepped down. He took some lengths of pigginstring from the mochila behind the saddle and looped them through his belt and unlimbered the catchrope and walked around the wolf. The horse was no use to him because if it leaned back on the rope it would kill the wolf or pull it from the trap or both. He circled the wolf and looked for something to tie to that he could stretch her. There was nothing that his rope would reach and double and finally he took off his coat and blindfolded the horse with it and led it forward upwind of the wolf and dropped the reins that it would stand. Then he paid out the rope and built his loop and dropped it over her. She stepped through it with the trap and looked at it and looked at him. Now he had the rope over the trapchain. He looked at it in disgust and dropped the rope and walked out in the desert until he found a paloverde and he cut from it a pole some seven feet long with a forked branch at the end and came back trimming off the limbs with his knife. She watched him. He snared the loop with the end of the pole and pulled it toward him. He thought she might bite at the pole but she did not. When he got the loop in his hand he had to pay the whole forty feet of rope back through the honda and begin again. She watched the rope make its traverse with great attention and when the end of it had passed over the trapchain and withdrew through the dead grass she lay down again.

He built a smaller loop and came forward. She stood. He swung the loop and she flattened her ears and ducked and bared her teeth at him. He made two more tries and on the third the loop dropped over her neck and he snatched the rope taut.

She stood twisting on her hindlegs holding the heavy trap up at her chest and snapping at the rope and pawing with her free foot. She let out a low whine which was the first sound she had made.

He stepped back and stretched her out till she lay gasping on the ground and he backed toward the horse paying out rope and then looped the rope about the saddlehorn and came back carrying the free end. He winced to see her bloodied foreleg stretched in the trap but there was no help for it. She got her hindquarters up off the ground and scrabbled sideways and she twisted and fought the rope and slung her head from side to side and even once got completely to her feet again before he pulled her down. He squatted holding the rope just a few feet from her and after a while she lay gasping quietly in the dirt. She looked toward him with her yellow eyes and closed them slowly and then looked away.

He stood on the rope with one foot and took out his knife again and reached carefully and got hold of the paloverde pole. He cut a threefoot length from the end of it and put the knife back in his pocket and took a length of the pigginstring from his belt and made a noose with it and took it in his teeth. Then he stepped off the rope and picked up the end of it and moved toward her with the stick. She watched with one almond eye, deep yellow, deepening to amber at the iris. She strained at the rope, her face in the dirt, her mouth open and her teeth so white, so perfectly made. He pulled the rope tighter where it was belayed around the saddlehorn. He pulled until he'd shut off her air and then he jammed the stick between her teeth.

She made no sound. She bowed up and twisted her head and bit at the stick and tried to get quit of it. He hauled on the rope and stretched her out wild and gagging and forced her lower jaw to the ground with the stick and stepped on the rope again with his boot not a foot from those teeth. Then he took the pigginstring from his mouth and dropped the loop of it over her muzzle and jerked it tight and seized her by one ear and made three turns of the cord about her jaws faster than eye could follow and halfhitched it and fell upon her, kneeling with the living wolf gasping between his legs and sucking air and her tongue working within the teeth all stuck with dirt and debris. She looked up at him, the eye delicately aslant, the knowledge of the world it held sufficient to the day if not to the day's evil. Then she closed her eyes and he slacked the rope and stood and stepped away and she lay breathing heavily with her forefoot stretched behind her in the trap and the stick in her mouth. He stood gasping himself. Cold as it was he was wringing wet with sweat. He turned and looked at the horse where it stood with his coat over its head. By damn, he said. By damn. He coiled the loose rope from off the ground and walked back to the horse and lifted the rope up and over the saddlehorn and untied the coatsleeves from under the horse's jaw and unhooded it and laid the coat across the saddle. The horse lifted its head and blew and looked toward the wolf and he patted it on the neck and spoke to it and got the clamps out of the mochila and pulled the coil of rope up over his shoulder and turned back to the wolf.

Before he could reach her she leapt up and lunged against the trapchain twisting and slinging her head and pawing at her mouth with her free foot. He pulled her down with the rope and held her. A white foam seethed between her teeth. He approached slowly and reached and held her by the stick in her jaws and spoke to her but his voice seemed only to make her shudder. He looked at the leg in the trap. It looked bad. He got hold of the trap and put the clamp over the spring and screwed it down and then did the second spring. When the eye of the spring dropped past the hinges in the plate the jaws fell open and her wrecked forefoot spilled out limp and bloody with the white bone shining. He reached to touch it but she snatched it away and stood. He was amazed at her quickness. She stood squared off at him, her eyes level with his where he knelt, still not meeting his gaze. He slid the coil of rope off his shoulder to the ground and picked up the end of it and wrapped it around his fist in a double grip. Then he let go slack the short end of the rope by which he held her. She tested the injured foot on the ground and drew it up again.

Go on, he said. If you think you can.

She turned and wheeled away. So quick. He hardly had time to get one heel in front of him in the dirt before she hit the end of the rope. She did a cartwheel and landed on her back and jerked him forward onto his elbows. He scrambled up but she was already off in another direction and when she hit the end of the rope again she almost snatched him off the ground. He turned and dug both heels in and took a turn of the rope around his wrist. She had swung toward the horse now and the horse snorted and set off toward the road at a trot with the reins trailing. She ran at the end of the rope in a circle until she passed the cholla that had first caught the trapchain drag and here the rope brought her around until she stood snubbed and gasping among the thorns.

He rose and walked up to her. She squatted and flattened her ears. Slobber swung in white strings from her jaw. He took out his knife and reached and got hold of the stick in her mouth and he spoke to her and stroked her head but she only winced and shivered.

It aint no use to fight it, he told her.

He cut the trailing length of the paloverde off short at the side of her mouth and put the knife away and walked the end of the rope around the cholla till it was free and then led her twisting and shaking her head out onto the open ground. He could not believe how strong she was. He stood spraddlelegged with the rope in both hands across his thighs and turned and scanned the country for some sight of his horse. She would not quit struggling and he got hold of the rope end again and sat with it doubled in his fist and dug both heels in and let her go. When she hit the end of the rope this time she flew into the air and landed on her back and lay there. He hauled on the rope and dragged her towards him through the dirt.

Get up, he said. You aint hurt.

He walked down and stood over her where she lay panting. He looked at the injured leg. There was a flap of loose skin pushed down around her ankle like a sock and the wound was dirty and stuck with twigs and leaves. He knelt and touched her. Come on, he said. You've done run my horse off so let's go find him.

By the time he'd dragged her out to the road he was all but exhausted. The horse was standing a hundred yards away grazing in the bar ditch. It raised its head and looked at him and bent to graze again. He halfhitched the catchrope to a fencepost and took the last length of cord from his belt and tied the honda to the rope that the noose could not back off loose and then he rose and walked back across the pasture to pick his coat up off the ground and to get the trap.

When he got back she was snubbed up against the fencepost and half strangling where she'd gone back and forth. He dropped the trap and knelt and unhitched the rope from the post and paid the whole length of it back and forth through the wires until he had her free again. She got up and sat in the dusty grass and looked off wildly up the road toward the mountains with the foam seething between her teeth and dripping from the paloverde stick.

You aint got no damn sense, he told her.

He rose and put on his coat and jammed the clamps into his coatpocket and slung the trap over his shoulder by the chain and then dragged her out into the middle of the road and set off with her behind him sliding stifflegged and raking a trail through the dust and gravel.

The horse raised its head to study them, chewing ruminatively. Then it turned and set off down the road.

He stopped and stood looking after it. He turned and looked back at the wolf. In the distance he could hear the chug of the old rancher's Model A and he realized that she had heard it some time ago. He shortened up the rope a couple of reaches and dragged the wolf through the bar ditch and stood by the fence and watched the truck come over the hill and approach in its attendant dust and clatter.

The old man slowed and leaned and peered. The wolf was jerking and twisting and the boy stood behind her and held her with both hands. By the time the truck had pulled abreast of them he was lying on the ground with his legs scissored about her midriff and his arms around her neck. The old man stopped and sat the idling truck and leaned across and rolled down the window. What in the hell, he said. What in the hell.

You reckon you could turn that thing off? the boy said.

That's a damn wolf.

Yessir it is.

What in the hell.

The truck's scarin her.

Scarin her?

Yessir.

Boy what's wrong with you? That thing comes out of that riggin it'll eat you alive.

Yessir.

What are you doin with him?

It's a she.

It's a what?

A she. It's a she.

Hell fire, it dont make a damn he or she. What are you doin with it?

Fixin to take it home.

Home?

Yessir.

Whatever in the contumacious hell for?

Can you not turn that thing off?

It aint all that easy to start again.

Well could I maybe get you to drive down there and catch my horse for me and bring him back. I'd tie her up but she gets all fuzzled up in the fencewire.

What I'd like to do is to try and save you the trouble of bein eat, the old man said. What are you takin it home for?

It's kindly a long story.

Well I'd sure like to hear it.

The boy looked down the road where the horse stood grazing. He looked at the old man. Well, he said. My daddy wanted me to come and get him if I caught her but I didnt want to leave her cause they's been some vaqueros takin their dinner over yonder and I figured they'd probably shoot her so I just decided to take her on home with me.

Have you always been crazy?

I dont know. I never was much put to the test before today.

How old are you?

Sixteen.

Sixteen.

Yessir.

Well you aint got the sense God give a goose. Did you know that?

You may be right.

How do you expect your horse to tolerate a bunch of nonsense such as this.

If I can get him caught he wont have a whole lot of say about it.

You plan on leadin that thing behind a horse?

Yessir.

How you expect to get her to do that?

She aint got a whole lot of choice either.

The old man sat looking at him. Then he climbed out of the truck and shut the door and adjusted his hat and walked around and stood at the edge of the bar ditch. He had on canvas pants and a blanketlined canvas coat with a corduroy collar and he wore boots with walkingheels and a full beaver John B Stetson hat.

How close can I get? he said.

Close as you want.

He crossed the ditch and came up and stood looking at the wolf. He looked at the boy and he looked at the wolf some more.

She's fixin to have pups.

Yessir.

Damn good thing you caught her.

Yessir.

Can you touch her?

Yessir. You can touch her.

The old man squatted and put his hand on the wolf. The wolf bowed and writhed and he snatched his hand away. Then he touched her again. He looked at the boy. Wolf, he said.

Yessir.

What do you aim to do with her?

I dont know.

I guess you'll collect the bounty. Sell the hide.

Yessir.

She dont much like bein touched, does she?

No sir. Not much.

When we used to bring cattle up the valley from down around Ciénega Springs why first night we'd generally hit in about Government Draw and make camp there. And you could hear em all across the valley. Them first warm nights. You'd nearly always hear em in that part of the valley. I aint heard one in years.

She come up from Mexico.

I dont doubt it. Ever other damn thing does.

He rose and looked off down the road to where the horse was grazing. You want my advice, he said, you'll let me fetch you that rifle I see sticking out of the boot yonder and shoot this son of a bitch right between the eyes and be done with it.

If I can just get my horse caught I'll be all right, the boy said.

Well. You suit yourself.

Yessir. I aim to.

The old man shook his head. All right, he said. Wait here and I'll go get him.

I aint goin nowheres, the boy said.

He went back to the truck and got in and drove down to where the horse was standing. When the horse saw the truck coming it crossed through the bar ditch and stood against the fence and the old man got out and walked the horse down along the fence until he could catch the trailing reins and then he led the horse back up the road. The boy sat holding the wolf. It was very quiet. The only sound along the road was the faint dry clop of the horse's hooves in the gravel and the steady chugging of the truck where the old man had left it idling by the roadside.

When he dragged the wolf out to the road the horse backed and stood facing her.

Maybe you better tie the horse, the old man said.

If you'll just hold him a minute I'll be all right.

I aint sure but what I'd about as soon hold the wolf.

The boy paid out enough slack so that the wolf could get to the bar ditch but not enough for her to reach the fence. He dallied the rope to the saddlehorn and turned the wolf loose and she scampered for the ditch on three legs and hit the rope end and flipped endwise and got up and crouched in the ditch and lay waiting. The boy turned and took the reins from the old man and put one knuckle to his hatbrim.

I'm much obliged, he said.

That's all right. It's been a interestin day.

Yessir. Mine aint over.

No it aint. You mind she dont get that mouth loose, you hear? She'll take a chunk out of you you couldnt put in your hat.

Yessir.

He stood in the stirrup and swung up and checked the dally and nudged his hat back and nodded to the old man. I'm much obliged, he said.

When he put the horse forward the wolf came up out of the ditch at the end of the rope with the game foot to her chest and swung into the road and went dragging after the horse stifflegged and rigid as a piece of taxidermy. He stopped and looked back. The old man was standing in the road watching them.

Sir? he said.

Yes.

Maybe you better go on by and get your truck. So you wont have to pass us.

I think that's a good idea.

He walked down and got into the truck and turned and looked back at them. The boy raised his hand. The old man looked like he might be going to call something to him but he didnt and he lifted his hand and turned and pulled away down the road toward Cloverdale.

He went on. Gusts of wind were blowing dust off the top of the road. When he looked back at her she had her windward eye asquint against the blowing grit and she was hobbling along after the horse with her head lowered. He stopped and she came slightly forward to slack the rope and then turned and went down into the bar ditch again. He was about to put the horse forward when she squatted in the ditch and began to make water. When she was done she turned and sniffed at the spot and checked the wind with her nose and then came up into the road and stood with her tail between her hocks and the wind making little furrows in her hair.

The boy sat the horse a long time watching her. Then he got down and dropped the reins and got his canteen and walked around to where she was standing. She backed along the reach of the rope. He slung the canteen over his shoulder and stepped over the rope and held it between his knee and pulled her to him. She twisted and stood but he got hold of the noose and doubled it in his fist and forced her down into the grass by the side of the road and got astraddle of her. It was all he could do to hold her. He slung the canteen around and unscrewed the cap with his teeth. The horse stamped in the road and he spoke to it and then holding the wolf by the stick in her mouth with her head against his knee he began slowly to pour water into the side of her mouth. She lay still. Her eye stopped moving. Then she began to swallow.

Most of the water ran out on the ground but he continued to trickle it between her teeth along the greenstick bit. When the canteen was empty he let go of the stick and she lay quietly getting her breath. He stood and stepped back but she didnt move. He swung the cap up by its chain and screwed it back onto the canteen and walked back out to the horse and slung the canteen over the mochila and looked back at her. She was standing watching him. He mounted up and nudged the horse forward. When he looked back she was limping along at the end of the rope. When he stopped she stopped. An hour down the road he stopped for a long time. He was at Robertson's crossfence. Ahead an hour's ride lay Cloverdale and the road north. South lay the open country. The yellow grass heeled under the blowing wind and sunlight was running over the country before the moving clouds. The horse shook its head and stamped and stood. Damn all of it, the boy said. Just damn all of it.

He turned the horse and crossed through the ditch and rode up onto the broad plain that stretched away before him south toward the mountains of Mexico.

Midday they crossed through a low pass in the easternmost spur of the Guadalupes and rode out down the open valley. They saw riders on the plain in the distance but the riders rode on. Late afternoon they passed through the last low cones of hills on that volcanic ground and an hour later they came to the last fence in the country.

It was a crossfence running east and west. On the other side was a dirt track. He turned the horse east and followed the fence. There was a cattletrail along the fence but he rode a rope length from it that the wolf not cross under the wires and by and by he came to a ranch house.

He sat the horse on a slight rise of ground and studied the house. He could see no safe place to leave the wolf so he continued on. At the gate he dismounted and unpinned the chain and swung the gate open and led horse and wolf through and closed the gate again and remounted. The wolf was standing bowed up in the road with its hair all wrong like something pulled backwards out of a pipe and when he put the horse forward she came skidding behind with her legs locked. He looked back at her. If I'd been eatin these people's cows, he said, I wouldnt want to come callin neither.

Before he could put the horse forward again there was a great howl from the direction of the house and when he looked three large hounds were coming up the road very low and very fast.

Shit almighty, he said.

He stepped down and snubbed the reins to the top fencewire and snatched the rifle out of the scabbard. Bird's eyes were rolling and he began to stamp about in the road. The wolf stood stock still with her tail up and her hair straight out. The horse turned and backed at the reins, the fencewire bowed. He heard in the melee a staple pop and he suddenly saw as in an evil dream the specter of the horse at full gallop on the plain with the wolf behind at the end of the rope and the dogs in wild pursuit and he snatched the rope from about the saddlehorn just as the reins broke and the horse wheeled and went pounding and he turned with the rifle and the wolf to stand off the dogs suddenly all about him in a bedlam of howling and teeth and whited eyes.

They circled scrabbling in the dirt of the road and he pulled the wolf hard up against his leg and yelled at them and whacked them away with the barrel of the rifle. Two were carrying broken lengths of chain at their collar and the third wore no collar at all. In all that whirling pandemonium he could feel the wolf trembling electrically against him and her heart hammering.

They were working hounds and although they circled and bayed he knew that they would be loath to attack anything a man held in absolute custody even if it was a wolf. He turned with them and caught one of them in the side of the head with the barrel of the rifle. Git, he shouted. Git. By now two men were coming from the house at a trot.

They called the dogs by name and two of the dogs actually stopped and looked back down the road. The third arched its back and came at the wolf with a mincing sidelong step and popped its teeth at her and drew away again and stood howling. One of the men had a dinnernapkin hanging from the neck of his shirt and he was breathing heavily. You Julie, he called. Git. Damnation. Get a stick or somethin, RL. Good God.

The other man unlatched his buckle and whipped his belt out through the loops and began to lay about him with the buckle end. Instantly the dogs were yelping and scurrying. The older man stopped and stood with his hands on his hips catching his breath. He turned to the boy. He saw the napkin in his shirt and pulled it free and wiped his forehead with it and stuck the napkin in his back pocket. You mind tellin me what the hell you're doin? he said.

Tryin to keep these damn dogs off of my wolf.

Dont give me no smart answer.

I aint. I come up on your fence and went to huntin a gate is all. I didnt know all hell was fixin to bust loose.

What the hell did you expect was goin to happen?

I didnt know there was dogs here.

Well hell, you seen the house didnt you?

Yessir.

The man squinted at him. You're Will Parham's boy. Aint you?

Yessir.

What's your name?

Billy Parham.

Well Billy this might sound to you like a ignorant question but what in the hell are you doin with that thing?

I caught it.

Well I reckon you did. It's the one with the stick in its mouth. Where are you started with it?

I was started home.

No you wasnt. You was headed yonway.

I was started home with it when I changed my mind.

What did you change it to?

The boy didnt answer. The dogs were pacing up and down, the hair standing along their backs.

RL, take the dogs on to the house and put em up. Tell Mama I'll be there directly.

He turned to the boy again. How do you aim to get your horse back?

Walk him down, I reckon.

Well it's about two miles to the first cattleguard.

The boy stood holding the wolf. He looked off down the road in the direction the horse had gone.

Will that thing ride in a truck? the man said.

The boy gave him a peculiar look.

Hell, the man said. I want you to listen at me. RL can you take him in the truck to catch his horse?

Yessir. Is his horse hard to catch?

Your horse hard to catch? the man said.

No sir.

He says it aint.

Well unless he just wants to go ridin I reckon I can get his horse for him.

You dont want to ride with that wolf is what it is, the man said.

It aint that I dont want to. It's that I aint goin to.

Well I was fixin to say that since it's liable to jump out of the bed of the truck why dont you take it up front in the cab with you and the boy can ride in the back?

RL had the dogs by their trailing pieces of chain and was fastening the third dog to them with his belt. I got a life sized picture of me ridin up the road with a wolf in the cab of my truck, he said. I can just see it plain as day.

The man stood looking at the wolf. He reached to adjust his hat but he had no hat on so he scratched his head. He looked at the boy. And here I thought I knowed all the lunatics in this valley, he said. Country crowdin up the way it is. You caint hardly keep up with your own neighbors even. Have you had your supper?

No sir.

Well come on to the house.

What do you want me to do with her?

Her?

This here wolf.

Well I guess it'll just have to lay around the kitchen till we get done eatin.

Lay around the kitchen?

It's a joke, son. Hell fire. You brought that thing in the house you could hear my wife in Albuquerque with the wires down.

I dont want to leave her outside. Somethin's liable to jump her.

I know that. Just come on. I wouldnt leave her out for nobody to see noways. They'd come and get me with a butterfly net.

They put the wolf in the smokehouse and left her and walked back to the kitchen. The man looked at the rifle the boy was carrying but he didnt say anything. When they got to the kitchen door the boy stood the rifle against the side of the house and the man held the door for him and they went in.

The woman had put the supper above the oven to warm and she brought everything out again and set a plate for the boy. Outside they heard RL start the truck. They passed the dishes, bowls of mashed potatoes and pinto beans and a platter of fried steaks. When he had his plate loaded with about all it could hold he looked up at the man. The man nodded at his plate.

We done blessed the food once, he said. So unless you got some personal business to conduct just tuck on in.

Yessir.

They began to eat.

Mama, the man said, see if you can get him to tell us where it is he's headed with that lobo.

If he dont want to say he dont have to, the woman said.

I'm takin her to Mexico.

The man reached for the butter. Well, he said. That seems like a good idea.

I'm goin to take her down there and turn her loose.

The man nodded. Turn her loose, he said.

Yessir.

She's got some pups somewheres, aint she?

No sir. Not yet she dont.

You sure about that?

Yessir. She's fixin to have some.

What have you got against the Mexicans?

I dont have nothin against em.

You just figured they might could use another wolf or two.

The boy cut a piece from his steak and forked it up. The man watched him.

How are they fixed for rattlesnakes down there do you reckon?

I aint takin her to give to nobody. I'm just takin her down there and turnin her loose. It's where she come from.

The man troweled butter very methodically along the edge of a biscuit with his knife. He put the top back on the biscuit and looked at the boy.

You a very peculiar kid, he said. Did you know that?

No sir. I was always just like everbody else far as I know.

Well you aint.

Yessir.

Tell me this. You aint plannin on just dumpin that thing across the line are you? Cause if you are I'm goin to follow you out there with a rifle.

I was goin to take her back to the mountains.

Take her back to the mountains, the man said. He looked at the biscuit speculatively and then bit slowly into it.

Where all is your family from? the woman said.

We're up at the Charcas.

She means before that, the man said.

We come out of Grant County. And De Baca fore that.

The man nodded.

We been down here a long time.

What's a long time?

Goin on ten years.

Ten years, the man said. Time just flies, dont it?

Go on and eat your supper, the woman said. Dont pay no attention to him.

They ate. After a while the truck pulled into the yard and passed the house and the woman got up from the table and went to get RL's plate from the warmer over the stove.

When they walked out after supper it was evening and growing cold and the sun was low over the mountains to the west. Bird stood in the yard tied by a rope halter to the gate and the bridle and reins were hung over the saddlehorn. The woman stood in the kitchen door and watched them cross toward the smokehouse.

Let's be careful about openin this door, the man said. If that thing has come out of that muzzletie you'll wish you was in a bathtub with a alligator.

Yessir, the boy said.

The man lifted the open lock from the haspstaple and the boy pushed the door in carefully. She was standing, backed into the corner. There was no window in the little adobe building and she blinked when the light fell across her.

She's all right, the boy said.

He pushed the door open.

That poor thing, the woman said.

The rancher turned patiently. Jane Ellen, he said, what are you doin out here?

That leg looks awful. I'm goin to get Jaime.

You're goin to what?

Just wait here.

She turned and set off across the yard. Half way she pulled off the coat she'd thrown over her shoulders and put it on. The man leaned in the door and shook his head.

Where was she goin? the boy said.

More craziness, the man said. We could be in a epidemic.

He stood in the doorway and rolled a smoke while the boy sat holding the wolf by the rope.

You dont use these do you? the man said.

No sir.

That's good. Dont start.

He smoked. He looked at the boy. What would you take for her cash money? he said.

She aint for sale.

What would you take if she was?

I wouldnt. Cause she aint.

When the woman came back she had with her an old Mexican who carried a small green tin deedbox under his arm. He greeted the rancher and nudged his hat and entered the smokehouse with the woman behind him. The woman was carrying a bundle of clean sheeting. The Mexican nodded to the boy and touched his hat again and knelt in front of the wolf and looked at it.

Puede detenerla? he said.

Sí, said the boy.

Necesitas más luz? the woman said.

Sí, said the Mexican.

The man stepped out into the yard and dropped the cigarette and stepped on it. They moved the wolf toward the door and the boy held her while the Mexican took her by the elbow and studied the damaged foreleg. The woman set the tin box on the floor and opened it and took out a bottle of witch-hazel and doped a piece of the sheeting with it. She handed it to the Mexican and he took it and looked at the boy.

Estás listo, joven?

Listo.

He renewed his grip on the wolf and wrapped his legs around her. The Mexican took hold of the wolf's foreleg and began to clean the wound.

She let out a strangled yelp and reared twisting in the boy's arms and snatched her foot out of the Mexican's grip.

Otra vez, the Mexican said.

They began again.

On the second attempt she slung the boy about the room and the Mexican stepped back quickly. The woman had already backed away. The wolf was standing with the slobber seething in and out between her teeth and the boy was lying on the floor beneath her hanging on to her neck. The rancher out in the yard had started to roll another cigarette but now he put the sack back in his shirtpocket and adjusted his hat.

Hang on a minute, he said. Damnation. Just hold it a minute.

He climbed through the door and reached and got hold of the wolf by the rope and twisted the rope in his fist.

People hear about me givin first aid to a damn wolf I wont be able to live in this county, he said. All right. Do your damndest. Ándale.

They finished their surgery in the last light of the sun. The Mexican had pulled the loose flap of skin into place and he sat patiently sewing it with a small curved needle clamped in a hemostat and when he was done he daubed it with Corona Salve and wrapped it in sheeting and tied it. RL had come out and stood watching them and picking his teeth.

Did you give her some water? the woman said.

Yes mam. It's kindly hard for her to drink.

I guess if you took that thing off of her she'd bite.

The rancher stepped over the wolf and out into the yard. Bite, he said. Good God almighty.

When he rode out thirty minutes later it was all but dark. He'd given the trap to the rancher to keep for him and he had a huge lunch wrapped in a cloth packed away in the mochila along with the rest of the sheeting and the jar of Corona Salve and he had an old Saltillo blanket rolled and tied behind the saddle. Someone had spliced new leather into the broken bridle-reins and the wolf was wearing a harnessleather dogcollar with a brass plate that had the rancher's name and RFD number and Cloverdale NM stamped into it. The rancher walked out to the gate with him and undid the gatelatch and swung it open and the boy led the horse through with the wolf behind and mounted up.

You take care, son, the man said.

Yessir. I will. Thank you.

I thought about keepin you here. Send for your daddy.

Yessir. I know you did.

He may want to whip me over it.

No he wont.

Well. Watch out for the banditos.

Yessir. I will. I thank you and the missus.

The man nodded. The boy raised one hand and reined the horse about and set out across the darkening land with the wolf hobbling behind. The man stood at the gate watching after him. All to the south was the dark of the mountains where they rode and he could not skylight them there and soon they were swallowed up and lost horse and rider in the oncoming night. The last thing he saw on that windblown waste was the white bandaged leg of the wolf moving random and staccato like some pale djinn out there antic in the growing cold and dark. Then it too vanished and he closed the gate and turned toward the house.

THEY CROSSED in that deep twilight a broad volcanic plain bounded within the rim of hills. The hills were a deep blue in the blue dusk and the round feet of the pony clopped flatly on the gravel of the desert floor. The night was falling down from the east and the darkness that passed over them came in a sudden breath of cold and stillness and passed on. As if the darkness had a soul itself that was the sun's assassin hurrying to the west

as once men did believe, as they may believe again. They rode
up off the plain in the final dying light man and wolf and horse
over a terraceland of low hills much eroded by the wind and
they crossed through a fenceline or crossed where a fenceline
once had been, the wires long down and rolled and carried off
and the little naked mesquite posts wandering singlefile away
into the night like an enfilade of bent and twisted pensioners.
They rode through the pass in the dark and there he sat the
horse and watched lightning to the south far over the plains of
Mexico. The wind was thrashing softly through the trees in the
pass and in the wind were spits of sleet. He made his camp in
the lee of an arroyo south of the pass and gathered wood and
made a fire and gave the wolf all the water she would drink.
Then he tied her to the washedout elbow of a cottonwood and
walked back and unsaddled and hobbled the horse. He unrolled
the blanket and threw it over his shoulders and took the mochila
and went and sat before the fire. The wolf sat on her haunches
below him in the draw and watched him with her intractable
eyes so red in the firelight. From time to time she would bend
to try the bindings on her leg with her sideteeth but she could
not grip them for the stick in her jaws.

He took a sandwich of steak and lightbread from the mochila
and unwrapped it and sat eating. The little fire sawed about in
the wind and the fine sleet fell slant upon them out of the
darkness and hissed in the coals. He ate and watched the wolf.
She pricked her ears and turned and looked out at the night but
whatever was passing passed and after a while she stood and
looked bleakly at the ground that was not of her choosing and
circled three times and lay down facing the fire with her tail
over her nose.

He woke all night with the cold. He'd rise and mend back
the fire and she was always watching him. When the flames
came up her eyes burned out there like gatelamps to another
world. A world burning on the shore of an unknowable void.
A world construed out of blood and blood's alcahest and blood
in its core and in its integument because it was that nothing save

blood had power to resonate against that void which threatened hourly to devour it. He wrapped himself in the blanket and watched her. When those eyes and the nation to which they stood witness were gone at last with their dignity back into their origins there would perhaps be other fires and other witnesses and other worlds otherwise beheld. But they would not be this one.

The last few hours before dawn he did sleep, cold or no. He rose in the gray light and pulled the blanket about him and knelt and tried to blow life into the dead ashes of the fire. He walked out to where he could watch the east for the sunrise. A mottled scud of clouds lay across the neutral desert sky. The wind had abated and the dawn was soundless.

When he approached the wolf holding the canteen she did not bridle or arch her back at him. He touched her and she edged away. He held her by the collar and pushed her down and sat trickling the water between her teeth while her tongue worked and her gullet jerked and the cold slant eye watched his hand. He held his hand under her jaw at the far side to save the water running out on the ground and she drank the canteen dry. He sat stroking her. Then he reached down and felt her belly. She struggled and her eye rolled wildly. He spoke to her softly. He put the flat of his hand between her warm and naked teats. He held it there for a long time. Then he felt something move.

When he set out across the valley to the south the grass was golden in the morning sun. Antelope were grazing on the plain a half mile to the east. He looked back to see if she had taken notice of them but she had not. She limped along behind the horse steadfast and doglike and in this fashion they crossed sometime near noon the international boundary line into Mexico, State of Sonora, undifferentiated in its terrain from the country they quit and yet wholly alien and wholly strange. He sat the horse and looked out over the red hills. To the east he could see one of the concrete obelisks that stood for a boundary marker. In that desert waste it had the look of some monument to a lost expedition.

Two hours later they'd left the valley and begun to climb through the low hills. Sparse grass and ocotillo. A few thin cattle trotted off before them. By and by they struck the Cajón Bonita which was the main trail south through the mountains and by the side of this track an hour later they came upon a small rancho.

He sat the horse and pulled the wolf close to him by the rope and he called out and waited to see if dogs would show but none did. He rode slowly. There were three crumbling adobe houses and a man dressed in rags stood in the doorway of one of them. The place had the look of an old waystation fallen into ruin. He rode forward and halted in front of the man and sat with his hands crossed at the wrists and resting on the pommel of his saddle.

Adónde va? the man said.

A las montañas.

The man nodded. He wiped his nose with his sleeve and turned and looked toward the mountains so spoken. As if he had not properly considered them before. He looked at the boy and at the horse and at the wolf and at the boy again.

Es cazador usted?

Sí.

Bueno, said the man. Bueno.

The day was cold for all that the sun shone and yet the man was half naked nor was there any smoke coming from the buildings. He looked at the wolf.

Es buena cazadora su perra?

The boy looked at the wolf. Sí, he said. Mejor no hay.

Es feroz?

A veces.

Bueno, said the man. Bueno. He asked the boy if he had tobacco, if he had coffee, if he had meat. The boy had none of these things and the man seemed to accept the inevitable truth of it. He stood leaning in the doorway, looking at the ground. After a while the boy realized that he was discussing something with himself.

Bueno, the boy said. Hasta luego.

The man flung up one arm. His rags flapped about him.
Ándale, he said.

He rode on. When he looked back the man was still in the
doorway. He was looking out back down the trail as if perhaps
to see who might be coming next.

By late afternoon when he would dismount and advance toward her with the canteen she would dip slowly to the ground
like a circus animal and roll onto her side waiting. The yellow
eye watching, the ear shifting with little movements within the
arc of its rotation. He didnt know how much of the water she
was getting or how much she needed. He sat trickling the water
between her teeth and looking into her eye. He touched the
pleated corner of her mouth. He studied the veined and velvet
grotto into which the audible world poured. He began to talk
to her. The horse raised its head from its trailside grazing and
looked back at him.

They rode on. The country was high rolling desert and the
trail ran the crests of the ridges and although it seemed traveled
he saw no one. On the slopes were acacia, scrub oak. Open
parks of juniper. In the evening a rabbit appeared in the middle
of the trail a hundred feet in front of him and he reined the
horse up and put two fingers to his teeth and whistled and the
rabbit froze and he stepped down and shucked the rifle backward
out of the scabbard and cocked it all in a single movement and
raised the rifle and fired.

The horse shied wildly and he snatched the reins out of the
air and hauled it around and got it calmed. The wolf had vanished into the trailside brush. He held the rifle at his waist and
levered the spent shell out of the chamber and caught it and put
it in his pocket and levered a fresh shell in and let down the
hammer with his thumb and undallied the rope and let the reins
drop and walked back to see about the wolf.

She was trembling in the weeds just short of a small twisted
juniper where she'd sought to hide. At his approach she sprang
against the rope and stood thrashing. He stood the rifle against

a tree and walked her down along the rope and held her and talked to her but he could not calm her and she did not stop trembling. After a while he took the rifle and went back out to the horse and shoved the rifle into the scabbard and walked back up the trail to look for the rabbit.

There was a long furrow down the center of the track that the rifle slug had plowed and the rabbit had been slung up into the bushes where it lay with its guts hanging in gray loops. It was all but in two pieces and he pooled it up all warm and downy in his hands with the head lolling and carried it out through the woods till he could find a windfall tree. There he kicked away the loose pinebark with the heel of his boot and brushed and blew it clean and laid the rabbit across the wood and took out his knife and straddling the log he skinned the rabbit out and gutted it and cut off the head and feet. He diced up the liver and heart on the log with his knife and sat looking at it. It didnt look much. He wiped his hand in the dead grass and took the rabbit and began to fillet strips from the back and hindquarters and to dice them as well until what he did have made a handful and then he wrapped them in the skin of the rabbit and folded away the knife.

He walked back and spiked the dead rabbit on a broken pine limb and went to where the wolf lay crouched. He squatted and held his hand out to her but she backed away at the end of the rope. He took a small piece of the rabbit's liver and held it to her. She sniffed it delicately. He watched her eyes and the speculation in them. He watched the leather nostrils. She turned her head to one side and when he offered the piece again she tried to back away.

Maybe you just aint hungry enough yet, he said. But you're fixin to get that way.

He made camp that night in a little swale under the windward side of the ridge and he skewered the rabbit on a paloverde pole and set it to broil in front of the fire before he even went to see about the horse and the wolf. When he approached her she stood and the first thing he saw was that the wrapping was gone from her leg. Then he saw that the stick between her teeth was gone. Then he saw that the cord with which her mouth was tied was gone.

She stood square to him with the hackles standing along her back. The catchrope tied to her collar and looped along the ground was frayed and wet where she'd been chewing it.

He stopped and stood dead still. He backed along the rope until he reached the horse and then untied the rope from the saddlehorn. He didnt take his eyes from her.

Holding the free end of the rope he began to circle the wolf. She turned in place watching him. He put a small pine tree between them. He tried to move in a casual manner but he felt all his motives naked to her. He handed the rope in a loop over the top of a high limb and caught it again and then backed away and pulled the rope taut. The slack came uncoiled out of the weeds and pine needles and tugged at her collar. She lowered her head and followed.

When she was standing under the limb he pulled the rope until her forefeet were all but off the ground and then slacked it just slightly and tied the rope off and stood looking at her. She bared her teeth at him and turned and tried to move away but she could not. She seemed to be at odds what to do. After a while she raised her injured leg and began to lick it.

He went back to the fire and piled on all the wood he'd collected. Then he got the canteen and he took one of the last of the sandwiches from the mochila and shucked it out of its wrapper and carried the canteen and the paper back to the wolf.

She watched while he scooped out a hole in the soft turf and she watched while he beat it smooth with the back of his bootheel. Then he spread the paper in the depression and weighed it with a rock and poured it full from the canteen.

He untied the rope and paid out slack as he backed away. She stood watching him. He stepped back a few more paces and squatted on the ground holding the rope. She looked at the fire and she looked at him. She sat on her haunches and licked her sore chops. He rose and went to the hole and poured in more water and splashed it about. Then he screwed the cap back on the canteen and stood it beside the waterhole and backed away again and sat. They watched each other. It was almost dark. She stood and tested the air with small nudging motions of her nose. Then she began to come forward.

When she reached the water she sniffed at it tentatively and raised her head to look at him. She looked at the fire again and at the shape of the horse beyond the fire. Her eyes glowed in the light. She lowered her nose to sniff at the water. Her eyes did not leave him or cease to burn and as she lowered her head to drink the reflection of her eyes came up in the dark water like some other self of wolf that did inhere in the earth or wait in every secret place even to such false waterholes as this that the wolf would be always corroborate to herself and never wholly abandoned in the world.

He squatted there watching her with the rope in both hands. Like a man entrusted with the keeping of something which he hardly knew the use of. When she'd drunk the hole dry she licked her mouth and looked at him and then leaned and sniffed at the canteen. The canteen fell over and she jerked away from it and then backed off to her site under the limb and sat again and began to lick her foot again.

He pulled the rope snug overhead and tied it and then walked back to the fire. He turned the rabbit on its spit and got the rabbitskin with the diced pieces and walked back and wafted it in front of her. Then he spread the skin open on the ground and untied and slacked the rope and backed away with it.

He watched her.

She leaned and sniffed the air.

It's rabbit, he said. I guess you aint ever eat any rabbit before.

He waited to see if she would come forward but she would not. He took the wind's direction by the smoke from the fire and gathered up the skin and carried it around upwind of her and held it out again in one hand while he held the rope with the other. He laid the skin down and backed away but still she made no move.

He walked around and tied off the rope as before and went back to the fire. The rabbit on the spit was half burnt and half raw and he sat and ate it and then with his knife constructed a muzzle out of his belt and out of two long pieces of leather that he cut from the fender of the saddle. He fitted the pieces with slits and latigos, studying the wolf from time to time where she lay curled under the tree with the rope ascending vertically in the firelight.

I reckon you think you'll wait till I'm asleep and then you can see about gettin loose, he said.

She raised her head and looked at him.

Yeah, he said. I'm talkin to you.

When he had the muzzle done he turned it in his hand and tried the buckle. It looked pretty good. He folded the knife away and stuffed the muzzle into his back pocket and got the last lengths of pigginstring from out of the mochila and hung them through his beltloop and took the horse's hobbles and put them in his other back pocket. Then he walked over to where the rope was tied. The wolf rose and stood waiting.

He pulled her slowly up by her collar. She pawed at the rope and tried to get at it with her teeth. He spoke to her and tried to calm her but there seemed no point in it so he just hauled her up and halfhitched the rope with her standing upright and half garrotted and her head almost touching the limb overhead. Then he dropped to the ground and crawled to where she stood twisting and tied her back feet together with one of the hobbles and looped the free end of the catchrope around the hobble and tied it and rolled away from under her and stood and backed away. He pulled the halfhitch free and paying out slack to the collar end of the rope with one hand he began to pull her towards him by the legs with the other. If anybody was to see this, he told her, they'd come and carry me off to the loonybin in a rig just like it.

When he had her stretched out he took out the other hobble and tied her back legs to the little jackpine he'd been using for a snubbingpost and then freed the end of the catchrope from her legs and looped up the slack and slung it over his shoulder. When she felt the rope go slack she wrenched herself up and began to snap at the ropes on her legs. He hauled her down again and then walked in a wide swath around her till he could reach the limb the rope was looped over. He paid the free end of the rope back over the limb and stepped away and stretched her out flat on the ground.

I know you think I'm tryin to kill you, he said. But I aint.

He tied the rope off to another of the little jackpines and took the pigginstring from his beltloop and approached her where she lay taut and quivering and gasping between the ropes. He made a noose of the cord and tried to drop it over her nose. On the second try she grabbed it in her mouth. He stood over her, waiting for her to turn loose of it. The yellow eyes watched him.

Turn loose, he said.

He got hold of the cord and pulled at it.

All right, he said. Dont get stupid on me now. He wasnt talking to the wolf. She gets hold of you, he said, they wont even find a beltbuckle.

When she would not turn loose of the pigginstring he got hold of the rope to her collar and pulled on it until he'd cut off her air. Then he reached and got the pigginstring and still holding the rope taut he slung it loose and slipped it over her mouth and pulled her mouth shut and made three passes with the cord and halfhitched it and let go the rope again. He sat back. The fire was dying and with it the light. All right, he said. Dont quit now. Hell, you still got ten fingers.

He pulled the muzzle from his pocket and fitted it over her nose. It fit pretty well. The nosepiece was too loose and he took it off again and took out his knife and made new slits and redid the latigos and refitted it and then buckled it behind her ears. Then buckled it a notch tighter. He fastened the two trailing jesses to her collar and then he reached through the side of the muzzle with the knife and cut the pigginstring he'd tied her mouth with.

The first thing she did was to suck in a long drink of air. Then she tried to bite the leather. But he'd used the saddle leather around her nose in a broad bosal and she couldnt get it between her teeth for the stiffness of it. He untied her back legs and stepped away. She got up and began to pitch and toss at the end of the rope. He squatted in the pine needles watching her. When she finally quit he rose and untied the rope and led her to the fire.

He thought she'd be terrifed of it but she was not. He hitched the rope midlength to the horn of the saddle where it stood drying before the fire and he got out the sheeting and the jar of salve and sat astraddle of her and cleaned and dressed the leg and rewrapped it. He thought she'd try to bite him even with the muzzle on but she did not. When he was done he let her up and she rose and walked to the end of the rope and sniffed at the wrapping and lay down watching him.

He slept with the saddle for a pillow. Twice in the night he woke with the saddle moving under his head and he reached and snatched at the rope and spoke to her. He lay with his feet to the fire so that if she circled in the night and dragged the rope through the fire she'd have to drag it over him and so wake him. He already knew that she was smarter than any dog but he didnt know how much smarter. Coyotes were yapping in the hills below them and he turned to see if she paid any mind to them but she appeared to be asleep. Yet as soon as his glance fell on her she opened her eyes. He looked away. He waited and then tried it again with more stealth. The eyes opened as before.

He nodded and slept and the fire drew down to coals and he woke in the cold to find the wolf watching him. When he woke again the moon was down and the fire was all but out. It was bitter cold. The stars stood fixed in their places like stampings in a tin lantern. He got up and fed wood to the fire and coaxed back the flame with his hat. The coyotes had hushed and the night was all darkness and silence. He'd had a dream and in the dream a messenger had come in off the plains from the south with something writ upon a ledgerscrap but he could

not read it. He looked at the messenger but that face was obscured in shadow and featureless and he knew that the messenger was messenger alone and could tell him nothing of the news
he bore.

In the morning he rose and built back the fire and squatted
shivering before it wrapped in the blanket. He ate the last sandwich the rancher's wife had made for him and then he got the
rabbitskin from the mochila and walked over to where the wolf
was lying. She stood at his approach. He unwrapped the stiffen-
ing skin and held it out to her. She sniffed at it and glanced at
him and circled two steps and stood looking at it with her ears
slightly forward.

I believe you'd almost eat, he said.

He walked off and found a broken section of limb and cut it
to length and with his knife carved one end of it into a thin
spatula. Then he walked back and sat on the ground and got
hold of the wolf by the collar and pulled her down against his
leg and held her till she quit struggling. He spread the skin on
the ground and scooped up a bit of the dark heartmeat and held
that feral head to him and passed the spatula back and forth for
her to smell. Then cupping her long nose in his hand he raised
with his thumb the strange black leather fold of her upper lip.
She opened her mouth and when she did he slid the spatula
through the leather straps and between her teeth and turned it
over and wiped it clean on her tongue and withdrew it.

He thought she would very likely bite the spatula but she
didnt. She closed her mouth. He saw her tongue move. Her
gullet jerk. When she opened her mouth again she had swallowed the meat.

When she had eaten all of the small handful of the rabbit he
had for her he pitched away the skin and wiped the stick in the
grass and put it in his pocket and walked out to where he'd last
seen the horse. The horse stood half way down the mountain
in a swale of winter grass and he walked it down with the bridle
in his hand and led it back up to the camp and saddled it and
tied the wolf's rope to the saddlehorn and mounted up and rode

out south along the Cajón Bonita deeper into the mountains with the wolf at heel.

He rode all day. The wolf seemed to take an interest in the country and she would raise her head and look out over the rolling meadowlands of yellow grass and standing lechugilla that fell away to the west of the saddleridges. He'd stop at the crest of a rise to let the horse blow and she would skulk into the trailside weeds and squat and make water and turn to sniff at the spot. The first pilgrims they encountered trekking north with their loaded burros halted a hundred yards out and gave the trail at his approach. They greeted him sparingly. The wolf crouched and pressed herself into the grass with her hackles up. Then the first of the burros caught her scent.

The animal's nostrils opened like two holes in wet mud and its eyes went blind white. It flattened its ears back and bowed up and shot out both hind heels and stove a leg from under the burro behind it. This animal fell down screaming beside the trail and in the space of a heartbeat all bedlam was loosed. The burros snapped their leads on every side and went rocketing off down the side of the mountain like enormous partridges with the arrieros after them and the animals careening off the sides of the trees and falling and rolling and righting again and running and the rude wood kiacks breaking up and the panniers breaking open and trailing down the mountainside behind them the baled pelts and hides and blankets and chattelgoods they contained.

He reined in the horse where it stamped and skittered and reached and untied the rope from the saddlehorn. The wolf had run off down the mountain and wrapped herself around a tree and he rode down to get her. By the time he came back dragging her behind him stifflegged and half crazed the trail was deserted save for an old woman and a young girl who sat in the grass by the trailside passing tobacco and cut cornhusks between them and rolling cigarettes. The girl was a year or two younger than he was and she lit her cigarette with an esclarajo and passed it to the old woman and blew smoke and tossed her head and stared at him boldly.

He coiled the rope and dismounted and dropped the reins and hung the coiled rope over the saddlehorn and touched the brim of his hat with two fingers.

Buenos días, he said.

They nodded, the older woman spoke his greeting back. The girl watched him. He walked the wolf down along the rope to where it crouched in the weeds and knelt and talked to it and led it by the collar back out into the trail.

Es Americano, the woman said.

Sí.

She sucked fiercely on the cigarette and squinted at him through the smoke.

Es feroz la perra, no?

Bastante.

They wore homemade dresses and huaraches cobbled up out of leather scraps and rawhide. The woman had on a black shawl or rebozo about her shoulders but the girl was all but naked in the thin cotton dress. Their skin was dark like an indian's and their eyes coal black and they smoked the way poor people eat which is a form of prayer.

Es una loba, he said.

Cómo? said the woman.

Es una loba.

The woman looked at the wolf. The girl looked at the wolf and at the woman.

De veras? said the woman.

Sí.

The girl looked as if she might be about to rise and back away but the woman laughed at her and told her that the caballero was only having a joke with them. She put the cigarette in the corner of her mouth and called to the wolf. She patted the ground for it to come.

Qué pasó con la pata? she said.

He shrugged. He said that she had caught it in a trap. Far below them on the side of the mountain they could hear the cries of the arrieros.

She offered their tobacco but the boy thanked her no. She shrugged. He said that he was sorry about the burros but the old woman said that the arrieros were inexperienced and had little control over their animals anyway. She said that the revolution had killed off all the real men in the country and left only the tontos. She said moreover that fools beget their own kind and here was the proof of it and that as only foolish women would have aught to do with them their progeny were twice doomed. She sucked again on the cigarette which was now little more than ash and let it fall to the ground and squinted at him.

Me entiende? she said.

Sí, claro.

She studied the wolf. She looked at him again. The eye half closed was probably from some injury but it lent her the air of one demanding candor. Va a parir, she said.

Sí.

Como la jovencita.

He looked at the girl. She didnt look pregnant. She had turned her back on them and sat smoking and looking out over the country where there was nothing to be seen although a few faint cries still drifted up the slope.

Es su hija? he said.

She shook her head. She said that the girl was the wife of her son. She said that they were married but that they had no money to pay the priest so they were not married by the priest.

Los sacerdotes son ladrónes, the girl said. It was the first she had spoken. The woman nodded her head at the girl and rolled her eyes. Una revolucionaria, she said. Soldadera. Los que no pueden recordar la sangre de la guerra son siempre los más ardientes para la lucha.

He said that he had to go. She paid no mind. She said that when she was a child she'd seen a priest shot in the village of Ascención. They'd stood him against the wall of his own church and shot him with rifles and gone away. When they were gone the women of the village came forward and knelt and lifted up the priest but the priest was dead or dying and some of the women dipped their handkerchiefs in the blood of the priest and blessed themselves with the blood as if it were the blood of Christ. She said that when young people see priests shot in the streets it changes their view of religion. She said that the young nowadays cared nothing for religion or priest or family or country or God. She said that she thought the land was under a curse and asked him for his opinion but he said he knew little of the country.

Una maldición, she said. Es cierto.

All sound of the arrieros had died away on the slopes below them. Only the wind blew. The girl finished her cigarette and rose and dropped it in the trail and stomped on it with her huarache and twisted it into the dirt as if it contained some malevolent life. The wind blew her hair and it blew her thin dress against her. She looked at the boy. She said the old woman was always talking about curses and dead priests and that she was half crazy and to pay her no mind.

Sabemos lo que sabemos, the old woman said.

Sí, said the girl. Lo que es nada.

The old woman held out one hand palm up in the direction of the girl. As if to offer her in evidence of all that she claimed. She invited him to observe the one who knew. The girl tossed her head. She said that at least she knew who was the father of her child. The woman threw her hand up. Ay ay, she said.

The boy held the wolf against his leg by the rope. He said that he had to go.

The old woman jutted her chin at the wolf. She said that the wolf's time was very near at hand.

Sí. De acuerdo.

Debe quitar el bosal, said the girl.

The woman looked at the girl. The girl said that if the perra should have her puppies in the night she should lick them. She said that he should not leave her muzzled at night because who could say how near her time was? She said that she would have to lick the pups. She said that all the world knew this.

Es verdad, the woman said.

The boy touched his hat. He wished them a good day.

Es tan feroz la perra? the girl said.

He said that she was. He said that she could not be trusted.

She said that she would like to have a little dog from such a bitch because it would grow up to be a watchdog and it would bite everyone who came around. Todos que vengas alrededor, she said. She made a sweep with her hand that took in the pines and the wind in the pines and the vanished arrieros and the woman watching her out of the dark rebozo. She said that such a dog would bark in the night if there were thieves about or anyone at all who was not wanted.

Ay ay, said the woman, rolling her eyes.

He said that he had to go. The woman told him to go with God and the jovencita just told him to go if he wished and he walked out the trail with the wolf and caught his horse and tied the rope to the saddlehorn and mounted up. When he looked back the girl was sitting beside the woman. They werent talking but just sitting side by side, waiting for the arrieros to return. He rode out along the ridge to the first turning in the trail and looked back again but they had not moved or changed in attitude and they seemed at that distance much subdued. As if his departure had wrested something from them.

The country itself was changeless. He rode on and the high mountains to the southwest seemed no nearer at the day's end than had they been some image in the eye itself. Toward evening riding up through a stand of dwarf oak he flushed a flock of turkeys.

They'd been feeding in the wood below him and they sailed out over a wash and disappeared into the trees on the far side. He sat the horse and marked them with his eye. Then he rode down off the trail and stepped down and tied the horse and unhitched the rope and tied the wolf to a tree and took the rifle and jacked forward the lever to see that there was a shell chambered and then set off across the little valley with one eye on the sun where it was already backlighting the trees at the head of the draw to the west.

The turkeys were on the ground in a glade, passing back and forth among the slatted treetrunks in the deepening dusk like gallery birds in a carnival booth. He squatted and got his breath and began to advance slowly upon them. When he was still the better part of a hundred yards above them one of the hens stepped clear of the banded shadows and stood in the open and paused and craned her neck and stepped again. He cocked the rifle and took a grip on the trunk of a small ashtree and laid the barrel over his foreknuckle and wedged it against the side of the tree with the back of his thumb and took a sight on the bird. He allowed for drop and he allowed for the way the light lay sidelong in the riflesights and fired.

The heavy rifle bucked and the echo of the shot went caroming out over the country. The turkey lay flopping and twisting on the ground. The other birds came boring out of the trees in every direction, some of them passing almost directly over him. He stood and ran toward the bird that was down.

There was blood everywhere in the leaves. She was lying on her side and her legs were running in the leaves and her neck was doubled back oddly. He grabbed her and pressed her to the ground and held her. The shot had broken her neck low and torn open the shoulder of one wing and he saw that he had very nearly missed her altogether.

He and the wolf between them ate the whole bird and then they sat by the fire side by side. The wolf snubbed up close on the rope and starting and quivering at every small eruption among the coals. When he touched her her skin ran and quivered under his hand like a horse's. He talked to her about his life but it didnt seem to rest her fears. After a while he sang to her.

In the morning riding out he came upon a party of mounted men, the first such he'd seen in the country. They were five in number and they rode good horses and all of them were armed. They reined up in the trail before him and hailed him in a man-

ner half amused while their eyes took inventory of everything
about him. Clothes, boots, hat. Horse and rifle. The mutilated
saddle. Lastly they studied the wolf. Who'd gone to try to hide
herself in the thin highcountry bracken a few feet off the trail.

Qué tienes allá, joven? they called.

He sat with his hands crossed on the pommel of his saddle.
He leaned and spat. He studied them from under the brim of
his hat. One of them had put his horse forward the better to see
the wolf but the horse balked and did not want to go and he
leaned forward and slapped its cheek and hauled it about roughly
with the reins. The wolf lay flat on the ground with her ears
back at the end of the rope.

Cuánto quieres por tu lobo? the man said.

He gathered the small slack out of the rope and rehitched it.
No puedo venderlo, he said.

Por qué no?

He studied the horseman. No es mia, he said.

No? De quién es?

He looked at the wolf where she lay quivering. He looked at
the blue mountains to the south. He said that the wolf had been
entrusted into his care but that it was not his wolf and he could
not sell it.

The man sat holding the reins loosely in one hand, the other
hand on his thigh. He turned his head and spat without taking
his eyes from the boy.

De quién es? he said again.

The boy looked at him and at the waiting riders in the trail.
He said that the wolf was the property of a great hacendado and
that it had been put in his care that no harm come to it.

Y este hacendado, said the rider, él vive en la colonia Morales?

The boy said that he did indeed live there and in other places
as well. The man studied him for a long time. Then he put his
horse forward and the other riders put their horses forward with
him. As if they were joined together by some unseen cord
or unseen principle. They rode past. They rode according to
seniority and the last to pass was much the youngest and as he

passed he looked at the boy and put his forefinger to the brim of his hat. Suerte, muchacho, he said. Then all rode on and none looked back.

It was cold in the mountains and there was yet snow in the high passes and snow on the Sierra de la Cabellera. Above the Cabellera Canyon snow lay in the trail for the better part of a mile. The snow in the trail was new snow and he was surprised to see the number of travelers who had been upon it and it occurred to him to wonder if there might not be in that country pilgrims so fearful as to quit the track entirely at the approach of any horseman. He studied the ground more closely. Tracks of men and burros. Tracks of women. A few bootprints but mostly the flat heelless prints of huaraches leaving the improbable imprint of tiretracks in that high wilderness. He saw the tracks of children and the tracks of the horses of the riders he had passed that morning. He saw the tracks of people barefoot in the snow. He rode on and as he rode he watched the wolf to see if she might betray the proximity of any travelers crouched in hiding by the wayside but she only trotted on behind the horse swinging her nose to test the air and leaving her own big tracks in the snow for the serranos to wonder at themselves.

They camped that night in the floor of a stone ravine and he led the wolf to a pool of standing water in the rocks below them and held the rope while she stepped down into the water and lowered her mouth into the pool to drink. She raised her head and he could see her gullet moving and the water running from her jaws. He sat in the rocks and held the rope and watched her. The water was black among the rocks in the deepening blue dusk and her breath smoked over the surface of it. She lowered and raised her head, drinking in the manner of birds.

For his supper he had a couple of tortillas with beans wrapped in them given to him by the sole other party he'd passed that day. They were Mennonites making their way north with a young girl to seek medical help. They looked like rustics out of a painting from the century before and they spoke little. They did not say what the girl's trouble was. The tortillas were leathery and the beans were beginning to sour but he ate them. The wolf watched. It aint nothin a wolf would eat, he told her. So dont be lookin.

He finished eating and took a long drink from the new cold water in the canteen and then he built up the fire and circled the perimeter of its light for all the wood he could collect. He'd pitched his little camp a good way below the trail but the glow of it could be seen at some distance in that country and he half expected late travelers might make their way to him in the night. None did. He sat wrapped in the blanket while the night grew cold and the stars ran burning down the sky to the south over the black shapes of the mountains where it must be that the wolves lived and had their home.

The day following in a southfacing valley he saw small blue flowers among the rocks and toward noon he passed through a broad gap in the mountains and stood looking out over the Bavispe River Valley. A faint blue haze hung over the trail in the switchback below. He was very hungry and he sat the horse and he and the wolf tested the air with their noses and then they rode on more cautiously.

The smoke was coming from a draw below the trail where a party of indians had nooned for their meal. They were laborers from the mines in western Chihuahua and they bore the mark of the tumpline across their narrow brows. There were six of them journeying overland to their village in Sonora bearing with them the body of one of their number killed under a scaffolding. They had been three days enroute and three days more lay before them and they had been fortunate in the weather. The dead body lay apart from them in the leaves upon a rude bier of poles and cowhide. It was wrapped in canvas and tied with bindings of grass and rope and the canvas of the shroud was worked with red and green ribbons and laid over with branches of the mountain ilex and one of the indians sat by it to guard it or perhaps to keep the dead man company. They spoke some spanish and they invited him to eat with little ceremony, such was the custom of the country. To the wolf they paid no attention whatever. They squatted in their thin homemade clothing eating pozole out of painted tin bowls with their fingers and passing from hand to hand a common pail that held tea made from some herb they favored. They sucked their fingers and dried them on the backs of their arms and rolled in cornhusks their punche cigarettes. None asked his business. Where he was from or where bound. They told him of uncles and fathers who'd fled to Arizona to escape the wars visited upon them by the Mexicans and one of them had been in that country himself just to see it, walking nine days through mountain and desert till he got there and nine days back. He asked the boy if he were from Arizona and the boy said that he was not and the indian nodded and said that it was customary among men to overstate the virtues of their own country.

That night from the edge of the meadow where he made his camp he could see the yellow windowlights of houses in a colonia on the Bavispe ten miles distant. The meadow was filled with flowers that shrank in the dusk and came forth again at the moon's rising. He made no fire. He and the wolf sat side by side in the dark and watched the shadows of things emerge on the meadow and step and trot and vanish and return. The wolf sat watching with her ears forward and her nose making constant small correction in the air. As if to make acts of abetment to the life in the world. He sat with the blanket over his shoulders and watched the moving shadows while the moon rose over the mountains behind him and the distant lights on the Bavispe winked out one by one till there were none.

In the morning he sat the horse on a gravel bar and studied the moving water where the broad clear river ran down and he studied the light on the riffles downriver where it bowed in the river's bend. He loosed the wolf's rope from the saddlehorn and dismounted. He led horse and wolf into the shallows and all three drank from the river and the water was cold and slatey to the taste. He rose and wiped his mouth and looked out across the country to the south where the high wild ranges of the Pilares Teras stood in the morning sun.

He could find no ford shallow enough for the wolf to cross

without swimming. Still he thought he could keep her afloat and he rode back upriver to the gravel bar and here he put the horse into the river.

He'd not gone far before the wolf was swimming and he'd not gone far before he saw that she was in trouble. Perhaps she could not breathe for the muzzle. She began to chop the water with rising desperation and the wrapping on her foreleg came loose and was flailing about in the water and this seemed to terrify her and she was trying to turn back against the rope. He halted the horse and the horse turned and stood with the water in flumes about its legs and faced the pull of the rope on the horn but by then he had dropped the reins in the river and stood down into water half way up his thigh.

He caught her by the collar and held her up and it was all he could do to stand. He got his other hand under her brisket to lift her up, his hand under the cold leather nipples that were almost naked of hair. He tried to calm her but she was trudging the water wildly. The catchrope lay in a long loop downriver and it was tugging at her collar and he held her up and worked his way back to the horse with the stones on the bottom of the river shifting under his boots and the water surging about his legs and he unhitched the rope and let the end of it float free. It uncoiled itself down the river and straightened and lay swaying in the current. The wrap of sheeting about the wolf's leg had come loose and floated off. He looked back toward the river bank. As he did so the horse surged past him and went clambering and half trotting across the shallows and up onto the gravel bar where it turned and stood smoking in the morning cold and then walked on downriver shaking its head.

He struggled back with the wolf, talking to her and keeping her head up. When they reached the shallows where she could get her footing he let go of her and walked up out of the river and stood on the bar and coiled the trailing rope out of the water while the wolf shook herself. When he had the rope coiled and hung over his shoulder he turned and looked for his horse.

Downriver on the gravel bar side by side were two horsemen watching him.

There was nothing about them that he liked. He looked past them to where his horse stood browsing in the willows with the stock of the rifle sticking out of the bootscabbard. He looked at the wolf. She was watching the riders.

They were dressed in dirty chino workclothes and they wore hats and boots and they had U S Government 45 automatic pistols in black leather holsters hanging from their belts. They had already put their horses forward and they rode at an insolent slouch. They rode up on his left side and one halted his horse and the other rode past and halted behind him. He turned, watching them. The first rider nodded to him. Then he looked back downriver at his horse and he looked at the wolf and he looked at him again.

De dónde viene? he said.

America.

He nodded. He looked out across the river. He leaned and spat. Sus documentos, he said.

Documentos?

Sí. Documentos.

No tengo ningunos documentos.

The man watched him for a while.

Qué es su nombre, he said.

Billy Parham.

The man gestured downriver with a slight jerk of his chin. Es su caballo?

Sí. Claro.

La factura por favor.

The boy looked at the other rider but the sun was behind him and his features were darkened. He looked to his inquisitor again. Yo no tengo esos papeles, he said.

Pasaporte?

Nada.

The rider sat his horse, his hands crossed loosely at the wrist.

He nodded to the other rider and the other rider detached himself and rode off down the gravel bar and caught the boy's horse and brought it back. The boy sat down in the gravel and pulled off his boots, one, the other, and poured the river water out of them and pulled them on again. He sat there with his elbows over his knees and he looked at the wolf and he looked across the river to the high Pilares rising in the sun. He knew that this day at least he would not be going there.

They took the path downriver, the leader riding with the boy's rifle across the bow of his saddle and the boy riding behind with the wolf close at the horse's heels and the third rider bringing up the rear a hundred feet behind. The path diverged from the river and ran out through a broad meadow where cattle were grazing. The cattle raised their heads with their slow jaws milling sideways and studied the riders and then bent to graze again. The riders rode on through the meadow until they struck a road and then turned south along the road and went on until they entered a settlement consisting of a handful of mud houses decomposing by the roadside.

They passed along the rutted street looking neither left nor right. A few dogs rose from their particular places in the sun and fell in behind the horses and sniffed after them. At an adobe building at the end of the street the riders halted and dismounted and the boy tied the wolf to the hounds of a wagon standing there and all entered.

The room had a musty odor to it. On the walls were faded frescoes and faded traces of a painted dado. The ruins of a linen ceiling hung in rags from the high vigas overhead. The floor was of large unglazed clay tiles and like the walls was badly out of true and the tiles were broken in many places where horses had walked upon them. The windows ran only along the south and east walls and contained no glass and they were shuttered that still had shutters while through the others the wind and dust blew and swallows passed in and out. At the far end of the room stood an old refectory table and a carved and ornate chair with a high back and against the wall behind it stood a steel filing cabinet whose top drawer had at one time been opened with an axe. There were tracks everywhere over the dusty tiles of birds and mice and lizards and dogs and cats. As if the room were a constant enigma to all things living in its vicinity. The riders stood under the mosslike hangings of the ceiling and the leader crossed to the double doors at the side of the room with the rifle cradled in one arm and tapped at the door and called out and then removed his hat and stood waiting.

In a few minutes the door opened and a young mozo stood there and he and the rider spoke and the man nodded toward the outside and the mozo looked toward the outer door and at the other rider and at the boy and then withdrew and shut the door. They waited. Outside in the street dogs had begun to assemble in front of the building. Some of them were visible through the open door. They sat looking at the tethered wolf and looking at each other while a rangy cur the color of ashes paced up and back before them with its tail up and the hair roached along its back.

It was a young and halelooking alguacil appeared in the door. He glanced briefly at the boy and turned to the man standing with the boy's rifle.

Dónde está la loba? he said.

Afuera.

He nodded.

They donned their hats and crossed the room. The man holding the rifle pushed the boy forward and the alguacil looked at him again.

Cuántos años tiene? he said.

Dieciseis.

Es su rifle?

Es de mi padre.

No es ladrón usted? Asesino?

No.

He jerked his chin at the man and told him to give the boy his rifle and then stepped out through the open door.

In the road in front of the house were upward of two dozen

dogs and almost as many children. The wolf had crawled up under the wagon and was backed against the wall of the building. Through the webs of the homemade muzzle you could see every tooth in its mouth. The alguacil crouched and pushed back his hat and set his hands palm down on his thighs and studied her. He looked at the boy. He asked if she were vicious and the boy said that she was. He asked him where he'd caught her and he said in the mountains. The man nodded. He rose and spoke to his deputies and then turned and went back into the building. The deputies stood uneasily and looked at the wolf.

Finally they untied the rope and dragged her from under the wagon. The dogs had begun to howl and to pace back and forth and the big gray dog darted in and snapped at the wolf's hindquarters. The wolf spun and bowed up in the road. The deputies pulled her away. The gray dog circled in for another sally and one of the deputies turned and fetched it a kick with his boot that caught it underneath the jaw and clapped its mouth shut with a slap of a sound that set the children to laughing.

By now the mozo had come from the house with a key and they dragged the wolf across the street and unlocked and unchained the doors to an adobe shed and put the wolf inside and locked the doors again. The boy asked them what they intended to do with the wolf but they only shrugged and they got their horses and mounted up and trotted back down the road, curbing the horses' heads this way and that and setting them to prancing as if there were women about. The mozo shook his head and went back inside with the key.

He sat by the door of the house all through the noon. He'd levered the shells out of the rifle and dried them and dried the rifle and reloaded it and put it back in the scabbard and he drank from the canteen and poured the rest of the water into the crown of his hat and watered the horse out of the hat and drove the pack of dogs away from the shed door. The streets were empty, the day cool and sunny. In the afternoon the mozo appeared at the door and said that he'd been sent to ask what he wanted. He said that he wanted his wolf. The mozo nodded and went back in again. When he came out again he said that he'd been sent to say that the wolf was seized as contraband but that he was free to go thanks to the clemency of the alguacil who had considered his youth. The boy said that the wolf was not contraband but was property entrusted into his care and that he must have it back. The mozo heard him out and then turned and went back into the house.

He sat. No one came. Late in the afternoon one of the pair of deputies returned at the head of a small and illsorted procession. Immediately behind came a small dark mule of the type used in the mines of that country and behind the mule an oldfashioned carreta with patched wooden wheels. Behind the cart a motley of people of the country all afoot, women and children, young boys, many of them bearing parcels or carrying baskets or pails.

They halted in front of the shed and the deputy stepped down and the cartdriver climbed down from the rude wood box of the carreta. They stood in the road drinking from a bottle of mescal and after a while the mozo came from the house and unlocked the shed doors and the deputy drew the chains rattling through the wooden barslots and flung the doors open and stood.

The wolf was in the farthest corner and she rose and stood blinking. The carretero stepped back and divested himself of his coat and put it over the mule's head and tied the sleeves under its jaws and stood holding the animal by the cheekstrap. The deputy entered the shed and picked up the rope and dragged the wolf into the doorway. The crowd fell back. Made bold by drink and by the awe of the onlookers the deputy seized the wolf by the collar and dragged her out into the road and then picked her up by the collar and by the tail and hefted her into the bed of the cart with one knee beneath her in the manner of men accustomed to loading sacks. He passed the rope along the side of the cart and halfhitched it through the boards at the front. The people in the road watched every movement. They watched with the attention of those who might be called upon to tell what they had seen. The deputy nodded to the carretero and the carretero loosed the knotted sleeves from under the mule's jaw and drew away the coat. He gathered the drivingreins together up under the mule's throat and stood holding the animal to see how it would do. The mule raised its head slightly to test the air. Then it jacked itself up onto its forelegs and kicked through the leather strap and stove in the bottom board of the carreta where the wolf was tied. The wolf came sliding and scrambling out of the open back of the cart dragging the broken board after it and the people cried out and turned to run. The mule screamed and flung itself sideways in the harness and broke away the offside cartshaft and fell into the road and lay kicking.

The carretero was strong and nimble and he managed to leap astride the little mule's neck and seize the mule's ear in his teeth till he could cover its head with the coat again. He looked about, gasping. The deputy who had been in the act of remounting his horse now stepped into the road again and seized the trailing rope and snatched the wolf up short. He untied the rope where it was hitched about the broken board and flung the board away and dragged the wolf back into the shed and shut the doors. Mire, called the carretero, lying in the road holding his coat over the mule's head, waving a hand at the wreckage. Mire. The deputy spat into the dust and walked across the road and into the house.

By the time they'd sent for someone to repair the cartshaft with lath and rawhide and by the time he'd done these repairs the day was well advanced. The pilgrims who had followed the cart into the town had deployed themselves under the shade of the buildings on the west side of the road and were eating their lunches and drinking lemonade. By late afternoon the cart was ready but the deputy was nowhere to be found. A boy was sent to the house to inquire. Another hour passed before he made his appearance and he adjusted his hat and eyed the sun and bent to examine the repair to the cartshaft as if he were deputized also to inspect such work and then he went back into the house. When he came out again he was accompanied by the mozo and they crossed the road to the shed and unlocked and unchained the doors and the deputy brought out the wolf again.

The carretero stood with the mule's blindfold head against his chest. The deputy studied him and then called for a mozo de cuadra. A young boy stepped forward. He instructed the boy to take charge of the mule and told the carretero to get in the wagon. The carretero relinquished the mule with some misgiving. He gave the muzzled shewolf a wide berth and climbed into the cart and unwrapped the reins from the stanchion and stood at the ready. The deputy once more lifted the wolf into the carreta and tied it close against the boards at the rear. The carretero looked back at the animal and looked at the deputy. His eyes moved over the waiting pilgrims now reassembled until he met the eyes of the young extranjero from whom the wolf had been appropriated. The deputy nodded to the mozo de cuadra and the mozo pulled away the carretero's coat from the mule's head and stepped away. The mule sprang forward wildly in the traces. The carretero fell back clutching at the topmost boards of the cart and trying not to fall on the wolf and the wolf lunged at her lead and let out a wild sad cry. The deputy laughed and booted his horse forward and snatched the coat from the mozo and swung it overhead like a lariat and threw it after the carretero and then reined up again in the road laughing while mule and cart and wolf and driver went bowling out through the settlement in a great clatter of wood and creation of dust.

The people were already gathering up their parcels. The boy went and got his saddle from the side of the house and saddled the horse and buckled up the saddlescabbard and mounted up and turned the horse into the rutted track. Those afoot pressed to the side of the road when the horse's shadow fell upon them. He nodded down to them. Adónde vamos? he said.

They looked up at him. Old women in rebozos. Young girls carrying baskets between them. A la feria, they said.

La feria?

Sí señor.

Adónde?

En el pueblo de Morelos.

Es lejos? he said.

They said that it was not far by horseback. Unas pocas leguas, they said.

He walked the horse beside them. Y adónde va con la loba? he said.

A la feria, sin duda.

He asked what was the purpose in taking the wolf to the fair but they seemed not to know. They shrugged, they tramped beside the horse. An old woman said that the wolf had been brought from the sierras where it had eaten many school-children. Another woman said that it had been captured in the company of a young boy who had run away naked into the woods. A third said that the hunters who had brought the wolf down out of the sierras had been followed by other wolves who howled at night from the darkness beyond their fire and some of the hunters had said that these wolves were no right wolves.

The road left the river and the river flats and led away to the north through a broad mountain valley. With dusk the company fell out in a high meadow and built a fire and set about cooking their supper. The boy tied his horse and sat in the grass, not quite one of them and not quite apart. He twisted the cap from his canteen and drank the last of his water and put the cap back and sat holding the empty container in his hands. After a while a boy came up to him and invited him to the fire.

They were elaborately polite. They called him caballero for all his sixteen years and he sat with his hat pushed back and his boots crossed before him and ate beans and napolitos and a machaca made from dried goatmeat that was rank and black and stringy and dusted with dry red pepper for traveling. Le gusta? they said. He said he liked it very much. They asked him where he came from and he said Nuevo Mexico and they glanced at one another and they said that he must be very sad to be so far from his home.

In the dusk the meadow looked a camp of gypsies or refugees. Their number had swelled with new arrivals along the road and there were new fires built and figures drifted back and forth across the darkened spaces between. Burros grazed on the meadow slope where it banked away against the dark lilac sky to the west and the little carretas stood tilted on their tongues in silhouette one behind the next like orecarts. Several men were in the company by now and were passing a bottle of mescal among themselves. In the dawn two of them were sitting yet before the cold dead ashes. The women turned out to cook breakfast, building back the fire and setting about slapping tortillas from the masa and laying them out on a comal cut from roofingtin. They worked around the seated drunks and around the packsaddles over which blankets had been hung to dry all with equal disregard.

It was midmorning before the caravan was under way. Those too drunk to travel were shown every consideration and room made for them among the chattels in the carts. As if some misfortune had befallen them that could as easily have visited any among them.

The road they traveled led through wilderness enough that they passed no habitation nor met upon it any other traveler at all. They made no stop at noon but soon thereafter passed through a gap in the mountains where two miles below them the river ran and the sparse houses of Colonia Morelos stood along the quadrature of its four streets like markers in a child's game drawn in the dust.

He left the company while they set up their camp on the floodplain south of the town and he turned his horse into the road downriver to see if he could find the wolf. The road was dried clay corrugated with cart tracks set so hard they would not break under the horse's hooves. The river was clear and cold where it came out of the high sierras to the south and it turned at the settlement to run south again under the western wall of the Pilares. He turned off the road and followed a path out along the river and stood the horse to drink from the cold riffles. An old man with a burro was gathering driftwood out on the gravel flats. The pale and twisted shapes of wood arranged atop the burro looked like some tapestry of bones. The boy put his horse forward upriver, the horse's hooves trudging in the round river gravels.

The town that he entered was an old Mormon settlement from the century before and he passed brick buildings with tin roofs, a brick store with a false wood front. In the alameda opposite the store bunting had been strung tree to tree and the members of a small brass band sat in the little kiosk as if perhaps awaiting the arrival of some dignitary. Along the streetfront and in the alameda were vendors selling cacahuates and ears of steamed corn dusted with red pepper and buñuelos and natillas and paper spills of fruit. He dismounted and tied the horse and took the rifle from the scabbard lest it be stolen and walked toward the alameda. Among the fairgoers in that little park of dried mud and starveling trees were visitors more alien than even he, families in rags that moved agape among the patched canvas pitchtents and Mennonites got up like medicineshow rubes in their straw hats and bib overalls and a row of children halted half dumbstruck before a painted canvas drop depicting garish human abnormalities and Tarahumara indians and Yaquis carrying bows and quivers of arrows and two Apache boys in deerskin boots with grave and coalblack eyes who'd come from their camp in the sierras where the last free remnants of their tribe lived like shadowfolk of the nation they had been and all of them with such gravity that the shabby circus of their beholding could as well have been the pageantry of some dread new dispensation visited upon them.

He found the wolf readily enough but he lacked the ten centavos required to see her. They'd rigged a makeshift tent of sheeting over the little tumbril of a cart and they'd put up a sign at the front that gave her history and the number of people she was known to have eaten. He stood and watched the few people filing in and out. They did not seem much animated by what they'd seen. When he asked them about the wolf they shrugged. They said a wolf was a wolf. They did not believe that she'd eaten anyone.

The man collecting the money at the fly of the pitchtent listened with his head bowed while the boy explained to him his situation. He raised his head and looked into the boy's eyes. Pásale, he said.

She was lying in the floor of the cart in a bed of straw. They'd taken the rope from her collar and fitted the collar with a chain and run the chain through the floorboards of the cart so that it was all that she could do to rise and stand. Beside her in the straw was a clay bowl that perhaps had held water. A young boy stood with his elbows hung over the top board of the cart with a jockeystick held loosely across his shoulder. When he saw enter what he took for a paying spectator he stood up and began to prod the wolf with the stick and to hiss at her.

She ignored the prodding. She was lying on her side breathing in and out quietly. He looked at the injured leg. He stood the rifle against the cart and called to her.

She rose instantly and turned and stood looking at him with her ears erect. The boy holding the jockeystick looked up at him across the top of the cart.

He talked to her a long time and as the boy tending the wolf could not understand what it was he said he said what was in his heart. He made her promises that he swore to keep in the making. That he would take her to the mountains where she would find others of her kind. She watched him with her yellow eyes and in them was no despair but only that same reckonless deep of loneliness that cored the world to its heart. He turned and looked at the boy. He was about to speak when the pitchman ducked inside under the canopy and hissed at them. Él viene, he said. Él viene.

Maldiciónes, the boy said. He threw aside his stick and he and the pitchman set about taking down the sheets and untying the cords from the stakes they'd driven into the mud. As the sheets fell the carretero came at a trot across the alameda and fell in to help them, snatching up the sheets and hissing at them to hurry. Soon they were backing the little blindfold mule between the shafts of the cart and fitting the harness and buckling it about.

La tablilla, cried the carretero. The boy snatched up the sign and pushed it under the pile of ropes and sheeting and the carretero mounted up into the cart and called out to the pitchman and the pitchman snatched away the blindfold from the mule's eyes and mule and cart and wolf and driver went rattling and clattering out into the street. Fairgoers scattered away before them and the carretero looked back wildly up the road where the alguacil and his entourage were just entering the town from the south—alguacil and attendants and retainers and friends and mozos de estribo and mozos de cuadra all with their equipage winking in the sun and trotting among the legs of the horses upwards of two dozen hunting dogs.

The boy had already turned and started toward the street to get his horse. By the time he'd untied it and shoved the rifle into the scabbard and mounted up and swung the horse into the street the alguacil and his party were passing along the alameda four and six abreast, calling out to one another, many of them garbed in the gaudy attire of the norteño and of the charro all spangled and trimmed with silver braid, the seams of their trousers done with silver shells. They rode saddles worked in silver with flat pommels the size of plates and some were drunk riding and doffed their enormous hats in gestures of outlandish courtliness at women their horses had forced against buildings or into doorways. The hunting dogs trotting neat of foot beneath them seemed alone sober and purposive and they paid no mind at all to the town dogs that sallied out bristling behind them or indeed to anything at all. They were some of them black in color or black and tan but for the most part they were bluetick dogs brought into the country from the north years before and some were so like in pattern and color to the speckled horses they paced that they seemed tailored from the same piece of hide. The horses sidled and stepped and tossed their heads and the riders pulled them about but the dogs trotted steadily upon the road before them as if they had a lot on their minds.

He waited in the crossroads for them to pass. Some nodded to him and wished him a good day as to a fellow horseman but if the alguacil in passing recognized him sitting his horse in this new wayplace he gave no sign so. When they had passed horses dogs and all he put his horse into the road again and set out behind them and behind the carreta now vanished upriver in the distance.

THE HACIENDA through whose gates they passed was sited on a level plain between the road and the braided flats of the Bato- pito River and it was named for the mountains to the east through which they'd ridden. It lay hazy in the distance in a long thin bight of limewashed walls under the thin green spires of a cypress grove. Downriver were groves of fruit trees and pecans in ordered rows. He turned down the long drive as the hunting party was entering the gates of the portal ahead of him. In the fields were crossbred bulls with long ears and humped backs of a kind new to the country and workers raised up and stood with their short hoes in their hands and watched him pass. He raised his hand in greeting but they only bent to their work again.

When he rode through the standing gate of the portal there was no sign of the party. A mozo came to take his horse and he stepped down and handed over the reins. The mozo appraised him by his clothes and nodded toward the kitchen door and a few minutes later he was seated at a table along with the retainers of the newly arrived party some dozen in number and all of them eating great slabs of fried steak with beans and flour tortillas hot from the comal. At the end of the table sat the carretero.

He stepped over the bench with his plate and sat and the carretero nodded to him but when he asked about the wolf the carretero said only that the wolf was for the feria and more he would not say.

When he'd eaten he rose and carried his plate to the sideboard and asked the cocinera where the patrón might be but she only glanced at him and then made a sweeping gesture that took in the thousands of hectares of land running north along the river which comprised the hacienda. He thanked her and touched his hat and walked out and crossed the compound. On the far side stood stables and a bodega or granary and the long row of mud houses where the workers were billeted.

He found the wolf chained in an empty stall. She was standing backed into the corner and two boys were leaning over the stall door hissing at her and trying to spit on her. He went down the stable hall looking for his horse but there were no horses in the stable. He walked back out into the compound. From upriver where they'd gone to course the dogs the alguacil and his party were returning toward the house. In the yard behind the house the carretero had harnessed the little mule into his cart again and had mounted up into the box. The flat pop of the reins carried across the compound like a distant pistolshot and mule and cart set forth. They passed out through the portal gate just as the first of the riders and the first of the dogs swung into the road before them.

Such a company makes no way for mules and carts and the carretero pulled his rig off into the grass by the side of the road to let them pass, standing in the box and taking off his hat with a flourish and searching with his eyes among the approaching riders for the alguacil. He slapped the reins again. The mule trudged sullenly and the cart tilted and creaked and rattled over the bad ground by the roadside. As the dogs and riders passed the lead dog raised its nose and caught the scent from the cart on the wind and let out a deep bay and turned and swung in behind the cart where it trundled past just off the road. The other dogs surged about, the hair bristling along their shoulders, swinging their muzzles in the air. The carretero looked back in alarm. As he did so the mule humped and kicked and snatched the little cart about and set off across the fields at a gallop with the dogs in full cry behind.

The alguacil and his minions stood in their stirrups and shouted after them, laughing and whooping. Some of the younger horsemen of the company roweled their mounts forward and set out after the runaway mule and cart, calling out to the carretero and laughing. The carretero clutched the boards and leaned over the side with his hat to slap at the dogs leaping and scrabbling at the cart. Tall as the cart was they yet began to leap in, three or four of them, and to rummage through the straw howling and whining and finally raising a leg and urinating and lurching and falling against the side of the cart and spraying the carretero and spraying each other and fighting briefly and then standing with their forefeet along the top boards of the cart and barking down at the dogs that raced beside.

The riders overtook them laughing and circled the cart at a full gallop until one of them took down his reata and dropped a loop over the mule's head and brought it to a halt. They whooped and called out to one another and beat away the dogs with their doubled rope ends and led the cart back to the road. The dogs coursed out over the fields and the girls and young women working there squealed and put their hands atop their heads while the men stood with their hoes clubbed in their hands. In the road the alguacil called to the carretero and fished a silver coin from his pocket and pitched it to him with great accuracy. The carretero caught the coin and touched the brim of his hat with it and stood down into the road to inspect the cart and the rudely cottered wooden wheels and the harness and the fresh repair to the cartshaft. The alguacil looked past the riders to where the boy stood afoot in the road. He took another coin from his pocket and pitched it spinning.

Por el Americano, he called.

No one caught it. It fell in the dust and lay there. The alguacil sat his horse. He nodded to the boy.

Es for you, he said.

The riders watched him. He stooped and picked up the coin

and the alguacil nodded and smiled but there was no thanking or touching the hat. The boy walked up to him and held the coin up.

No puedo aceptarlo, he said.

The alguacil arched his brow and nodded his head vigorously. Sí, he said. Sí.

The boy stood at the alguacil's stirrup and gestured at him with the outheld coin. No, he said.

No? said the alguacil. Y cómo no?

The boy said that he wanted the wolf. He said that he could not sell her. He said that if there was a fine that he would work to pay the fine or if there was a fee for a permit or a toll to cross into the country he would work for that but that he could not part with the wolf because the wolf had been put in his care.

The alguacil heard him out and when he was done he accepted the coin and then pitched it to the watching carretero as a coin once given cannot be taken back and then he turned his horse in the road and called to his men and driving the dogs before them they all rode on toward the hacienda and vanished through the standing gates of the portal.

The boy looked at the carretero. The carretero had climbed again into his cart and he unwrapped the reins and looked down at the boy. He said that the alguacil had given the coin to him. He said that if the boy had wanted the coin he should have taken it when it was offered. The boy said he did not want the man's money then or now. He said that the carretero might work for such a man but he did not. But the carretero only nodded as if to say he did not expect the boy would understand but that someday with luck he might. Nadie sabe para quien trabaja, he said. Then he slapped the drivingreins against the mule's rump and set off down the road.

He walked back out to the stable where they'd chained the wolf. An old mozo from the house had been set to guard her and to see that she not be molested. He sat with his back to the stable door in the half dark smoking a cigarette. His hat lay in the straw beside him. When the boy asked if he could see the wolf he drew deeply on the cigarette as if contemplating the request. Then he said that no one could see the wolf without the permission of the hacendado and in any case there was no light to see her by.

The boy stood in the doorway. The mozo spoke no more and after a while he turned and went out again. He walked back across the compound to the house and stood looking in at the patio gates. Men were laughing and drinking and there was a veal calf roasting on a spit under the wall at the far side of the enclosure and under the smoky light of the cressetlamps burning in the long blue desert dusk were tables laden with savories and sweets and fruits to feed a hundred people and more. He turned and went back around the side of the house to find one of the mozos de cuadra and to see about his horse. Mariachi music struck up behind him in the courtyard and new arrivals were dismounting at the gates, coming out of the darkening shapes of the mountains to the east along the road accompanied by dogs at their horses' heels and hoving up in the light at the gateposts where torches burned in iron pipes driven into the ground.

The horses of the lesser guests such as himself were tied by halter ropes along a rail at the rear of the establos and he found Bird standing among them. He was still saddled and the bridle and bridlereins hung from the pommel and he was eating feed from a two-board tinsheathed trough nailed along the wall. He raised his head when Billy spoke to him and looked back chewing.

Es su caballo? said the mozo.

Sí. Claro.

Todo está bien?

Sí. Bien. Gracias.

The mozos were working their way along the line of horses pulling off saddles and brushing horses and pouring feed. He asked that they leave his horse saddled and they said that they would do as he wished. He looked at his horse again. You fell into it pretty good, didnt you? he said.

He walked around to the stable and entered the door at the

far end and stood. It was almost dark in the stable hall and the mozo in charge of the wolf seemed to be sleeping. He found an empty stall and walked in and kicked up the hay in one corner with his boots and lay down with his hat on his chest and closed his eyes. He could hear the cries of the mariachis and the howling of the chained hounds in an outbuilding somewhere and after a while he slept.

He slept and as he slept he dreamt and the dream was of his father and in the dream his father was afoot and lost in the desert. In the dying light of that day he could see his father's eyes. His father stood looking toward the west where the sun had gone and where the wind was rising out of the darkness. The small sands in that waste was all there was for the wind to move and it moved with a constant migratory seething upon itself. As if in its ultimate granulation the world sought some stay against its own eternal wheeling. His father's eyes searched the coming of the night in the deepening redness beyond the rim of the world and those eyes seemed to contemplate with a terrible equanimity the cold and the dark and the silence that moved upon him and then all was dark and all was swallowed up and in the silence he heard somewhere a solitary bell that tolled and ceased and then he woke.

Men with torches were passing singlefile down the stable past the open door of the stall where he'd been sleeping, their figures reeling outsized across the farther walls. He rose and put on his hat and went out. They were dragging the wolf from her stall by her chain and she cringed in the smoky light and drew back and tried to keep low to the ground to protect her underbelly. Someone with an old rakehandle fell in behind her to goad her on and in the distance somewhere beyond the domicilios the hounds had set up a fresh clamor.

He followed them out and across the darkened lot. They passed through an open wooden carriage gate where the doors were hung in stone piers and the howling of the hounds grew louder and the wolf shrank back and struggled against the chain.

Some of the men following behind were stumbling drunk and they kicked at her and called her cobarde. They passed along the stone bodega where the light from the eaves fell along the upper walls and carried the shadows of the interior rafters out into the dark of the yard. The illumination from within seemed to bow the walls and in the apron of light before the open doors the shadows of figures inside reeled and fell away and the company entered dragging the wolf over the packed clay. A way was made for them with much cheering and calling out. They handed off their torches to mozos who snuffed them in the dirt of the floor and when all had entered and were inside the mozos pushed shut the heavy wooden doors and dropped the bar.

He made his way along the edge of the crowd. They were a strange egality of witnesses there gathered and among the merchants from adjacent towns and the neighboring hacendados and the petty hidalgos de gotera come from as far as Agua Prieta and Casas Grandes in their tightly fitted suits there were tradesmen and hunters and gerentes and mayordomos from the haciendas and from the ejidos and there were caporals and vaqueros and a few favored peons. There were no women. Along the far side of the building were bleachers or stands scaffolded up on poles and in the center of the bodega was a round pit or estacada perhaps twenty feet in diameter defined by a low wooden palisade. The boards of the palisade were black with the dried blood of the ten thousand gamecocks that had died there and in the center of the pit was an iron pipe newly driven into the ground.

He shouldered his way through from the rear just as they were dragging the wolf over the boards and into the pit. Those along the bleachers stood to see. The man in the pit chained the wolf to the pipe and then dragged her to the end of the chain and stretched her out while they removed the homemade muzzle. Then they stepped back and slipped the noose of the rope they'd stretched her with. She stood up and looked about. She looked small and ragged and she stood with her back bowed like a cat. The wrapping was gone from her leg and she favored it as she moved sideways to the end of the chain and back, her white teeth shining in the light from the tin reflectors overhead.

The first casts of dogs had already been brought in by their handlers and they leaped and tugged at their leads and bayed and stood upright against their collars. Two of them were led forward and spectators in the crowd called out to the owners and whistled and named their wagers. The hounds were young and uncertain. The handlers boosted them over the parapet into the pit where they circled bristling and bayed at the wolf and looked at each other. The handlers hissed them on and they circled the wolf warily. The wolf crouched and bared her teeth. The crowd began to hoot and catcall and after a while a man at the far side of the pit blew a whistle and the handlers came forward and grabbed the ends of the trailing chains and hauled the dogs back and dragged them over the parapet and led them away, the dogs standing at their collars again and baying back at the wolf.

The wolf paced and circled limping on three legs and then crouched by the iron stake where it seemed she'd made her querencia. Her almond eyes ran the circle of faces beyond the pit and she glanced briefly up at the lights. She crouched on her elbows and then rose and circled and came back and crouched again. Then she stood. A fresh cast of dogs was being handed scrabbling over the parapet.

When the handlers slipped loose the dogs they sprang forward with their backs roached and bowled into the wolf and the three of them rolled into a ball of snarling and popping teeth and a rattle of chain. The wolf fought in absolute silence. They scrabbled over the ground and then there was a high yip and one of the dogs was circling and holding up one foreleg. The wolf had seized the other dog by the lower jaw and she threw it to the ground and straddled it and snatched her grip from the dog's jaw and buried her teeth in its throat and bit again to improve her grip where the muscled neck slid away in the loose folds of skin.

The boy had worked his way around to the bleachers. He stood by one of the stone piers and he took off his hat so that those behind could see but then he realized no one else had taken off theirs so he put it back on. Left alone the wolf might well have killed the dog but the arbitro blew his whistle and one of the handlers came forward with a sixfoot length of cane and with it blew into the wolf's ear. She abandoned her hold and leaped back and spun on her haunches. The handlers got hold of their dogs by the chains and led them away. A man came forward and stepped over the low wooden barricade and began to circle about with a pail out of which he laved and flung water like some bemused and halfwitted horticulturist, methodically slaking the dust in the floor of the pit while the wolf lay panting. The boy turned and made his way along the edge of the crowd to the door at the rear through which the hounds had gone and stepped outside into the cool dark. A handler with two fresh dogs was already coming through the door.

Some boys smoking cigarettes at the back wall of the bodega turned and looked at him in the light of the door's opening. The howling of the dogs in the crib beyond was loud and continuous.

Cuántos perros tienen? he asked them.

The nearest boy looked at him. He said they had four dogs. Y usted? he said.

He explained that he meant all the dogs how many but they only shrugged.

Quién sabe? they said. Bastante.

He walked past them and out to the crib. It was a long building with a tin roof and he took a lantern down from a pole and lifted the wooden stake from out of the doorhasp and pushed open the door and entered with the lantern aloft. Along the wall the hounds leaped and bayed and lunged at their chains. There were upwards of thirty of them in the shed, mostly redbone and bluetick dogs bred in the country to the north but also nondescript animals from new-world bloodlines and dogs that were little more than pitbulls bred to fight. Chained at the end of the shed separate from the others were two enormous airedales and when the light from the lantern ignited their eyes the boy saw a thing that not even the pit dogs possessed in such absolute purity and he backed away mistrustful of the chains that held them. He backed out and shut the door and dropped the stake into the hasp and rehung the lantern on the pole. He nodded to the boys standing along the wall and went past and entered the bodega again.

The crowd seemed actually to have swelled in his brief absence. On the far side of the arena stood the members of the mariachi band in their white and illfitting suits. Through the crowd he could glimpse the wolf. She was squatting on her haunches with her mouth wide and she was alternately darting at one and then the other of the two dogs circling her. One of the dogs had been bitten through the ear and both handlers were freckled with blood where it had circled shaking its head. He pushed his way through the crowd and when he reached the wooden parapet he stepped over it and walked out into the pit.

He was taken at first for yet another handler but it was the handlers he approached. They were now at the farther side of the pit crouching and feinting in such postures of attack and defense as they would have the dogs adopt and calling out in highpitched chants to seek the dogs on and twisting and gesturing with their hands in an antic simulation of the contest before them. When the nearer of them saw him coming he raised up and looked toward the arbitro. The arbitro stood with the whistle to his mouth but he seemed not to know what to make of what he saw. The boy stepped past the handlers and entered the perimeter of the twelvefoot circle of torn ground defined by the chain to which the wolf was tethered. Someone called out a warning and the arbitro blew his whistle and then there was a hush fell over the bodega. The wolf stood panting. The boy stepped past her and seized the first dog by the loose skin of the saddle and hauled its hindquarters up off the ground and squatted and got hold of its chain and backed away with it and turned and handed the chain to the handler. The handler took the chain and pulled the lunging dog against his leg. Qué pasó? he said.

But the boy had already started after the second dog. By now some of the spectators had begun to call out and there was an ugly murmur running through the bodega. The handlers looked toward the arbitro. The arbitro blew the whistle again and gestured toward the intruder. He in turn hauled up the second dog by its chain and walked it on its hindlegs to the other handler and then turned and went back after the wolf.

She stood spraddlelegged with her sides heaving and her black mouth pleated back from the white and perfect teeth. He crouched and spoke to her. He had no way to know if she would bite him or not. A handful of men had climbed over the estacada and were advancing toward him but when they reached the perimeter of the torn ground they stopped as if they'd come to a wall. No one spoke to him. All seemed to be watching to see what he would do. He rose and stepped to the iron stake piked in the ground and wrapped a turn of chain about his forearm and squatted and seized the chain at the ring and tried to rise with it. No one moved, no one spoke. He doubled his grip and tried again. The beaded sweat on his forehead shone in the light. He tried yet a third time but he could not pull the stake and he rose and turned and took hold of the actual wolf by the collar and unsnapped the swivelhook and drew the bloody and slobbering head to his side and stood.

That the wolf was loose save for his grip on her collar did not escape the notice of the men who had entered the ring. They looked at one another. Some began to back away. The wolf stood against the güero's thigh with her teeth bared and her flanks sucking in and out and she made no move.

Es mia, the boy said.

People in the stands began to call out but those in any proximity to the unchained wolf seemed hesitant as to what course to take. In the end it was neither the alguacil nor the hacendado who came forward but the hacendado's son. They gave way before him, a young man who bore on the braided jacket he wore the scent of the young women he'd so recently danced with. He stepped into the pit and advanced and stood with his boots spread and his thumbs hung loosely in the blue sash about his waist. If he was afraid of the wolf he gave no evidence so.

Qué quieres, joven? he said.

The boy repeated what he'd said to the riders he'd met with on the Cajón Bonita in the mountains to the north. He said that he was custodian to the wolf and charged with her care but the young hacendado smiled ruefully and shook his head and said that the wolf had been caught in a trap in the Pilares Teras which mountains are barbarous and wild and that the deputies of Don Beto had encountered him crossing the river at the Colonia de Oaxaca and that he had been intent on taking the wolf to his own country where he would sell the animal at some price.

He spoke in a high clear voice like one declaiming to the crowd and when he was done he stood with his hands folded one across the other before him as if there were no more to be said.

The boy stood holding the wolf. He could feel the movement of her breathing and the light tremor of her body against him. He looked at the young don and he looked at the ring of faces in the light. He said that he had come from Hidalgo County in the state of New Mexico and that he had brought the wolf with him from that place. He said that he had caught her in a steeltrap and that he and the wolf had been on the trail six days coming into this country and had not come out of the Pilares at all but were in the act of attempting to cross the river and enter those same mountains when they were turned back because of the swiftness of the water.

The young hacendado took his hands from before him and clasped them behind. He turned and took a few steps in contemplation and turned again and looked up.

Para qué trajo la loba aquí? De que sirvió?

He stood holding the wolf. All waited for him to answer but he had no answer. His eyes ran the assemblage, searching the eyes that watched him. The arbitro stood with his pocketwatch still outheld before him. The handlers stood with doubled grip upon the collars of the dogs. The man with the watercan waited. The young hacendado turned to look at the gallery.

He smiled and turned again to the boy. Then he spoke in english.

You think that this country is some country you can come here and do what you like.

I never thought that. I never thought about this country one way or the other.

Yes, said the hacendado.

We was just passin through, the boy said. We wasnt botherin nobody. Queríamos pasar, no más.

Pasar o traspasar?

The boy turned and spat into the dirt. He could feel the wolf lean against his leg. He said that the tracks of the wolf had led out of Mexico. He said the wolf knew nothing of boundaries. The young don nodded as if in agreement but what he said was that whatever the wolf knew or did not know was irrelevant and that if the wolf had crossed that boundary it was perhaps so much the worse for the wolf but the boundary stood without regard.

The spectators nodded and murmured among themselves. They looked to the boy to see how he would reply. The boy only said that if he were allowed to go he would return with the wolf to America and that he would pay whatever fine he had incurred but the hacendado shook his head. He said that it was too late for that and that anyway the alguacil had taken the wolf into custody and it was forfeit in lieu of the portazgo. When the boy said that he had not known that he would be required to pay in order to pass through the country the hacendado said that then he was in much the same situation as the wolf.

They waited. The boy looked aloft toward the roofbeams where the dust and the smoke had risen and where it moved slowly in slow coils across the lights. He looked among the faces for any there to whom he might plead his case but he saw nothing. He reached down and unbuckled the leather dogcollar from about the wolf's neck and pulled it away and stood. Those nearest tried to back into the crowd. The young gentryman drew a small revolver from his waistband.

Agarrala, he said.

He stood. Some several other of the spectators had also drawn their arms. He looked like a man standing on a scaffold seeking in the crowd some likeness to his own heart. Nothing to come of the looking even though all there might arrive at their own such standing soon or late. He looked at the young don. He knew that he would shoot the wolf. He reached down and pulled the collar back around the bloodied ruff of the wolf's neck and rebuckled it.

Ponga la cadena, said the hacendado.

He did so. Stooping and picking up the snap end of the chain and hooking it through the ring of the collar. Then he dropped the chain into the dirt and stepped away from the wolf. The little pistols disappeared as silently as they had come.

They made a path for him and watched him as he went. Outside the night had grown colder yet and the air smelled of woodsmoke from the cookfires over in the domicilios of the workers. Someone closed the door behind him. The square of the light in which he stood drew narrow slowly in the door's shadow to darkness. The tranca dropped woodenly into place within. He walked back up in the dark to the establo where the horses were being tended. A young mozo stood up and greeted him. He nodded and walked down and got his horse and slipped off the halter and hung it over the hitchrail and bridled the horse. He unrolled his blanket from behind the saddle and pulled it around his shoulders. Then he mounted up and rode out past the standing horses and nodded down to the mozo and touched his hat and rode toward the house.

The gate to the patio was closed. He stood down and opened it and then mounted up again. He bent forward in the saddle to clear the gateway arch and rode through with the stirrups dragging along the plaster and clicking off the iron jambs. The patio was paved with clay tiles and the sound of the horse's hooves upon them caused the servant girls to look up from their tasks. They stood holding tablecloths and plates and wicker baskets. Along the wall the oil lamps still burned atop their poles and the staccato shadows of hunting bats crossed the tiles and vanished and reappeared and crossed back. He crossed the courtyard horseback and nodded to the women and leaned from the saddle and took an empanada from a platter and sat eating it. The horse leaned its long nose down over the table but he pulled it away. The empanada was filled with seasoned meat and he ate it and leaned down and took another. The women went on with their work. He finished the empanada and then took a sweet pastry from a tray and ate that, putting the horse forward along the tables. The women moved away before him. He nodded to them again and wished them a good evening. He took another pastry and rode the circuit of the courtyard eating it while the horse shied at the passing bats and then he rode out through the gate again and down the drive. After a while one of the women crossed the patio and shut the gate behind him.

When he struck the road he turned south toward the town riding slowly. The howling of the dogs receded behind him. A half moon hung cocked in the east over the mountains like an eye narrowed in anger.

He'd reached the outer lights of the colonia before he halted the horse in the road. Then he reined it about and turned back.

When he pulled up before the door of the bodega he slid one foot out of the stirrup and slammed at the door with the heel of his boot. The door rattled against the crossbar within. He could hear the shouts of the men and he could hear the snarling of the dogs in the shed at the far side of the bodega. No one came. He rode around to the rear of the building and down along the narrow walled passageway between the bodega and the crib where the hounds were penned. Some men who had been squatting along the wall stood up. He nodded to them and stepped down and slid the rifle out of the scabbard and tied the reins together and dropped them over the post at the corner of the shed and walked past the men and pushed open the door and entered.

No one paid him any mind. He made his way through the crowd and when he reached the estacada the wolf was alone in the pit and she was a sorry thing to see. She'd returned to the stake and crouched by it but her head lay in the dirt and her tongue lolled in the dirt and her fur was matted with dirt and blood and the yellow eyes looked at nothing at all. She had been fighting for almost two hours and she had fought in casts of two the better part of all the dogs brought to the feria. At the far side of the estacada a pair of handlers were holding on to the airedales and there was a discussion going on with the arbitro and with the young hacendado. No one was anywhere near the airedales and they stood at their leashes and popped their wet teeth and jerked the handlers roughly about. The dust hanging in the lights glistened like silica. The aguador stood by with his pail of water.

He stepped over the parapet and walked toward the wolf and levered a shell into the chamber of the rifle and halted ten feet from her and raised the rifle to his shoulder and took aim at the bloodied head and fired.

The echo of the shot in the closed space of the barn rattled all else into silence. The airedales dropped to all fours and whined and circled behind the handlers. No one moved. The blue riflesmoke hung in the air. The wolf lay stretched out dead.

He lowered the rifle and ratcheted the spent casing out and caught it where it spun and put it in his pocket and levered the breech of the rifle shut again and stood with his thumb over the hammer. He looked at the crowd surrounding him. No one spoke. Some of them were looking toward the rear but it was not the young don who made his way to the estacada but the alguacil's deputy last seen hazing the carretero with his own coat down the street of the upriver colonia. He stepped over the barricade and walked out into the pit and demanded of the boy his rifle. The boy stood. The deputy unsnapped the flap on his holster and drew the 45 automatic already cocked.

Déme la carabina, he said.

The boy looked at the wolf. He looked at the crowd. His eyes were swimming but he did not let down the hammer of the rifle or move to relinquish it. The deputy raised the pistol and sighted

it upon his upper chest. Spectators at the far side of the estacada
squatted or dropped to their knees and some of them lay face
down in the dirt with their hands over their heads. In the silence
the only sound was the low whining of one of the dogs. Then
someone spoke from the bleachers. Bastante, he said. No le
molesta.

It was the alguacil. All turned to him. He was standing in
the upper tiers of the rough board scaffolding with men at either
side of him in their seven x beaver hats, some smoking puros as
was the alguacil. He gestured with one hand. He said it was
finished. He said for the boy to put up his rifle and that he would
not be harmed. The deputy lowered the pistol, the watchers in
the gallery rose from the ground and dusted themselves off. The
boy laid the barrel of the rifle across his shoulder and lowered
the hammer with his thumb. He turned and looked up at the
alguacil. The alguacil made a small sweeping motion with the
back of his hand. Whether to him or to the crowd at large he
knew not but the spectators began to talk among themselves
once more and someone opened the doors of the bodega onto
the cool Mexican night.

The man to whom the hide had been promised had stepped
across the boards and come forward. He walked around the
dead wolf and stood facing her with his beltknife in his hand.
The boy asked him what the hide was worth and he shrugged.
He watched the boy carefully.

Cuánto quiere por él? the boy said.

El cuero?

La loba.

The claimant to the hide looked at the wolf and he looked at
the boy. He said that the hide was worth fifty pesos.

Acepta la carabina? the boy said.

The claimant's eyebrows rose but he regained his composure.
En un huinche? he said.

Claro. Cuarenta y cuatro.

He unlimbered the rifle from his shoulder and pitched it
across to the man. The claimant jacked open the lever and closed

it again. He bent and picked up the ejected cartridge from the dirt and wiped it on his shirtsleeve and fed it back into the receiver. He raised the rifle and sighted at the lights overhead. It was worth a dozen mutilated wolfhides but he held it and weighed it in his hand and looked at the boy before nodding. Bueno, he said. He put the rifle over his shoulder and held out his hand. The boy looked down at the hand, then slowly took it and they sealed their barter by handclasp in the center of the pit while the populace filed past toward the open door. They studied him with their dark eyes in passing but if they were disappointed in their sport they gave no notice for they also were guests of hacendado and alguacil and they kept their own counsel as the custom of the country decreed. The claimant of the hide asked the boy if he had any more cartridges for the rifle but he only shook his head and knelt down and gathered up the limp shape of the shewolf in his arms which thin as she was yet was all he could carry and he crossed the pit and stepped over the barricade and went on toward the door at the rear with the head lolling and the slow blood dripping in his tracks.

When he rode out from the shadow of the building with the wolf across the bow of the saddle he had wrapped her in the remainder of the sheeting the rancher's wife had given him. The yard was filled with departing horsemen and with their shouts to each other. Dogs swarmed baying about the legs of his horse and the horse shied and stamped and kicked out at them and he rode past the open door of the bodega and on through the gate and out across the fields toward the river, leaning from the saddle and batting away the last of the dogs with his hat. To the south over the town rockets were rising in long sputtering arcs and breaking open in the darkness and falling in a slow hot confetti. The crack of their bursting reached him well behind the flare of light and in each flare of light hung the smudged ghosts of those gone before. He reached the river and turned downstream and rode through the shallow riffles and out along the broad gravel flats. A flight of ducks passed him going downriver in the dark. He could hear their wings. He

could see them where they rose against the sky and flared away
over the dark country to the west. He rode past the town and
the small lights of the carnival and the shapes of the lights that
lay slurred in the slow black coils of water along the river shore.
A burntout catherinewheel stood smoking beyond the willow
bracken. He studied the rise of the mountains, how they lay.
The wind coming off the water smelled like wet metal. He could
feel the blood of the wolf against his thigh where it had soaked
through the sheeting and through his breeches and he put his
hand to his leg and tasted the blood which tasted no different
than his own. The fireworks died away. The moon's half hung
over the black cape of the mountains.

At the junction of the rivers he rode across the broad gravel
beach and sat the horse at the ford and he and the horse looked
away to the north where the river was running clear and cold
down out of the darkness of the country. He almost reached to
draw the rifle from the scabbard to keep it out of the river but
then he just put the horse forward into the shoals.

He could feel the horse's hooves muted on the cobbled rocks
of the river floor and hear the water sucking at the horse's legs.
The water came up under the animal's belly and he could feel
the cold of it where it leaked into his boots. A last lone rocket
rose over the town and revealed them midriver and revealed all
the country about them, the shoreland trees strangely enshadowed, the pale rocks. A solitary dog from the town that had
caught the scent of the wolf on the wind and followed him out
stood frozen on the beach on three legs standing in that false
light and then all faded again into the darkness out of which it
had been summoned.

They crossed through the ford and rode dripping up out of
the river and he looked back at the darkening town and then put
the horse forward through the shore willows and standing cane
and rode west toward the mountains. As he rode he sang old
songs his father once had sung in the used to be and a soft
corrido in spanish from his grandmother that told of the death
of a brave soldadera who took up her fallen soldierman's gun

and faced the enemy in some old waste of death. The night was clear and as he rode the moon dropped under the rim of the mountain and stars began to come up in the east where it was darkest. They rode up the dry course of a creekbed in a night suddenly colder, as if the moon had had warmth to it. Up through the low hills where he would ride all night singing softly as he rode.

By the time he reached the first talus slides under the tall escarpments of the Pilares the dawn was not far to come. He reined the horse in a grassy swale and stood down and dropped the reins. His trousers were stiff with blood. He cradled the wolf in his arms and lowered her to the ground and unfolded the sheet. She was stiff and cold and her fur was bristly with the blood dried upon it. He walked the horse back to the creek and left it standing to water and scouted the banks for wood with which to make a fire. Coyotes were yapping along the hills to the south and they were calling from the dark shapes of the rimlands above him where their cries seemed to have no origin other than the night itself.

He got the fire going and lifted the wolf from the sheet and took the sheet to the creek and crouched in the dark and washed the blood out of it and brought it back and he cut forked sticks from a mountain hackberry and drove them into the ground with a rock and hung the sheet on a trestlepole where it steamed in the firelight like a burning scrim standing in a wilderness where celebrants of some sacred passion had been carried off by rival sects or perhaps had simply fled in the night at the fear of their own doing. He pulled the blanket about his shoulders and sat shivering in the cold and waiting for the dawn that he could find the place where he would bury the wolf. After a while the horse came up from the creek trailing the wet reins through the leaves and stood at the edge of the fire.

He fell asleep with his hands palm up before him like some dozing penitent. When he woke it was still dark. The fire had died to a few low flames seething over the coals. He took off his hat and fanned the fire with it and coaxed it back and fed the

wood he'd gathered. He looked for the horse but could not see
it. The coyotes were still calling all along the stone ramparts of
the Pilares and it was graying faintly in the east. He squatted
over the wolf and touched her fur. He touched the cold and
perfect teeth. The eye turned to the fire gave back no light and
he closed it with his thumb and sat by her and put his hand
upon her bloodied forehead and closed his own eyes that he
could see her running in the mountains, running in the starlight
where the grass was wet and the sun's coming as yet had not
undone the rich matrix of creatures passed in the night before
her. Deer and hare and dove and groundvole all richly empan-
eled on the air for her delight, all nations of the possible world
ordained by God of which she was one among and not separate
from. Where she ran the cries of the coyotes clapped shut as if
a door had closed upon them and all was fear and marvel. He
took up her stiff head out of the leaves and held it or he reached
to hold what cannot be held, what already ran among the mountains at once terrible and of a great beauty, like flowers that feed
on flesh. What blood and bone are made of but can themselves
not make on any altar nor by any wound of war. What we may
well believe has power to cut and shape and hollow out the dark
form of the world surely if wind can, if rain can. But which
cannot be held never be held and is no flower but is swift and
a huntress and the wind itself is in terror of it and the world
cannot lose it.

II

DOOMED ENTERPRISES divide lives forever into the then and the now. He'd carried the wolf up into the mountains in the bow of the saddle and buried her in a high pass under a cairn of scree. The little wolves in her belly felt the cold draw all about them and they cried out mutely in the dark and he buried them all and piled the rocks over them and led the horse away. He wandered on into the mountains. He whittled a bow from a holly limb, made arrows from cane. He thought to become again the child he never was.

They rode the high country for weeks and they grew thin and gaunted man and horse and the horse grazed on the sparse winter grass in the mountains and gnawed the lichens from the rock and the boy shot trout with his arrows where they stood above their shadows on the cold stone floors of the pools and he ate them and ate green nopal and then on a windy day traversing a high saddle in the mountains a hawk passed before the sun and its shadow ran so quick in the grass before them that it caused the horse to shy and the boy looked up where the bird turned high above them and he took the bow from his shoulder and nocked and loosed an arrow and watched it rise with the wind rattling the fletching slotted into the cane and watched it turning and arcing and the hawk wheeling and then flaring suddenly with the arrow locked in its pale breast.

The hawk turned and skated off down the wind and vanished beyond the cape of the mountain, a single feather fell. He rode out to look for it but he never found it. He found a single drop of blood that had dried on the rocks and darkened in the wind and nothing more. He dismounted and sat on the ground beside the horse where the wind blew and he made a cut in the heel of his hand with his knife and watched the slow blood dropping on the stone. Two days later he sat the horse on a promontory overlooking the Bavispe River and the river was running backwards. That or the sun was setting in the east behind him. He made his rough camp in a windbreak of juniper and waited out the night to see what the sun would do or what the river and in the morning when day broke over the distant mountains and across the broad plain before him he realized that he had crossed back through the mountains to where the river ran north again along the eastern side of the sierras.

He rode deeper into the mountains. He sat on a windfall tree in a high forest of madroño and ash and with his knife cut to length a piece of rope while the horse watched. He stood and strung the rope through the beltloops of his jeans where they hung from his hips and folded away the knife. It aint nothin to eat, he told the horse.

In that wild high country he'd lie in the cold and the dark and listen to the wind and watch the last few embers of his fire at their dying and the red crazings in the woodcoals where they broke along their unguessed gridlines. As if in the trying of the wood were elicited hidden geometries and their orders which could only stand fully revealed, such is the way of the world, in darkness and ashes. He heard no wolves. Ragged and half starving and his horse dismayed he rode a week later into the mining town of El Tigre.

A dozen houses sited senselessly along a slope overlooking a small mountain valley. There was no one about. He sat the horse in the middle of the mud street and the horse stared bleakly at the town, at the rude jacales of mud and sticks with their cowhide doors. He put the horse forward and a woman came out into the street and approached him and stood at his stirrup and looked up into the child's face under the hat and asked if he were sick. He said that he was not. That he was only hungry. She told him to get down and he did so and slid the bow from his shoulder and hung it over the horn of the saddle and followed her down to her house while the horse walked behind.

He sat in a kitchen that was all but dark so sheltered was it from the sun and he ate frijoles from a clay bowl with a huge spoon of enameled tin. The sole light fell from a smokehole in the ceiling and the woman knelt there at a low clay brasero and turned tortillas on a cracked and ancient clay comal while the thin smoke rose up the blackened wall and vanished overhead. He could hear chickens clucking outside and in a room darker yet beyond a curtain of pieced sacking some sleeper was sleeping. The house smelled of smoke and rancid grease and the smoke bore the faintly antiseptic odor of piñon wood. She turned the tortillas with her bare fingers and put them on a clay plate and brought them to him. He thanked her and folded one of the tortillas and dipped it into the beans and ate.

De dónde viene? she said.

De los Estados Unidos.

De Tejas?

Nuevo Mexico.

Que lindo, she said.

Lo conoce?

No.

She watched him eat.

Es minero? she said.

Vaquero.

Ay, vaquero.

When he'd finished and wiped the bowl clean with the last piece of tortilla she took the dishes and carried them across the room and put them in a bucket. When she came back she sat down on the slab-board bench across the table from him and studied him. Adónde va? she said.

He didnt know. He looked vaguely around the room. Pinned to the bare mud wall with a wooden peg was a calendar with a color print of a 1927 Buick. A woman in a fur coat and a turban stood beside it. He said that he did not know where he was going. They sat. He nodded toward the curtained doorway. Es su marido? he said.

She said that it was not. She said that it was her sister.

He nodded. He looked about the room again which his first look had in any case exhausted and then he reached over his shoulder and took his hat from the stile of the chair at his back and pushed the chair back on the clay floor and stood.

Muchísimas gracias, he said.

Clarita, called the woman.

She hadnt taken her eyes from him and it occurred to him that she might be a little bit crazy. She called again. She turned and looked toward the darkened room beyond the curtain, she held up one finger. Momentito, she said. She rose and went into the other room. In a few minutes she appeared again. She held aside the sacking against the doorjamb in a faintly theatrical gesture. The woman who had been asleep stepped through and stood before him in a wrapper of stained pink rayon. She looked at him and turned and looked back at her sister. She was perhaps the younger but they looked much alike. She looked again at the boy. He stood with his hat in his hands. The sister stood behind her in the doorway with the frayed and dusty sacking pulled against her in a way to suggest perhaps that the emergence of the sleeper was a rare and transitory thing. She herself no more than a herald of coming good. The sleeping sister pulled her wrap about herself and reached and touched the boy's face with one hand. Then she turned and passed back through the doorway to be seen no more. The boy thanked his hostess and put on his hat and pushed open the clattery hide door and walked outside into the sunlight where the horse stood waiting.

Riding out the road wherein were neither ruts nor hoofprints nor any sign of commerce at all he passed two men standing in a doorway who called out and made signs to him. He'd hung the bow again across his shoulder and he thought that riding so armed in his blackened rags atop the bony horse he must cut a sad or foolish figure but when he regarded his hecklers more closely he reckoned he could scarce look worse than they and he rode on.

He crossed the small valley and rode west into the mountains. He'd no way to know how long he'd been in that country but for all he'd seen of it good or ill which he pondered as he rode he knew that he no longer feared whatever he might find there. Days to come he would encounter wild indians deep in the sierras living in the chozas and wickiups of their squalid rancherías and indians wilder yet who lived in caves and all of whom may well have thought him mad for the regard with which they treated him. They fed him and the women washed his clothes and mended them and sewed his boots with a home-made awl and ligaments from a hawk's foot. They spoke among themselves in their own tongue or with him in their broken spanish. They said that most of their young people had gone to work in the mines or in the cities or on the haciendas of the Mexicans but that they did not trust the Mexicans. They traded with them in the small villages along the river and sometimes they would stand in the outer ring of light and watch them at their festivals but otherwise they kept to themselves. They said that it was the way of the Mexicans to blame them for the crimes they committed among themselves and that the Mexicans would get drunk and kill each other and then send soldiers into the mountains to seek them out. When he told them where he came from he was surprised to find that they knew that country also but of it they would not speak. No one tried to trade horses with him. No one asked him why he had come. They cautioned him only to lay clear of the Yaqui country to the west because the Yaqui would kill him. Then the women packed for him a dinner of some dried and leathern meat or machaca and parched corn and sootstained tortillas and an old man came forward and addressed him in a spanish he could scarcely understand, speaking with great earnestness into the boy's eyes and holding his saddle fore and aft so that the boy sat almost in his arms. He was dressed in odd and garish fashion and his clothes were embroidered with signs that had about them the geometric look of instructions, perhaps a game. He wore jewelry of jade and silver and his hair was long and blacker than his age would seem to warrant. He told the boy that although he was huérfano still he must cease his wanderings and make for himself some place in the world because to wander in this way would become for him a passion and by this passion he would become estranged from men and so ultimately from himself. He said that the world could only be known as it existed in men's hearts. For while it seemed a place which contained men it was in reality a place contained within them and therefore to know it one must look there and come to know those hearts and to do this one must live with men and not simply pass among them. He said that while the huérfano might feel that he no longer belonged among men he must set this feeling aside for he contained within him a largeness of spirit which men could see and that men would wish to know him and that the world would need him even as he needed the world for they were one. Lastly he said that while this itself was a good thing like all good things it was also a danger. Then he removed his hands from the boy's saddle and stepped away and stood. The boy thanked him for his words but he said that he was in fact not an orphan and then he thanked the women standing there and turned the horse and rode out. They stood watching him go. As he passed the last of the brush wickiups he turned and looked back and as he did so the old man called out to him. Eres, he said. Eres huérfano. But the boy only raised one hand and touched his hat and rode on.

In two days he struck a wagonroad passing east and west across the sierras. The woods were green with ilex and madroño, the road seemed little used. In a day's travel he passed no soul. He crossed through a high pass where the way was so narrow that the rocks bore old scars of wagonhubs and below the pass were scattered stone cairns, the mojoneras de muerte of that country where travelers had been slain by indians years before. The country seemed depopulate and barren and he saw no game and saw no birds and there was nothing about but the wind and the silence.

At the eastern escarpment he dismounted and led the horse along a shelf of gray rock. The scrub juniper that grew along the rim leaned in a wind that had long since passed. Along the face of the stone bluffs were old pictographs of men and animals and suns and moons as well as other representations that seemed to have no referent in the world although they once may have. He sat in the sun and looked out over the country to the east, the broad barranca of the Bavispe and the ensuing Carretas Plain that was once a seafloor and the small pieced fields and the new corn greening in the old lands of the Chichimeca where the priests had passed and soldiers passed and the missions fallen into mud and the ranges of mountains beyond the plain range on range in pales of blue where the terrain lay clawed open north and south, canyon and range, sierra and barranca, all of it waiting like a dream for the world to come to be, world to pass. He saw a single vulture hanging motionless in some high vector that the wind had chosen for it. He saw the smoke of a locomotive passing slowly downcountry over the plain forty miles away.

He took a handful of piñon nuts from one tattered pocket and spread them on a rock and cracked them with a handstone. He'd taken to talking to the horse and he talked to it now as he cracked the nuts and when he had them free of their hulls he scooped them up and held them out. The horse looked at him and looked at the piñon nuts and shuffled forward two steps and placed its rubbery mouth in his palm.

He wiped the slobber from his hand on the leg of his trousers and sat cracking and eating the rest of the nuts himself while the horse watched. Then he stood and walked to the edge of the escarpment and threw the handstone. It sailed out turning and fell and fell and vanished in the silence. He stood listening. From far below the faint clatter of stone on stone. He walked back and stretched out on the warm rock shelving and cradled his head in the crook of his arm and stared into the dark of his hatcrown. His home had come to seem remote and dreamlike. There were times he could not call to mind his father's face.

He slept and in his sleep he dreamt of wild men who came to

him with clubs and their teeth were filed to points and they gathered round him and warned him of their work before they even set about it. He woke and lay listening. As if they might yet be there just beyond the darkness of his hat. Squatting among the rocks. Chiseling in stone with stones those semblances of the living world they'd have endure and the world dead at their hands. He lifted his hat and placed it on his chest and looked at the blue sky. He sat up and looked for the horse but the horse was only a few feet away standing waiting for him. He rose and rolled the stiffness out of his shoulders and put on his hat and took up the trailing reins and ran his hand down the horse's foreleg till it lifted its foot and he cradled the hoof between his knees and looked at it. The horse had long since shed its shoes and the hooves were long and broomed and he took out his pocketknife and pared back the hoof wall where the edges were splayed and then let down the horse's foot and walked around the animal inspecting and paring the other hooves in turn. The constant currying of the brush and greenwood in the mountains had carried off all trace of the stable and the horse gave off a warm and rooty smell. The horse had dark hooves with heavy hoof walls and the horse had in him enough grullo blood to make a mountain horse by both conformation and inclination and as the boy had grown up where talk of horses was more or less continual he knew that where the blood carries the shape of a hock or the breadth of a face it carries also an inner being of a certain design and no other and the wilder their life became in the mountains the more he felt the horse subtly at war with itself. He didnt think the horse would quit him but he was sure the horse had thought about it. He pared the last hind hoof and led the animal back out to the narrow track and mounted up and turned and started down into the gorge.

The road descended the granite face of the sierra like a hairspring. He was amazed that wagons could have negotiated those narrow switchbacks. There were caveouts along the edges of the road where he dismounted and led the horse and there were rocks in the road no man could move. The way descended down out of the pine forests through oak and juniper. A wild and jumbled terrain. Everywhere the green spring invasive in the barrancas. In the evening light a trembling celadon. He was at the descent some seven hours, the last of them in darkness.

He slept that night in a wash in the river sand with the cane and willow thick about him and in the morning he rode north along the river track until he came to a ford. Shored up on the red alluvial plain on the far side of the river were the ruins of a town slumping back into the mud out of which it had been raised. A single smoke stood in the blue air. He put the horse into the ford and halted to let the animal drink and he leaned down from the saddle and raised a palmful of water and passed it over his face and raised another to drink. The water was cold and clear. Upriver swifts or swallows were circling and flaring low over the water and the morning sun was warm on his face. He pressed the heels of his boots into the horse's flank and the horse raised its dripping mouth out of the river and waded slowly out into the ford. Midstream he halted again and slid the bow from his shoulder and let it go in the river. It turned and jostled in the riffles and floated out into the pool below. A crescent of pale wood, turning and drifting, lost in the sun on the water. Legacy of some drowned archer, musician, maker of fire. He rode on through the ford and up through the shore willows and carrizal and into the town.

Most of those buildings still standing were at the farther end of the town and toward these he rode. He passed the wreckage of an ancient coach half crushed in a zaguán where the doors were fallen in. He passed a mud horno in a yard from within which the eyes of some animal watched and he passed the ruins of a huge adobe church whose roofbeams lay in the rubble. The man who stood in the doorway at the rear of the church was paler of skin than even he and had sandy hair and pale blue eyes and the man called out to him first in spanish and then in english. He told him to get down and to come in.

He left the horse at the door of the church and followed the man into a small room where a fire burned in a homemade sheetiron stove. The room contained a small bed or cot and a long pine table with turned legs and several ladderback chairs such as were made by the Mennonites of that country. A number of cats of every color lay about the room. The man gestured at the cats vaguely as if they were to be excused in some way and then motioned for the boy to take a chair. The boy pulled the blanket from about his shoulders and stood holding it. The room was very warm and yet the man had bent and opened the stove door and was at chunking in more wood. On top of the stove stood an iron skillet and a kettle and a few blackened pans together with a clawfooted silver teapot deeply dented and dark with tarnish that sorted oddly with the other housewares. He rose and shut the stove door with his foot and reached and took down a pair of china cups and saucers and set them on the table. One of the cats got up and walked down the table and looked into each of the cups in turn and then sat. The man took the teapot from the stove and poured the cups and put the pot back and looked at the boy.

Eres puros huesos, he said.

Tengo miedo es verdad.

Please. Be comfortable. Would you like some eggs?

I guess I could eat some eggs.

How many will you eat?

I'll eat three.

There is no bread.

I'll eat four.

You must sit.

Yessir.

He took down a small enameled pail and went out through the low door. The boy pulled back a chair and sat. He folded the blanket roughly and laid it in the chair beside him and took up the nearer cup and sipped the coffee. It wasnt real coffee. He didnt know what it was. He looked around the room. The cats watched him. After a while the man returned with eggs rolling around in the floor of the pail. He picked up the frypan and held it by the handle and peered into it as into some black looking-glass and then set it down again and spooned grease into it from a clay jar. He watched the grease melt and then broke the eggs into the pan and stirred them about with the same spoon. Four eggs, he said.

Yessir.

The man turned and looked at him and then turned back to his cooking. It occurred to the boy that he hadnt been speaking to him. When the eggs were done he took down a plate and scooped them out onto it and placed a blackened silver fork on the edge of the plate and set it on the table in front of the boy. He poured more coffee and put the pot back on the stove and sat down across the table to watch him eat.

You are lost, he said.

The boy paused with a forkful of the eggs and studied the question. I dont think so, he said.

The last man to come here was sick. He was a sick man.

When was that?

The man gestured vaguely in the air with one hand.

What happened to him? the boy said.

He died.

The boy went on eating. I aint sick, he said.

He is buried in the churchyard.

The boy ate. I aint sick, he said, and I aint lost.

He is the first to be buried there in many a year, I can tell you.

How many a year?

I dont know.

What did he come here for?

He was a miner from the mountains. A barretero. He became sick and so he came here. But it was too late. No one could do anything for him.

How many other people live here?

No one. Only me.

Then you was the only one that tried?

Tried what?

To do anything for him.

Yes.

The boy looked up at the man. He ate. What day is it? he said.

It is Sunday.

I meant what day of the month.

I dont know.

Do you know what month it is?

No.

How do you know it's Sunday.

Because it comes every seven days.

The boy ate.

I am a Mormon. Or I was. I was a Mormon born.

He wasnt sure what a Mormon was. He looked at the room. He looked at the cats.

They came here many years ago. Eighteen and ninety-six. From Utah. They came because of the statehood. In Utah. I was a Mormon. Then I converted to the church. Then I became I dont know what. Then I became me.

What do you do here?

I am the custodian. The caretaker.

What do you take care of?

The church.

It's done fell down.

Yes. Of course. It fell down in the terremoto.

Were you here then?

I was not born.

When was it?

In eighteen eighty-seven.

The boy finished the eggs and put the fork on the plate. He looked at the man.

How long have you been here?

Since six years now.

It was like this when you got here.

Yes.

He raised and drained his cup and set it back in the saucer. I thank you for the breakfast, he said.

You are welcome.

He looked like he might be getting ready to rise and leave. The man reached into his shirtpocket and took out tobacco and a small cloth folder in which were papers cut from cornhusks. One of the cats on the bunk had risen and stretched, hindleg and fore, and it leapt silently to the table and walked to the boy's plate and sniffed at it and squatted on bowed elbows and began delicately to pick bits of egg from the tines of the fork. The man had pinched tobacco into a paper and sat rolling it back and forth. He pushed the makings across the table toward the boy.

Thanks, the boy said. I aint never took it up.

The man nodded and twisted the cigarette he'd made into the corner of his mouth and rose and went to the stove. He took a long splinter of wood from a can of them in the floor and opened the stove door and leaned and lit the splinter and with it lit the cigarette. Then he blew out the splinter and put it back in the can and shut the stove door and returned to the table with the pot and refilled the boy's cup. His own cup stood black and cold untouched. He set the pot back on the stove and walked around the table and sat as before. The cat rose and looked at itself in the white porcelain of the plate and stepped away and sat and yawned and set about cleaning itself.

What did you come here for? the boy said.

What did you?

Sir?

What did you come here for?

I didnt come here. I'm just passin through.

The man drew on the cigarette. Myself also, he said. I am the same.

You been passin through for six years?

The man gestured with a small toss of one hand. I came here as a heretic fleeing a prior life. I was running away.

You come here to hide out?

I came because of the devastation.

Sir?

The devastation. From the terremoto.

Yessir.

I was seeking evidence for the hand of God in the world. I had come to believe that hand a wrathful one and I thought that men had not inquired sufficiently into miracles of destruction. Into disasters of a certain magnitude. I thought there might be evidence that had been overlooked. I thought He would not trouble himself to wipe away every handprint. My desire to know was very strong. I thought it might even amuse Him to leave some clue.

What sort of clue?

I dont know. Something. Something unforeseen. Something out of place. Something untrue or out of round. A track in the dirt. A fallen bauble. Not some cause. I can tell you that. Not some cause. Causes only multiply themselves. They lead to chaos. What I wanted was to know his mind. I could not believe He would destroy his own church without reason.

You think maybe the people that lived here had done somethin bad?

The man smoked thoughtfully. I thought it possible, yes. Possible. As in the cities of the plain. I thought there might be evidence of something suitably unspeakable such that He might be goaded into raising his hand against it. Something in the rubble. In the dirt. Under the vigas. Something dark. Who could say?

What did you find?

Nothing. A doll. A dish. A bone.

He leaned and stubbed out the cigarette in a clay bowl on the table.

I am here because of a certain man. I came to retrace his steps. Perhaps to see if there were not some alternate course. What was here to be found was not a thing. Things separate from their stories have no meaning. They are only shapes. Of a certain size and color. A certain weight. When their meaning has become lost to us they no longer have even a name. The story on the other hand can never be lost from its place in the world for it is that place. And that is what was to be found here. The corrido. The tale. And like all corridos it ultimately told one story only, for there is only one to tell.

The cats shifted and stirred, the fire creaked in the stove. Outside in the abandoned village the profoundest silence.

What is the story? the boy said.

In the town of Caborca on the Altar River there was a man who lived there who was an old man. He was born in Caborca and in Caborca he died. Yet he lived once in this town. In Huisiachepic.

What does Caborca know of Huisiachepic, Huisiachepic of Caborca? They are different worlds, you must agree. Yet even so there is but one world and everything that is imaginable is necessary to it. For this world also which seems to us a thing of stone and flower and blood is not a thing at all but is a tale. And all in it is a tale and each tale the sum of all lesser tales and yet these also are the selfsame tale and contain as well all else within them. So everything is necessary. Every least thing. This is the hard lesson. Nothing can be dispensed with. Nothing despised. Because the seams are hid from us, you see. The joinery. The way in which the world is made. We have no way to know what could be taken away. What omitted. We have no way to tell what might stand and what might fall. And those seams that are hid from us are of course in the tale itself and the tale has no abode or place of being except in the telling only and there it lives and makes its home and therefore we can never be done with the telling. Of the telling there is no end. And whether in Caborca or in Huisiachepic or in whatever other place by what-ever other name or by no name at all I say again all tales are one. Rightly heard all tales are one.

The boy looked into the dark disc of liquid in his cup that was not coffee. He looked at the man and he looked at the cats. They seemed to be sleeping to a cat and it occurred to him that the man's voice was to them no novelty and that he must talk to himself in the absence of any godsent ear from the outer world. Or talk to the cats.

What about the man that used to live here? he said.

Yes. This man's parents were killed by a cannonshot in the church at Caborca where they had gone with others to defend themselves against the outlaw American invaders. Perhaps you know something of the history of this country. When the stones and rubble were cleared away the boy lay in the arms of his dead mother. The boy's father lay nearby and he tried to speak. They raised him up. The blood ran from his mouth. They bent to hear what he would say but he said nothing. His chest was crushed and he breathed blood and he lifted one hand as if in farewell and then he died.

The boy was brought to this town. Of Caborca he remembered little. He remembered his father. Certain things. He remembered his father lifting him in his arms to see puppets performing in the alameda. Of his mother he remembered less. Perhaps nothing. The particulars of his life are strange particulars. This is a story of misfortune. Or so it would seem. The end is not yet told.

Here he grew to manhood. In this town. Here he married a wife and all in God's good time was himself blessed with a son.

In the first week of May in the year eighteen eighty-seven this man takes his son and sets out on a journey. He will go to Bavispe and there leave the boy in the care of an uncle who is also the boy's padrino. From Bavispe he will continue on to Batopite where he will arrange for the sale of sugar from certain estancias to the south. In Batopite he will stay the night. This is a journey I have thought of many times. This journey and this man. He is youthful. Perhaps not thirty years of age. He rides a mule. The boy rides in the bow of the saddle before him. It is in the springtime and the wildflowers are blooming in the meadows along the river. He has promised to return with a gift for his young wife. He sees her standing there. She waves goodbye to him as he sets out. He has no likeness of her other than that which he carries in his heart. Think of that. Perhaps she is crying. Standing there watching him out of sight. Standing in the very shadow of this church that is doomed to fall. Life is a memory, then it is nothing. All law is writ in a seed.

The man had arched his fingers above the table to place the scene. He passed one hand from left to right to show where things had been and how it must have been with the sun and with the rider or with the woman where she stood. As if he'd shape out in the present air the spaces where such things had been.

At Bavispe there was a fair. A traveling circus. And the man held his young son aloft under the paper lanterns as his father before him so that the child might see. A clown, a magician, a man who held up serpents in his naked hands. The next morning he departed alone for Batopite as told, leaving the child behind. And there in Bavispe the child died, crushed in the terremoto. The padrino held the boy in his arms and wept. The town of Batopite was spared. Even today you can see the great crack in the mountain wall across the river like an enormous laugh. And that was all the news they had of disaster in Batopite. Nothing else was known. Returning to Bavispe the following day this man met a traveler afoot who told him the news. He could not believe the man's words and he urged the mule on and when he arrived at Bavispe all was in ruin as the traveler had told and death was everywhere in great abundance.

He entered the town already in terror of what he should find. He heard gunshots. Dogs ran out that had been at the bodies in the rubble and scampered past him and men with guns ran out and stood in the street shouting. In the alameda the dead lay on mats of river reed and old women dressed in black walked to and fro among the rows with green fronds to keep the flies away. The padrino came to him and wept at the mule's stirrup and could not speak but only took the reins in his own hands and led him sobbing. Through the alameda where lay dead merchants and farmers and the wives of merchants and farmers. Dead schoolgirls. Lying on reeds in the alameda of Bavispe. A dead dog in a carnival costume. A dead clown. Youngest of them all his son crushed and lifeless. He dismounted and there he knelt and clasped the bloody ruin of the child to his breast. The year is eighteen eighty-seven.

What thoughts must have been his? Who cannot feel his anguish? He returns to Huisiachepic bearing across the mule's haunches the corpse of the child with which God had blessed his house. Waiting for him in Huisiachepic is the mother of the child and this is the gift he brings her.

Such a man is like a dreamer who wakes from a dream of grief to a greater sorrow yet. All that he loves is now become a torment to him. The pin has been pulled from the axis of the universe. Whatever one takes one's eye from threatens to flee away. Such a man is lost to us. He moves and speaks. But he is himself less than the merest shadow among all that he beholds. There is no picture of him possible. The smallest mark upon the page exaggerates his presence.

Who would seek the company of such a man? That which speaks in us one to another and is beyond our words or beyond the lifting or the turning of a hand to say that this is the way my heart is, or this. That thing was lost in him. So.

The boy watched him. His eyes were bright and he had placed one hand palm upward on the table as if within it lay the very thing lost. He closed his fist upon it.

We lose sight of him for some years. He abandons his wife in the ruins of this town. Many friends are dead. Of his wife nothing more is known. He is in Guatemala. He is in Trinidad. How could he return? Had he but saved some part of the burial of his life then perhaps there would have been no need to come with flowers and grief. And yet as it was there was no part of him left to do so. You see?

Men spared their lives in great disasters often feel in their deliverance the workings of fate. The hand of Providence. This man saw in himself again what he'd perhaps forgot. That long ago he'd been elected out of the common lot of men. For what he was asked now to reckon with was that he'd been called forth twice out of the ashes, out of the dust and rubble. For what?

You must not suppose such elections to be happy ones for they are not. In his sparing he found himself severed from both antecedents and posterity alike. He was but some brevity of a being. His claims to the common life of men became tenuous, insubstantial. He was a trunk without root or branch. Perhaps there was yet even then a moment when he would have gone to the church to pray. But the church lay in pieces on the ground. And in the darkened chancel within him had the ground also shifted, also cracked. There also was a ruin. A waste had opened in his soul and perhaps he saw with some new clarity how like the church he was himself but a thing of clay and perhaps he thought that the church would not be raised again as to do such work requires first that God be in men's hearts for it is there alone that it truly has its being and there failing no power can build it back again. He became a heretic. So.

After many a youthful wandering this man appeared at last in the capital and there he worked for some years. He was a bearer of messages. He carried a satchel of leather and canvas secured with a lock. He had no way to know what the messages said nor had he any curiosity concerning them. The stone facades of the buildings among which he went on his daily rounds were pitted with the marks of old gunfire. In places above the reach of people to collect them there yet remained smeared here and there the thin dark medallions of lead which had been rounds from machinegun emplacements in the streets. The rooms in which he stood waiting were rooms from which men in high office had been dragged to their execution. Need one say he was a man without politics? He was simply a messenger. He had no faith in the power of men to act wisely in their own behalf. It was his view rather that every act soon eluded the grasp of its propagator to be swept away in a clamorous tide of unforeseen consequence. He believed that in the world was another agenda, another order, and with this power lay whatever brief he may have held. In the meantime he waited to be called to he knew not what.

The man leaned back, he looked up at the boy and smiled.

Do not misunderstand me, he said. The events of the world can have no separate life from the world. And yet the world itself can have no temporal view of things. It can have no cause to favor certain enterprises over others. The passing of armies and the passing of sands in the desert are one. There is no favoring, you see. How could there be? At whose behest? This man did not cease to believe in God. Nor did he come to have some modern view of God. There was God and there was the world. He knew that the world would forget him but that God could not. And yet that was the very thing he wished for.

Easy to see that naught save sorrow could bring a man to such a view of things. And yet a sorrow for which there can be no help is no sorrow. It is some dark sister traveling in sorrow's clothing. Men do not turn from God so easily you see. Not so easily. Deep in each man is the knowledge that something knows of his existence. Something knows, and cannot be fled nor hid from. To imagine otherwise is to imagine the unspeakable. It was never that this man ceased to believe in God. No. It was rather that he came to believe terrible things of Him.

By now he is a pensioner in Mexico. He has no friends. By day he sits in the park. The very ground under his feet is composted with the blood of the ancients. He watches passersby. He has become convinced that those aims and purposes with which they imagine their movements to be invested are in reality but a means by which to describe them. He believes that their movements are the subject of larger movements in patterns unknown to them and these in turn to others. He finds no comfort in these speculations I can tell you. He sees the world slipping away. All about him an enormous emptiness without echo. It was at this time that he began to pray. From no very pure motive perhaps. But then what would such a motive look like? Can God be cajoled? Can He be pled with or asked to see the reason in one's argument? Can anything from his own hand do aught to please Him more than had it acted otherwise? Can He be surprised? In his heart this man had already begun to plot against God but he did not know it yet. He would not know it until he began to dream of Him.

Who can dream of God? This man did. In his dreams God was much occupied. Spoken to He did not answer. Called to did not hear. The man could see Him bent at his work. As if through a glass. Seated solely in the light of his own presence. Weaving the world. In his hands it flowed out of nothing and in his hands it vanished into nothing once again. Endlessly. Endlessly. So. Here was a God to study. A God who seemed a slave to his own selfordinated duties. A God with a fathomless capacity to bend all to an inscrutable purpose. Not chaos itself lay outside of that matrix. And somewhere in that tapestry that was the world in its making and in its unmaking was a thread that was he and he woke weeping.

On a certain day he rose and put his few possessions into an old valise he'd kept beneath his bed these years and descended the stairwell for the last time. He carried his bible beneath his arm. Like the peregrine minister of some paltry sect. In three days' time he was in the town of Caborca of sacred memory. Standing there by the river squinting up in the sunshine where the dome of the broken transept of the church of La Purísima Concepción de Nuestra Señora de Caborca floated in the pure desert air. So.

The man shook his head slowly. He'd taken up his makings from the table and begun to roll another cigarette. Very thoughtfully. As if its construction were a puzzle to him. He rose and went to the stove and lit the cigarette with the same blackened splinter of wood and inspected the fire and shut the stove door and returned to the table and sat as before.

Perhaps you know the town of Caborca. The church is very beautiful. By the flooding of the river through the years much has been destroyed. The sanctuary and two bell towers. The rear of the nave and most of the south transept. What remains of it stands on three legs, so to speak. The dome hangs in the sky like an apparition and so it has hung for many years. Most improbably. No mason could devise such a structure. For years the people of Caborca waited for it to fall. It was like a thing unfinished in their lives. Events of doubtful outcome were made subject to its standing. It was said of certain old and venerable men that when they died the dome would fall and they died and their children died and the dome floated on in the pure air until at last it came to bear such import in the minds of the people of that town that they scarce would speak of it at all.

This was what he came to. Perhaps he did not even consider the question as to how he had been brought to this place. Yet it was the very thing he sought. Beneath that perilous roof he threw down his pallet and made his fire and there he made ready to receive that which had eluded him. By whatever name. There in the ruins of that church out of whose dust and rubble he had been raised up seventy years before and sent forth to live his life. Such as it was. Such as it had become. Such as it would be.

He drew slowly on the cigarette. He studied the rising smoke. As if in its slow uncoiling lay the lineaments of the history he told. Dream or memory or builded stone. He tapped the ash into the bowl.

The people of the town came and they stood about. At a certain distance. They were interested to see what God would do with such a man. Perhaps he was a crazy person. Perhaps a saint. He paid them no mind. He paced and muttered into his bible and he thumbed the pages. Overhead in the vault were frescoes depicting the very events he pondered. On the west wall of the dome the clay nests of golondrinas mortared up among the fading vestments of the saints. From time to time in his circling he'd pause and hold his book aloft and thump at a page with his finger and address his God at large. This is what they saw. An old hermit. A man with no history. Some said a holy man come among them and some a lunatic and many were scandalized who'd not heard God addressed before in such a manner. Not seen God bearded in his very house.

It seemed that what he wished, this man, was to strike some colindancia with his Maker. Assess boundaries and metes. See that lines were drawn and respected. Who could think such a reckoning possible? The boundaries of the world are those of God's devising. With God there can be no reckoning. With what would one bargain?

They sent for the priest. The priest came and spoke with the man. The priest outside the church. The solitary parishioner within. Beneath the shadow of the perilous vault. The priest spoke to this misguided man of the nature of God and of the spirit and the will and of the meaning of grace in men's lives and the old man heard him out and nodded his head at certain salient points and when the priest was done this old man raised his book aloft and shouted at the priest. You know nothing. That is what he shouted. You know nothing.

The people looked at the priest. To see how he would respond. The priest studied the man and then went away again. The conviction with which the old man spoke had jarred his heart and he weighed the old man's words and was troubled because of course the old man's words were true ones. And if the old man knew that then what else must he know?

He returned the next day. And the day after. People came to attend. Scholars of the town. To hear what was said on either side. The old man at his pacing under the shadow of the vault. The priest outside. The old man thumbing his book with a terrible dexterity. Like a moneycounter. The priest countering from those high canonical principles to which he gave such latitude. Both of them heretics to the bone.

He leaned forward and stubbed out the cigarette. He held up a finger. As if to countenance caution. The sun had entered the room by the south window and certain of the cats had risen to stretch, to rearrange themselves.

With this difference, he said. With this difference. The priest wagered nothing. He'd nothing at hazard. He stood on no such ground as the crazed old man. Under no such shadow. Rather he chose to stand outside the critical edifice of his own church and by this choice he sacrificed his words of their power to witness.

The old man by whatever instinct stood on ground at once blessed and fraughtful. This was his choice, this his gesture. All agreed his testimony was a powerful one. The strength of his conviction was plain to them. In his words there was little measure and little of restraint. In his new life the libertine was out. Do you see? By his arrogance he had engaged the living thing. On that perilous ground he had made of himself the only witness there can ever be and if some saw in his eyes the rapture of madness what else would one look for in one who had enjoined the God of the universe on ground of that God's own choosing? For that is always the nature of such ground, perilous and transitory. And it is indeed so that you must make your case there or nowhere.

And the priest? A man of broad principles. Of liberal sentiments. Even a generous man. Something of a philosopher. Yet one might say that his way through the world was so broad it scarcely made a path at all. He carried within himself a great reverence for the world, this priest. He heard the voice of the Deity in the murmur of the wind in the trees. Even the stones were sacred. He was a reasonable man and he believed that there was love in his heart.

There was not. Nor does God whisper through the trees. His voice is not to be mistaken. When men hear it they fall to their knees and their souls are riven and they cry out to Him and there is no fear in them but only that wildness of heart that springs from such longing and they cry out to stay his presence for they know at once that while godless men may live well enough in their exile those to whom He has spoken can contemplate no life without Him but only darkness and despair. Trees and stones are no part of it. So. The priest in the very generosity of his spirit stood in mortal peril and knew it not. He believed in a boundless God without center or circumference. By this very formlessness he'd sought to make God manageable. This was his colindancia. In his grandness he had ceded all terrain. And in this colindancia God had no say at all.

To see God everywhere is to see Him nowhere. We go from day to day, one day much like the next, and then on a certain day all unannounced we come upon a man or we see this man who is perhaps already known to us and is a man like all men but who makes a certain gesture of himself that is like the piling of one's goods upon an altar and in this gesture we recognize that which is buried in our hearts and is never truly lost to us nor ever can be and it is this moment, you see. This same moment. It is this which we long for and are afraid to seek and which alone can save us.

So. The priest went away. He returned to the town. The old man to his testament. To his pacing and to his argufying. He'd become something like a barrister. He pored over the record not for the honor and glory of his Maker but rather to find against Him. To seek out in nice subtleties some darker nature. False favors. Small deceptions. Promises forsaken or a hand too quickly raised. To make cause against Him, you see. He understood what the priest could not. That what we seek is the worthy adversary. For we strike out to fall flailing through demons of wire and crepe and we long for something of substance to oppose us. Something to contain us or to stay our hand. Otherwise there were no boundaries to our own being and we too must extend our claims until we lose all definition. Until we must be swallowed up at last by the very void to which we wished to stand opposed.

The church at Caborca continued to stand as before. Even the priest could see that the ragged pensioner encamped in the rubble was all of parishioner it was ever like to have. He went away. He left the old man to his claim there under the shadow of that dome which some said could be seen to yaw visibly in the wind. He tried to smile at the old man's posture. What news of God that this church should stand or fall? What more than the wind's whim whether the faltering dome should prove sanctuary or sepulchre to a deranged old anchorite? Nothing would be changed. Nothing known. In the end all would be as before.

Acts have their being in the witness. Without him who can speak of it? In the end one could even say that the act is nothing, the witness all. It may be that the old man saw certain contradictions in his position. If men were the drones he imagined them to be then had he not rather been appointed to take up his brief by the very Being against whom it was directed? As has been the case with many a philosopher that which at first seemed an insurmountable objection to his theories came gradually to be seen as a necessary component to them and finally the centerpiece itself. He saw the world pass into nothing in the very multiplicity of its instancing. Only the witness stood firm. And the witness to that witness. For what is deeply true is true also in men's hearts and it can therefore never be mistold through all and any tellings. This then was his thought. If the world was a tale who but the witness could give it life? Where else could it have its being? This was the view of things that began to speak to him. And he began to see in God a terrible tragedy. That the existence of the Deity lay imperiled for want of this simple thing. That for God there could be no witness. Nothing against which He terminated. Nothing by way of which his being could be announced to Him. Nothing to stand apart from and to say I am this and that is other. Where that is I am not. He could create everything save that which would say him no.

Now we may speak of madness. Now it is safe to do so. Perhaps one could say that only a madman could pace and rend his clothes over the accountability of God. What then to make of this man with claim that God had preserved him not once but twice out of the ruins of the earth solely in order to raise up a witness against Himself?

The fire ticked in the stove. He leaned back in his chair. He pressed the tips of his fingers together five to five and flexed his hands thoughtfully against each other. As if testing the strength of some membranous proposition. A large gray cat came up the table and stood looking at him. It had one ear missing almost entirely and its teeth hung down outside. The man pushed back slightly from the table and the cat stepped down into his lap and curled up and subsided and turned its head and gravely regarded the boy across the table in the manner of a consultant. A cat of counsel. The man placed one hand upon it as if to secure it there. He looked at the boy. The task of the narrator is not an easy one, he said. He appears to be required to choose his tale from among the many that are possible. But of course that is not the case. The case is rather to make many of the one. Always the teller must be at pains to devise against his listener's claim—perhaps spoken, perhaps not—that he has heard the tale before. He sets forth the categories into which the listener will wish to fit the narrative as he hears it. But he understands that the narrative is itself in fact no category but is rather the category of all categories for there is nothing which falls outside its purview. All is telling. Do not doubt it.

The priest visited the old man no more, the story stood unfinished. The old man of course in no wise ceased to pace and rail. He at least had no plans for forgetting the injustices of his past life. The ten thousand insults. The catalog of woes. He had the mind of the injured party, you see. Nothing was lost to him. Of the priest what can be said? As with all priests his mind had become clouded by the illusion of its proximity to God. What priest will denounce his robes even to save himself? And yet the old man was not so far from his thoughts and one day they sent for him and they told him that the old man had fallen ill. That he lay on his pallet and spoke to no one. Not even God. The priest went to see him and it was as they said. He stood without the transept and addressed the old man. He asked if he were indeed ill. The old man lay staring at the fading frescoes. At the coming and going of the golondrinas. He cast his eyes upon the priest and his look was haggard and hollow and he looked away again. The priest seeing opportunity in the weakness of others in the normal human way took up where he'd left off those weeks before and began to declaim to the old man concerning the goodness of God. The old man clapped his hands to his ears but the priest only drew nearer. At last the old man staggered up from his pallet and began to scrabble up stones from the rubble and to pelt the priest with them and so drove him away.

He returned in three days' time and spoke again to the old man but the old man no longer heard him. The food, the pitcher of milk—which the people of Caborca had become accustomed to leave for him at the edge of the shadowline—these remained untouched. God had outwitted him, of course. How could there have been another possibility? In the end it seemed He'd turned even the old man's heretical usurpations to his own service. The sense of election which had at once sustained and tormented the pensioner these years now stood fulfilled in a way he'd not foreseen and before his troubled gaze stood the truth in its awful purity. He saw that he was indeed elect and that the God of the universe was yet more terrible than men reckoned. He could not be eluded nor yet set aside nor circumscribed about and it was true that He did indeed contain all else within Him even to the reasoning of the heretic else He were no God at all.

The priest was greatly moved by what he saw and this surprised him. In the end he even overcame his fears and ventured in beneath the dome of the ruinous church to the old man's side. Perhaps this gave the old man heart. Perhaps even at this late juncture he thought the priest might bring the structure toppling down where he himself had failed. But the dome of course only hung in the air and after a while the old man began to speak. He took the priest's hand as of the hand of a comrade and he spoke of his life and what it had been and what it had become. He told the priest what he had learned. In the end he said that no man can see his life until his life is done and where then to make a mending? It is God's grace alone that we are bound by this thread of life. He held the priest's hand in his own and he bade the priest look at their joined hands and he said see the likeness. This flesh is but a memento, yet it tells the true. Ultimately every man's path is every other's. There are no separate journeys for there are no separate men to make them. All men are one and there is no other tale to tell. But the priest only took his telling for confession and when the old man was done he began the words of absolution. At this the old man seized his arm midway in its crossing there in the still air by his deathbedside and stayed him with his eyes. He let go the priest's other hand and raised his own. Like a man going on a journey. Save yourself, he hissed. Save yourself. Then he died.

Outside in the weedgrown streets all was silence. The man passed his cupped hand over the cat's head, sleeking back its ears. The good, the damaged. The cat lay with its forepaws curled against its chest, its eyes half closed. This is my warrior cat, the man said. Pero es el más dulce de todo. Y el más simpático.

He looked up. He smiled. The storyteller's task is not so simple. You will have guessed by now of course who was the priest. Or perhaps not so much priest as advocate of priestly things. Priestly views. This priest for a while yet would strive to cling to his calling but in the end he was no longer able to bear the look in the eyes of those who came to him for counsel. What counsel had he to give, this man of words? He'd no answers to the questions the old messenger had brought from the capital. The more he considered them the more knotted they became. The more he attempted even to formulate them the more they eluded his every representation and finally he came to see that they were not the old pensioner's queries at all but his own.

The old man was buried in the churchyard at Caborca among those of his own blood. Such was the working out of God's arrangement with this man. Such was his colindancia and such perhaps is every man's. At his dying he had told the priest that he'd been wrong in his every reckoning of God and yet had come at last to an understanding of Him anyway. He saw that his demands upon God resided intact and unspoken also in even the simplest heart. His contention. His argument. They had their being in the humblest history. For the path of the world also is one and not many and there is no alter course in any least part of it for that course is fixed by God and contains all consequence in the way of its going and outside of that going there is neither path nor consequence nor anything at all. There never was. In the end what the priest came to believe was that the truth may often be carried about by those who themselves remain all unaware of it. They bear that which has weight and substance and yet for them has no name whereby it may be evoked or called forth. They go about ignorant of the true nature of their condition, such are the wiles of truth and such its stratagems. Then one day in that casual gesture, that subtle movement of divestiture, they wreak all unknown upon some ancillary soul a havoc such that that soul is forever changed, forever wrenched about in the road it was intended upon and set instead upon a road heretofore unknown to it. This new man will hardly know the hour of his turning nor the source of it. He will himself have done nothing that such great good befall him. Yet he will have the very thing, you see. Unsought for and undeserved. He will have in his possession that elusive freedom which men seek with such unending desperation.

What the priest saw at last was that the lesson of a life can never be its own. Only the witness has power to take its measure. It is lived for the other only. The priest therefore saw what the anchorite could not. That God needs no witness. Neither to Himself nor against. The truth is rather that if there were no God then there could be no witness for there could be no identity to the world but only each man's opinion of it. The priest saw that there is no man who is elect because there is no man who is not. To God every man is a heretic. The heretic's first act is to name his brother. So that he may step free of him. Every word we speak is a vanity. Every breath taken that does not bless is an affront. Bear closely with me now. There is another who will hear what you never spoke. Stones themselves are made of air. What they have power to crush never lived. In the end we shall all of us be only what we have made of God. For nothing is real save his grace.

* * *

WHEN HE HAD mounted up the man stood at his stirrup and squinted up at him in the midmorning sun. You ride to America? he said.

Yessir.

To return to your family.

Yes.

How long since you have seen them?

I dont know.

He looked out down the street. Lost in weeds between the rows of fallen buildings. The mudbrick rubble slumped by the episodic rains of the region into shapes suggesting the work of enormous insect colonies. There was no sound anywhere. He looked down at the man. I dont even know what month it is, he said.

Yes. Of course.

Spring's comin.

Go home.

Yessir. I aim to.

The man stepped back. The boy touched his hat.

I thank you for the breakfast.

Vaya con Dios, joven.

Gracias. Adiós.

He turned the horse and rode out down the street. At the end of the town he reined the horse toward the river and he looked back a last time but the man was gone.

HE WOULD CROSS and recross the river countless times in the days following where the road went ford by ford or along those alluvial fans stepped into the base of the hills where the river shoaled and bended and ran. He passed through the town of Tamichopa which was leveled and burned by the Apaches on the day before Palm Sunday in the year seventeen fifty-eight and in the early afternoon he entered the town of Bacerac which was the old town of Santa María founded in the year sixteen forty-two and where a child came out unbidden and took his horse by the headstall and led him through the street.

They passed through a portal where he was obliged to bend low over the horse's neck and they went on through a white-washed zaguán into a patio where a burro tethered to a pole turned a stone wheatmill. He dismounted and was given a cloth with which to wash and then he was taken into the house and given his supper.

He sat at a scrubbed wooden table with two other young men and they ate very well on baked squash and onion soup and tortillas and beans. The boys were even younger than he and they eyed him furtively and waited for him to speak as the oldest but he did not and so they ate in silence. They fed his horse and at nightfall he was put to bed on an iron cot with a shuck tick at the rear of the house. He'd spoken to no one other than to say thank you. He thought he'd been mistaken for someone else. He woke once at some unknown hour and started up to see a figure watching him from the doorway but it was only the clay olla hanging there in the half darkness to cool the water in the night and not some other kind of figure of some other kind of clay. The next sound he heard was the slapping of hands making the tortillas for breakfast at daylight.

One of the boys brought him coffee in a bowl on a tray. He walked out into the patio drinking it. He could hear women talking somewhere in another part of the house and he stood in the sun drinking the coffee and watching the hummingbirds that tilted and darted and stood among the flowers hanging down over the wall. After a while a woman came to the door and called him to his breakfast. He turned holding the cup and turning saw his father's horse pass in the street.

He walked out through the zaguán and stood in the street but it was empty. He walked up to the corner and looked east and west and he walked up to the square and looked out along the main road north but horse or rider there was none. He turned and started back to the house. He listened as he went for the sound of a horse anywhere behind the walls or the portals that he passed. He stood in front of the house for a long time and then he went in to get his breakfast.

He ate alone in the kitchen. There seemed no one about. He finished and rose and went out to see about his horse and then returned to the house to thank the women but he could not find them. He called but no one answered. He stood in the doorway to a room with high ceilings sheathed in cane and furnished with an old dark wood armoire from another country and two wooden beds painted blue. On the far wall in a niche a painted tin retablo of the Virgin with a slender daycandle burning before it. In the corner a child's cradle and in the cradle a small dog with clouded eyes that raised its head and listened for his presence. He went back to the kitchen and looked for something with which to write. In the end he dusted flour from the bowl on the sideboard over the wooden table and wrote his thanks in that and went out and got his horse and led it afoot down the zaguán and out through the portal. Behind in the patio the little mule turned the pugmill tirelessly. He mounted up and rode out down the little dusty street nodding to those he passed on his way. Riding like a young squire for all his rags. Carrying in his belly the gift of the meal he'd received which both sustained him and laid claim upon him. For the sharing of bread is not such a simple thing nor is its acknowledgement. Whatever thanks be given, however spoke or written down.

Midmorning he rode through the town of Bavispe. He did not stop. A meatvendor's cart stood in the plaza before the church and old women in black muslin wraps were at lifting the dull red strips that hung from the racks and looking underneath with a strange prurience. He rode on. By noon he was in Colonia de Oaxaca and he halted his horse in the road before the alguacil's house and then spat quietly in the dust and rode on. Noon of the day following he passed again through the town of Morelos and took the road north toward Ojito. All day black thunderclouds were making up to the north. He crossed the river a final time and rode up through the low broken hills where the storm overtook him in a hail of ice. He and the horse took shelter in a compound of old abandoned buildings by the roadside. The hail passed and a steady rain set in. Water ran everywhere down through the clay roof overhead and the horse was restless and stood uneasily. Some scent of old troubles or perhaps just the closeness of the walls. It grew dark and he pulled the saddle from the horse and made a bed in the corner out of the loose straw he kicked up. The horse walked out into the rain and he lay under his blanket where he could see out through the broken walls the shape of the horse standing by the side of the road and the shape of the horse in the mute erratic glare of the lightning where the storm moved off to the west. He slept. Late in the night he woke but what had woke him was only the rain's ceasing. He rose and walked out. The moon was in the east over the dark escarpment of the mountains. Sheetwater standing in the flats beyond the narrow road. There was no wind and yet the dead flat of the water shimmered in the bonecolored light as if something had passed over it and the galled moon in the water shivered and yawed and righted itself again and then all lay as before.

In the morning he rode the horse through the border crossing at Douglas Arizona. The guard nodded to him and he nodded back.

You look like maybe you stayed a little longer than what you intended, the guard said.

The boy sat the horse, his hands resting on the pommel of the saddle. He looked down at the guard. You wouldnt loan a man a half dollar to eat on would you? he said.

The guard stood a minute. Then he reached into his pocket.

I live over towards Cloverdale, the boy said. You tell me your name and I'll see that you get it back.

Here you go.

The boy cupped the spinning coin out of the air and nodded and dropped it into his shirtpocket. What's your name?

John Gilchrist.

You aint from around here.

No.

I'm Billy Parham.

Well I'm pleased to meet you.

I'll send you that half dollar soon as I catch somebody comin back this way. You neednt to worry about it.

I aint worried about it.

The boy sat holding the reins loosely. He looked out up the broad street lying before him and at the barren hills about. He looked at Gilchrist again.

How do you like this country? he said.

I like it fine.

The boy nodded. I do too, he said. He touched the brim of his hat. Thanks, he said. I appreciate it. Then he touched the wildlooking horse with his heels and rode off up the street into America.

HE WAS ALL DAY on the old road from Douglas to Cloverdale. By evening he was high in the Guadalupes and it was cold and cold in the pass with the early dark coming and the wind that shunted through the gap. He rode slouched loosely in the saddle with his elbows at his side. He read names and dates where they'd been written in the rock by men long dead who'd passed the same as he. Below him in the long enshadowed twilight lay the beautiful Animas Plain. Coming down the eastern side of the pass the horse suddenly knew where it was and it raised its nose and nickered and quickened its step.

It was past midnight when he reached the house. There were no lights. He went to the barn to put the horse up and there were no horses in the barn and there was no dog and before he'd even traversed half the length of the barn bay he knew that something was bad wrong. He pulled the saddle off the horse and hung it up and pulled down some hay and shut the stall door and walked down to the house and opened the kitchen door and walked in.

The house was empty. He walked through all the rooms.

Most of the furniture was gone. His own small iron bed stood alone in the room off the kitchen, bare save for the tick. In the closet a few wire hangers. He went into the pantry and found some canned peaches and he stood in the dark at the sink eating them out of the glass jar with a cookingspoon and looking out through the window at the pastureland to the south blue and silent under the rising moon and the fence running out into the darkness under the mountains and the shadow of the fence crossing the land in the moonlight like a suture. He turned on the tap at the sink but it gave only a dry gasp and then nothing. He finished the peaches and went to his parents' room and stood in the doorway looking at the empty bedstead, the few rags of clothes in the floor. He went to the front door and opened it and walked out onto the porch. He walked down to the creek and stood listening. After a while he went back to the house and went to his room and lay down on his bed and after a while he slept.

He was up in the morning at daylight sorting through the jars on the shelves in the pantry. He found some stewed tomatoes and ate them and he walked out to the barn and found a brush and led the horse out into the sun and stood brushing him for a long time. Then he led him back into the barn bay and saddled him and mounted up and rode out through the standing gate and took the road north toward the SK Bar.

When he rode into the yard old man Sanders was sitting on the porch much as he'd left him. He didnt know the boy. He didnt even know the horse. He called for him to get down anyway.

It's Billy Parham, the boy called. The old man didnt answer for a minute. Then he called into the house. Leona, he called. Leona.

The girl came to the door and shaded her eyes with one hand and looked at the rider. Then she came out and stood with her hand on her grandfather's shoulder. As if it was the rider had come with bad news for the old man.

* * *

WHEN HE GOT BACK to the house again it was past noon. He left the horse saddled and standing in the yard and walked in and took off his hat. He walked through all the rooms. He thought the old man was crazy but he couldnt account for the girl. He walked into his parents' room and stood. He stood for a long time. He saw how the ticking of the mattress bore the rusty imprint of the springcoils and he looked at that for a long time. Then he hung his hat on the doorknob and walked over to the bed. He stood beside it. He reached down and got hold of the mattress and dragged it off the bed and stood it up and let it fall over backwards in the floor. What came to light beneath was an enormous bloodstain dried near black and soaked so thick it cracked and splintered like some dark ceramic glaze. A faint sour dust rose. He stood there. His hands reached about in the air and finally he took hold of the bedpost and gripped it for support. After a while he looked up and after a while he walked over to the window. Where the noon light lay over the fields. Over the new green of the cottonwoods along the creek. Bright on the Animas Peaks. He looked at it all and he fell to his knees in the floor and sobbed into his hands.

When he rode through Animas the houses seemed deserted. He stopped at the store and filled his canteen from the spigot at the side of the building but he didnt go in. He slept that night on the plains north of the town. He'd nothing to eat and he made no fire. He woke all night and at each waking the signature of Cassiopeia had swung further about the polestar and at each wakening all was as it had been and would forever be. At noon the following day he rode into Lordsburg.

THE SHERIFF LOOKED UP from his desk. He pursed his thin lips.

My name's Billy Parham, the boy said.

I know who you are. Come on in. Set down.

He sat in a chair opposite the sheriff's desk and put his hat on his knee.

Where have you been, son?

Mexico.

Mexico.

Yessir.

What caused you to run off?

I didnt run off.

Were you havin trouble at home?

No sir. Pap never allowed it.

The sheriff leaned back in his chair. He tapped his lower lip with his forefinger and contemplated the ragged figure before him. Pale with road dust. Thin to emaciation. A rope holding up his trousers.

What were you doin in Mexico?

I dont know. I just went down there.

You just got a wild hair up your ass and there wouldnt nothin else do but for you to go off to Mexico. Is that what you're tellin me?

Yessir. I reckon.

The sheriff reached and pushed a stapled set of papers from the edge of the desk and squared them with this thumb. He looked at the boy.

What do you know about this business, son?

I dont know nothin about it. I come here to ask you.

The sheriff sat watching him. All right, he said. If that's your story you'll be held to it.

It aint a story.

All right. We took trackers down there. There was six horses left out of there. Mr Sanders says he thinks that's all the horses there was on the place. Is that right?

Yessir. There was seven countin mine.

Jay Tom and his boy said that there was two of em and that they left out with the horses about two hours before daylight.

They could tell that?

They could tell that.

They showed up down there on foot.

Yes.

What does Boyd say?

Boyd dont say nothin. He run off and hid. He laid out in the cold all night and walked up to Sanders' the next day and they couldnt get no sense out of him. Miller had to get in the truck and drive down there and find that mess. They'd been shot with a shotgun.

Billy looked past the sheriff out to the street. He tried to swallow but he couldnt. The sheriff watched him.

First thing they done was they caught the dog and cut its throat. Then they set and waited to see would anybody come out. They waited there long enough that one of em went to take a leak. They waited to see that everbody was asleep again after the dog quit barkin and all.

Were they Mexicans?

They was indians. Or Jay Tom says they was indians. I reckon he would know. The dog never died.

What?

I said the dog never died. Boyd's got it. It's mute as a stone.

The boy sat looking at the greasestained hat cocked on his knee.

What kind of guns did they get? the sheriff said.

There wasnt any to get. The only gun on the place was a forty-four forty carbine and I had that with me.

It wasnt much use to em, was it?

No sir.

We got nothin to go on. You know that.

Yessir.

Have you?

Have I what?

Do you know anything you aint told me.

Have you got jurisdiction in Mexico?

No.

Then what difference does it make?

That aint much of a answer.

No it aint. It's about like yours.

The sheriff watched him for a while.

If you think I dont care about this, he said, you're wrong as hell.

The boy sat. He put the back of his forearm to one eye and then the other and turned and looked out the window again. There was no traffic in the street. Out on the sidewalk two women were talking in spanish.

Could you give me a description of the horses?

Yessir.

Was any of em branded?

One of em was. That Niño horse. Pap bought him off of a Mexican.

The sheriff nodded. All right, he said. He leaned down and pulled out a drawer in his desk and took out a tin deedbox and put it on top of the desk and opened it.

I dont guess I'm supposed to give you this stuff, he said. But I dont always do what I'm told. You got any place to keep it?

I dont know. What's in there?

Papers. Marriage license. Birth certificates. There's some papers on horses in here but most of em goes back a few years. Your mama's weddin ring is in here.

What about Pap's watch?

There wasnt no watch. There's some household effects out at the Websters'. If you want I'll put these papers in the bank. They aint even appointed a conservator so I dont know what else to do with em.

There ought to be papers on Niño and on that Bailey horse.

The sheriff turned the box around and slid it across the desk. The boy began to thumb through the documents.

Who's Margarita Evelyn Parham? the sheriff said.

My sister.

Where is she at?

She's dead.

How come her to have a Mexican name?

She was named after my grandmother.

He pushed the deedbox back on the desk and refolded the two papers he'd removed from it along their three lines and slid them inside his shirt.

Is that everthing you want? the sheriff said.

Yessir.

He closed the lid on the box and put it back in the drawer of his desk and shut the drawer and leaned back in his chair and looked at the boy. You aint fixin to go back down there are you? he said.

I aint decided what all I'm goin to do. First thing I got to do is go get Boyd.

Go get Boyd?

Yessir.

Boyd aint goin nowhere.

If I am he is.

Boyd's a juvenile. They aint goin to turn him over to you. Hell. You're a juvenile yourself.

I aint askin.

Son, dont get crosswise of the law over this.

I dont intend to. I dont intend for it to get crosswise of me neither.

He took his hat off his knee and held it briefly in both hands and then stood. I thank you for the papers, he said.

The sheriff put his hands on the arms of his chair as if he might be going to rise but he didnt. What about the descriptions on them horses? he said. You want to write them out for me?

What would be the use in it?

You didnt learn no manners down there while you was gone, did you?

No sir. I guess not. I learned some things but they sure wasnt manners.

The sheriff nodded toward the window. Is that your horse out there?

Yessir.

I see that scabbard boot. Where's the rifle at?

I traded it.

What did you trade it for?

I dont think I could say.

You mean you wont say.

No sir. I mean I aint sure I could put a name to it.

When he walked out into the sun and untied the horse from the parking meter people passing in the street turned to look at him. Something in off the wild mesas, something out of the past. Ragged, dirty, hungry in eye and belly. Totally unspoken for. In that outlandish figure they beheld what they envied most and what they most reviled. If their hearts went out to him it was yet true that for very small cause they might also have killed him.

THE HOUSE where his brother was staying was out on the east side of town. A small stucco house with a fenced yard and a front porch. He tied Bird at the fence and pushed open the gate and started up the walk. The dog came around the corner of the house and bared its teeth at him and raised its hackles.

It's me, numbnuts, he said.

When it heard his voice it flattened its ears and began to squirm across the yard toward him. It hadnt barked and it didnt whine.

Hello the house, he called.

The dog twisted itself against him. Git away, he said.

He called the house again and then went up on the porch and knocked at the front door and stood. No one came. He walked around to the back. When he tried the kitchen door it was unlocked and he pushed it open and looked in. It's Billy Parham, he called.

He entered and shut the door. Hello, he called. He walked through the kitchen and stood in the hallway. He was about to call again when the kitchen door opened behind him. He turned and Boyd was standing there. He stood with a steel pail in one hand and his other hand on the doorknob. He was taller. He leaned against the jamb.

I reckon you thought I was dead, Billy said.

If I'd of thought you was dead I wouldnt be here.

He shut the door and set the pail on the kitchen table. He looked at Billy and he looked out the window. When Billy spoke to him again his brother wouldnt look at him but Billy could see that his eyes were wet.

Are you ready to go? he said.

Yeah, said Boyd. Just waitin on you.

They took a shotgun from a closet in the bedroom and they took nineteen dollars in coins and small bills from a white china box in a bureau drawer and stuffed it all into an oldfashioned leather changepurse. They took the blanket off the bed and they found Billy a belt and some clothes and they took all the shotshells out of a Carhart coat hanging on the wall at the back door, one double-ought buckshot and the rest number five and number seven shot, and they took a laundry bag and filled it with canned goods and bread and bacon and crackers and apples from the pantry and they walked out and tied the bag to the horn of the saddle and mounted up and rode out the little sandy street riding double with the dog trotting after them. A woman with clothespins in her mouth in a yard they passed nodded to them. They crossed the highway and they crossed the tracks of the Southern Pacific Railway and turned west. Come dark they were camped on the alkali flats fifteen miles west of Lordsburg before a fire made of fenceposts they'd dragged out of the ground with the horse. East and to the south there was water on the flats and two sandhill cranes stood tethered to their reflections out there in the last of the day's light like statues of such birds in some waste of a garden where calamity had swept all else away. All about them the dry cracked platelets of mud lay curing and the fencepost fire ran tattered in the wind and the balled papers from the groceries they opened loped away one by one downwind into the gathering dark.

They fed the horse on oatmeal they'd taken from the house

and Billy skewered bacon along a length of fencewire and hung it to cook. He looked at Boyd where he sat with the shotgun across his lap.

You and Pap ever get your differences patched up?

Yeah. About half way.

Which half?

Boyd didn't answer.

What is that you're eatin?

A raisin sandwich.

Billy shook his head. He poured water from the canteen into a fruitcan and set it in the coals.

What happened to your saddle? Boyd said.

Billy looked at the saddle with the mutilated offside fender but he didnt answer.

They'll be huntin us, Boyd said.

Let em hunt.

How are we goin to pay em back for what all we took?

Billy looked up at him. Maybe you better just get used to the idea of bein a outlaw, he said.

Even a outlaw dont rob them that's took him in and befriended him.

How much of this are we goin to have to listen to?

Boyd didnt answer. They ate and unrolled their beds and turned in to sleep. The wind blew all night. It burned up the fire and burned up the coals of the fire and the balled and twisted shape of redhot wire burned briefly like the incandescent armature of an enormous heart in the night's darkness and then faded to black and the wind blew the coals to ash and blew the ash away and scoured the clay where coals and ash had been till other than the blackened wire there was no trace of fire at all and all night things passed in the dark that had of themselves no articulation yet had a destination for that.

Are you awake? Billy said.

Yeah.

What did you tell em?

Nothin.

Why?

What would be the use in it?

The wind blew. The migrant sands seethed past.

Billy?

What?

They knew my name.

Knew your name?

They called for me. Called Boyd. Boyd.

It dont mean nothin. Go to sleep.

Like we was friends.

Go to sleep.

Billy?

What?

You dont have to try and make it better than what it is.

Billy didnt answer.

It is what it is.

I know it. Go to sleep.

In the morning they sat eating and they watched across the flats where something was articulating in the sunrise far out on the steelcolored clay of the playa. After a while they could see that it was a rider. He was perhaps a mile out and he approached in a series of thin and trembling images which in those places where the footground was flooded would suddenly augment in their length and then shrivel and draw up again so that the rider appeared to advance and recede and advance again. The sun rose into the red reefs of cloud along the eastern shore and the rider came on, crossing a lake ten miles wide and three inches deep. Billy got up and got the shotgun and came back and put it under the blanket and sat again.

The horse was either the color of the terrain or was stained so by it. The rider advanced over the shallow standing water and the water displaced under the hooves of the horse brightened in the light and vanished instantly like lead dishing in a vat. He rode off of the lake and threaded a path along the sandy soda shore through the sparse tussocks of grass until he sat the clay-colored horse before them and looked down at them from under the shade of his hat. He didnt speak. He looked at them and he looked back across the playa and leaned and spat and looked at them again. You aint who I thought you was, he said.

Who'd you think we was?

The rider ignored him. What are you all doin out here? he said.

Aint doin nothin.

He looked at Boyd. He looked at the horse. What have you got under that blanket? he said.

A shotgun.

Are you fixin to shoot me?

No sir.

Is that your brother?

He can answer for hisself.

Are you his brother?

Yeah.

What are you all doin out here?

Passin through.

Passin through?

Yeah.

Passin through to where?

We're goin to Douglas Arizona.

Yeah?

We got friends over there.

You aint got none over here?

We aint cut out for town life.

Is that your all's horse?

Yeah.

I know who you are, the man said.

They didnt answer. The man looked back out across the flats of the dry lake where the thin standing water lay like lead in the windless morning. He leaned and spat again and looked at Billy.

I'm goin to tell Mr Boruff what you told me. That it's just a pair of drifters. Or if you want I'll wait on you and you can ride back with me.

We aint ridin back. I appreciate it.

I'll tell you somethin else if you dont know it.

Tell it.

You got a long row to hoe.

Billy didnt answer.

How old are you?

Seventeen.

The man shook his head. Well, he said. You all take care.

Tell me somethin, Billy said.

All right.

How could you see us from way out yonder?

I seen your reflection. Certain times you can see things out on a playa that's too far to see. Some of the boys claimed you all was a mirage but Mr Boruff knowed you wasnt. He studies this country. He knows what's in it and what aint in it. So do I.

You study it again in about a hour and see if you see us.

I aim to.

He nodded to them each separately where they sat on that barren inland strand and he looked at the mute dog.

He aint much shucks as a watchdog, is he?

He's had his throat cut.

I know it, the rider said. You all take care. Then he turned the horse and rode back out across the flats and across the lake. He rode into the sun and he rode in silhouette but even though the sun was well up and no longer in their eyes when they themselves were mounted and set out south along the edge of the pan they still could see nothing at all on the far shore of the lake where the rider had vanished.

Some time midmorning they crossed the boundary line into the state of Arizona. They rode through a low range of mountains and descended into the San Simon Valley where it ran down from the north and they nooned at the river in a grove of cottonwoods. They hobbled and watered the horses and sat naked in the shallow gravel pool. Pale, thin, dirty. Billy watched his brother until his brother raised up and looked at him.

It aint no use you askin me a bunch of stuff.

I wasnt goin to ask you nothin.

You will.

They sat in the water. The dog sat in the grass watching them.

He's wearin daddy's boots, aint he? Billy said.

There you go.

You're lucky you aint dead too.

I dont know what's so lucky about it.

That's a ignorant thing to say.

You dont know.

What dont I know?

But Boyd didnt say what it was he didnt know.

They ate sardines and crackers in the shade of the cotton-woods and they slept and in the afternoon they rode on again.

I thought one time maybe you'd gone to California, Boyd said.

What would I do in California?

I dont know. They got cowboys in California.

California cowboys.

I wouldnt want to go to California.

I wouldnt either.

I might go to Texas.

What for?

I dont know. I aint never been.

You aint never been noplace. So what reason is that?

Only one I got.

They rode. In the long shadows jackrabbits bolted and loped and froze again. The mute dog paid them no mind.

Why caint the law go to Mexico? Boyd said.

Cause it's American law. It aint worth nothin in Mexico.

What about the Mexican law?

There aint no law in Mexico. It's just a pack of rogues.

Will number five shot kill a man?

It will if you get close enough. It'll make a hole you can run your arm through.

In the evening they crossed the highway just east of Bowie and struck the old road south through the Dos Cabezas range.

They made camp and Billy rustled wood out along a shallow stone arroyo and they ate and sat by the fire.

You reckon they will come after us? Boyd said.

I dont know. They might.

He leaned and jostled the coals with a stick and put the stick in the fire. Billy watched him.

They wont catch us.

I know it.

Why dont you say what's on your mind.

There aint nothin on my mind.

It wasnt nobody's fault.

Boyd sat staring into the fire. Coyotes were yapping out along the ridge to the north of the camp.

You'll just make yourself crazy, Billy said.

I done already have.

He looked up. His pale hair looked white. He looked fourteen going on some age that never was. He looked as if he'd been sitting there and God had made the trees and rocks around him. He looked like his own reincarnation and then his own again. Above all else he looked to be filled with a terrible sadness. As if he harbored news of some horrendous loss that no one else had heard of yet. Some vast tragedy not of fact or incident or event but of the way the world was.

The day following they crossed through the high gap at Apache Pass. Boyd sat behind him with his thin legs dangling on the horse's flanks and together they looked over the country to the south. The day was sunny and there was a wind blowing and there were ravens in the mountains riding the updrafts over the southfacing slopes.

This is one more place you aint been, Billy said.

They're everwhere, aint they?

You see that line yonder where the color changes?

Yeah.

That's Mexico.

It dont look like it's gettin no closer.

What does that mean?

It means let's ride if we're goin to.

Noon the following day they struck route 666 and followed the blacktop down out of the Sulphur Springs Valley. They rode through the town of Elfrida. They rode through the town of McNeal. In the evening they rode through the main street of Douglas and halted at the gateshack on the border. The guard stood in the doorway and nodded at them. He looked at the dog.

Where's Gilchrist at? said Billy.

He's off. He dont come on till in the mornin.

Can I leave some money for him?

Yeah. You can leave it.

Let me have a half dollar, Boyd.

Boyd dug the leather changepurse out of his pocket and unsnapped it. The money was all nickels and dimes and pennies and he counted the requisite coins out and cupped them and handed them across Billy's shoulder to him. Billy took the coins and poked them apart in his own hand and recounted them and then cupped them together again and leaned down and held out his fist.

I owe him a half dollar.

All right, said the guard.

Billy touched the brim of his hat with his forefinger and put the horse forward.

You takin that dog with you? the guard said.

If he wants to come.

The guard watched them go, the dog trotting after. They crossed the little bridge. The Mexican guard looked up at them and nodded them on and they rode into Agua Prieta.

I know how to count, Boyd said.

What?

I know how to count. There wasnt no need for you to count it a second time.

Billy turned and looked at him and turned back again.

All right, he said. I wont do it again.

They bought paletas of icecream from a streetvendor and sat on the curb at the horse's feet and watched the street coming to life in the evening. The dog lay uneasily in the dust in front of them while town dogs passed and circled with their backs roached taking his scent.

They bought meal and dried beans in a grocery and salt and coffee and dried fruit and dried peppers and they bought a small enameled frypan and a pot with a lid and a box of kitchen matches and a few utensils and they changed the remainder of their money into pesos.

Now you're rich, Billy said.

Nigger-rich, said Boyd.

It's moren what I had when I come down here.

That aint no big comfort.

They left the road at the south end of town and followed the river along its course of pale gray cobbles out into the desert and made camp in the dark. Billy fixed their supper and they ate and sat watching the fire.

You need to quit thinkin about it, Billy said.

I aint thinkin about it.

What are you thinkin about?

Nothin.

That's hard to do.

What if somethin was to happen to you?

Dont be thinkin all the time about what would happen.

What if it was?

You could go back.

To the Websters?

Yeah.

After we robbed em and all?

You didnt rob em. I thought you wasnt thinkin about nothin.

I aint. I just got a uneasy feelin.

Billy leaned and spat into the fire. You'll be all right.

I'm all right now.

They rode all the day following along the secular river in its bed of stones and in the early evening they entered the roadside hamlet of Ojito. Boyd had been sleeping with his face against his brother's back and he raised up all sweaty and rumpled and got his hat from where he'd crushed it in his lap between them and put it on.

Where are we at? he said.

I dont know.

I'm hungry.

I know it. I am too.

You reckon they got anything to eat here?

I dont know.

They halted the horse before a man in a crumbling mud doorway and asked if there was anything to eat in the town and the man reflected a moment and then offered to sell them a chicken. They rode on. Where the empty road ran out into the desert to the south a storm was making up and the country was bluelooking under the clouds and the thin wires of lightning that stood repeatedly over the raw blue mountains in the distance broke in utter silence like a storm in a belljar. It caught them just before dark. The rain came ripping across the desert driving flights of wild doves before it and they rode into a wall of water and were wet instantly. A hundred yards along they dismounted and stood in a grove of roadside trees and held the horse and watched the rain roar in the mud. By the time the storm had passed it was dead black of night about them and they stood shivering in the starless dark and listened to the water dripping in the silence.

What do you want to do now? Boyd said.

Mount up and ride, I reckon.

That's a awful wet horse to have to climb aboard.

He might say the same about you.

It was past midnight when they rode through the town of Morelos. Lamps dimmed out down the street as if they were bringing the darkness with them. He'd wrapped his coat around Boyd and Boyd was tottering asleep against his back and the horse went sucking through the mud with its head down and the dog tacked before them among the pools of standing water and they took the road south where he had followed the pilgrims to the fair in the spring of that same year so long ago.

They passed what was left of the night in a jacal just off the road and in the morning they built a fire and made breakfast and dried their clothes and then saddled the horse and set out again on the road south. In three more days of such riding and seven days into the country passing one by one through the squalid mud towns along the river they entered the town of Bacerac. In front of a whitewashed house under an elder tree were two horses standing head down. One was a big roan gelding with a fresh brand on its left hip and the other was their horse Keno wearing a tooled mexican saddle.

Look yonder, said Boyd.

I see him. Get down.

Boyd slid from the horse and Billy dismounted and passed him the reins and pulled the shotgun from the saddlescabbard. The dog had stopped in the road and stood looking back at them. Billy unbreeched the gun to see that it was loaded and breeched it shut again and looked at Boyd.

Take the horse over yonder and keep out of the way.

All right.

He watched while Boyd walked the horse across the road and then he turned and started for the house. The dog stood looking from one to the other until Boyd whistled for it.

He walked around Keno and patted his neck and the horse pushed its forehead against his shirt and breathed a long sweet breath against him. He stood the shotgun against the elder tree and lifted the stirrup and hung it over the horn and pulled the latigo and slid the strap free and pulled loose the backcinch and took hold of the saddle by horn and cantle and lifted it down and stood it in the dirt. Then he pulled off the saddleblanket and hung it over the horn of the saddle and picked up the shotgun and untied the horse and led it back across the street to where Boyd stood.

He jammed the shotgun back into the scabbard and looked again toward the house. Ride Bird, he said.

Boyd stood up into the saddle and looked down at him.

Take the horses up here and keep out of sight of the house.

I'll meet you at the south end of town. Just stay hid. I'll find you.

What do you aim to do?

I want to see who all's in there.

What if it's them?

It aint.

Who all do you think is in there?

I dont know. I think somebody has died. Go on now.

You better take the shotgun.

I dont need it. Go on.

He watched him ride up the narrow dirt street and then he turned and walked back to the house.

He knocked at the door and stood with his hat in his hands. No one came. He put his hat on and walked down and pushed at an old weathered carriage door in the wall but it was barred shut. He looked at the top of the wall. There were broken bottle ends set into the mud masonry there. He took out his knife and put it between the doors and began to walk the ancient wooden tranca a half inch at a time across the gates until the end of it slipped free of the cradle and he pushed the door open and stepped inside and pushed it shut again. There were no drag-marks in the dirt, nothing come and gone. There were chickens sitting in a tree in broad daylight. He crossed the patio to the rear of the house and stood in a doorway that gave onto a long hall. On a low bench were clay pots with plants in them which had been recently watered and the dirt was damp and the tiles under the bench were wet. He took off his hat again and walked down the hallway and stood in the door at the far end. In a darkened room a woman lay in a bed. About her were sister figures clothed in dark rebozos. On a table a candle burning.

The woman in the bed was lying with her eyes closed and she held a glass rosary in her hands. She was dead. One of the women kneeling turned her head and looked at him. Then she looked toward a part of the room he could not see. After a while a man came out pulling on his coat and he nodded politely to the boy standing at the door.

Quién es? he said.

He was tall and blond and he spoke spanish with a foreign accent. Billy stepped to one side and they stood in the hall.

Estaba su caballo enfrente de la casa?

The man stopped, his coat on one shoulder. He looked at Billy and he looked down the hallway. Estaba? he said.

HE FOUND BOYD laid up with the horses in a stand of carrizo cane at the river's edge south of the town.

Anybody could of tracked you here, he said.

Boyd didnt answer. Billy squatted on the ground and broke off a reed and broke it again in his hands.

He's a German doctor. He had a factura for the horse. Or said he did. He said he had papers from a broker in Casas Grandes named Soto.

Boyd had been standing holding the shotgun. He reholstered it in the scabbard and leaned and spat. Well, he said. Whatever papers he has it's moren what we got.

We got the horse.

Boyd stood looking past the horse at the river running. They're goin to shoot us, he said.

Come on, Billy said. Let's go.

You just walked in there?

Yeah.

What did you tell him?

Let's go. We aint down here for the fun of it.

What did you tell him.

Told him the truth. Told him his horse was stole by indians.

Where's he at now?

He took the mozo's horse and rode off downriver to hunt em.

Did he have a gun?

Yeah. He had a gun.

What are we goin to do?

Ride to Casas Grandes.

Where's it at?

I dont know.

They left Keno in the brake doublehobbled with the dog tied to him and rode back into the town. They sat on the ground in the dusty square while a thin old man squatted opposite and drew for them with a whittled stick a portrait of the country they said they wished to visit. He sketched in the dust streams and promontories and pueblos and mountain ranges. He commenced to draw trees and houses. Clouds. A bird. He penciled in the horsemen themselves doubled upon their mount. Billy leaned forward from time to time to question the measure of some part of their route whereupon the old man would turn and squint at the horse standing in the street and then give an answer in hours. All the while there sat watching on a bench a few feet away four men dressed in ancient and sunfaded suits. By the time the old man was done the map he'd drawn covered an area in the dirt the size of a blanket. He stood and dusted the seat of his trousers with a swipe of his flattened hand.

Give him a peso, Billy said.

Boyd dug out the pocketbook and unsnapped it and took out the coin and Billy gave it to the old man and the old man took it with grace and dignity and removed his hat and put it on again and they shook hands all around and the old man pocketed the coin and turned and walked out across the little blighted zócalo and disappeared up the street without looking back. When he was gone the men on the bench began to laugh. One of them rose to better see the map.

Es un fantasma, he said.

Fantasma?

Sí, sí. Claro.

Cómo?

Cómo? Porque el viejo está loco es como.

Loco?

Completamente.

Billy stood looking at the map. No es correcto? he said.

The man threw up his hands. He said that what they beheld was but a decoration. He said that anyway it was not so much a question of a correct map but of any map at all. He said that in that country were fires and earthquakes and floods and that one needed to know the country itself and not simply the landmarks therein. Besides, he said, when had that old man last journeyed to those mountains? Or journeyed anywhere at all? His map was after all not really so much a map as a picture of a voyage. And what voyage was that? And when?

Un dibujo de un viaje, he said. Un viaje pasado, un viaje antiguo.

He threw up one hand in dismissal. As if no more could be said. Billy looked at the other three men on the bench. They watched with a certain brightness of eye so that he wondered if he were being made a fool of. But the one seated at the right leaned forward and tapped the ash from his cigarette and addressed the man standing and said that as far as that went there were certainly other dangers to a journey than losing one's way. He said that plans were one thing and journeys another. He said it was a mistake to discount the good will inherent in the old man's desire to guide them for it too must be taken into account and would in itself lend strength and resolution to them in their journey.

The man who was standing weighed these words and then erased them in the air before him with a slow fanning motion of his forefinger. He said that the jovenes could hardly be expected to apportion credence in the matter of the map. He said that in any case a bad map was worse than no map at all for it engendered in the traveler a false confidence and might easily cause him to set aside those instincts which would otherwise guide him if he would but place himself in their care. He said that to follow a false map was to invite disaster. He gestured at the sketching in the dirt. As if to invite them to behold its futility. The second man on the bench nodded his agreement in this and said that the map in question was a folly and that the dogs in the street would piss upon it. But man on the right only smiled and said that for that matter the dogs would piss upon their graves as well and how was this an argument?

The man standing said that what argued for one case argued for all and that in any event our graves make no claims outside of their own simple coordinates and no advice as to how to arrive there but only the assurance that arrive we shall. It may even be that those who lie in desecrated graves—by dogs of whatever manner—could have words of a more cautionary nature and better suited to the realities of the world. At this the man at the left who'd so far not spoke at all rose laughing and gestured for the two boys to follow and they went with him out of the square and into the street leaving the disputants to their rustic parkbench tertulia. Billy untied the horse and they stood while the man pointed out to them the track to the east and told them certain landmarks in the mountains and that the track terminated at a station called Las Ramadas and that they must trust in their luck or their friendship with God to make their way across the divide to Los Horcones. He shook hands with them and smiled and wished them luck and they asked how far it was to Casas Grandes and he held up one hand with his thumb folded across the palm. Cuatro días, he said. He looked toward the square where the other men were yet haranguing one another and he said that they must attend a funeral that very evening for the wife of a friend and that their mood was idiosincrasico and to pay them no mind. He said that far from making men reflective or wise it was his experience that death often leads them to attribute great consequence to trivial things. He asked if they were brothers and they said that they were and he told them to care for one another in the world. He nodded again toward the mountains and he said that the serranos had good hearts but that elsewhere was another matter. Then he wished them luck again and called upon God to be with them and stepped back and raised his hand in farewell.

When they were out of sight of the old men they quit the road and went down to the river and followed the river path until they had picked up the other horse and the dog. Boyd mounted Keno and they rode on until they came to the ford where they crossed the river and took the road east into the mountains.

Such road as it was soon ceased to be road at all. Where it first left the river it was the width of a wagon or more and had in recent times been scraped or graded with a fresno and the brush cut back yet once clear of the town the heart seemed to have gone out of this enterprise and they found themselves on a common footpath following the course of a dry arroyo up into the hills. At just dark they came upon a small holding, a clutch of pole huts staked out upon a trinchera or terrace shored up with rock. They made their camp just above this place on the next level ground and hobbled the horses and made a fire. Below them through the scrub pine and juniper they could see a yellow houselamp. A little later as they were boiling their pail of beans a man came up the road carrying a lantern. He called to them from the road and Billy stepped to where the shotgun stood leaning against a tree and called back for him to approach. He came to the fire and stood. He looked at the dog.

Buenas noches, he said.

Buenas noches.

Son Americanos?

Sí.

He held the lantern up. He looked at the shapes of the horses in the dark beyond the fire.

Dónde está el caballero?

No hay otro caballero más que nosotros, Billy said.

The man's eyes wandered over their meager possessions. Billy knew that he'd been sent to invite them to the house but he did not do so. They spoke briefly of nothing at all and then he took his leave. He walked back out to the road and through the trees they saw him raise the lamp to his face and lift the glass in its bail and blow out the flame. Then he walked back down to the house in the dark.

The day following their way led them into the mountains shutting in the Bavispe River Valley under the western slope.

The trail grew more wretched yet with washouts where the riders were obliged to dismount and lead the horses clambering along the narrow floor of the arroyo and up along the switchbacks and there were places where the track diverged and where separate schools of thought wandered off through the pine and scrub oak. They camped that night in an old burn among the bones of trees and among the shapes of boulders that had broken open in the earthquake half a century before and slid down the mountain on the face of their cleavings and grinding stone on stone had struck the fire with which they'd burnt the woods alive. The trunks of the pollarded and broken trees stood at every angle pale and dead in the twilight and in the twilight small owls flew in utter silence hither and yon about the darkening glade.

They sat by the fire and cooked and ate the last of their bacon with beans and tortillas and they slept on the ground in their blankets and the wind in the dead gray pilings about them made no sound and the owls when they called in the night called with soft watery calls like the calls of doves.

They rode for two days through the high country. A fine rain fell. It was cold and they rode with their blankets about them and the dog trotted ahead like some mute and mindless bellwether and the breath from the horses' nostrils plumed whitely in the thin air. Billy offered that they take turn about riding the saddled horse but Boyd said that he would ride the Keno horse by preference saddle or no. When Billy then offered to swap the saddle to the other horse Boyd only shook his head and booted the bareback horse forward.

They rode through the ruins of old sawmills and they rode through a mountain meadow dotted with the dark stumps of trees. Across a valley in the evening with the sun on it they could see the tailings of an old silvermine and camped in withy huts among the rusted shapes of antique machinery a family of gypsy miners working the abandoned shaft who now stood aligned all sizes of them before the evening cookfire watching the riders pass along the opposing slope and shading their eyes against the sun with their hands like some encampment of ragged and deranged militants at review. That same evening he shot a rabbit and they halted in the long mountain light and made a fire and cooked the rabbit and ate it and fed the guts to the dog and then the bones and when they were done they sat gazing into the coals.

You reckon the horses know where we're at? Boyd said.

What do you mean?

He looked up from the fire. I mean do you reckon they know where we're at.

What the hell kind of question is that?

Well. I reckon it's a question about horses and what they know about where they're at.

Hell, they dont know nothin. They're just in some mountains somewheres. You mean do they know they're in Mexico?

No. But if we was up in the Peloncillos or somewheres they'd know where they was at. They could find their way back if you turned em out.

Are you askin me if they could find their way back from here if you cut em loose?

I dont know.

Well what are you askin.

I'm askin if they know where they're at.

Billy stared at the coals. I dont know what the hell you're talkin about.

Well. Forget it.

You mean like they got a picture in their head of where the ranch is at?

I dont know.

Even if they did it wouldnt mean they could find it.

I didnt mean they could find it. Maybe they could and maybe they couldnt.

They couldnt backtrack the whole way. Hell.

I dont think they backtrack. I think they just know where things are.

Well you know moren me then.

I didnt say that.

No, I said it.

He looked at Boyd. Boyd sat with the blanket over his shoulders and his cheap boots crossed before him. Why dont you go to bed? he said.

Boyd leaned and spat into the coals. He sat watching the spittle boil. Why dont you, he said.

When they set forth in the morning it was still gray light. Mist moving through the trees. They rode out to see what the day would bring and within the hour they sat the horses on the eastern rim of the escarpment and watched while the sun ballooned like boiling glass up out of the plains of Chihuahua to make the world again from darkness.

By noon they were on the prairie again riding through better grass than any they had seen before, riding through bluestem and through sideoats grama. In the afternoon they saw far to the south a standing palisade of thin green cypress trees and the thin white walls of a hacienda. Shimmering in the heat like a white boat on the horizon. Distant and unknowable. Billy looked back at Boyd to see if he had seen it but Boyd was watching it as he rode. It shimmered and was lost in the heat and then it reappeared again just above the horizon and hung there suspended in the sky. When he looked again it had vanished altogether.

In the long twilight they walked the horses to cool them. There was a stand of trees in the middle distance and they mounted up again and rode toward them. The dog trotted ahead with lolling tongue and the darkening prairieland sank about them cool and blue and the shapes of the mountains they'd quit stood behind them black and without dimension against the evening sky.

They kept the trees skylighted before them and as they approached the glade they rode the groaning shapes of cattle up out of their beds. The cattle shook their necks and trotted off in the dark and the horses sniffed at the air and at the trampled grass. They rode into the trees and the horses slowed and stopped and then walked carefully out into the dark standing water.

They hobbled Bird and then staked Keno where he would keep the cows off of them while they slept. They'd nothing to eat and they made no fire but only rolled themselves in their blankets on the ground. Twice in the night in his grazing the horse passed the catchrope over them and he woke and lifted the rope over his brother where he slept and laid it in the grass again. He lay in the dark wrapped in the blanket and listened to the horses cropping the grass and smelling the good rich smell of the cattle and then he slept again.

In the morning they were sitting naked in the dark water of the ciénega when a party of vaqueros rode up. They watered their mounts at the far end and nodded and wished them a good morning and sat astride the drinking horses rolling cigarettes and taking in the country.

Adónde van? they called.

A Casas Grandes, said Billy.

They nodded. Their horses raised their dripping muzzles and regarded the pale shapes crouched in the water with no great curiosity and lowered their heads and drank again. When they were done the vaqueros wished them a safe journey and turned the horses out of the ciénega and rode them at a trot out through the trees and set off across the country south the way they'd come.

They washed their clothes out with soapweed and hung them in an acacia tree where they could not blow away for the thorns. Clothes much consumed by the country through which they'd ridden and which they had little way to repair. Their shirts all but transparent, his own coming apart down the center of the back. They spread their blankets and lay naked under the cottonwoods and slept with their hats over their eyes while the cows came up through the trees and stood looking at them.

When he woke Boyd was sitting up and looking out through the trees.

What is it?

Look yonder.

He raised up and looked across the ciénega. Three indian children were crouched in the reeds watching them. When he stood up with the blanket about his shoulders they went trotting off.

Where the hell's the dog at?

I dont know. What's he supposed to do?

Beyond the trees woodsmoke was rising and he could hear voices. He pulled the blanket about him and walked out and got their clothes and came back.

They were Tarahumaras and they were afoot as their kind always were and they were headed back into the sierras. They drove no stock, they had no dogs. They spoke no spanish. The men wore white breechclouts and straw hats and little else but the women and girls had on brightly colored dresses with many petticoats. A few among them wore huaraches but for the most part they were barefoot and their feet shod or no were clublike and stubby and thick with callus. Their equipage was done up in bundles of handwoven cloth and all of it piled under a tree together with half a dozen morawood bows and goathide quivers with long reed arrows standing in them.

The women at the cookfire regarded them with little interest where they stood at the edge of the glade in their newly laundered rags. An old man and a young boy were playing homemade violins and the boy stopped playing but the old man played on. The Tarahumara had watered here a thousand years and a good deal of what could be seen in the world had passed this way. Armored Spaniards and hunters and trappers and grandees and their women and slaves and fugitives and armies and revolutions and the dead and the dying. And all that was seen was told and all that was told remembered. Two pale and wasted orphans from the north in outsized hats were easily accommodated. They sat on the ground a little apart from the others and ate from tin plates too hot to hold a kind of succotash in which they recognized the seeds of squash and mesquite beans and bits of wild celery. They ate with the plates balanced on the insides of their boots where they'd drawn them up before them heel to heel. While they were eating a woman came from the fire and dished up from a gourd a brickcolored mucilage made from God knew what. They sat looking at it. There was nothing to drink. No one spoke. The indians were dark almost to blackness and their reticence and their silence bespoke a view of a world provisional, contingent, deeply suspect. They had about them a wary absorption, as if they observed some hazardous truce. They seemed in a state of improvident and hopeless vigilance. Like men committed upon uncertain ice.

When they'd done eating they said their thanks and withdrew. Nothing was acknowledged. Nothing spoken. As they passed out through the trees Billy looked back but not even the children had been watching them leave.

The Tarahumara moved on in the evening. A great quiet settled over the glade. Billy took the shotgun and walked out through the grass with the dog and studied the country in the long red twilight. The lean and tallowcolored cattle watched from the cottonwoods and acacia and snorted and went trotting. There was nothing to shoot save the little ringdoves coming in to water and he would not waste a shell on them. He stood on a slight rise out on the prairie and watched the sun set beyond the mountains to the west and he walked back in the dark and in the morning they caught the horses and saddled Bird and set out once more.

They reached the Mormon settlement at Colonia Juárez in the late afternoon and rode the horses through the orchards and vineyards and picked apples from the trees and put them in their clothing. They crossed the Casas Grandes River on the narrow plank bridge and rode past the tidy whitewashed clapboard houses. Trees lined the little street and the houses were kept with garden and lawn and white picket fences.

What kind of a place is this? Boyd said.

I dont know.

They rode on to the end of the street and when they turned the first bend in the narrow dusty road they were on the desert again as if the little town were no more than a dream. In the evening on the road to Casas Grandes they rode past the walled ruins of the ancient mud city of the Chichimeca. Among those clay warrens and mazes there burned here and there in the dusk the fires of squatters and where the squatters rose and moved about they cast their shadows lurching across the crumbling walls like drunken stewards and the moon rose over the dead city and shone upon the terraced embattlements and shone upon the roofless crypts and the pitovens and upon the mud corrals and upon the darkened ballcourt where nighthawks were hunting and upon the dry acequias where bits of pottery and stone tools together with the bones of their makers lay enleavened in the cracked clay floors.

They rode into Casas Grandes across the high banked tracks of the Mexican Northeast Railroad and they rode past the depot and up the street and tied their horses in front of a cafe and entered. Screwed into their receptacles in the ceiling and casting a hard yellow light over the tables were the first electric lightbulbs they'd seen since leaving Agua Prieta on the American border. They sat at a table and Boyd took off his hat and put it on the floor. There was no one in the place. After a while a woman came from behind the curtained doorway at the rear and walked over and stood at their table and looked down at them. She had no pad to write on and there seemed to be no menu. Billy asked her if she had any steaks and she nodded and said that she did. They ordered and sat looking out the small window at the darkened street where the horses stood.

What do you think? Billy said.

About what?

About anything.

Boyd shook his head. His thin legs stretched out before him. On the far side of the street a family of Mennonites passed along before the dimly lighted shopfronts in their overalls with the women behind them in their sunfaded motherhubbards carrying marketbaskets.

You aint sullin up on me are you?

No.

What are you thinkin?

Nothin.

All right.

Boyd watched the street. After a while he turned and looked at Billy. I was thinkin it was too easy, he said.

What was?

Comin up on Keno thataway. Gettin him back.

Yeah. Maybe.

He knew that they wouldnt have the horse back until they crossed the border with it and that nothing was easy but he didnt say so.

You dont trust nothin, he said.

No.

Things change.

I know. Some things.

You worry about everthing. But that dont change nothin. Does it?

Boyd sat studying the street. Two riders passed in what looked to be band uniforms. They both looked at the horses tied in front of the cafe.

Does it, Billy said.

Boyd shook his head. I dont know, he said. I dont know how it would of turned out if I hadnt worried.

They slept that night in a field of dusty weeds just off the railroad right of way and in the morning they washed in an irrigation ditch and mounted up and rode back into town and ate at the same cafe. Billy asked the woman if she knew the whereabouts of the offices of a ganadero named Soto but she did not. They ate a huge breakfast of eggs and chorizo and tortillas made from wheat flour such as they had not seen before in that country and they paid with what proved to be very nearly the last of their money and walked out and mounted up and rode through the town. Soto's offices were in a brick building three blocks south of the cafe. Billy was watching the reflections of two riders passing in the glass of the building's window across the street where the gaunted horses slouched by segments through the wonky panes when he saw the illjoined dog appear also and realized that the rider at the head of this unprepossessing parade was he himself. Then he saw that the lettering on the glass above the rider's head said Ganaderos and above that it said Soto y Gillian.

Look yonder, he said.

I see it, said Boyd.

Why didnt you say somethin if you seen it?

I'm sayin it now.

They sat the horses in the street. The dog sat in the dirt and waited. Billy leaned and spat and looked back at Boyd.

You care for me to ask you somethin?

Ask it.

How long do you aim to stay sulled up like this?

Till I get unsulled.

Billy nodded. He sat looking at their reflections in the glass. He seemed at odds to account for their appearance there. I thought you might say that, he said. But Boyd had seen him studying the tableau of ragged pilgrims paired with their horses all askew in the puzzled grid of the ganadero's glass with the mute dog at their heels and he nodded toward the window. I'm lookin at the same thing you are, he said.

They returned twice more to the ganadero's office before they found him in. Billy left Boyd to tend the horses. You keep Keno out of sight, he said.

I aint ignorant, said Boyd.

He crossed the street and raised one hand at the door to break the glare on the glass and looked in. An oldfashioned office with dark varnished wainscotting, dark oak furniture. He opened the door and entered. The glass in the door rattled when he closed it and the man at the desk looked up. He was holding the receiver of an oldfashioned pedestal telephone to his ear. Bueno, he said. Bueno. He winked at Billy. He gestured with one hand for him to come forward. Billy took off his hat.

Sí, sí. Bueno, said the ganadero. Gracias. Es muy amable. He hung the receiver back in the cradle and pushed the telephone away from him. Bueno, he said. Pendejo. Completamente sin verguenza. He looked up at the boy. Pásale, pásale.

Billy stood holding his hat. Busco al señor Soto, he said.

No está.

Cuándo regresa?

Todo el mundo quiere saber. Who are you?

Billy Parham.

And who is that?

I'm from Cloverdale New Mexico.

Is that a fact?

Yessir. It is.

And what was your business with señor Soto?

Billy turned his hat a quarter turn through his hands. He looked toward the window. The man looked with him.

I am Señor Gillian, he said. Perhaps I can help you.

He pronounced it Geeyan. He waited.

Well, Billy said. You all sold a horse to a German doctor named Haas.

The man nodded. He seemed anxious for the story to unfold.

And I was huntin the man you bought the horse off of. It might could of been a indian.

Gillian leaned back in his chair. He tapped his lower teeth.

It was a dark bay gelding about fifteen and a half hands high. What you might call a castaño oscuro.

I am familiar with the particulars of this horse. Needless to say.

Yessir. You might of sold him moren one horse.

Yes. I might have but I did not. What was your interest in this horse?

I aint really concerned about the horse. I was just huntin the man that sold him.

Who is the boy in the street?

Sir?

The boy in the street.

That's my brother.

Why is he outside?

He's all right outside.

Why dont you bring him in?

He's all right.

Why dont you bring him in?

Billy looked out the window. He put on his hat and went out.

I thought you was watchin the horses, he said.

Yonder they stand, said Boyd.

The horses were in the sidestreet tethered by their bridlereins to a spike in a telegraph pole.

That's a sorry way to leave a horse.

I aint left em. I'm right here.

He seen you settin out here. He wants you to come in.

What for?

I didnt ask him.

You dont think we might be better off to just keep ridin?

It'll be all right. Come on.

Boyd looked toward the ganadero's window but the sun was on the glass and he couldnt see in.

Come on, said Billy. We dont go back in he'll think somethin.

He thinks somethin now.

No he dont.

He looked at Boyd. He looked off up the street at the horses. Them horses look terrible, he said.

I know it.

He stood with his hands in the back of his overall pants and chopped his bootheel into the dirt of the street. He looked at Boyd. We come a pretty hard ride to see this man, he said.

Boyd leaned and spat between his boots. All right, he said.

Gillian looked up when they entered. Billy held the door for his brother and Boyd walked in. He didnt take off his hat. The ganadero leaned back and studied them one and then the other. As if he'd been called upon to judge their consanguinity.

This here's my brother Boyd, Billy said.

Gillian gestured for him to come forward.

He was worried about the way we look, Billy said.

He can tell me himself what are his worries.

Boyd stood with his thumbs in his belt. He still hadnt taken off his hat. I wasnt worried about how we look, he said.

The ganadero studied him anew. You are from Texas, he said.

Texas?

Yes.

Where'd you get a notion like that?

You came here from Texas, no?

I aint never been in Texas in my life.

How do you know Dr Haas?

I dont know him. I never laid eyes on the man.

What is your interest in his horse?

It aint his horse. The horse was stole off our ranch by indians.

And your father sent you to Mexico to recover this horse.

He didnt send us nowhere. He's dead. They killed him and my mother with a shotgun and stole the horses.

The ganadero frowned. He looked at Billy. You agree with this? he said.

I'm like you, said Billy. Just waitin to hear what's comin next.

The ganadero studied them for a long time. Finally he said that he had come to his present position by way of trading horses on the road in both their own country and his and that he had learned as all such traders must how to reconstruct the histories of those with whom he came in contact largely by eliminating their own alternatives. He said that he was seldom wrong and seldom surprised.

What you have told me is preposterous, he said.

Well, said Boyd. You have it your own way.

The ganadero swiveled slightly in his chair. He tapped his teeth. He looked at Billy. Your brother thinks I am a fool.

Yessir.

The ganadero arched his brows. You agree with him?

No sir. I dont agree with him.

How come you believe him and not me? said Boyd.

Who would not? the ganadero said.

I reckon you just enjoy to hear people lie.

The ganadero said that yes he did. He said that it was a prerequisite for being in this business at all. He looked at Billy.

Hay otro más, he said. Something else. What is it?

That's all I know to tell.

But not all there is to be told.

He looked at Boyd. Is it? he said.

I dont know what you'd be askin me for.

The ganadero smiled. He rose laboriously from his desk. He was a smaller man standing. He went to an oak filecabinet and opened a drawer and thumbed through some papers and came back with a folder and sat and placed the folder on the desk before him and opened it.

Do you read spanish? he said.

Yessir.

The ganadero was tracing the document with his forefinger.

The horse was purchased at auction on March the second. It was a lot purchase of twenty-three horses.

Who was the seller?

La Babícora.

He turned the open folder and pushed it across the desk. Billy didnt look at it. What's La Babícora? he said.

The ganadero's unkempt eyebrows lifted. What is the Babícora? he said.

Yessir.

It is a ranch. It is owned by one of your countrymen, a señor Hearst.

Do they sell a lot of horses?

Not so many as they buy.

Why did they sell the horse?

Quién sabe? The capón is not so popular in this country. There is a prejudice I think is how you would say.

Billy looked down at the sales sheet.

Please, said the ganadero. You may look.

He picked up the folder and scanned the list of horses detailed under lot number forty-one eighty-six.

Qué es un bayo lobo? he said.

The ganadero shrugged.

He turned the page. He scanned the descriptions. Ruano. Bayo. Bayo cebruno. Alazán. Alazán Quemado. Half the horses were colors he'd never heard of. Yeguas and caballos, capones and potros. He saw a horse he thought could have been Niño. Then he saw another that could also have been. He closed the folder and placed it back upon the ganadero's desk.

What do you think? said the ganadero.

What do I think about what?

You told me it was the seller of the horse that brought you here and not the horse itself.

Yessir.

Perhaps your friend works for señor Hearst. That could be.

Yessir. That could be.

It is not such an easy thing to find a man in Mexico.

No sir.

The monte is extensive.

Yessir.

A man can be lost.

Yessir. He can.

The ganadero sat. He tapped the arm of his chair with his forefinger. Like a retired telegrapher. Otro más, he said. What is it?

I dont know.

He leaned forward on his desk. He looked at Boyd and he looked down at Boyd's boots. Billy followed his gaze. He was looking for the marks of spur straps.

You are far from home, he said. Needless to say. He looked up at Billy.

Yessir, said Billy.

Let me advise you. I feel the obligation.

All right.

Return to your home.

We aint got one to return to, Boyd said.

Billy looked at him. He still hadnt taken off his hat.

Why dont you ask him why he wants us to go home, said Boyd.

I will tell you why he wants this, said the ganadero. Because he knows what perhaps you do not. That the past cannot be mended. You think everyone is a fool. But there are not so many reasons for you to be in Mexico. Think of that.

Let's go, said Boyd.

We are close to the truth here. I do not know what that truth is. I am no gypsy fortuneteller. But I see great trouble in store. Great trouble. You should listen to your brother. He is older.

So are you.

The ganadero leaned back in the chair again. He looked at Billy. Your brother is young enough to believe that the past still exists, he said. That the injustices within it await his remedy. Perhaps you believe this also?

I dont have a opinion. I'm just down here about some horses.

What remedy can there be? What remedy can there be for what is not? You see? And where is the remedy that has no unforeseen consequence? What act does not assume a future that is itself unknown?

I quit this country once before, Billy said. It wasnt the future that brought me back here.

The ganadero was holding his hands forward one above the other, a space between. As if he held something unseen shut within an unseen box. You do not know what things you set in motion, he said. No man can know. No prophet foresee. The consequences of an act are often quite different from what one would guess. You must be sure that the intention in your heart is large enough to contain all wrong turnings, all disappointments. Do you see? Not everything has such a value.

Boyd was standing at the door. Billy turned and looked at him. He looked at the ganadero. The ganadero dismissed the air before him with the back of his hand. Yes, yes, he said. Go.

In the street Billy looked back to see if the ganadero was watching from his window.

Dont be lookin back, said Boyd. You know he's watchin us.

They rode south out of the town and took the road toward San Diego. They rode in silence, the mute and footsore dog trotting and walking by turns before them down the center of the shadowless noon road.

Do you know what he was talkin about? said Billy.

Boyd turned slightly on the bareback horse he rode and looked back.

Yeah. I know what he was talkin about. Do you?

They rode out through the last of the small colonias south of the town. In the fields they passed there were men and women picking cotton among the gray and brittle plants. They watered the horses at a roadside acequia and loosed the latigos to let them blow. Across the pieced land they watched a man turning the earth with an ox yoked by its horns to a singlehanded plow. The plow was of a type that was old in Egypt and was little more than a treeroot. They mounted up and rode on. He looked back at Boyd. Thin atop the unfurnished horse. Thinner yet in shadow. The tall dark horse that trod the road with its great angular articulations arch and slanting in the dust more true of horse than horse he rode. Late in the day from the crest of a rise in the road they halted the horses and looked out over the broken plats of dark ground below them where the sluicegates had been opened into the newplowed fields and where the water standing in the furrows shone in the evening light like grids of burnished barmetal stretching away in the distance. As if the boundary gates to some ancient enterprise lay fallen there beyond the ditchside cottonwoods, the evening's singing birds.

By and by they overtook on the darkening road a young girl walking barefoot and carrying upon her head a cloth bundle that hung to either side like a great soft hat. So that as they clopped slowly past she was obliged to turn her whole body sideways to see them. They nodded and Billy wished her a good evening and she wished them one back and they rode on. A little farther and they came to a place where the overflow from the acequias had left water standing in the bar ditch and they dismounted and led the horses along the bank and sat in the grass and watched geese walk stiffly about on the darkening fields. The girl passed along the road. They thought at first that she was singing softly to herself but she was crying. When she saw the horses she stopped. The horses raised their heads and looked toward the road. She went on and they lowered their heads and drank again. When they led the horses back up into the road she was very small and almost motionless in the distance before them. They mounted up and set out and after a while they overtook her once again.

Billy crossed his horse to the far side of the road. So that she must turn her face to the west in the last of the light to answer him if he spoke to her as he rode past. But when she heard the horses on the road behind her she crossed also and when he spoke to her she did not turn at all and if she answered he did not hear it. They rode on. A hundred yards and he stopped and got down into the road.

What are you doin? said Boyd.

He looked back at the girl. She had stopped. There was nowhere for her to go. Billy turned and lifted the near stirrup and hung it over the horn and checked the latigo.

It's gettin dark, said Boyd.

It is dark.

Well let's go on.

We're goin.

The girl had begun to walk again. She approached slowly keeping to the farthest edge of the road. As she came abreast of them Billy asked her if she wanted to ride. She didnt answer. She shook her head under the bundle and then she hurried past. Billy watched her go. He stroked the horse and took up the reins and started down the road afoot leading the horse behind. Boyd sat Keno and watched him.

What's got into you? he said.

What?

Askin her to ride.

What's wrong with that?

Boyd put his horse forward and rode beside his brother. What are you doin? he said.

Walkin my horse.

What the hell's wrong with you?

Aint nothin wrong with me.

Well what are you doin?

I'm just walkin my horse. Like you're ridin yours.

The hell you are.

Are you scared of girls?

Scared of girls?

Yeah.

He looked up at Boyd. But Boyd just shook his head and rode on.

The girl's small figure receded into the darkness ahead. Doves were still coming into the fields to the west of the road. They could hear them cross overhead even after it was too dark to see. Boyd rode on, he waited in the road. After a while Billy caught him up. He was riding again and they went on side by side.

They passed out of the irrigated land and they passed in a grove of roadside trees a jacal of mud and sticks where the faint orange light of a slutlamp burned. They thought it must be the place where the girl lived and were surprised to come upon her in the road before them once again.

When they overtook her now it was black of night and Billy slowed the horse beside her and asked her if she had far to go and she hesitated for a moment and then said that she did not. He offered that he would carry her bundle behind him on the horse and she could walk beside but she refused politely. She called him señor. She looked at Boyd. It occurred to him that she could have hidden in the roadside chaparral but she had not done so. They wished her a good evening and rode on and a short while later they encountered two horsemen on the road riding back the way they'd come who spoke to them briefly out of the darkness and passed on. He halted his horse and sat watching after them and Boyd halted beside him.

Are you thinkin what I am? Billy said.

Boyd sat with his forearms crossed on the pommel of his saddle. You want to wait on her?

Yeah.

All right. You think they'll bother her?

Billy didnt answer. The horses shifted and stood. After a while he said: Let's just wait here a minute. She'll be along in a minute. Then we can go.

But she wasnt along in a minute and she wasnt along in ten minutes or in thirty.

Let's go back, Billy said.

Boyd leaned and spat slowly into the road and turned his horse.

They'd gone no more than a mile when they saw a fire somewhere ahead of them through the iron shapes of the brush. The road turned and the fire swung slowly off to the right. Then it swung back. A half mile further and they halted their horses. The fire was burning in a small grove of oaks off to the east. The light of it was caught under the dark canopy of the leaves and shadows moved and moved back and a horse nickered from the dark beyond.

What do you want to do? said Boyd.

I dont know. Let me think.

They sat their horses in the darkened road.

You thought yet?

I guess there aint nothin to do but just ride on in.

They'll know we backtracked em.

I know it. It caint be helped.

Boyd sat watching the fire through the trees.

What do you want to do? said Billy.

If we're goin to go on in there then let's just do it.

They got down and led the horses. The dog sat in the road and watched them. Then it got up and followed.

When they entered the clear ground under the trees the two men were standing on the far side of the fire watching them approach. Their horses were not in sight. The girl was sitting on the ground with her legs tucked under her and clutching the bundle in her lap. When she saw who it was she looked away and sat staring into the fire.

Buenas noches, called Billy.

Buenas noches, they said.

They stood holding the horses. They had not been invited forward. The dog when it struck the circle of light stopped in its tracks and then backed away slightly and stood waiting. The men were watching them. One of them was smoking a cigarette and he raised it to his lips and sucked thinly at it and blew a thin stream of smoke toward the fire. He made a circling motion with his arm, his finger pointed down. He told them to take their horses around and into the trees behind them. Nuestros caballos están allá, he said.

Está bien, said Billy. He stood.

The man said that it was not all right. He said that he did not want their horses soiling the ground on which they were to sleep.

Billy looked at him. He turned slightly and looked at his horse. He could see curved like a dark triptych in a glass paperweight the figures of the two men and the girl burning in the fugitive light of the fire at the black center of the animal's eye. He passed the reins behind him to Boyd. Take them out yonder, he said. Dont unsaddle Bird and dont loose the latigo and dont put them with their horses.

Boyd passed in front of him leading the horses and went on past the men and into the dark of the trees. Billy came forward and nodded to them and pushed his hat back slightly from his eyes. He stood before the fire and looked down into it. He looked at the girl.

Cómo está, he said.

She didnt answer. When he looked across the fire the man who was smoking had squatted on his heels and was watching him through the warp of heat with eyes the color of wet coal. On the ground at his side stood a bottle stoppered with a corncob.

De dónde viene? he said.

America.

Tejas.

Nuevo Mexico.

Nuevo Mexico, the man said. Adónde va?

Billy watched him. He had his right arm folded across his chest and held in place with the elbow of his left so that his left forearm stood vertically before him holding the cigarette in a pose strangely formal, strangely delicate. Billy looked at the girl again and he looked again at the man across the fire. He had no answer to his query.

Hemos perdido un caballo, he said. Lo buscamos.

The man didnt answer. He held the cigarette between his forefingers and dipped his wrist in a birdlike motion and smoked and then raised the cigarette aloft again. Boyd came out of the trees and circled the fire and stood but the man did not look at him. He pitched the butt of the cigarette into the fire before him and wrapped his arms around his knees and began to rock back and forth in a motion barely perceptible. He jutted his chin at Billy and asked if he had followed them in order to see their horses.

No, said Billy. Nuestro caballo es un caballo muy distinto. Lo conoceríamos en cualquier luz.

As soon as he'd said it he knew that he'd given up his only plausible answer to the man's next question. He looked at Boyd. Boyd knew it too. The man rocked, he studied them. Qué quieren pues? he said.

Nada, said Billy. No queremos nada.

Nada, said the man. He formed the word as if tasting it. He gave his chin a slight sideways turn as a man might in pondering likelihoods. Two horsemen who meet two others on a dark road and pass on and thereafter meet also a traveler afoot know that those riders have overtaken the foot-traveler and passed on. That was what was known. The man's teeth shone in the firelight. He picked something from between them and examined it and then ate it. Cuántos años tiene? he said.

Yo?

Quién más.

Diecisiete.

The man nodded. Cuántos años tiene la muchacha?

No lo sé.

Qué opina.

Billy looked at the girl. She sat staring into her lap. She looked to be maybe fourteen.

Es muy joven, he said.

Bastante.

Doce quizás.

The man shrugged. He reached and took up the bottle from the ground and pulled the stopper and drank and sat holding the bottle by the neck. He said that if they were old enough to bleed they were old enough to butcher. Then he held the bottle up over his shoulder. The man behind him stepped forward and took it from him and drank. Out in the road a horse was passing. The dog had stood to listen. The rider did not stop and the slow clop of the hooves on the dried mud of the roadway faded and the dog lay down again. The man standing drank a second time and then handed the bottle back. The other man took it and pushed the cob back into the neck of the bottle with the heel of his hand and then weighed the bottle.

Quiere tomar? he said.

No. Gracias.

He weighed the bottle in his hand again and then pitched it underhand across the fire. Billy caught it and looked at the man. He held the bottle to the light. The smoky yellow mescal rolled viscously inside the glass and the curled form of the dead gusano circled the floor of the bottle in a slow drift like a small wandering fetus.

No quiero tomar, he said.

Tome, the man said.

He looked at the bottle again. The greaseprints on the glass shone in the firelight. He looked at the man and then he twisted the cob out of the neck.

Get the horses, he said.

Boyd stepped behind him. The man watched him. Adónde vas? he said.

Go on, said Billy.

Adónde va el muchacho?

Está enfermo.

Boyd crossed and went on toward the trees. The dog stood up and looked after him. The man turned and looked at Billy again. Billy raised the bottle and began to drink. He drank and lowered the bottle. Water ran from his eyes and he wiped them with his forearm and looked at the man and raised the bottle and drank again.

When he lowered the bottle it was all but empty. He sucked in air and looked at the man but the man was looking at the girl. She'd stood and was looking toward the trees. They could feel the ground shudder. The man rose and turned. Behind him the second man had stepped away from the fire and went trotting holding up his arms in silent exhortation. He was trying to head the horses where they came out of the trees tossing their heads and trotting sideways to keep from treading on the trailing stakeropes.

Demonios, said the man. Billy dropped the bottle and pitched the cob stopper into the fire and reached and grabbed the girl by the hand.

Vámonos, he said.

She bent and scooped up her bundle. Boyd came out of the trees at a gallop. He was bent low over Keno's neck and he was holding the bridlereins of Billy's horse in one hand and the shotgun in the other and he carried the reins of his own horse in his teeth like a circus rider.

Vámonos, hissed Billy, but she was already clutching his arm.

Boyd rode the horses almost through the fire and pulled Keno up stamping and wild-eyed. He caught the reins in his teeth again and pitched the shotgun to Billy. Billy caught it and took the girl by the elbow and swung her toward the horse. The other two horses had vanished out on the darkened plain to the south of the camp and the man who'd pitched him the bottle of mescal was coming back out of the darkness carrying in his left hand a long thin knife. Other than the sound of the horses blowing and stamping all was silence. No one spoke. The dog circled nervously behind the horses. Vámonos, said Billy. When he looked the girl was already seated on the horse's crupper behind saddle and blanketroll. He grabbed the reins from Boyd and swung them over the horse's head and cocked the shotgun in one hand like a pistol. He didnt know whether it was loaded or not. The mescal sat in his stomach like some unholy incubus. He stepped into the stirrup and the girl flattened herself expertly along the horse's flank and he swung his leg over her and sawed the horse around. The man was already upon him and he pointed the shotgun at the man's chest. The man made a lunge for the bridle but the horse shied and Billy shucked his boot out of the stirrup and kicked at the man and the man ducked and passed the blade of the knife across the outside of Billy's leg cutting through his boot and trouser both. He hauled the horse around and dug his heels in and the man lunged at the girl and got a handful of her dress but the cloth ripped away and then they were pounding out across the low grass swale and out onto the roadway where Boyd sat his stamping horse in the starlight waiting for them. He pulled the horse up squatting and tossing its head and spoke to the girl over his shoulder. Está bien? he said.

Sí, sí, she whispered. She was leaning forward over her bundle with both arms around his waist.

Let's go, said Boyd.

They set out south down the road side by side at a hard gallop with the dog behind them losing ground by the yard. There was no moon but the stars in that country were so many that the riders cast shadows on the road anyway. Ten minutes later Boyd sat holding Billy's horse by the reins while Billy stood at the roadside and gripped his knees and vomited into the roadside grass. The dog came wheezing up out of the dark and the horses looked at Billy and stamped in the road. Billy looked up and wiped his weeping eyes. He looked at the girl. She sat the horse half naked, her bare legs hanging down the side of the horse's haunches. He spat and wiped his mouth on the back of his sleeve and looked at his boot. Then he sat in the road and pulled the boot off and looked at his leg. He pulled the boot back on again and got up and picked the shotgun up out of the road and walked back to the horses. The leg of his jeans flapped about his ankle.

We need to get off this road, he said. It aint goin to take them all that long to catch their horses.

Are you cut?

I'm all right. Let's go.

Let's listen a minute.

They listened.

You caint hear nothin for the damn dog pantin.

Listen a minute.

Billy took the reins and raised them over the horse's head and put his boot in the stirrup and the girl ducked and he swung up into the saddle. A crazy man, he said. I got a crazy man for a brother.

Mánde? said the girl.

Listen a minute, Boyd said.

What do you hear?

Nothin. How do you feel?

About like you'd expect.

She dont speak no english, does she?

Hell no. How would she speak english?

Boyd sat looking off up the road into the darkness. You know they're goin to follow us.

Billy jammed the shotgun into the scabbard. Hell yes I know it, he said.

Dont be cussin in front of her.

What?

I said dont be cussin in front of her.

You just now got done sayin she dont speak no english.

That dont make it not cussin.

You dont make no sense. And what made you think them

sumbucks back yonder didnt have pistols in their clothes somewheres?

I didnt think it. That's why I thowed you the shotgun.

Billy leaned and spat. Damn, he said.

What do you aim to do with her?

I dont know. Hell. How would I know?

They turned the horses off of the road and set out upon a
treeless plain. The flat black mountains in the distance made a
jagged hem along the lower reach of the heavens. The girl sat
small and erect with one hand holding on to Billy by his belt.
Trekking in the starlight between the dark boundaries of the
mountain ranges east and west they had the look of storybook
riders conveying again to her homeland some stolen backland
queen.

They made camp in the dry country on a rise where the night
sank about them in an infinite deep and they staked the horses
and left Bird saddled. The girl had yet to speak. She walked
out in the darkness and they saw her no more till morning.

When they woke there was a fire on the ground and she was
pouring water from the canteen and setting it to heat, moving
quietly about in the gray light. Billy lay in his blanket watching
her. She must have found more clothes among her possessions
for she was wearing a skirt again. She stirred the water in the
tin, though what she stirred he could not guess. He closed his
eyes. He heard his brother say something in spanish and when
he looked out from his blanket Boyd was squatting by the fire
crosslegged and drinking from his tinware cup.

He turned out and rolled his bedding and she brought him a
cup of hot chocolate and went back to the fire. She'd browned
tortillas in their small skillet and spooned them full of beans and
they sat by the fire and ate their breakfast while the day paled
about them.

Did you unsaddle Bird? Billy said.

No. She did.

He nodded. They ate.

How bad are you cut? Boyd said.

It's just a scratch. He cut through my boot pretty good.

This country's hell on clothes.

It's gettin that reputation with me. What possessed you to run their horses off thataway?

I dont know. I just took a notion to do it.

Did you hear what he said about her?

Yeah. I heard it.

By sunup they'd broke camp and were set out once more across the gravel and creosote plain south. They nooned at a well in the desert where oak and elder grew clumped in the flats and they turned the horses out and slept on the ground. Billy slept with the shotgun cradled in his arm and when he woke the girl was sitting watching him. He asked her if she could ride caballo en pelo and she said that she could. When they set out again she rode behind Boyd so as to spell the horses. He thought Boyd would have something to say about it but he didnt. When he looked back the girl was riding with both arms around his waist. When he looked back later her dark hair was spilled over his brother's shoulder and she was sleeping against his back.

In the evening they reached the hacienda of San Diego sited on a hill overlooking the tilled lands that ran on to the Casas Grandes River and to the Piedras Verdes. A windmill turned on the plain below them like a chinese toy and dogs barked in the distance. In the long steep light the raw umber mountains stood deeply shadowed in their folds and in the sky to the south a dozen buzzards turned in a slow crepe carousel.

III

I T WAS ALL BUT DARK when they rode past the main house
and along the drive, past the porticoes with their slender
carved iron posts, past the white plaster walls quoined with
red sandstone blocks and the terracotta filigree along the upper
parapets. The front of the house was faced with three stone
arches and above them were carved the words Hacienda de San
Diego in letters arched over the initials L.T. The tall palladian
windows were shuttered and the shutters were weathered and
broken and paint and plaster were flaking from the walls and
the portico ceiling was no more than bare wood lath all water-
stained and buckled. They went on across the yard toward what
looked to be the domicilios where smoke was rising against the
evening sky and rode through the standing wooden gates into
the courtyard and sat the horses side by side.

In one corner of the enclosure stood the carcass of an antique
Dodge touring car long stripped of wheels and axles, of glass
and seats. At the far end of the compound a cookfire burned on
the ground and by its light they could see two gaudy caravan
wagons with wash hung between them and passing back and
forth before the fire both men and women in robes and kimonos
who appeared to belong to a circus.

Qué clase de lugar es éste? Billy said.

Es ejido, said the girl.

Qué clase de gente?

No lo sé.

He swung down and the girl slid from the back of Boyd's
horse and came and took the reins.

What are them? said Boyd.

I dont know.

They entered the compound, Billy and the girl afoot, the girl leading the horse. Boyd rode behind them. The figures at the far end paid them no mind at all. Two boys were lighting lamps from a burning split of wood at the fire and passing the lit lamps by their bails on a forked pole to a boy on the azotea who moved against the deepening sky hanging the lamps from the parapet. The ground in the compound became more illuminated as he went and soon a rooster began to call. Other boys were stacking haybales against a wall and under the farther portal men were unrolling a painted canvas drop much cracked and weathered from its travels.

Two of the costumed figures seemed engaged in a controversy and one of them stepped back and flung his arms wide. As if to demonstrate the measure of something outsized. Then he burst into song in some alien tongue. All movement ceased until he had done. Then all began again.

Dónde están los domicilios? said Billy.

The girl nodded toward the dark beyond the walls. Afuera, she said.

Let's go.

I'd like to see it, Boyd said.

You dont even know what it is.

It's somethin.

Billy took the bridlereins from the girl. He looked back at the fire, at the figures there. We can come back, he said. They're just gettin set up.

They rode out to where the three long adobe buildings stood that housed the workers and they rode up the passageway between the first two paced the way by a gauntlet of bristling and snarling curdogs. The evening was warm and there were cookfires burning out of doors and in the soft light a muted clink of utensils and the delicate slapping of hands shaping out tortillas. People drifted from fire to fire and their voices carried on the darkness and more distantly yet the sound of a guitar on the sweetness of the summer night.

They were given rooms at the far end of the row and the girl unsaddled Billy's horse and led both animals off to water them. Billy fished a wooden match from his shirtpocket and struck it alight with his thumbnail. The two rooms had a single door and a single window and high ceilings of vigas with latillas of sticks. A low door connected them and in the corner of the second room was a fireplace and a small altar with a Virgin of painted wood. A jar that held dead weeds. A drinking glass in the bottom of which lay a medallion of blackened wax. Against the wall stood a contrivance of poles lashed together into a frame and webbed with strips of rawhide with the hair on. It had the look of some rude agrarian implement but was in fact a bed. He blew out the match and walked out and stood in the door. Boyd was sitting on the stoop watching the girl. She was at the watering trough at the far end of the compound holding the horses while they drank. She and the two horses and the dog were surrounded by a semicircle of sitting dogs of every stripe and color but she paid them no mind. She stood very patiently with the horses while they drank. While they raised their dripping mouths and looked about and while they drank again. She did not touch the horses nor talk to them. She just waited while they drank and they drank for a long time.

They ate with a family named Muñoz. They must have looked hard used by the road for the woman kept urging food upon them and the man made little lifting motions with his outheld hands that they take more. He asked Billy where it was that they had come from and received the news with a certain sadness or resignation. As of things that could not be helped. They ate squatting on the ground with spoons and clay plates. The girl offered nothing in the way of her own origins and no one asked. While they were eating a strong tenor voice came floating on the night over the roofs of the domicilios. It ran up the scales and down twice in succession. Silence fell over the camp. A dog began to howl. Only after it seemed there would be nothing more forthcoming did the ejiditarios commence to talk again. A little later a bell tolled from somewhere off in the compound and in the long afterclang they began to rise and call out to one another.

The woman had carried her comal and her pots to the house and she now stood in the lamplit doorway with a small child on one arm. She saw Billy still sitting on the ground and she motioned him up. Vámonos, she called. He looked up at her. He said that he had no money but she only stared at him as if she did not understand. Then she said that everyone was going and that those who had money would pay for those who did not. She said that everyone must go. There could be no thought of people being left behind. Who would permit such a thing?

He rose and stood. He looked for Boyd but he could not see him or the girl. Stragglers were hurrying through the smoke of the dying cookfires. The woman had shifted the child to her other hip and come forward and took him by the hand as if he were himself a child. Vámonos, she said. Está bien.

They followed the others up the hill, the crowd moving slowly for the old people and the old people urging them to pass and go on. None would. The empty house on the crest of the rise above them stood bleak and lightless but music was coming from the long walled compound where the shops and establos were once sited, the domiciles of the overseers. Light fell out through the tall bay doors and cressets of oil or pitch fashioned out of buckets burned at either side of the stone archway at the entrance and here the ejiditarios were queued and they shuffled forward with their centavos and their pesos clutched in their hands to offer them up to the doorman where he stood in his polished black suit. Two young men carrying a litter passed through the crowd. The litter was made from poles and sheeting and the old man lying on it was dressed in coat and tie and he clutched a wooden rosary and stared grimly at the arch of sky above him. Billy looked at the child the woman was carrying but the child was asleep. When they reached the gates the woman paid and the gatekeeper thanked her and rattled the coppers into a bucket on the ground beside him and they passed through into the courtyard.

The gaudy little wagons had been drawn up at the farther end of the enclosure. Lamps stood in a semicircle on the packed clay ground before them and lamps had been hung from a rope stretched overhead and in the uplight overhead the faces of young boys watched along the parapet like rows of theatrical masks displayed there. The mules that stood between the wagonshafts were fitted out in braid and tinsel and velvet trappings and the mules and caravans alike were the same that conveyed the little company over the back roads of the republic to stand at night in just these costumes while the lamps were lit and the crowds pushed forward in some backland plaza or alameda where a man passed up and back and swung before him like a censer a waterpail pierced with nailholes by which to lay the dust and the primadonna moved in lascivious silhouette behind a wagonsheet donning her costume or turning to regard herself in a mirror which none could see but all could imagine to be present.

He watched the play with interest but could make little of it. The company was perhaps describing some adventure of their own in their travels and they sang into each other's faces and wept and in the end the man in buffoon's motley slew the woman and slew another man perhaps his rival with a dagger and young boys ran forward with the curtain hems to draw them shut and the mules standing in their traces raised their heads up out of their sleep and began to shift and step.

There was no applause. The crowd sat quietly on the ground. Some of the women were crying. After a while the majordomo who had spoken to them prior to the performance stepped out through the curtain and thanked them for their attendance and stepped to one side and bowed as the boys carried the curtains open again. The actors stood before them hand in hand and bowed and curtseyed and there was a smattering of applause and then the curtain closed for good.

In the morning before it was quite light he walked out of the compound and down to the river. He walked out over the plank bridge on its stone piers and stood looking down at the clear cold waters of the Casas Grandes running out of the mountains to the south. He turned and looked downstream. A hundred feet away in water to her thighs stood the primadonna naked. Her hair was down and it was wet and clinging to her back and it reached to the water. He stood frozen. She turned and swung her hair before her and bent and lowered it into the river. Her breasts swung above the water. He took off his hat and stood with his heart laboring under his shirt. She raised up and gathered her hair and twisted out the water. Her skin so white. The dark hair under her belly almost an indelicacy.

She bent once more and trailed her hair in the water with a swaying motion sideways and then stood and swung it about her in a great hoop of spray and stood with her head back and her eyes closed. The sun rising over the gray ranges to the east lit the upper air. She held one hand up. She moved her body, she swept both hands before her. She bent and caught her falling hair in her arms and held it and she passed one hand over the surface of the water as if to bless it and he watched and as he watched he saw that the world which had always been before him everywhere had been veiled from his sight. She turned and he thought she might sing to the sun. She opened her eyes and saw him there on the bridge and she turned her back and walked slowly up out of the river and was lost to his view among the pale standing trunks of the cottonwoods and the sun rose and the river ran as before but nothing was the same nor did he think it ever would be.

He walked slowly back up to the compound. In the new sunrise the shadows of workers setting out for the fields with their shouldered hoes passed one by one along the eastern facing wall of the granary like figures in some agrarian drama. He got his breakfast from the Muñoz woman and walked out with his saddle over his shoulder and caught his horse and saddled him and mounted up and rode out to see the country.

It was midday before the caravans bearing the opera company sallied forth out through the gates and down the hill and across the bridge to set out south along the road to Mata Ortíz, to Las

Varas and Babícora. In the hard noon light the faded gilt of the lettering and the weathered red paint and sunbleached tapestries seemed some fallen grace from the pageantry of the prior night and the caravans in their trundling and swaying slowly south and in their diminishing in the heat and desolation seemed charged with some new and more austere enterprise. As if the light of God's day had sobered their hopes. As if the light and the country thereby made visible were alien to their true purpose. He watched from a rise in the rolling lands south of the hacienda where the grass seethed in the wind underfoot. The caravans moved slowly through the cottonwoods on the far side of the river, the little mules plodded. He leaned and spat and put the horse forward with his heels.

In the afternoon he walked through the empty rooms of the old residencia. The rooms were stripped of their fixtures and chandeliers and the parquet flooring was mostly gone. Turkeys stepped and moved away through the rooms before him. The house smelled of damp and old straw and waterstains had wrought upon the swagged and crumbling plasterwork great freeform sepia maps as of old antique kingdoms, ancient worlds. In the corner of the parlor a dead animal, dry hide and bones. A dog perhaps. He walked out into the courtyard. The raw mud brickwork showing through the plaster of the enclosing walls. In the center of the open space a stonework well. A bell rang in the distance.

In the evening the men smoked and talked and drifted in small groups from fire to fire. The Muñoz woman brought his boot to him and he examined it in the firelight. The long slice in the leather had been mended back with awl and cord. He thanked her and pulled it on. The women knelt on the packed dirt and leaned over the coals and turned with their bare hands the tortillas off the hot sheetiron comals leaving along the unleavened edges like tallymarks fingerprints of black from where they'd fed the charcoal fire. An endless ritual endlessly repeated, the propagation of the great secular host of the Mexicans. The girl helped the woman prepare the meal and after the men had been fed she came and sat beside Boyd and ate in silence. Boyd seemed to pay her little mind. He'd told Boyd that they'd be leaving in two days' time and in the way she raised her eyes to look at him across the fire he knew that Boyd had told her.

She worked all the day following in the fields and in the evening she came in and went to wash herself with bowl and rag behind the curtain and then went out to sit and watch small boys playing ball in the clay court between the buildings. When he rode in she stood and came over and took the bridlereins and she asked him if she could go with them.

He stepped down and took off his hat and clawed his fingers through his sweaty hair and put his hat back on again and looked at her. No, he said.

She stood holding the horse. She looked away. Her dark eyes swimming. He asked her why she wanted to go with them but she only shook her head. He asked her if she was afraid, if there was something here of which she was afraid. She didnt answer. He asked how old she was and she said fourteen. He nodded. He punched a crescent in the dirt underfoot with the heel of his boot. He looked at her.

Alguien le busca, he said.

She didnt answer.

No se puede quedar aquí?

She shook her head. She said she could not stay. She said she had no place to go.

He looked out across the compound in the tranquil evening light. He said that he had no place to go either so what help could he be to her but she only shook her head and said that she would go wherever they went she didnt care.

At dawn the day following while he saddled his horse the workers came out bringing gifts of food. They brought tortillas and chiles and carne seca and live chickens and whole hoops of cheese until they were burdened with provisions beyond their means to carry them. The Muñoz woman gave Billy something which when she stepped back he saw was a clutch of coins knotted into a rag. He tried to give it back but she turned away and walked back to her house without speaking. When they rode out of the compound the girl was riding behind Boyd on the bareback horse with her arms around his waist.

They rode all day south and nooned by the river and ate an enormous lunch out of the provisions they carried and slept under the trees. Late in the day a few miles south of Las Varas on the Madera road they came to a place where the horses balked and stood blowing in the road.

Look yonder, said Boyd.

The opera company was camped beyond the road in a field of wildflowers. The caravans were parked side by side and a canvas awning had been hung between them for a ramada and in the afforded shade the primadonna was taking her ease in a great canvas hammock with a pot of tea on the table at her side and a japanese fan. A victrola was playing from the open door of the caravan and in the field beyond their encampment a number of workers leaned on their implements with their hats in their hands and listened to the music.

She'd heard the horses on the road and she sat in her hammock and raised one hand to shade her eyes and look out although the sun was behind her and the awning shaded her anyway.

I guess they just camp out like gypsies, Billy said.

They are gypsies.

Who says?

Everbody.

The horse's ears quartered the compass for the source of the music.

They're broke down.

What makes you say that?

They'd of got farthern this.

Maybe they just decided to stop here.

What for? There aint nothin here.

Billy leaned and spat. You reckon she's here just by herself?

I dont know.

What do you reckon's got into the horses?

I dont know.

She's done went and put the spyglasses to us now.

The primadonna had fetched up from the table a small pair of lorgnette operaglasses and was peering toward the road with them.

Let's get down.

All right.

They walked the horses along the road and he sent the girl over to see if the woman needed anything. The music stopped. The woman called into the caravan and after a while the music began again.

There's a mule's died, Boyd said.

How do you know?

There just has.

Billy looked over the camp. There were no animals of any description about.

Likely the mules is hobbled up in them oaks yonder, he said.

No they aint.

When the girl came back she said that one of the mules had died.

Shit, said Billy.

What, said Boyd.

You all set that up.

Set what up?

About the mule. She's made a signal or somethin.

A dead mule signal.

Yeah.

Boyd leaned and spat and shook his head. The girl stood with one hand shading her eyes waiting. Billy looked at her. Her thin clothes. Her dusty legs. Her feet in huaraches made from strapleather and rawhide. He asked her how long the men had been gone and she said two days.

We better go over and see if she's all right.

What do you aim to do if she aint? Boyd said.

Hell if I know.

Well why dont we just keep ridin.

I thought you was the one liked to go around rescuin people.

Boyd didnt answer. He mounted up and Billy turned and looked up at him. He shucked one boot out of the stirrup and leaned down and gave the girl his hand and she put her foot in the stirrup and he swung her up and then put the horse forward. Well let's go, he said. If they aint nothin else will satisfy you.

He followed them out across the field. When the workers saw them coming they began once again to grub in the ground with their short hoes. He rode up alongside Boyd and they sat their horses side by side before the reclining primadonna and wished her a good afternoon. She nodded. She studied them across the top of the splayed fan. It was painted with some oriental scene and the bolsters were of ivory inlaid with silver wire.

Los hombres han salido por Madero? said Billy.

She nodded. She said that they would be returning at any moment. She lowered the fan slightly and looked out down the road south. As if they might be appearing even now.

Billy sat his horse. He didnt seem to be able to think what else to say. After a while he took his hat off.

You are Americans, the woman said.

Yes mam. I reckon the girl told you.

There is nothing to hide.

We dont have nothin to hide. I just come over to see if there was anything we could do for you.

She arched her painted brows in surprise.

I thought maybe you all was broke down out here.

She looked at Boyd. Boyd looked off toward the mountains to the south.

We're headed yonway, Billy said. If you wanted us to carry a message or anything.

She sat up slightly in the hammock and called out into the caravan. Basta, she called. Basta la música.

She sat listening, one hand balanced on the table. In a moment the music ceased and she subsided again into the hammock and spread the fan and looked across the top of it at the young jinete who sat his horse before her. Billy looked toward the caravan thinking someone might appear in the doorway but no one did.

What all did the mule die of? he said.

That mule, she said. That mule died because its blood all fell out in the road.

Mam?

She raised a hand languidly before her, her ringed and tapered fingers weaving. As if she described the ascending of the animal's soul.

That mule was having his troubles but no one could reason with that mule. Gasparito should not have been put to attend to the wants of that mule. He had no temperament for such a mule. Now you see what has come to pass.

No mam.

Drinking too. In these matters drinking is always present. And then the fear. The other mules are screaming. Tienen mucho miedo. Screaming. Sliding and falling in the blood and screaming. What does one say to these animals? How does one put their minds at rest?

She made a peremptory gesture to one side. As of some casting to the winds in the dry hot solitude, the birdcalls in the little glade, the evening's onset. Can such animals ever be restored to their former state? There can be no question. Especially in the case of dramatic mules such as these mules. These mules can have no peace now. No peace. You see?

What was it he done to the mule?

He tried to cut off the head with a machete. Of course. What did the girl say to you? She speaks no english?

No mam. She just said it died was all.

The primadonna looked at the girl suspiciously. Where did you find this girl?

She was just walkin along the road. I wouldnt of thought you could cut off a mule's head with a machete.

Of course not. Only a drunken fool would attempt such a feat. When the hacking availed not he began to saw. When Rogelio seized him he would have hacked at Rogelio. Rogelio was disgusted. Disgusted. They fell in the road. In the blood and the dust. Rolling about under the feet of the animals. The carriage threatening to overturn and all in it. Disgusting. What if someone should come along on this road? What if people appeared on this road at such a time to see this spectacle?

What happened to the mule?

The mule? The mule died. Of course.

They wouldnt nobody shoot it or nothin?

Yes. There is a story. I myself was the one. I came forward to shoot this mule, what do you think? Rogelio prohibited this act. Because it will frighten the other mules he says to me. Can you imagine this? At this point in history? Then he wishes to dismiss Gasparito. He says that Gasparito is a lunatic but Gasparito is only a borrachon. From Vera Cruz of course. And a gypsy. Can you imagine this?

I thought you was all gypsies.

She sat up in the hammock. Cómo? she said. Cómo? Quién lo dice?

Todo el mundo.

Es mentira. Mentira. Me entiendes? She leaned over and spat twice into the dirt.

At this moment the door did darken and a small dark man in shirtsleeves stood glaring out. The primadonna turned in her hammock and looked up at him. As if his appearance in the doorway had cast a shadow visible to see. He looked over the visitors and their mounts and took from his shirtpocket a package of El Toro cigarettes and put one in his mouth and fished about in his pocket for a match.

Buenas tardes, Billy said.

The man nodded.

You think a gypsy can sing an opera? the woman said. A gypsy? All gypsies can do is play the guitar and paint horses. And dance their primitive dances.

She sat upright in the hammock and hiked her shoulders and spread her hands before her. Then she uttered a long piercing note that was not quite a cry of pain and not quite anything else. The horses shied and arched their necks and the riders had to haul them around and still they twisted and stepped and rolled their eyes. Out in the fields the workers stood stock still in their furrows.

Do you know what that was? she said.

No mam. It sure was loud.

That was the do agudo. You think some gypsy can sing that note? Some croaking gypsy?

I guess I never give it a lot of thought.

Show me this gypsy, said the primadonna. This gypsy I wish to see.

Who would paint a horse?

Gypsies of course. Who else? Horsepainters. Dentists of horses.

Billy took off his hat and wiped his forehead with the back of his shirtsleeve and put the hat back on. The man in the door had come partway down the painted wooden steps and sat smoking. He leaned and snapped his fingers at the dog. The dog backed away.

Where abouts did this happen about the mule? Billy said.

She raised up and pointed with the folded fan. On the road, she said. Not one hundred meters. We could go no farther. A trained mule. A mule with theatrical experience. Slaughtered in its traces by a drunken fool.

The man on the steps took a last deep draw on his cigarette and flipped the stub at the dog.

You got any message for your party if we see em? said Billy.

Tell Jaime that we are well and that he is to come at his own pace.

Who is Jaime?

Punchinello. He is Punchinello.

Mam?

The payaso. The clowen.

The clown.

Yes. The clown.

In the show.

Yes.

I wont know him without his warpaint.

Mánde?

How will I know him.

You will know him.

Does he make people laugh?

He makes people do what he wishes them to do. Sometimes he makes the young girls cry but that is another history.

Why does he kill you?

The primadonna leaned back in her hammock. She studied him. She looked out at the workers in the field. After a while she turned to the man on the steps.

Díganos, Gaspar. Por qué me mata el punchinello?

He looked up at her. He looked at the riders. Te mata, he said, porque él sabe su secreto.

Paff, said the primadonna. No es porque le sé el suyo?

No.

A pesar de lo que piensa la gente?

A pesar de cualquier.

Y qué es este secreto?

The man raised one foot before him and turned his boot to examine it. It was a boot of black leather with lacing up the side, a kind seldom seen in that country. El secreto, he said, es que en este mundo la mascara es la que es verdadera.

Le entendió? said the primadonna.

He said that he understood. He asked her if that was her opinion also but she only waved one hand languidly. So says the arriero, she said. Quién sabe?

He said it was your secret.

Paff. I have no secret. Anyway it no longer interests me. To be killed night after night. It drains one's strength. One's powers of speculation. It is better to concentrate on small things.

I reckon I would of thought he was just jealous.

Yes. Of course. But even to be jealous is a test of one's strength. Jealous in Durango and again in Monclova and in Monterrey. Jealous in heat and in rain and in cold. Such a jealousy must empty out the malice of a thousand hearts, no? How is one to do this? I think it is better to make a study of smaller things.

Then the larger will follow. In smaller things one can progress.
There one's efforts are repaid. Perhaps just the attitude of the
head. The movement of a hand. The arriero is only a spectator
in these matters. He cannot see that for the wearer of the mask
nothing is changed. The actor has no power to act but only as the
world tells him. Mask or no mask is all one to him.

She picked up the operaglasses by their stem and scanned the
countryside. The road. The long shadows upon the road. And
where do you go, you three? she said.

We're down here huntin some horses that was stole.

In whose charge were these horses?

No one answered.

She looked at Boyd. She spread the fan. Painted across the
folded bellows of the ricepaper was a dragon with great round
eyes. She folded it shut. For how long will you seek these
horses? she said.

Ever how long it takes.

Podría ser un viaje largo.

Quizás.

Long voyages often lose themselves.

Mam?

You will see. It is difficult even for brothers to travel together
on such a voyage. The road has its own reasons and no two
travelers will have the same understanding of those reasons. If
indeed they come to an understanding of them at all. Listen to
the corridos of the country. They will tell you. Then you will
see in your own life what is the cost of things. Perhaps it is true
that nothing is hidden. Yet many do not wish to see what lies
before them in plain sight. You will see. The shape of the road
is the road. There is not some other road that wears that shape
but only the one. And every voyage begun upon it will be
completed. Whether horses are found or not.

I reckon we better get on, Billy said.

Ándale pues, said the primadonna. May God go with you.

I see this Punchinello on the road I'll tell him you're waitin
on him.

Paff, said the primadonna. Do not waste your breath.
Adiós.
Adiós.
He looked at the man on the steps. Hasta luego, he said.
The man nodded. Adiós, he said.
Billy reined the horse around. He looked back and touched
the brim of his hat. The primadonna opened the fan in a graceful
falling gesture. The arriero leaned forward with his hands on
his kneecaps and tried a last time to spit upon the dog and then
they all rode out across the field to the road. When he looked
back at the primadonna she was watching them through the
spyglasses. As if she might better assess them in that way where
they set forth upon the shadowbanded road, the coming twilight. Inhabiting only that ocular ground in which the country
appeared out of nothing and vanished again into nothing, tree
and rock and the darkening mountains beyond, all of it contained
and itself containing only what was needed and nothing more.

THEY MADE CAMP in an oakgrove beside the river and built a
fire and sat while the girl prepared their dinner out of the bounty
they'd carried off from the ejido. When they'd eaten she fed the
dog the scraps and washed the plates and the pot and went to
see about the horses. They rode out again late the next morning
and at noon they turned the horses out of the dirt roadway and
took a path along the lower edge of a field of peppers and on to
the trees and to the river where it shimmered quietly in the
heat. The horses quickened their pace. The path turned and ran
along an irrigation ditch and then descended into the trees and
out again and along a growth of river willows and through a
stand of cane. A cool wind was coming off the water, the white
tassels of the cane bending and hissing gently in the wind.
Beyond the bracken the sound of water falling.
    They came out of the canebrake at a trodden ford in the
runoff from the irrigation channel. Above them was a pool
where water ran from an old corrugated culvertpipe. The water

spilled heavily into the pool and splashing there in the water were half a dozen boys stark naked. They saw the riders at the ford and they saw the girl but they paid them no mind.

Damn, said Boyd.

He clapped his heels into the horse's ribs and put it forward through the sandy shallows. He didnt look back at the girl. She was watching the boys with goodnatured interest. She looked behind at Billy and put her other arm around Boyd's waist and they rode on.

When they reached the river she slid from the horse and took the reins and led both animals out into the water and loosed the latigo on Bird and stood with the horses while they drank. Boyd sat on the bank of the river with one of his boots in his hand.

What's the matter? said Billy.

Nothin.

He limped down along the gravel bar carrying his boot and got a round rock and sat and ran his arm down into the boot and began to pound with the rock.

You got a nail?

Yeah.

Tell her to bring the shotgun.

You tell her.

The girl was standing in the river with the horses.

Tráigame la escopeta, Billy called.

She looked at him. She waded around to the offside of his horse and took the shotgun out of the scabbard and brought it to him. He pried off the forearm and unbreeched the gun and took out the shell and lifted away the barrel and squatted in front of Boyd.

Here, he said. Let me have it.

Boyd handed him the boot and he set it on the ground and reached down and felt inside for the nail and then dropped the breech end of the barrel down into the boot and pounded down the nail with the barrel lug and reached in and felt again and then handed the boot back to Boyd.

Them things smell awful, he said.

Boyd pulled on the boot and stood and walked up and back.

Billy put the shotgun back together and pushed the shell into the chamber with his thumb and breeched the gun and stood it upright on the gravels and sat holding it. The girl was back out in the river with the horses.

You reckon she seen em? Boyd said.

Seen what?

Them boys naked.

He squinted up at Boyd where he stood against the sun. Well, he said, I reckon she did. She aint been struck blind since yesterday has she?

Boyd looked out to where the girl stood in the river.

She didnt see nothin she aint seen before, Billy said.

What's that supposed to mean?

It dont mean nothin.

The hell it dont.

It dont mean nothin. People see people naked, that's all. Dont start gettin crazy on me again. Hell. I seen that opera woman in the river naked as a jaybird.

You never.

The hell I didnt. She was takin a bath. She was washin her hair.

When was all this?

She washed her hair and wrung it out like a shirt.

You mean buck naked?

I mean not stitch one.

How come you never said nothin about it?

You dont need to know everthing.

Boyd stood chewing his lip. You went up and talked to her, he said.

What?

You went up and talked to her. Just like you never seen nothin.

Well what did you want me to do? Tell her I seen her jaybird naked and then start talkin to her?

Boyd had squatted on the gravel spit and he took off his hat and sat holding it in both hands before him. He looked out at the passing river. You think maybe we ought to of stayed back yonder? he said.

At the ejido?

Yeah.

And wait for the horses to come to us I reckon.

He didnt answer. Billy rose and walked out along the gravel bar. The girl brought the horses up and he put the shotgun back in the scabbard and looked at Boyd.

Are you ready to ride? he called.

Yeah.

He pulled the cinches on his horse and took the reins from the girl. When he looked at Boyd Boyd was still sitting there.

What is it now? he said.

Boyd got up slowly. It aint nothin now, he said. It aint nothin from what it was before.

He looked at Billy. You know what I mean?

Yeah, said Billy. I know what you mean.

IN THREE DAYS' RIDING they reached the crossing where the old wagonroad came down out of La Norteña in the western sierras and crossed the high plains of the Babícora and on through the valley of the Santa María to Namiquipa. The days were hot and dry and the riders and their horses by each day's end were the color of the road. They'd ride the horses out across the fields to the river and Billy would throw down the saddle and bedrolls and while the girl made camp he'd take the horses downriver and strip off his boots and clothes and ride bareback into the river leading Boyd's horse by the reins and sit the horse naked save for his hat and watch the dust of the road leach away in a pale stain downstream in the clear cold water.

The animals drank. They lifted their heads and looked out downriver. After a while an old man came through the woods on the far side driving a pair of oxen with a jockeystick. The oxen were yoked with a homemade yoke of poplar wood so whitened by the sun it seemed some ancient weathered bone they bore upon their necks. They waded out into the river with their slow rolling motion and looked upstream and down and across at the horses before they bent to drink. The old man stood at the water's edge and looked at the naked boy horseback.

Cómo le va? said Billy.

Bien, gracias a Dios, said the old man. Y usted?

Bien.

They spoke of the weather. They spoke of the crops, of which the old man knew a great deal and the boy nothing. The old man asked the boy if he was a vaquero and he said he was and the old man nodded. He said that the horses were good horses. Everyone could see that. His eyes drifted upstream to where the thin blue column of smoke from their camp stood in the windless air.

Mi hermano, said Billy.

The old man nodded. He was dressed in the dirty white manta of that country in which the workers tended the fields like soiled inmates wandered from some ultimate Bedlam to stand at last hacking in slow and mindless rage at the earth itself. The oxen raised their dripping mouths out of the river first one and then the other. The old man tilted his stick toward them as if to bless.

Le gustan, he said.

Claro, said Billy.

He watched them drink. He asked the old man if the oxen were willing workers and the old man weighed the question and then said that he did not know. He said that the oxen had no choice. He looked at the horses. Y los caballos? he said.

The boy said he thought that horses were willing enough. He said that some horses enjoyed their work. They enjoyed working cattle. He said that horses were different from oxen.

A kingfisher flew up the river and veered and chattered and then swung back above the river again and continued upstream. No one looked at it. The old man said that the ox was an animal close to God as all the world knew and that perhaps the silence and the rumination of the ox was something like the shadow of a greater silence, a deeper thought.

He looked up. He smiled. He said that in any case the ox knew enough to work so as to keep from being killed and eaten and that was a useful thing to know.

He came forward and hazed the animals up out of the river. They clambered out along the gravel shore and blew and craned their necks. The old man turned, his stick on one shoulder.

Está lejos de su casa? he said.

The boy said that he had no home.

The old man's face grew troubled. He said that the boy must have a home but the boy said that he did not. The old man said that there was a place for everyone in the world and that he would pray for the boy. Then he drove the oxen out through the willows and the sycamore wood in the new dusk and was soon gone from sight.

When he got back to the fire it was almost dark. The dog stood up and the girl came forward to take the sleek and dripping animals. He walked around the fire and turned his saddle where it stood to dry.

She wants to go to Namiquipa to see her mother, Boyd said.

He stood looking down at his brother. I guess she can go wherever she's a mind to, he said.

She wants me to go with her.

Wants you to go with her?

Yeah.

What for?

I dont know. Because she's afraid.

Billy stared into the coals. Is that what you want to do? he said.

No.

Then what are we jawin about?

I told her she could take the horse.

Billy squatted slowly with his elbows on his knees. He shook his head. No, he said.

She aint got no other way to go.

What the hell do you think is goin to happen if somebody sees her ridin a stolen horse? Hell. Any horse.

It aint stole.

The hell it aint. And how do you aim to get it back?

She'll bring it back.

It and the sheriff. What did she run off for if she wants to go back?

I dont know.

I dont either. We come a long ways to get that horse.

I know it.

Billy spat into the fire. I sure would hate to be a woman in this country. What does she aim to do after she gets back?

Boyd didnt answer.

Does she know the kind of shape we're in?

Yeah.

Why wont she talk to me?

She's afraid you'll leave her.

That's why she wants to take the horse.

Yeah. I guess.

What if I wont let her take it?

I reckon she'd go anyways.

Then let her.

The girl came back. They stopped talking even though she could not have understood what they said. She arranged their cookware in the coals and went off to the river for water. Billy looked at Boyd.

You aint above runnin off with her. Are you?

I aint goin nowheres.

If push come to shove.

I dont know what that would be.

If you thought she'd be left on her own or they wouldnt be nobody to look after her or somebody would bother her. Like that. You aint above just goin with her. Are you?

Boyd leaned and pushed the blackened billet ends of two

sticks forward into the small coals with his fingers and wiped his fingers on the leg of his jeans. He didnt look at his brother. No, he said. I guess I aint.

In the morning they rode out to the crossroads and here they took leave of the girl.

How much money have we got? Boyd said.

Damn near none.

Why dont you give it to her?

I knew this was comin. What do you propose to eat on?

Give her half of it.

All right.

She sat the horse bareback and looked down at Boyd with her black eyes brimming and then she slid from the horse and put her arms around him. Billy watched them. He looked at the sky to the south all troubled with weather clouds. He leaned and spat dryly into the road. Let's go, he said.

Boyd boosted her onto the horse and she turned and looked down at him with her hand to her mouth and then reined the horse around and set off on the narrow dirt road east.

THEY RODE ON SOUTH along the dusty road, doubled once more upon Billy's horse. The dust blew off the crown of the road before them and the roadside acacias twisted and hissed in the wind. Late in the afternoon it darkened over and rain began to splatter in the dirt and to rattle in their hatbrims. They passed three men in the road riding. Illsorted horses and worse tack. When Billy looked back two of them were looking back at him.

Would you know them Mexicans we took the girl off of? he said.

I dont know. I dont think so. Would you?

I dont know. Probably not.

They rode on in the rain. After a while Boyd said: They'd know us.

Yeah, said Billy. They'd know us.

The road narrowed going up into the mountains. The country

was all barren pinewood and the spare and reedy grass in the parklands looked poor fare for the sustenance of a horse. They took turns walking on the switchbacks, leading the horse or walking beside it. They camped in the pinewoods at night and the nights were cold again and when they rode into the town of Las Varas they had not eaten in two days. They crossed the railroad tracks and rode past the big adobe warehouses with their mud buttresses and their signs that said puro maíz and compro maíz. There were stacks of raw yellow slabcut pine lumber along the sidings and the air was rank with piñon smoke. They rode past the low stuccoed railstation with its tin roof and descended into the town. The houses were adobe with pitched roofs of wood shake and there were stacks of firewood in the yards and fences made from pine slabs. A boldlooking dog with one leg off limped into the street before them and turned to stand them off.

Sic him, Trooper, said Boyd.

Shit, said Billy.

They ate in what passed for a cafe in that rawlooking country. Three tables in an empty room and no fire.

I believe it's warmer outside than what it is in here, Billy said.

Boyd looked out the window at the horse standing in the street. He looked toward the rear of the cafe.

You reckon this place is even open?

After a while a woman came through the door at the rear and stood before them.

Qué tiene de comer? Billy said.

Tenemos cabrito.

Qué más?

Enchiladas de pollo.

Qué más?

Cabrito.

I aint eatin no goat, Billy said.

I aint either.

Dos ordenes de las enchiladas, Billy said. Y café.

She nodded and went away.

Boyd sat with his hands between his knees to warm them. Outside gray smoke blew through the streets. No one was about.

You think it's worse to be cold or be hungry?

I think it's worse to be both.

When the woman brought the plates she set them down and then made a shooing motion toward the front of the cafe. The dog was standing at the window looking in. Boyd took off his hat and made a pass at the glass with it and the dog went away. He put his hat back on again and picked up his fork. The woman went to the rear and returned with two mugs of coffee in one hand and a basket of corn tortillas in the other. Boyd pulled something from his mouth and laid it on the plate and sat looking at it.

What's that? said Billy.

I dont know. It looks like a feather.

They poked the enchiladas apart trying to find something edible inside. Two men came in and looked at them and went on to sit at the table at the back.

Eat the beans, Billy said.

Yeah, said Boyd.

They spooned the beans into the tortillas and ate them and drank the coffee. The two men at the rear sat quietly waiting for their meal.

She's goin to ask us what was wrong with the enchiladas, Billy said.

I dont know if she will or not. You reckon people eat them things?

I dont know. We can take em and give em to the dog.

You propose to take the woman's food out and feed it to the dog right in front of her own cafe?

If the dog'll eat it.

Boyd pushed back his chair and rose. Let me go out and get the pot, he said. We can feed the dog down the road.

All right.

We'll just tell her we're takin it with us.

When he came back in with the pot they scraped the food off the plates and put the lid on and sat drinking their coffee. The woman came out with two platters of richlooking meat with gravy and rice and pico de gallo.

Damn, said Billy. Dont that look good.

He called for the bill and the woman came over and told them it was seven pesos. Billy paid and nodded toward the rear and asked the woman what those men were eating.

Cabrito, she said.

When they walked out into the street the dog got up and stood waiting.

Hell, said Billy. Just go on and give it to him.

In the evening on the road to Boquilla they encountered a bunch of vaqueros looseherding perhaps a thousand head of raw corriente steers upcountry toward the Naco pens at the border. They'd been trailing the herd three days from the Quemada deep at the southern end of La Babícora and they were dirty and outlandishlooking and the cattle wild and spooky. They passed bawling in a sea of dust and the ghostcolored horses trod among them sullen and red-eyed with their heads lowered. A few of the riders raised a hand in greeting. The young güeros had pulled to a piece of high ground and swung down and they stood with the horse and watched the slow pale chaos drift west with the sun leaving the ground behind them smoking gently and the last cries of the riders and the last moans of the cattle drifting away into the deep blue silence of the evening. They mounted up and rode on again. At dark they passed through a hamlet on that high plain where the houses were of logs with woodshingle roofs. Smoke and the smell of cooking drifted on the cold air. They rode through the bands of yellow light that fell over the road from the lamplit windows and on into the dark and the cold again. In the morning on that same road they encountered wet and sleek coming up from the high-country laguna south of the road the horses Bailey and Tom and Niño.

They'd clambered up into the road with half a dozen other horses all of them still dripping water and they trotted and tossed their heads in the cool of the morning. Two riders came into the road behind them and hazed them up out of their cropping at the roadside grass and drove them on.

Billy neckreined the horse to the side of the road and swung his leg over the pommel of the saddle and slid down and handed the reins up to Boyd. The bunched horses advanced curiously, their ears up. Their father's horse tossed its head and let out a long whicker.

Aint this somethin? said Billy. Aint this somethin?

He watched the riders. Young boys themselves. Perhaps his age. They were wet to the knees and the horses they rode were wet. They'd seen the riders and seen them rein to the side and they came on more cautiously. Billy pulled the shotgun from the scabbard and unbreeched it to see that it was loaded and breeched it shut again with a quick upward jerk. The advancing horses stopped in the road.

Shake out a loop, he said. Dont let that Niño by.

He stepped out into the road with the shotgun in the crook of his arm. Boyd boosted himself over the cantle and pulled the lasso tie and paid out the rope in his hands. The other horses had stopped but Niño came on along the edge of the road, his head up, testing the air.

Whoa Niño, Billy said. Whoa boy.

The two riders coming along behind stopped. They sat their horses uncertainly. Billy had crossed the road to head Niño and Niño tossed his head and came back into the road.

Qué pasa? called the vaqueros.

Drop a loop on that son of a bitch or take the shotgun one, Billy said.

Boyd brought the loop up. Niño had already sized up the space between the man afoot and the man horseback and he bolted forward. When he saw the rope come up he tried to check but he lost footing on the packed clay of the roadway and Boyd

swung the loop once and dropped it over his head and dallied
the rope to the saddlehorn. Bird turned and planted himself in
the road and squatted on his haunches but the Niño horse
stopped when the rope hit him and stood and whinnied and
looked back at the riders and the horses behind.

Qué están haciendo? the riders called. They were sitting their
horses where they'd first stopped. The other horses had turned
and taken to grazing by the roadside again.

Pull a piece of that small rope and build me a hackamore,
Billy said.

You aim to ride him?

Yes.

I can ride him.

I'll ride him. Make it longer. Longer.

Boyd looped and tied the hackamore and cut the rope with
his claspknife and pitched the hackamore to Billy. Billy caught
it and walked Niño down along the length of the catchrope
talking softly to him. The two riders put their horses forward.

He slipped the hackamore over Niño's head and loosed the
catchrope. He talked to the horse and patted it and then pulled
the catchrope off over the horse's head and let it fall to the
ground and led the horse over to where Boyd sat the other
horse. The loop of rope went scurrying over the dirt. The riders
stopped again. Qué pasa? they called.

Billy pitched the shotgun up to Boyd and then jumped and
pulled himself up over the horse's back with both hands and
swung a leg over and sat and reached for the shotgun again.
Niño stamped in the road and tossed his head.

Dab your twine on old Bailey yonder, Billy said.

Boyd looked out down the road at the two riders. He put the
horse forward.

No moleste esos caballos, the riders called.

Billy reined Niño to the side of the road. Boyd advanced upon
the horses where they stood leisurely cropping the roadside grass
and threw his loop. The throw anticipated the Bailey horse and

as he raised his head to move away he raised it into the loop. Billy sat his father's horse watching. I could do that, he told the horse. In about nine tries.

Quiénes son ustedes? the riders called.

Billy rode forward. Somos proprietarios de estos caballos, he called.

The vaqueros sat their horses. Behind them a truck had appeared in the road coming from Boquilla. It was too far off to hear but they must have seen the gaze of the other two riders shift for they turned and looked behind them. No one moved. The truck came on slowly in a thin and augmenting gearwhine. The dust from the wheels drifted slowly out over the country. Billy turned his horse out of the road and sat with the shotgun upright on his thigh. The truck came on. It labored past. The driver looked at the horses and at the boy sitting with the shotgun. In the bed of the truck were eight or ten workers all huddled like conscriptees and as the truck passed they sat looking out back down the road through the dust and motorsmoke at the horses and riders with no expression at all.

Billy nudged Niño forward. But when he looked for the vaqueros there was only one of them in the road. The other one was already riding back south across the campo. He crossed to the standing horses and cut the Tom horse out of the bunch and hazed the rest of the horses up out of the road and turned and looked at Boyd. Let's go, he said.

They advanced upon the lone rider with the loose horse trotting before them and Boyd trailing the Bailey horse behind by the catchrope. The young vaquero watched them come. Then he turned his horse off the road and out onto the grass swales and there he sat watching them pass. Billy looked off across the campo for the other rider but he had dropped from sight behind a rise. He slowed his horse and called out to the vaquero.

Adónde se fué su compadre?

The young vaquero did not answer.

He put the horse forward again, the shotgun upright against his shoulder. He looked back at the horses grazing by the roadside and he looked again at the vaquero and then he fell in alongside Boyd and they rode on. A quarter mile on when he looked back the vaquero was in the road riding slowly behind them. A little way more he stopped and sat the horse quarterwise in the road with the shotgun on his knee. The vaquero stopped also. When they rode on again he rode as well.

Well we're in it now.

We were in it when we left home, Boyd said.

The other old boy's gone for help.

I know it.

Old Niño aint been rode much, has he.

Not much.

He looked at Boyd. Dirty and ragged with his hat forward against the sun and his face enshadowed. He looked some new breed of child horseman left in the wake of war or plague or famine in that country.

At noon with the low walls of the hacienda at Boquilla shimmering in the distance five riders appeared in the road before them. Four of them had rifles which they carried across the bow of their saddles or held loosely in one hand. They curbed their horses sharply and the animals stamped and sidled in the road and the riders called loudly back and forth although they were none at any distance from another.

The two brothers checked their horses. The Tom horse went trotting forward with its ears up. Billy turned in the saddle and looked back. There were three more riders in the road behind them. He looked at Boyd. The dog walked over to the edge of the road and sat down. Boyd leaned and spat and looked south across the unfenced grasslands, the shape of the lake in the distance palely blown where it mirrored the cloudcover overhead. Five or six lean duncolored steers had raised their heads to stare at the horses in the road. He looked back at the riders behind and he looked at Billy.

You want to make a run for it?

No.

We got the fresher horses.

You dont know what kind of horses they got. Bird couldnt keep up with Niño anyways.

He studied the advancing horsemen. He handed the shotgun across to Boyd. Put this up, he said. Find the papers.

Boyd reached back and began to unwrap the thong from the rosette on the saddlebag pocket.

Dont set there with that thing, said Billy. Put it up.

He sheathed the shotgun in the scabbard. You got a lot more confidence in papers than what I got, he said.

Billy didnt answer. He was watching the riders advance along the road all five abreast now with their rifles upright save one. The Tom horse stood at the side of the road and neighed at the approaching horses. One of the riders scabbarded his rifle and took down his rope. The Tom horse watched him approach and then turned and started out of the road but the rider spurred forward and swung his loop and dropped it over the horse's neck. The horse stopped and stood just off the road and the rider let the coil of rope fall in the road and all came on.

Boyd handed Billy the brown envelope with Niño's papers and Billy sat holding them and holding the hackamore rope loosely in his other hand. The insides of his legs were wet from the horse and he could smell him and the horse stamped and nodded and whinnied at the approaching riders.

They halted a few feet out. The older man among them looked them over and nodded. Bueno, he said. Bueno. He was one-armed and his right shirtsleeve was pressed and pinned to his shoulder. He rode his horse with the reins tied and he wore a pistol at his belt and a plain flatcrowned hat of a type no longer much seen in that country and he wore tooled boots to his knees and carried a quirt. He looked at Boyd and he looked again at Billy and at the envelope he was holding.

Déme sus papeles, he said.

Dont give him them papers, Boyd said.

How else is he goin to see em?

Los papeles, said the man.

Billy nudged the horse forward and leaned and handed the

envelope over and then backed the horse and sat. The man put the envelope in his teeth and undid the tieclasp and then took out the papers and unfolded them and examined the seals and held them to the light. He looked through the papers and then refolded them and took the envelope from his armpit and put the papers back in the envelope and handed the envelope to the rider on his right.

Billy asked him if he could read the papers for they were in english but the man didnt answer. He leaned slightly to better see the horse that Boyd was riding. He said that the papers were of no value. He said that in consideration of their youth he would not bring charges against them. He said that if they wished to pursue the matter further they could see señor Lopez at Babícora. Then he turned and spoke to the man on his right and this man put the envelope inside his shirt and he and another man rode forward with their rifles upright in their left hands. Boyd looked at Billy.

Turn the horse loose, Billy said.

Boyd sat holding the rope.

Do like I told you, Billy said.

Boyd leaned and slacked the noose of the catchrope under Bailey's jaw and pulled the rope off over the animal's head. The horse turned and crossed through the roadside ditch and set off at a trot. Billy stepped down from Niño and pulled the hackamore off and slapped the animal across the rump with it and it turned and set out after the other horse. By now the riders behind them had come up and they set off after the horses without being told. The jefe smiled. He touched his hat at them and picked up the reins and turned his horse sharply in the road. Vámonos, he said. Then he and the four mounted riflemen set off back down the road toward Boquilla from whence they'd come. Out on the plain the young vaqueros had headed the loose horses and were driving them back into the road west again as they had first intended and soon all were lost to sight in the noon heatshimmer and there was only the silence left. Billy stood in the road and leaned and spat.

Say what's on your mind, he said.

I aint got nothin to say.

Well.

You ready?

Yeah.

Boyd shucked his boot backward out of the stirrup and Billy put his foot in and swung up behind him.

Bunch of damned ignorance if you ask me, Boyd said.

I thought you didnt have nothin to say.

Boyd didnt answer. The mute dog had gone to hide in the roadside weeds and now it reappeared and stood waiting. Boyd sat the horse.

Now what are you waitin on? said Billy.

Waitin on you to tell me which way you want to go.

Well what the hell way do you think we're goin?

We're supposed to be in Santa Ana de Babícora in three days' time.

Well we might just be late.

What about the papers?

What the hell good are the papers without the horse? Anyway you just got done seein what papers are worth in this country.

One of them boys that left out of here with the horses had a rifle in a boot.

I seen it. I aint blind.

Boyd turned the horse and they set out back west along the road. The dog fell in and trotted at the horse's offside in the horse's shadow.

You want to quit? Billy said.

I never said nothin about quittin.

It aint like home down here.

I never said it was.

You dont want to use common sense. We come too far down here to go back dead.

Boyd pressed the horse's flanks with the heels of his boots and the horse stepped out more smartly. You think there is a place that far? he said.

They picked up the tracks of the two riders and the three horses where they'd returned to the road and an hour later they were back at the place above the lake where they'd first seen the horses. Boyd rode slowly along the side of the road studying the ground underfoot until he saw where horses shod and shoeless had left the road and set out north across the high rolling grasslands.

Where do you reckon they're headed? he said.

I dont know, said Billy. I dont know where they come from for that matter.

They rode north all afternoon. From a rise just at twilight they saw the riders looseherding the horses now some dozen in number before them five miles away on the blue and cooling prairie.

You reckon that's them? Boyd said.

Pret near got to be, said Billy.

They rode on. They rode into the dark and when it was too dark to see they halted the horse and sat listening. There was no sound save the wind in the grass. The evening star sat low in the west round and red like a shrunken sun. Billy slid to the ground and took the bridlereins from his brother and led the horse.

It's dark as the inside of a cow.

I know it. It's all overcast.

That's a damned favorable way to get snakebit.

I got boots on. The horse dont.

They crested out on a knoll and Boyd stood in the stirrups.

Can you see em? said Billy.

No.

What do you see?

I dont see nothin. There aint nothin to see. It's just dark on dark and then more of it.

Maybe they aint had time to build a fire yet.

Maybe they aim to drive all night.

They moved on along the crest of the rise.

Yonder they are, said Boyd.

I see em.

They crossed down the far side into a low swale and looked for some sheltered place out of the wind. Boyd got down and stood in the grassy bajada and Billy handed him the reins.

Find somethin to tie him to. Dont hobble him and dont try to stake him. He'll wind up in their remuda.

He pulled down the saddle and blankets and saddlebag.

You want to build a fire? said Boyd.

What would you build it with?

Boyd walked off into the night with the horse. After a while he came back.

There aint nothin to tie him to that I can find.

Let me have him.

He looped the catchrope and slid it over the horse's head and dallied the other end to the saddlehorn.

I'll sleep with the saddle for a pillow, he said. He'll wake me if he gets farthern forty foot.

I never seen it no darker, said Boyd.

I know it. I think it's fixin to rain.

In the morning when they walked out along the crest of the rise and looked off to the north there was no fire nor smoke of fire. The weather had moved on and the day was clear and still. There was nothing at all out there on the rolling grasslands.

This is some country, said Billy.

You reckon they've done skeedaddled?

We'll find em.

They rode out and began to cut for sign a mile to the north. They found the cold dead fire and Billy squatted and blew into the ashes and spat into the coals but there was no faintest hiss to them.

They never built a fire this mornin.

You reckon they seen us?

No.

No tellin how early they might of left out of here.

I know it.

What if they're laid up somewheres fixin to drygulch us?

Drygulch us?

Yeah.

Where'd you hear that at?

I dont know.

They aint laid up noplace. They just got a early start is all.

They mounted up and rode on. They could see the trace of the horses where they'd gone through the grass.

We need to be careful and not top one of these rises and just come up on em, Boyd said.

I thought about that.

We could lose their track.

We wont lose it.

What if the ground turns off hard and rocky? You thought about that?

What if the world ends, said Billy. You thought about that?

Yeah. I thought about it.

Midmorning they saw the riders entrained along a ridge two miles to the east driving the horses before them. An hour later they came into a road running east and west and they sat the horse in the road and studied the ground. In the dust were the tracks of a large remuda of horses and they looked out down the road to the east the way the remuda had gone. They turned east along the road and by noon they could see before them the sometime haze of dust drifting off the low places in the road where the horses had gone. An hour later and they came to a crossroads. Or they came to a place where a gullied rut ran down out of the mountains from the north and crossed and continued on over the rolling country to the south. Sitting in the road astride a good american saddlehorse was a small dark man of indeterminate age in a John B Stetson hat and a pair of expensive latigo boots with steeply undershot heels. He'd pushed the hat back on his head and he was quietly smoking a cigarette and watching them approach along the road.

Billy slowed the horse, he studied the terrain about for other horses, other riders. He halted the horse at a small distance and thumbed back his own hat. Buenos días, he said.

The man studied them briefly with his black eyes. His hands were folded loosely over the pommel of his saddle before him and the cigarette burned loosely between his fingers. He shifted slightly in the saddle and looked off down the rutted track behind him where the faint dust of the driven remuda yet hung lightly in the air like a haze of summer pollen.

What are your plans? he said.

Sir? said Billy.

What are your plans. Tell me your plans.

He raised the cigarette and drew slowly upon it and blew the smoke slowly before him. He seemed not to be in a hurry about anything.

Who are you? said Billy.

My name is Quijada. I work for Mr Simmons. I am superintendent of the Nahuerichic.

He sat his horse. He drew slowly on the cigarette again.

Tell him we're huntin our horses, Boyd said.

I'll be the judge of what to tell him, Billy said.

What horses? the man said.

Horses stole off our ranch in New Mexico.

He studied them. He jutted his chin at Boyd. Is that your brother?

Yes.

He nodded. He smoked. He dropped the cigarette in the road. The horse looked at it.

You understand this is a serious matter, he said.

It is to us.

He nodded again. Follow me, he said.

He reined the horse about and set off up the road. He did not look back to see if they would follow but they did follow. Nor did they presume to ride beside him.

By midafternoon they were full in the dust of the driven horses. They could hear them on the road ahead although they could not see them. Quijada reined his horse off the road and out through the pine trees and reentered the road ahead of the remuda. The caporal was riding point and when he saw Quijada

he raised one hand and the vaqueros rode forward and headed
the herd and the caporal came up and he and Quijada sat their
horses and talked. The caporal looked back at the two boys
doubled on the bony horse. He called to the vaqueros. The
horses in the road were bunching and milling nervously and one
of the riders had gone back down the line hazing horses out of
the trees. When the horses had all come to rest and stood contained in the road Quijada turned to Billy.

Which are your horses? he said.

Billy turned in the saddle and looked over the remuda. Some
thirty horses standing or shifting sullenly from foot to foot in
the road, lifting and ducking their heads in the golden dust
where it shimmered in the sun.

The big bay, he said. And that lightcolored bay with him.
The one with the blaze. And that speckled horse at the back.
The tigre.

Cut them out, said Quijada.

Yessir, Billy said. He turned to Boyd. Get down.

Let me do it, said Boyd.

Get down.

Let him do it, said Quijada.

Billy looked at Quijada. The caporal had turned his horse
and the two men sat side by side. He swung his leg over the
fork of the saddle and slid to the ground and stepped back. Boyd
boosted himself into the saddle and took down the rope and
began to build a loop, putting the horse forward with his knees
and riding back along the edge of the remuda. The vaqueros sat
smoking, watching him. He rode slowly and he did not look at
the horses. He rode with the loop hanging down the near side
of the horse and then he swung it low along the roadside balk
of pines and brought up a hoolihan backhanded over the
heads of the now stirring horses and dropped the loop over
Niño's neck and raised his arm aloft to carry the slack rope off
of the backs of the interim horses all in one gesture and dallied
and began to cluck to the roped horse and talk him gently out
of the bunch. The vaqueros watched, they smoked.

Niño came forward. The Bailey horse followed, the two of them shouldering their way haltingly and wide of eye out through the strange horses. Boyd brought them close in behind him and continued on along the edge of the road. He undallied and fashioned a jimsaw loop from the home end of the rope and when he reached the rear of the bunch he dropped the loop over the head of the Tom horse without even looking at it. Then he led the three horses back up along the edge of the road past the remuda and stopped with the horses pressed up against Bird and against each other, raising and ducking their heads.

Quijada turned and spoke to the caporal and the caporal nodded. Then he turned and looked at Billy.

Take your horses, he said.

Billy reached and took the bridlereins from his brother and stood in the road holding the horses. I need you to write me a paper, he said.

What kind of paper.

A quitclaim or a conducta or a factura. Some kind of a voucher with your name on it till I can get these horses off of this range.

Quijada nodded. He turned and unfastened the flap on his saddlebag and rummaged through his possibles and came up with a small black leather notebook. He opened it and took a pencil from the binding and sat writing.

What is your name? he said.

Billy Parham.

He wrote. When he was done he tore the page from the notebook and put the pencil back in the binding and closed the book and handed the paper down to Billy. Billy took it and folded it without reading it and took off his hat and put the folded paper inside the sweatband and put the hat back on again.

Thank you, he said. I appreciate it.

Quijada nodded again and spoke again to the caporal. The caporal called to the vaqueros. Boyd leaned down and took the reins and walked the horse out into the dusty roadside pines and turned and sat the horse and he and the horses watched while the vaqueros hazed the remuda into motion again. They passed.

The horses bunched and sorted and rolled their eyes and the vaquero riding drag looked at Boyd sitting his horse with the horses among the trees and he raised one hand and made a small tossing motion with his jaw. Adiós, caballero, he said. Then he fell in behind the remuda and they all passed on up the road into the mountains.

IN THE EVENING they watered the horses at an abrevadero masoned up out of hewn limestone. The vanes of the mill turned slowly above them and the long and skewed shadow of the vanes lay turning out on the high prairie in a slow dark carousel. They'd saddled Niño to ride and Billy dismounted and loosed the cinch to let him blow and Boyd slid down from the Bailey horse he'd been riding and they drank from the pipe and then squatted and watched the horses drink.

You like to watch horses drink, Billy said.

Yeah.

He nodded. I do too.

What would you say that paper's worth?

On this spread I'd say it's worth gold.

And not much off of it.

No. Not much off of it.

Boyd pulled a grass stem and put it in his teeth.

Why do you reckon he let us have the horses?

Cause he knowed they was ours.

How did he know it?

He just knew it.

He could of kept em anyways.

Yeah. He could of.

Boyd spat and put the grass stem back in his teeth. He watched the horses. That was more blind luck, he said. Us runnin up on the horses.

I know it.

How much more luck you reckon we got comin?

You mean like findin the other two horses?

Yeah. That. Or anything.

I dont know.

I dont either.

You think the girl will be there like she said?

Yeah. She'll be there.

Yeah, Billy said. I guess she will be.

Doves coming in across the drylands to the south veered and flared away from the tank when they saw them sitting there. The water from the pipe ran with a cold metallic sound. The western sun descending under the banked clouds had sucked away the golden light and left the land all blue and cool and silent.

You think they've got the other horses, dont you? Boyd said.

Who.

You know who. Them riders that come out of Boquilla.

I dont know.

But that's what you think.

Yeah. That's what I think.

He took the paper Quijada had given him from the sweatband of his hat and unfolded it and read it and refolded it and put it back in his hat and put his hat on. You dont like it, do you? he said.

Who would like it?

I dont know. Hell.

What do you think the old man would of done?

You know what he'd of done.

Boyd took the stem from his teeth and threaded it through the buttonhole on the pocket of his ragged shirt and looped and tied it.

Yeah. He aint here to say though, is he?

I dont know. Someways I think he'll always have a say.

NOON THE FOLLOWING DAY they rode into Boquilla y Anexas looseherding the horses before them. Boyd stayed with the horses while Billy went into the tienda and bought forty feet of half inch grass rope to make hackamores out of. The woman at the counter was measuring cloth off of a bolt. She held the cloth to her chin and measured down the length of her arm and she cut the cloth with a straightedge and a knife and folded it and pushed it across the counter to a young girl. The young girl doled out coppers and ancient tlacos and pesos and crumpled bills and the woman counted the sum and thanked her and the girl left with the cloth folded under her arm. When she'd left the woman went to the window and watched her. She said that the cloth was for the girl's father. Billy said it would make a pretty shirt but the woman said that it was not to make a shirt but to line his coffinbox with. Billy looked out the window. The woman said that the girl's family was not rich. That she had learned these extravagances working for the wife of the hacendado and had spent the money she was saving for her boda. The girl was crossing the dusty street with the cloth under her arm. At the corner were three men and they looked away when she approached and two of them looked after her when she passed.

THEY SAT in the shade of a whitewashed mud wall and ate tacos off of greasy brown papers that they'd bought from a streetvendor. The dog watched. Billy balled the empty paper and wiped his hands on his jeans and got his knife out and measured a length of rope between his outstretched arms.

Are we goin to set here? said Boyd.

Yeah. Why? You got a appointment somewheres?

Why dont we go over yonder and set in the alameda?

All right.

How come do you reckon they never branded the horses?

I dont know. They probably been traded all over the country.

Maybe we ought to brand em.

What the hell you goin to brand em with?

I dont know.

Billy cut the rope and laid the knife by and looped the bosal. Boyd put the last corner of the taco in his mouth and sat chewing.

What do you reckon is in these tacos? he said.

Cats.

Cats?

Sure. You see how the dog was lookin at you?

They aint done it, said Boyd.

You see any cats in the street?

It's too hot for cats in the street.

You see any in the shade?

There could be some laid up in the shade somewheres.

How many cats have you seen anywheres?

You wouldnt eat a cat, Boyd said. Even to get to watch me eat one.

I might.

No you wouldnt.

I would if I was hungry enough.

You aint that hungry.

I was pretty hungry. Wasnt you?

Yeah. I aint now. We aint eat no cats have we?

No.

Would you know it if we had?

Yeah. You would too. I thought you wanted to go over in the alameda.

I'm waitin on you.

Lizards now, Billy said. You caint tell them from chicken hardly.

Shit, said Boyd.

They hazed the horses across the street and under the shade of the painted trees and Billy tied hackamores with trailing rope ends for the horses to walk on if they took a mind to quit them and Boyd lay in the parched and ratty grass with the dog for a pillow and his hat over his eyes and slept. The street was empty all through the afternoon. Billy put the hackamores on the horses and tied them and walked over and stretched out in the grass and after a while he was asleep too.

Toward evening a solitary rider on a horse somewhat above his station stopped in the street opposite the alameda and looked them over where they slept and looked their horses over. He leaned and spat. Then he turned and rode back the way he'd come.

When Billy woke he raised up and looked at Boyd. Boyd had turned on his side and had his arm around the dog. He reached and picked his brother's hat up out of the dust. The dog opened one eye and looked at him. Coming up the street were five riders.

Boyd, he said.

Boyd sat up and felt for his hat.

Yonder they come, said Billy. He rose and stepped into the street and cinched up the latigo on Bird and undid the reins and stepped up into the saddle. Boyd pulled on his hat and walked out to where the horses were standing. He untied Niño and walked him past one of the little ironslatted benches and stood onto the bench and forked one leg over the animal's bare back all in one motion without even stopping the horse and turned and rode past the trees and out to the street. The riders came on. Billy looked at Boyd. Boyd was sitting his horse leaning slightly forward with his hands palm down on the horse's withers. He leaned and spat and wiped his mouth with the back of his wrist.

They approached slowly. They didnt even look at the horses standing under the trees. Save for the one-armed rider they were all of them young men and they did not appear to be carrying guns.

Yonder's our buddy, said Billy.

The jefe.

I dont believe he's all that much of a jefe.

Why is that?

He wouldnt be here. He'd of sent somebody. You recognize any of them others?

No. Why?

I just wondered how big of a outfit it is that we're dealin with here.

The same man in the same tooled boots and the same flat hat turned his horse slightly sideways before them as if he might be going to ride past. Then he turned the horse back. Then he halted the horse in front of them and nodded. Bueno, he said.

Quiero mis papeles, Billy said.

The young men behind looked at each other. The manco studied the two boys. He asked them if they might perhaps be crazy. Billy didnt answer. He took the paper from his pocket and unfolded it. He said that he had a factura for the horses.

Factura de donde? said the manco.

De la Babícora.

The man turned his head and spat into the dust of the street without taking his eyes off Billy. La Babícora, he said.

Sí.

Firmado por quién?

Firmado por el señor Quijada.

He sat without expression. Quijada no es alguacil, he said.

Es gerente, said Billy.

The manco shrugged. He dropped the loop of the reins over the saddlehorn and held out his one hand. Permítame, he said.

Billy folded the paper and put it in his shirtpocket. He said that they had come for the other two horses. The man shrugged again. He said that he could not help them. He said that he could not help the young Americans.

We dont need your help, Billy said.

Cómo?

But Billy had already reined his horse to the right and put the horse forward into the middle of the street. Stay there, Boyd, he said. The jefe turned to the rider on his right. He told him to take the horses in charge. Te los encargo, he said.

No toque esos caballos, said Billy.

Cómo? said the jefe. Cómo?

Boyd rode out from under the trees.

Stay there, said Billy. Do like I said.

Two of the riders had advanced upon the tied horses. The third moved to head Boyd's horse but Boyd booted past him and put his horse out into the street.

Stay back, said Billy.

The rider reined his horse about. He looked at the jefe. Niño had begun to roll his eyes and to stamp in the street. The manco had taken the reins of his horse in his teeth and he had reached across and was in the act of unbuttoning the flap on the holster of his sidearm. Niño's rolling eye must have communicated some unwelcome intelligence to the other horses in the street for the jefe's horse also had begun to skitter and to jerk its head. Billy snatched off his hat and booted his horse forward and hazed his hat in front of the eyes of the jefe's horse and the jefe's horse stood bolt upright and squatted and took two steps backward. The jefe grabbed the great flat pommel of his saddle and when he did so the horse stepped again and made a quarter turn and fell backwards in the street. Billy sawed his horse about and the horse stepped in the jefe's hat and turned and sent it skittering. In turning Billy saw Niño stand and saw Boyd standing with his bootheels in the horse's flanks. The jefe's horse was on its knees scrabbling and it struggled and lunged up and set off down the street with the looped reins hanging and the stirrups flapping. The jefe lay in the road. His eyes moved from side to side taking in the rancorous movements of the horses all about him. He looked at his hat crushed in the road.

The pistol lay in the dirt. Of the riders in the jefe's party two were trying to snub down the horses under the trees where they lunged and jerked at their hackamore leads and one had dismounted and was coming to the assistance of the fallen man. The fourth rider turned and looked at the pistol. Boyd slid from his horse and swung the reins down over the horse's head all in one movement and kicked the pistol out into the middle of the street. Niño tried to rear again and snatched him half off the ground but he pulled the horse down and stepped in front of the mounted rider and cut him off where he had already turned and he ran two fingers up the nostrils of the man's horse which set it to backing and fighting its head. Then he trotted Niño out into the street behind him and bent and picked up the pistol and jammed it into his belt and grabbed a handful of mane and swung himself up and pulled the horse around.

Billy was standing in the street. One of the other vaqueros had also dismounted and now two of them were kneeling in the dust trying to get the jefe to sit up. But the jefe couldnt sit. They raised him up but he sloughed bonelessly to one side and fell over into their arms. They must have thought him only addled because they kept talking to him and patting his cheeks. Out in the street a collection of onlookers had begun to assemble. The other two riders stepped down and dropped their reins and came running.

There aint no use in that, Billy said.

One of the vaqueros turned and looked at him. Cómo? he said.

Es inútil, said Billy. Se quebró el espinazo.

Mánde?

His back's broke.

THEY LEFT THE ROAD a mile north of the town and traveled west till they came to the river. Boyd had hazed the other horses off while the riders were kneeling in the street and they now had all the horses with them. It was almost dark. They sat on a gravel bar and watched the horses standing in the water against the cooling sky. The dog walked into the water and drank and raised its head and looked back at them.

You got any ideas now? Boyd said.

No. I aint.

They sat looking at the horses, nine in number.

They probably got some old boy can track a lizard across a rockslide.

Probably.

What are we goin to do with their horses?

I dont know.

Boyd spat.

Maybe if they get their own horses back they'll leave us be.

Bullshit.

They aint goin to wait till in the mornin.

I know it.

You know what they'll do to us?

I got a pretty good notion.

Boyd threw a stone into the water. The dog turned and looked at the place where it had gone.

We caint looseherd these horses across this country in the dark, he said.

I dont intend to.

Well why dont you tell us what you do intend.

Billy rose and stood looking at the drinking horses. I think we ought to cut out their horses and drive em out to that rise yonder and chouse em back towards Boquilla. They'll get there sooner or later.

All right.

Let me have the pistol.

What do you aim to do with it?

Put it in the man's mochila it belongs to.

You think he's dead?

If he aint he will be.

Then what difference does it make?

Billy looked at the horses in the river. He looked down at Boyd. Well, he said, if it dont make no difference then just let me have it.

Boyd pulled the pistol out of his belt and handed it up. Billy stuck it in his own belt and waded out into the river and mounted Bird and cut the five Boquilla horses out and hazed them up from the river.

Dont let our horses foller, he said.

They aint goin to foller.

Dont entertain no company while I'm gone.

Go on.

Dont build no fires nor nothin.

Go on. I aint a idjit.

He rode out and disappeared over the rise. The sun was down and the long cool evening of the high country had set in. The other three horses came up out of the river one by one and began to graze in the good grass along the bank. It was dark by the time Billy got back. He rode directly in off the plain to their camp.

Boyd stood. You must of give him his head, he said.

I did. Are you ready.

Just waitin on you.

Well let's go.

They sorted out the horses and drove them across the river and set out upcountry. The plains about them blue and devoid of life. The thin horned moon lay on its back in the west like a grail and the bright shape of Venus hung directly above it like a star falling into a boat. They kept to the open country clear of the river and they rode all night and toward the morning they made a dry camp in a quemada of burned trees clustered dead and black and ragged on a slight rise a mile west of the river. They dismounted and looked for some sign of water but there was none.

There's got to of been water here at one time, Billy said.

Maybe the fire dried it up.

A spring or a seep. Somethin.

There aint no grass. There aint nothin.

It's a old burn. Years old.

What do you want to do?

Let's just tough it out. It'll be daylight directly.

All right.

Get your soogan. I'll watch for a while.

I wish I had a soogan.

Outlaws travel light.

They staked the horses and Billy sat with the shotgun in the dark ruin of trees about. The moon long down. No wind.

What was he goin to do with Niño's papers and no horse? Boyd said.

I dont know. Find a horse to fit them. Go to sleep.

Papers aint worth a damn noways.

I know it.

I'm a hungry son of a bitch.

When did you take to cussin so much?

When I quit eatin.

Drink some water.

I did.

Go to sleep.

It was already growing light in the east. Billy stood and listened.

What do you hear? said Boyd.

Nothin.

This is a spooky kind of place.

I know it. Go to sleep.

He sat and cradled the shotgun in his lap. He could hear the horses cropping grass out on the prairie.

You asleep? he said.

No.

I got the papers back.

Niño's papers?

Yeah.

Bullshit.

No, I did.

Where'd you get em from.

They were in the mochila. When I went to put his pistol back they were in the mochila.

I'll be damned.

He sat holding the shotgun and listening to the horses and to the silence of the world beyond. After a while Boyd said: Did you put the pistol back?

No.

How come?

I just didnt.

Have you got it?

Yeah. Go to sleep.

When it was light he rose and walked out to see what sort of country it was that they were in. The dog rose and followed. He walked out to the top of the rise and squatted and leaned on the shotgun. A mile away on the plain a band of palecolored rangecattle were grazing toward the north. Otherwise nothing. When he got back to the trees he stood looking down at his sleeping brother.

Boyd, he said.

Yeah.

Are you ready to ride?

His brother sat up and looked out at the country. Yeah, he said.

We could head back north to the hacienda. The old lady would hide us out.

Till what?

I dont know.

We're supposed to meet her tomorrow.

I know it. It caint be helped.

How long would it take to ride to the hacienda?

I dont know. Let's go.

They set out north and rode till they came in view of the river. There were cattle grazing along the edge of the trees at the river breaks. They sat the horses and looked back across the rolling high prairie to the south.

Could you kill a cow with a shotgun? said Boyd.

Get close enough. Yeah.

What about with a pistol?

You'd have to get close enough to where you could hit it.

How close would you have to get?

We aint shootin no cow. Come on.

We got to eat somethin.

I know it. Come on.

When they reached the river they crossed through the shallows and looked for a road on the other side but there was no road. They followed the river north and in the early afternoon they rode into the pueblito of San José, a clutch of low and graylooking mud hovels. As they passed along the rutted track with their string of horses a few women peered warily from out of the low doorways.

What do you think's wrong here? said Boyd.

I dont know.

Maybe they think we're gypsies.

Maybe they think we're horsethieves.

A goat watched them from a low roof with its agate eyes.

Ay cabrón, said Billy.

This is a hell of a place, said Boyd.

They found a woman to feed them and they sat on a mat of woven rushes on the clay floor and ate cold atole out of home-made bowls of unfired clay. When they wiped the bottoms of the bowls their tortillas came up gritty and stained with mud. They tried to pay the woman but she would take no money. Billy offered again for the niños but she said there were no niños.

They camped that night in a grove of cottonwoods by the river and staked out the horses in the river grass and they stripped off and swam in the river in the dark. The water was cold and silky. The dog sat on the bank and watched them. In the morning Billy rose before daybreak and walked out and unstaked Niño and led him back to camp and saddled him and mounted up with the shotgun.

Where you goin? said Boyd.

See if I can rustle us up somethin to eat.

All right.

Just stay here. I wont be gone long.

Where would I go?

I dont know.

What am I supposed to do if somebody comes?

There wont nobody come.

What if they do?

Billy looked at him. He was crouched with his blanket around his shoulders and he was so thin and ragged. He looked at him and he looked out past the pale boles of the cottonwoods and over the rolling desert grassland emerging in the gray dawn light.

I guess what it is is you want me to leave you the pistol.

I think it might be a good idea.

Do you know how to shoot it?

Yes, damn it.

It's got two safeties.

I know it.

All right.

He took the pistol out of the bag and handed it down to him.

There's one in the chamber.

All right.

Dont shoot it. That and what's in the clip is all the shells we got for it.

I aint goin to shoot it.

All right.

How long will you be gone?

I wont be gone long.

All right.

He rode off downriver with the shotgun across the bow of the saddle. He'd taken the buckshot shell from the chamber and rummaged through the shells in the bag and come up with a couple of number five shot and loaded the gun with one of them and buttoned the other into the pocket of his shirt. He rode slowly and he watched the river through the trees as he rode. A mile down he saw ducks on the water. He dismounted and dropped the reins and took the shotgun and began to stalk them through the shore willows. He took off his hat and laid it on the ground. The horse whinnied behind him and he looked back and swore at it under his breath and then raised up and looked out down the river. The ducks were still there. Three dark scaup motionless on the pewter calm of the tailwater. The mist rising off the river like smoke. He made his way carefully through the willows, crouching as he went. The horse nickered again. The ducks flew.

He stood up and looked back. Damn you, he said. But the horse was not looking at him. It was looking across the river. He turned and there he saw five men riding.

He dropped to his hands and knees. They were coming upriver singlefile through the trees on the far side. They had not seen him. The ducks wheeled overhead in the new sunlight and swung away downriver. The riders looked up, they rode on. Niño stood in plain sight among the willows but they did not see him and he did not whinny again and they passed on and disappeared upriver among the trees.

He rose and grabbed up his hat and jammed it on his head and walked carefully back out to where the horse stood that he not spook it and he caught the reins and mounted up and swung the horse around and put it into a lope.

He cut away from the river and made a swing out over the prairie. The upper branches of the cottonwoods were already in sunlight. He fished about in the mochila behind him as he rode trying to find the buckshot shell. He did not see the riders anywhere across the river and when he saw his own horses grazing at their stakeropes among the trees he turned toward the camp.

Boyd knew what was happening without he said a word and set off to get the horses. Billy swung down and grabbed their blankets and rolled and tied them. Boyd came up the river afoot at a run hazing the horses before him.

Get the ropes off of em, Billy called. We're goin to have to make a run for it.

Boyd turned. He put up one hand as if to reach for the first of the horses as they came up out of the trees and then his shirt belled out behind him redly and he fell down on the ground.

Billy knew afterward that he had seen the actual riflebullet. That the suck and whiff at his ear had been the bullet passing and that he had seen it for one frozen moment before his eyes with the sun on the side of the small revolving core of metal, the lead wiped bright by the rifling of the bore, slowed from having passed through his brother's body but still moving faster than sound and passing his left ear with the suck of the air like a whisper from the void and the small jar of the shockwave and then the bullet caroming off of a treebranch and singing away over the desert behind him that by a hairsbreadth had not carried his life away with it and then the sound of the shot come lagging after.

It rang out across the river lean and flat and echoed back from the desert. He was already running among the frantic and careening horses and he knelt and turned his brother over where he lay in the bloodstained dirt. Oh God, he said. Oh God.

He lifted his head out of the dust. His ragged shirt wet with blood. Boyd, he said. Boyd.

It hurts, Billy.

I know it.

It hurts.

The rifle cracked again from across the river. All of the horses had run out of the trees save Niño who stood stamping at the dropped reins. He turned toward the sound and raised one hand. No tire, he called. No tire. Nos rendimos. Nos rendimos aquí.

The rifle cracked again. He laid Boyd down and ran for the horse and caught the trailing reins just as the animal turned to quit the place. He hauled the horse around and trotted with it to where his brother lay and he stood on the reins while he picked his brother up and then he turned and pushed him up into the saddle and threw the reins over the horse's head and grabbed the pommel and swung up behind him and seized him around the waist where he sat tottering and leaned and dug his heels into Niño's belly.

Three more shots rang out as they came out of the trees and into the open country but by now he had put the horse into a gallop. His brother lolled against him all loose and bloody and he thought that he had died. He could see the other horses running on the plain before them. One of them had dropped back and appeared to be injured. The dog was nowhere in sight.

The horse he overtook was Bailey and he had been shot just above the rear hock and when they passed him he stopped altogether. When Billy looked back he was just standing there. As if the heart had gone out of him.

He overtook the other two horses in the length of perhaps a mile and they fell in behind. When he looked back he could see all five horsemen on the plain coming hard after him in a thin line of dust, some of them whipping over and under, all carrying their rifles held out at their side, all of it clear and stark in the new morning sun. When he looked ahead he saw nothing but grass and the sporadic palmilla that dotted the plain stretching away to the blue sierras. There was nowhere to run and nowhere to stand. He whacked Niño with the heels of his boots. Bird and the Tom horse were already beginning to fall back and he turned and called to them. When he looked ahead again he saw in the distance a small dark form crossing the landscape left to right in a trail of dust and he knew that there was a road there.

He leaned forward clutching his brother to him and he talked to Niño and dug in with his heels under the horse's flanks and they went pounding over the empty plain with the stirrups flapping and kicking out. When he looked back Bird and the Tom horse were still with him and he knew that Niño was tiring under the double riders he carried. He thought that the horsemen behind had dropped back some and then he saw that one of them had stopped and he saw the white puff of smoke from the rifle and heard the thin dead crack of it lost in the open space but that was all. Ahead the carrier on the road had vanished in the distance and left only a pale hovering of dust to mark its passage.

The road was raw dirt and as there was neither selvedge nor bar ditch to mark it he was in it before he knew it. He reined up skidding and hauled the gasping horse around. Bird was coming hard behind him and he tried to head him but then when he looked to the south he saw laboring towards him out of the emptiness an ancient flatbed truck carrying farmworkers. He forgot Bird and turned and put the horse south along the road toward the truck waving his hat.

The truck had no brakes and when the driver saw him he began to grind slowly down through the gears. The workers crowded forward along the bed looking down at the wounded boy.

Tómelo, he called to them. Tómelo. The horse stamped and rolled its eyes and a man reached and took the reins and half-hitched them about one of the stakes in the truckbed and other hands reached for the boy and some clambered down into the road to help lift him up. Blood was a condition of their lives and none asked what had befallen him or why. They called him el güerito and passed him up into the truck and wiped the blood from their hands on the front of their shirts. A lookout was standing with one hand on top of the cab watching the riders out on the plain.

Pronto, he called, pronto.

Vámonos, Billy shouted to the driver. He leaned and pulled the reins loose and hammered the truckdoor with the side of his fist. The men in the truck reached down their hands to help aboard those in the road and the driver put the truck in gear and they lurched forward. One of the men held out a blood-stained hand and Billy clasped it. They'd made a place for Boyd on the rough boards of the truckbed with shirts and serapes. He couldnt tell if he was alive or dead. The man gripped his hand. No te preocupes, he shouted.

Gracias, hombre. Es mi hermano.

Vámonos, the man shouted. The truck labored forward up the road in a low whine of gears. Out on the prairie the riders were already dividing, two of them cutting away to the north to follow the truck. The workers waved and whistled at him where he sat the horse in the road and they gestured with their hands in great circles over their heads to motion to him to go on. He'd already boosted himself forward into the saddle and found the stirrups and the blood was soaking cold through his trousers. He booted Niño forward. Bird was a mile ahead on the prairie. When he looked back the riders were less than a hundred yards out and he leaned along Niño's neck and called upon him to give his life.

He rode Bird down on the prairie but when he overtook him he had in his eye much the same look as the Bailey horse and he knew that he had lost him. He looked back at the riders and he called one last time to his old horse to give him heart and then he rode on. He heard again that distant flat report that a rifle makes over open ground and when he looked back one of the riders had dismounted and was kneeling beside his horse firing. He leaned low in the saddle and rode on. When he looked back again the two riders had diminished on the plain and when he looked one final time they were smaller yet and Bird was nowhere in sight. He never did see the Tom horse again.

Midmorning alone in that country he led the drenched and bottomed horse afoot up a cobbled arroyo. He talked to the horse and kept to the rocks and where the horse put a foot in the sand of the arroyo floor he dropped the reins and went back and repaired the mark with a whisk of grass. His trouserlegs were stiff with dried blood and he knew that both he and the horse were going to have to find water very soon.

He left the horse standing with the latigo loosed and climbed up and lay in the arroyo breaks and studied the country to the east and to the south. He saw nothing. He climbed back down and picked up the reins of the standing horse and took hold of the pommel of the saddle and he looked at the dark shape of the blood in the leather and he stood for a moment with the reins doubled in his fist and his forearm across the wet salt withers of his father's horse. Why couldnt the sons of bitches have shot me? he said.

In the blue dusk of that day he saw a light far to the north that first he took for the polestar. He watched to see if it would lift off of the horizon but it did not and he turned slightly in his course and leading the exhausted horse afoot set out across the desert prairie toward it. The horse faltered behind him and he dropped back and took hold of the bridle cheekstrap and walked beside the horse and talked to it. The horse so crusted with white salt rime it shone like some prodigy embarked upon the darkening plain. When he'd said all he knew to say he told it stories. He told it stories in spanish that his grandmother had told him as a child and when he'd told all of those that he could remember he sang to it.

The last thin paring of the old moon hung over the distant mountains to the west. Venus had moved away. With dark a gauzy swarm of stars. He could not guess what they were for, so many. He trekked on for another hour and then halted and felt the horse to see that it was dry and swung up into the saddle and rode on. When he looked for the light it was gone and he fixed his position by the stars and after a while the light appeared again out of the dark cape of desert headland that had obscured it. He'd quit singing and he tried to think how to pray. Finally he just prayed to Boyd. Dont be dead, he prayed. You're all I got.

IT WAS NEAR MIDNIGHT when they struck the fence and he turned east and rode till he came to a gate. He dismounted and led the horse through and closed the gate again and remounted and rode up the pale clay track toward the light where dogs had already risen and come forward howling.

The woman who came to the door was not young. She lived in this remote station with her husband who she said had given his eyes for the revolution. She shouted back the dogs and they slank away and when she stood aside for him to pass this husband was standing in the small lowceilinged room as if he'd risen to greet some dignitary. Quién es? he said.

She said that it was an American who had lost his way and the man nodded. He turned away and the weathercreased face caught for a moment the light from the oil lamp. There were no eyes in his sockets and the lids were pinched shut so that he wore a constant look of painful selfabsorption. As if old errors preoccupied him.

They sat at a pine table painted green and the woman brought him milk in a cup. He'd about forgotten that people even drank milk. She struck a match to the circular wick of the burner in the kerosene stove and adjusted the flame and put on a kettle and when it had boiled she spooned eggs one by one down into the kettle and put the lid back again. The blind man sat stiff and erect. As if he himself were the guest in his own house. When the eggs had boiled the woman brought them steaming in a bowl and sat down to watch the boy eat. He picked one up and put it down quickly. She smiled.

Le gustan los blanquillos? said the blind man.

Sí. Claro.

They sat. The eggs steamed in the bowl. In the unshaded light of the coaloil lamp their faces hung like masks.

Dígame, said the blind man. Qué novedades tiene?

He told them that he was in the country seeking to recover horses stolen from his family. He said that he was traveling with his brother but that he had become separated from him. The blind man inclined his head to hear. He asked for news of the revolution but the boy had no news to give. Then the blind man said that although the countryside was tranquil this was not necessarily a good sign. The boy looked at the woman. The woman nodded her head solemnly in agreement. She seemed to set great store by her husband. He took an egg from the bowl and cracked it on the rim and began to peel it. While he was eating the woman began to tell of their life.

She said that the blind man had been born of humble origins. Orígenes humildes, she said. She said that he had lost his eyes in the year of our Lord nineteen thirteen in the city of Durango. He'd ridden east in late winter of that year and joined Maclovio Herrera and on the third of February they had fought at Namiquipa and taken the town. In April he had fought at Durango with the rebels under Contreras and Pereyra. In the federal arsenal was an antique demiculverin of french manufacture which he was placed in charge of. They did not take the city. He could have saved himself, the woman said. But he would not leave his post. He was taken prisoner along with many others. The prisoners were given the opportunity to swear oaths of loyalty to the government and those who would not do so were stood against a wall and shot without ceremony. Among them were men of many nations. American and English and German. And men from lands no one had even heard of. Yet they went also to the wall and there they died in the terrible volleys of riflefire, the terrible smoke. They fell down soundlessly beside each other, their hearts' blood on the plasterwork behind them. He saw this.

Among the defenders of Durango there were of course few foreigners yet there was one such. A German Huertista named Wirtz who was a captain in the federal army. The captured rebels stood in the street chained together with fencewire like toys and this man walked their enfilade and bent to study each in turn and note in their eyes the workings of death as the assassinations continued behind him. The man spoke spanish well for all that he spoke it with a german accent and he told the artillero that only the most pathetic of fools would die for a cause that was both wrong and doomed and the captive spat in his face. The German then did something very strange. He smiled and licked the man's spittle from about his mouth. He was a very large man with enormous hands and he reached and seized the young captive's head in both these hands and bent as if to kiss him. But it was no kiss. He seized him by the face and it may well have looked to others that he bent to kiss him on each cheek perhaps in the military manner of the French but what he did instead with a great caving of his cheeks was to suck each in turn the man's eyes from his head and spit them out again and leave them dangling by their cords wet and strange and wobbling on his cheeks.

And so he stood. His pain was great but his agony at the disassembled world he now beheld which could never be put right again was greater. Nor could he bring himself to touch the eyes. He cried out in his despair and waved his hands about before him. He could not see the face of his enemy. The architect of his darkness, the thief of his light. He could see the trampled dust of the street beneath him. A crazed jumble of men's boots. He could see his own mouth. When the prisoners were turned and marched away his friends steadied him by the arm and led him along while the ground swang wildly underfoot. No one had ever seen such a thing. They spoke in awe. The red holes in his skull glowed like lamps. As if there were a deeper fire there that the demon had sucked forth.

They tried to put his eyes back into their sockets with a spoon but none could manage it and the eyes dried on his cheeks like grapes and the world grew dim and colorless and then it vanished forever.

Billy looked at the blind man. He sat erect and impassive. The woman waited. Then she continued.

Some said of course that this man Wirtz had saved his life for had he not been blinded he'd have surely gone to the wall. Some others said that would have been the better course. None asked the blind man for his views. He sat in the cold stone cárcel while the light did fade about him till at last he sat in darkness. The eyes dried and wrinkled and the cords they hung by dried and the world vanished and he slept at last and dreamt of the country through which he'd ridden in his campaigns in the mountains and the brightly colored birds thereof and the wildflowers and he dreamt of young girls barefoot by the roadside in the mountain towns whose own eyes were pools of promise deep and dark as the world itself and over all the taut blue sky of Mexico where the future of man stood at dress rehearsal daily and the figure of death in his paper skull and suit of painted bones strode up and back before the footlights in high declamation.

Hace veintiocho años, the woman said. Y mucho ha cambiado. Y a pesar de eso todo es lo mismo.

The boy reached and took the last egg from the bowl and cracked it and began to peel it. As he did so the blind man spoke. He said that on the contrary nothing had changed and

all was different. The world was new each day for God so made
it daily. Yet it contained within it all the evils as before, no
more, no less.

The boy bit into the egg. He looked at the woman. She
seemed to be waiting for the blind man to say more and when
he did not she continued as before.

The rebels returned and took Durango on June the eighteenth
and he was led from the cárcel and he stood in the street while
the sounds of gunfire echoed from the outskirts where the routed
federal soldiers were being hunted down and shot. He stood
and he listened for any voice he might know.

Quién es usted, ciego? they said. He told his name but none
knew him. Someone cut and gave to him a greenwood stave and
with this as his sole possession he set out alone afoot on the road
to Parral.

He told the time of day by turning his face to the sightless
sun like a worshipper. By the sounds of the countryside. The
coolness of the night, the damp. By the calls of birds and by the
first warmth of the rumored light upon his skin. People brought
him water and food from the houses he passed and provisioned
him for the road ahead. Dogs that came bristling into the road
to challenge him slank away again. He was surprised at the
authority which his blindness conferred upon him. He seemed
to want for nothing.

There had been rain in the country and wildflowers bloomed
by the roadside. He made his way slowly, tracking the ruts with
his greenwood stick. He'd no boots for they'd long been stolen
and those first days he walked barefoot and his heart was filled
with despair. More than filled. Despair was in him like a lodger.
Like a parasite that had turned out his very being from its abode
and taken up the shape of that space within him where it once
had been. He could feel it lodged against his throat. He could
not eat. He sipped water from a cup proffered anonymously out
of the world's dark and handed the cup away into that dark
again. His liberation from the cárcel meant little to him and
there were days his freedom seemed to him no more than just

some further curse and in this condition he tapped his way slowly north along the road to Parral.

In the cool dark of his first night alone in the country it had rained and he stopped and listened and he could hear the rain coming across the desert. Borne on the wind the smell of wet creosote bush. He lifted his face and stood by the roadside and his thoughts were that other than wind and rain nothing would ever come again to touch him out of that estrangement that was the world. Not in love, not in enmity. The bonds that fixed him in the world had become rigid. Where he moved the world moved also and he could never approach it and he could never escape it. He sat in the roadside weeds in the rain and wept.

On the morning of his third day abroad he entered the town of Juan Ceballos and there he stood in the road with his cane aloft and turned, listening, squinting his terrible squint. But the dogs had already crept away and a woman spoke to him at his right side and asked that she might take his hand and he gave it.

Y adónde va? she said.

He said he did not know. He said that he was going where the road went. The wind. The will of God.

La voluntad de Dios, she said. As if choosing.

She took him to her house. He sat at a rough board table and she gave him a pozole with fruit to eat but he could not eat it for all that she urged him. She asked him to tell her from whence he'd come but he was ashamed of his condition and he would not say how his calamity had befallen him. She asked him had he always been blind and he weighed this question and after a while he said that yes he had.

When he left he wore on his feet a pair of old patched huaraches and he carried over his shoulder a thin serape. In the pocket of his ragged breeches a few copper coins. Men talking in the street fell silent at his approach and spoke again when he had passed. As if it might be that he were some deputy of darkness sent to spy among them. As if words carried away by a blind man might thereby come to have a life unreckoned with and be met with elsewhere in the world bearing a meaning never intended by those who'd uttered them. He turned in the road and held his cane aloft. Ustedes no saben nada de mí, he shouted. They fell silent and he turned and went on and after a while he could hear them talking again.

That night he heard the sounds of battle far distant on the plain and he stood in the dark and listened. He tested the wind for the smell of cordite and listened for sounds of men and horses but all he could hear was the faint rattle of riflefire and the periodic heavy dull report of a howitzer firing cannister shot and after a while nothing.

The next morning early his cane clattered before him on the boards of a bridge. He stopped. He reached and tapped forward. He stepped carefully onto the boards and stood and listened. He could hear much muted beneath him the sound of water running.

He made his way down along the small river bank and pushed through the rushes till he came to the water. He reached out and touched it with his cane. He slashed at the water and then he stopped. He raised his head to listen.

Quién está? he called.

No one answered back.

He laid aside his serape and stripped out of his rags and took up his cane again and thin and naked and filthy he waded into the river.

He waded out wondering if the water might perhaps be deep enough to bear him away. He imagined that in his estate of eternal night he might somehow have already halved the distance to death. That the transition for him could not be so great for the world was already at some certain distance and if it were not death's terrain he encroached upon in his darkness then whose?

The water came but to his knees. He stood in the river, he steadied himself with his staff. Then he sat. The water was cool, it moved slowly about him. He lowered his face to take its odor, to taste it. He sat for a long time. In the distance he heard a bell that tolled slowly three times and ceased. He got to his knees and then leaned forward and lay facedown in the water. He placed the staff yokewise across his neck and held it in his two hands. He held his breath. He gripped his staff and he held it for a long time. When he could hold it no longer he breathed out and then tried to breathe the water in but he could not and the next thing he was kneeling in the river gasping and coughing. He'd let go his cane and it had drifted away and he rose and floundered about coughing and sucking in air and flailing at the river surface with the flat of his hand. To the man standing on the bridge he must have seemed deranged. Must have seemed to be attempting to calm the river, or something in the river. Until he saw those barren eyecups.

A la izquierda, he called.

The blind man stopped. He crouched with his arms crossed before him.

A su izquierda, called the man.

The blind man patted the water to his left.

A tres metros, called the man. Pronto. Se va.

He lurched forward. He groped about. The man on the bridge called out coordinates and finally his hand closed upon his staff and he sat down in the river for modesty and clutched the cane to him.

Qué hace, ciego? the man called.

Nada. No me molesta.

Yo? Le molesto? Ciego, ciego.

He said that he had thought the blind man was drowning and was on the point of coming to his rescue when he saw him raise up sputtering.

The blind man sat with his back turned to the bridge and the road. He could smell tobacco smoke and after a while he asked the man if he could have a cigarette.

Por supuesto.

He rose and waded ashore. Dónde está mi ropa? he called.

The man directed him to his clothes. When he had dressed he made his way up to the road and he and the man sat on the bridge smoking. The sun felt good on his back. The man said that there was not enough water in the river to drown oneself and the blind man nodded. He said that in any case there was not enough privacy.

The blind man said that there was a church nearby, no? His friend told him that there was no church. That there was nothing at all anywhere in sight. The blind man said that he had heard a bell and the man said that he had had an uncle who was blind and he too often heard things which were not.

The blind man shrugged. He said he was only newly blinded. The man asked him why he thought the sound of bells must be from a church but the blind man only shrugged again and smoked. He asked what other sound a church would make.

The man asked him why he wished to die but the blind man said that it was not important. The man asked if it was because he could not see and he said that it was a reason among reasons. They smoked. Finally the blind man told him about his conjecture that the blind had already partly quit the world anyway. He said that he had become but a voice to speak in a darkness incommensurable with the motives of life. He said that the world and all in it had become to him but a rumor. A suspicion. He shrugged. He said that he did not wish to be blind. That he had outlived his estate.

The man heard him out, they sat in silence. The blind man heard the faint hiss of the other's cigarette in the water beneath him. Finally the man said that it was a sin to lose heart and anyway the world remained as it had always been. That much was undeniable. When the blind man did not answer he told the blind man to touch him but the blind man was loath to do so.

Con permiso, the man said. He took the blind man's hand and placed his fingers on his lips. There the blind man's fingers lay. In the gesture of one adjuring another to silence.

Toca, the man said. The blind man would not. He took the blind man's hand again and he moved it upon his face. Toca, he said. Si el mundo es ilusión la perdida del mundo es ilusión también.

The blind man sat with his hand to the man's face. Then he began to move it. A face of no determinate age. Dark or fair. He touched the narrow nose. The coarse straight hair. He touched the balls of the man's eyes beneath the thin closed lids. No sound in the high desert morning save their breathing. He felt the eyeballs move under his fingers. Small quick movements like the movements in a tiny womb. He drew his hand away. He said that he could tell nothing. Es una cara, he said. Pues que?

The other man sat in silence. As if contemplating how to answer. He asked the blind man could he weep. The blind man said that any man could weep but what the man wished to know was could the blind weep tears from the places where their eyes had been, how could they do this? He did not know. He took a last draw from the cigarette and let it fall into the river. He said again that the world in which he made his way was very different from what men suppose and in fact was scarcely world at all. He said that to close one's eyes told nothing. Any more than sleeping told of death. He said that it was not a matter of illusion or no illusion. He spoke of the broad dryland barrial and the river and the road and the mountains beyond and the blue sky over them as entertainments to keep the world at bay, the true and ageless world. He said that the light of the world was in men's eyes only for the world itself moved in eternal darkness and darkness was its true nature and true condition and that in this darkness it turned with perfect cohesion in all its parts but that there was naught there to see. He said that the world was sentient to its core and secret and black beyond men's imagining and that its nature did not reside in what could be seen or not seen. He said that he could stare down the sun and what use was that?

These words seemed to silence his friend. They sat side by side on the bridge. The sun shone upon them. Finally the man asked him how he had come by such views and he answered that they were things he'd long suspected and that the blind have much to contemplate.

They rose to go. The blind man asked his friend which way he was going. The man hesitated. He asked the blind man which way he. The blind man pointed with his stave.

Al norte, he said.

Al sur, said the other.

He nodded. He offered his hand into the darkness and they said their farewell.

Hay luz en el mundo, ciego, the man said. Como antes, asi ahora. But the blind man only turned away and set out as before on the road to Parral.

Here the woman broke off her narrative and looked at the boy. The boy's eyelids were heavy. His head jerked.

Está despierto, el joven? said the blind man.

The boy sat upright.

Sí, the woman said. Está despierto.

Hay luz?

Sí. Hay luz.

The blind man sat erect and formal. His hands outspread palm down on the table before him. As if to steady the world, or himself in it. Continuas, he said.

Bueno, the woman said. Como en todos los cuentos hay tres viajeros con quienes nos encontramos en el camino. Ya nos hemos encontrado la mujer y el hombre. She looked at the boy. Puede acertar quien es el tercero?

Un niño?

Un niño. Exactamente.

Pero es verídica, esta historia?

The blind man broke in to say that indeed the tale was a true one. He said that they had no desire to entertain him nor yet even to instruct him. He said that it was their whole bent only to tell what was true and that otherwise they had no purpose at all.

Billy asked how it could be that on the long road to Parral he should meet only three people but the blind man said that he did meet other people on that road and that he received from them many kindnesses but that the three strangers at issue were those with whom he spoke of his blindness and that they must therefore be the principals in a cuento whose hero was a blind man, whose subject was sight. Verdad?

Es héroe, este ciego?

For a while the blind man forbore to answer. Finally he said that it was best to wait and see. That it was best to judge for oneself. Then he gestured with one hand to the woman and she continued as before.

He'd made his way north along the road as told until in nine days' time he reached the town of Rodeo on the Río Oro. Everywhere he attracted gifts. Women came out to him. They stopped him in the road. They pressed upon him their own possessions and they offered to attend him some part of the way along the road. Walking at his elbow they described to him the village and the fields and the condition of the crops and they named to him the names of the persons who lived in the houses they passed and confided to him details of their domestic arrangements or spoke of the illnesses of the old. They told him of the sorrows in their lives. The death of friends, the inconstancy of lovers. They spoke of the faithlessness of husbands in a way that was a trouble to him and they clutched his arm and hissed the names of whores. None swore him to secrecy, none asked his name. The world unfolded to him in a way it had not before in his life.

On the twenty-sixth of June of that year a company of Huertistas had passed through the town of Rodeo on their way east to Torreón. They arrived late in the night many of them drunk and all of them afoot and they bivouacked in the alameda and burned the benches for firewood and in the gray dawn rounded up those they said were rebel sympathizers and stood them against the mud wall of the granja and gave them cigarettes to smoke and then shot them dead while their children watched and their wives and mothers wailed and tore out their hair.

When the blind man arrived the following day he fell unwittingly into a funeral enfiled along the gray mud street and before he could properly judge the events occurring about him a young girl had taken his hand and he was led out to the dusty cemetery at the outskirts of the town. There amid the poor wooden crosses and the crockery jars and cheap glass dishes that stood for offertory the first of the three cratewood coffins imperfectly blacked with coaloil and chimneysoot was placed upon the ground while the attending trumpeter played a melancholy martial air and an elder of the village spoke in lieu of priest for there was none. The girl clutched his hand, she leaned to him.

Era mi hermano, she whispered.

Lo siento, said the blind man.

They lifted the dead man from the box and lowered him into the arms of two men who had scrambled down into the grave. There they laid him out on the raw dirt and composed his arms again upon his chest where they had fallen free and they laid a cloth across his face. Then these rude provisional sextons reached up and took the hands of their waiting friends and were helped up from the grave and the men shoveled each a spadeful of dirt down upon the dead man in his poor clothes, the gray caliche rattling dully and the women sobbing, and shouldered up the empty box and the lid to carry back to the village for the conveying of yet another body. The blind man could hear new people arriving in the little cemetery and soon he was led away a short distance through the shouldering crowd to stand again and hear yet another simple country oration.

Quién es? he hissed.

The girl clutched his hand. Otro hermano, she whispered.

As they stood for the third burial the blind man leaned and asked how many of her family were to be buried but she said that this was the last.

Otro hermano?

Mi padre.

The clods rattled, the women wailed anew. The blind man put on his hat.

Returning they passed in the road another cortege bound out for the cemetery and the blind man heard yet other weeping and other feet shuffling along under the dire weight of the dead they bore. No one spoke. When they had passed the girl led him forth into the road again and they went on as before.

He asked the girl if there were any left alive of her household but she said there were none save only she for her mother was dead years since.

It had rained in the night past and rained in the dead fire left by the assassins and the blind man could smell the wet ashes. They passed the clay granja where the wall that had been dark with blood was all washed clean again by women of the town as if no blood had ever been there. The girl told him of the executions and named each man who died and told who he was and how he stood and how he fell. The women were held back until the last man was shot and then the captain had stood aside and they rushed forward to try to hold the men in their arms as they died.

Y tú? said the blind man.

She'd gone first to her father but he was already dead. Then to each of her brothers in turn, the elder first. But they also were dead. She walked among the women where they squatted on the ground and held the dead bodies to themselves and rocked and wept. The soldiers went away. A dogfight broke out in the street. After a while some men came with carretas. She walked about carrying her father's hat. She didnt know what to do with it.

She was still holding the hat in her lap at midnight sitting in the church when the sepulturero stopped to speak to her. He told her that she should go home but she said that her father and her brothers were dead in her house on their mats and a candle burned in the floor and that she had nowhere to sleep. She said that all her house was taken up with the dead and so she had come to the church. The sepulturero listened. Then he sat beside her on the raw wood bench. The hour was late, the church empty. They sat side by side holding their hats, she the sombrero of woven straw, he the dusty black fedora. She was crying. He sighed and seemed himself weary and cast down. He said that while one would like to say that God will punish those who do such things and that people often speak in just this way it was his experience that God could not be spoken for and that men with wicked histories often enjoyed lives of comfort and that they died in peace and were buried with honor. He said that it was a mistake to expect too much of justice in this world. He said that the notion that evil is seldom rewarded was greatly overspoken for if there were no advantage to it then men would shun it and how could virtue then be attached to its repudiation? It was the nature of his profession that his experience with death should be greater than for most and he said that while it was true that time heals bereavement it does so only at the cost of the slow extinction of those loved ones from the heart's memory which is the sole place of their abode then or now. Faces fade, voices dim. Seize them back, whispered the sepulturero. Speak with them. Call their names. Do this and do not let sorrow die for it is the sweetening of every gift.

The girl respoke these words to the blind man where they stood before the granja wall. She said that the young girls had come and dipped their pañuelos in the blood of the slain where it pooled in the dirt or torn off strips from the hems of their pettiskirts. There was a great coming and going in this commerce as of some band of witless nurses wrenched from all memory of their right function. The blood soon soaked into the earth and with fall of dark before the rain began packs of dogs arrived and gouged up mouthfuls of the bloodsoaked mud and ate it down and snapped and quarreled and slank away again and in the day once more there was no sign remaining of death and blood and murder.

They stood in silence and then the blind man touched the girl, her face and cheek and lips. He did not ask to do so. She stood very still. He touched her eyes each in turn. She asked if he had been a soldier and he said that he had been and she asked if he had killed many men and he said none. She asked that he lean down so that she could close her eyes and touch his own face to see what could be known in that way and he did so. He did not say that it would not be the same for her. When she came to the eyes she hesitated.

Ándale, he said. Está bien.

She touched the wrinkled lids caved into the sockets. She touched them gently with the tips of her fingers and she asked if there were any pain there but he said there was only the pain of memory and that sometimes in the night he would dream that this darkness were itself a dream and he would wake and he would touch those eyes that were not there. He said such dreams were a torment to him and yet he would not wish them away. He said that as the memory of the world must fade so must it fade in his dreams until soon or late he feared that he would have darkness absolute and no shadow of the world that was. He said that he feared what that darkness held for he believed that the world hid more than it revealed.

In the street people were shuffling past. Persínese, the girl whispered. The blind man would not turn loose her hand but leaned his staff against his waist and blessed himself clumsily with his left hand. The cortege passed. The girl gripped his hand anew and they went on.

Among her father's clothes she found him coat and shirt and trousers. She put what few other clothes were in the house into a muslin sack and tied it shut and she took the kitchen knife and molcajete and some spoons together with what food there was and tied them up in an old Saltillo serape. The house was cool and smelled of the earth. Outside among the cloistered walls and warrens he could hear yardfowl, a goat, a child. She brought water in a bucket for him to wash himself and he did so with a rag and then put on the clothes. He stood in the one small room that was the house entire and waited for her to return. The door stood open to the road and people going past in the street on their way to the cemetery could see him standing there. When she came back she took his hand again and she said that he was guapo in his new clothes and she gave him an apple of those she had bought and they stood in the room eating the apples and then shouldered up the bundles and set out together.

The woman leaned back. The boy thought that she would continue but she did not. They sat in silence.

Era la muchacha, he said.

Sí.

He looked at the blind man. The blind man sat with his drawn face half enshadowed in the light of the oil lamp. He must have sensed the boy studying him. Es una carantoña, no? he said.

No, Billy said. Y ademas, no me dijo que los aspectos de las cosas son engañosas?

Because the blind man's face lacked all expression one could not tell when he would speak or if he would at all. After a while he raised one hand from the table in that odd gesture of blessing or despair. Para mi, sí, he said.

Billy looked at the woman. She sat as before, her hands folded upon the table. He asked the blind man had he heard of others who had suffered the same calamity as he at that man's hands but the blind man only said that he had heard, yes, but had not seen nor met. He said that the blind do not seek each other's company. He told how once in the alameda in Chihuahua he had heard a cane come tapping and he'd called out his own condition and asked if another such were there in that mutual darkness. The tapping ceased. No one spoke. Then the tapping commenced again and withdrew down the walkway and faded among the sounds of traffic in the street.

He leaned slightly forward. Entienda que ya existe este ogro. Este chupador de ojos. Él y otros como él. Ellos no han desaparecido del mundo. Y nunca lo haran.

Billy asked him if such men as had stole his eyes were only products of the war but the blind man said that since war itself was their very doing that could hardly be the case. He said that in his opinion no one could speak for the origins of such men nor where they might appear but only of their existence. He said that who steals one's eyes steals a world and himself remains thereby forever hidden. How to speak of his locality?

Y sus sueños, said the boy. Se han hecho más pálidos?

The blind man sat for some time. He could have been sleeping. He could have been waiting for word to be brought to him. Finally he said that in his first years of darkness his dreams had been vivid beyond all expectation and that he had come to thirst for them but that dreams and memories alike had faded one by one until they were no more. Of all that once had been no trace remained. The look of the world. The faces of loved ones. Finally even his own person was lost to him. Whatever he had been he was no more. He said that like every man who comes to the end of something there was nothing to be done but to begin again. No puedo recordar el mundo de luz, he said. Hace muchos años. Ese mundo es un mundo frágil. Ultimamente lo que vine a ver era más durable. Más verdadero.

He spoke of the first years of his blindness in which the world about him awaited his movements. He said that men with eyes may select what they wish to see but for the blind the world appears of its own will. He said that for the blind everything was abruptly at hand, that nothing ever announced its approach. Origins and destinations became but rumors. To move is to abut against the world. Sit quietly and it vanishes. En mis primeros años de la oscuridad pensé que la ceguedad fué una forma de la muerte. Estuve equivocado. Al perder la vista es como un sueño de caída. Se piensa que no hay ningún fondo de este abismo. Se cae y cae. La luz retrocede. La memoria de la luz. La memoria del mundo. De su propia cara. De la carantoña.

He raised one hand slowly and held it before him. As if in measure of something. He said that if this falling were a falling to death then it was death itself that was different than men supposed. Where is the world in this falling? Is it also receding away with the light and the memory of the light? Or does it not fall also? He said that in his blindness he had indeed lost himself and all memory of himself yet he had found in the deepest dark of that loss that there also was a ground and there one must begin.

En este viaje el mundo visible es no más que un distraimiento. Para los ciegos y para todos los hombres. Ultimamente sabemos que no podemos ver el buen Dios. Vamos escuchando. Me entiendes, joven? Debemos escuchar.

When he spoke no more the boy asked him if the advice then which the sepulturero had given to the girl in the church had been false advice but the blind man said that the sepulturero had advised according to his lights and should not be faulted. Such men even took it upon themselves to advise the dead. Or to commend them to God once priest and friends and children all have gone to their houses. He said that the sepulturero might presume to speak of a darkness of which he had no knowledge, for had he such knowledge he could not then be a sepulturero. When the boy asked him if this knowledge were a special knowledge only to the blind the blind man said that it was not. He said that most men were in their lives like the carpenter whose work went so slowly for the dullness of his tools that he had not time to sharpen them.

Y las palabras del sepulturero acerca de la justicia? the boy said. Qué opina?

At this the woman reached and took up the bowl of eggshells and said that it was late and that her husband should not tire himself. The boy said that he understood but the blind man said for them not to preoccupy themselves. He said that he had given a certain amount of thought to the question which the boy asked. As had many men before him and as men would after he was gone. He said that even the sepulturero would understand that every tale was a tale of dark and light and would perhaps not have it otherwise. Yet there was still a further order to the narrative and it was a thing of which men do not speak. He said the wicked know that if the ill they do be of sufficient horror men will not speak against it. That men have just enough stomach for small evils and only these will they oppose. He said that true evil has power to sober the smalldoer against his own deeds and in the contemplation of that evil he may even find the path of righteousness which has been foreign to his feet and may have no power but to go upon it. Even this man may be appalled at what is revealed to him and seek some order to stand against it. Yet in all of this there are two things which perhaps he will not know. He will not know that while the order which the righteous seek is never righteousness itself but is only order, the disorder of evil is in fact the thing itself. Nor will he know that while the righteous are hampered at every turn by their ignorance of evil to the evil all is plain, light and dark alike. This man of which we speak will seek to impose order and lineage upon things which rightly have none. He will call upon the world itself to testify as to the truth of what are in fact but his desires. In his final incarnation he may seek to indemnify his words with blood for by now he will have discovered that words pale and lose their savor while pain is always new.

Quizás hay poca de justicia en este mundo, the blind man said. But not for the reasons which the sepulturero supposes. It is rather that the picture of the world is all the world men know and this picture of the world is perilous. That which was given him to help him make his way in the world has power also to blind him to the way where his true path lies. The key to heaven has power to open the gates of hell. The world which he imagines to be the ciborium of all godlike things will come to naught but dust before him. For the world to survive it must be replenished daily. This man will be required to begin again whether he wishes to or no. Somos dolientes en la oscuridad. Todos nosotros. Me entiendes? Los que pueden ver, los que no pueden.

The boy studied the mask in the lamplight. Lo que debemos entender, said the blind man, es que ultimamente todo es polvo. Todo lo que podemos tocar. Todo lo que podemos ver. En éste tenemos la evidencia más profunda de la justicia, de la misericordia. En éste vemos la bendición más grande de Dios.

The woman rose. She said that it was late. The blind man made no move to do so. He sat as before. The boy looked at him. Finally he asked him why this was such a blessing and the blind man did not answer and did not answer and then at last he said that because what can be touched falls into dust there can be no mistaking these things for the real. At best they are only tracings of where the real has been. Perhaps they are not even that. Perhaps they are no more than obstacles to be negotiated in the ultimate sightlessness of the world.

In the morning when he walked out to saddle his horse the woman was scattering grain from a bota to the birds in the yard. Wild blackbirds flew down from the trees and stalked and fed among the poultry but she fed all without discrimination. The boy watched her. He thought she was very beautiful. He saddled the horse and left it standing and said his goodbyes and then mounted up and rode out. When he looked back she raised her hand. The birds were all about her. Vaya con Dios, she called.

He turned the horse into the road. He'd not gone far when the dog came out of the chaparral and fell in beside the horse. He had been in a fight and he was cut and bloody and held one paw to his chest. Billy halted the horse and looked down at him. The dog limped forward a few steps and stood.

Where's Boyd? Billy said.

The dog pricked its ears and looked about.

You dumb-ass.

The dog looked toward the house.

He was in the truck. He aint here.

He put the horse forward and the dog fell in behind and they set out north along the road.

Before noon they struck the main road north to Casas Grandes and he sat in that empty desert crossroads and looked off up-country and back to the south but there was nothing to be seen save sky and road and desert. The sun stood almost overhead. He slid the shotgun out of the dusty leather scabbard and unbreeched it and took out the shell and looked at the wad end to see what size shot it held. It was number five and he thought about putting in the buckshot load but in the end he put the number five shell back in the chamber and breeched the gun shut and put it back in the scabbard and set out north along the road to San Diego, the dog limping at the horse's heels. Where's Boyd? he said. Where's Boyd?

That night he slept in a field wrapped in the blanket the woman had given him. The breaks of a river lay across the plain perhaps a mile distant and that was the way the horse would have gone. He lay on the cooling earth and watched the stars. The dark shape of the horse off to his left where he'd staked it. The horse raising its head above the skyline to listen among the constellations and then bending to graze again. He studied those worlds sprawled in their pale ignitions upon the nameless night and he tried to speak to God about his brother and after a while he slept. He slept and woke from a troubling dream and could not sleep again.

He'd trudged in his dream through a deep snow along a ridge toward a darkened house and the wolves had followed him as far as the fence. They ran their lean mouths against each other's flanks and they flowed about his knees and furrowed the snow with their noses and tossed their heads and in the cold their pooled breath made a cauldron about him and the snow lay so blue in the moonlight and those eyes were palest topaz where they crouched and whined and tucked their tails and they fawned and shuddered as they drew close to the house and their teeth shone that were so white and their red tongues lolled. At the gate they would go no further. They looked back toward the dark shapes of the mountains. He knelt in the snow and reached out his arms to them and they touched his face with their wild muzzles and drew away again and their breath was warm and it smelled of the earth and the heart of the earth. When the last of them had come forward they stood in a crescent before him and their eyes were like footlights to the ordinate world and then they turned and wheeled away and loped off through the snow and vanished smoking into the winter night. In the house his parents slept and when he crawled into his bed Boyd turned to him and whispered that he'd had a dream and in the dream Billy had run away from home and when he woke from the dream and seen his empty bed he'd thought that it was true.

Go to sleep, Billy said.

You wont run off and leave me will you Billy?

No.

You promise?

Yes. I promise.

No matter what?

Yes. No matter what.

Billy?

Go to sleep.

Billy.

Hush. You'll wake them.

But in the dream Boyd only said softly that they would not wake.

The dawn was long in coming. He rose and walked out on the desert prairie and scanned the east for light. In the gray beginnings of the day the calls of doves from the acacias. A wind coming down from the north. He rolled the blanket and ate the last of the tortillas and the boiled eggs she'd given him and he saddled the horse and rode out as the sun came up out of the ground to the east.

Within the hour it was raining. He untied the blanket from behind him and pulled it over his shoulders. He could see the rain coming across the country in a gray wall and soon it was pounding the flat gray clay of the bajada through which he rode. The horse plodded on. The dog walked beside. They looked like what they were, outcasts in an alien land. Homeless, hunted, weary.

He rode all day the broad barrial between the breaks of the river and the long straight bight of the roadway to the west. The rain slacked but it did not stop. It rained all day. Twice he saw riders ahead on the plain and he halted the horse but the riders rode on. In the evening he crossed the railroad tracks and entered the pueblo of Mata Ortíz.

He halted before the door of a small blue tienda and got down and halfhitched the reins to a post and entered and stood in the partial darkness. A woman's voice spoke to him. He asked her if there was a doctor in this place.

Médico? she said. Médico?

She was sitting in a chair at the end of the counter with what looked like a flywhisk cradled in her arms.

En este pueblo, he said.

She studied him. As if trying to ascertain the nature of his illness. Or his wounds. She said that there was no doctor nearer than Casas Grandes. Then she half rose out of the chair and began to hiss and to make shooing gestures at him with the whisk.

Mam? he said.

She fell back laughing. She shook her head and put her hand to her mouth. No, she said. No. El perro. El perro. Dispensame.

He turned and saw the dog standing in the doorway behind him. The woman rose heavily still laughing and came forward tugging at a pair of old wirerimmed spectacles. She set them on the bridge of her nose and took him by the arm and turned him to the light.

Güero, she said. Busca el herido, no?

Es mi hermano.

They stood in silence. She had not turned loose of his arm. He tried to see into her eyes but the light played off the glass of her spectacles and one of the panes was half opaque with dirt as if perhaps she had no vision in that eye and saw no need to clean it.

El vivía? he said.

She said that he was living when he passed by her door and that people had followed the truck to the end of the town and that he was alive to the limits of Mata Ortíz and beyond that who could say?

He thanked her and turned to go.

Es su perro? she said.

He said that it was his brother's dog. She said that she'd

guessed as much for the dog wore a worried look. She looked out into the street where the horse stood.

Es su caballo, she said.

Sí.

She nodded. Bueno, she said. Monte, caballero. Monte y vaya con Dios.

He thanked her and walked out to the horse and untied it and mounted up. He turned and touched the brim of his hat to the old woman where she stood in the door.

Momento, she called.

He waited. In a moment a young girl came out and eased past the woman and came to the stirrup of his horse and looked up at him. She was very pretty and very shy. She held up one hand, her fist closed.

Qué tiene? he said.

Tómelo.

He held out his hand and she dropped into it a small silver heart. He turned it to the light and looked at it. He asked her what it was.

Un milagro, she said.

Milagro?

Sí. Para el güero. El güero herido.

He turned the heart in his hand and looked down at her.

No era herido en el corazón, he said. But she only looked away and did not answer and he thanked her and dropped the heart into his shirtpocket. Gracias, he said. Muchas gracias.

She stepped back from the horse. Que joven tan valiente, she said and he agreed that indeed his brother was brave and he touched his hat again and raised his hand to the old woman where she stood in the doorway still clutching the whisk and he put the horse forward down the single mud street of Mata Ortíz north toward San Diego.

It was dark and starless from the overcast of rain when he crossed the bridge and rode up the hill toward the domicilios. The same dogs sallied forth howling and circled the horse and he rode past the dimly lighted doorways and past the remains of the evening fires where the haze of woodsmoke hung over the compound in the damp air. He saw no one run to carry news of his arrival yet when he arrived at the door of the Muñoz house the woman was standing there waiting for him. People were coming out of the houses. He sat the horse and looked down at her.

Él está? he said.

Sí. Él está.

Él vive?

Él vive.

He dismounted and handed the reins to the boy standing nearest in the company gathered about him and took off his hat and entered the low doorway. The woman followed him. Boyd lay on a pallet at the far side of the room. The dog was already curled on the pallet with him. About him on the floor stood gifts of food and gifts of flowers and holy images of wood or clay or cloth and little handmade wooden boxes that held milagros and ollas and baskets and glass bottles and figurines. In the wall niche above him a candle in a glass burned at the feet of the poor wooden Madonna but there was no light other.

Regalos de los obreros, the woman whispered.

Del ejido?

She said that some of the gifts were from the ejido but that mostly they were from the workers who had carried him here. She said the truck had returned and the men had filed in holding their hats and placed these gifts before him.

Billy squatted and looked down at Boyd. He pulled back the blanket and pushed up the shirt he wore. Boyd was wrapped in muslin windings like someone dressed for death and he'd bled through the cloth and the blood was dry and black. He put his hand on his brother's forehead and Boyd opened his eyes.

How you doin, pardner? he said.

I thought they got you, Boyd whispered. I thought you was dead.

I'm right here.

That good Niño horse.

Yeah. That good Niño horse.

He was pale and hot. You know what I am today? he said.

No, what are you?

Fifteen. If I dont make it another day.

Dont you worry about that.

He turned to the woman. Qué dice el médico?

The woman shook her head. There was no doctor. They'd sent for an old woman no more than a bruja and she had bound his wounds with a poultice of herbs and given him a tea to drink.

Y qué dice la bruja? Es grave?

The woman turned away. In the light from the niche he could see the tears on her dark face. She bit her lower lip. She did not answer. Damn you, he whispered.

It was three oclock in the morning when he rode into Casas Grandes. He crossed the high embankment of the railroad track and rode up Alameda Street until he saw a light in a cantina. He dismounted and went in. At a table near the bar a man lay asleep in his crossed arms and otherwise the room was empty.

Hombre, Billy said.

The man jerked upright. The boy before him had every air of those bearing grave news. He sat warily with his hands on the table at either side.

El médico, Billy said. Dónde vive el médico.

THE DOCTOR'S MOZO unlocked and unlatched the door cut into the wooden gate and stood there just inside the darkened zaguán. He did not speak but only waited to hear the supplicant's tale. When Billy was done he nodded. Bueno, he said. Pásale.

He stepped aside and Billy entered and the mozo resecured the door. Espere aquí, he said. Then he went padding away over the cobbles and disappeared in the dark.

He waited a long time. From the rear of the zaguán came the smell of green plants and earth and humus. A rustle of wind. Of things disturbed that had been sleeping. Outside the gate

Niño whinnied softly. Finally a light came on in the patio and the mozo reappeared. Behind him the doctor.

He was not dressed but came forward in his robe, one hand in his robe pocket. A small and unkempt man.

Dónde está su hermano? he said.

En el ejido de San Diego.

Y cuándo ocurrió ese accidente?

Hace dos días.

The doctor studied the boy's face in the pale and yellow light.

He is very hot?

I dont know. Yes. Some.

The doctor nodded. Bueno, he said. He told the mozo to start the car and then turned back to Billy. I will need some minutes, he said. Five minutes.

He held up one hand and spread his fingers.

Yessir.

You have nothing to pay of course.

I got a good horse outside. I'll give you the horse.

I dont want your horse.

I got papers on him. Tengo los papeles.

The doctor had already turned to go. Bring in the horse, he said. You can put the horse here.

Have you got room to where we can take the saddle with us? The saddle?

I'd like to keep the saddle. My daddy give it to me. I got no way to carry it back.

You can carry it back on the horse.

You wont take the horse?

No. It is all right.

He stood outside in the street holding Niño while the mozo slid back the bars and opened the tall wooden gates. He started through leading the horse but the mozo cautioned him back and told him to wait and then turned and disappeared. After a while he heard the car start up and the mozo came driving up through the zaguán in an old Dodge opera coupe. He drove out into the street and got out and left the motor running and took the bridlereins and led the horse in through the gates and on toward the rear.

In a few minutes the doctor appeared. He was dressed in a dark suit and the mozo followed behind carrying his medical bag.

Listo? the doctor said.

Listo.

The doctor walked around the car and climbed in. The mozo handed in the bag and shut the door. Billy climbed in the other side and the doctor turned on the lights and the motor died.

He sat waiting. The mozo opened the door and reached under the seat and got the crank and walked around in front of the car and the doctor turned the lights off. The mozo bent and fitted the crank into the slot and raised up and gave it a turn and the motor started again. The doctor ran the engine up loudly and turned the lights back on and rolled down the window and took the crank from the mozo. Then he pulled the shiftlever in the floor down into first and they pulled away.

The street was narrow and ill lit and the yellow beams of the headlamps ran out to a wall at the end of it. A family of people were just entering the street, the man walking ahead, behind him a woman and two halfgrown girls carrying baskets and shabbily tied bundles. They froze in the headlights like deer and their postures mimicked the shadows volunteered outsized upon the wall behind them, the man standing upright and erect and the woman and the older girl throwing up one arm as if to protect themselves. The doctor levered the big wooden steering wheel to the left and the headlights swung away and the figures vanished once more into the indenominate dark of the Mexican night.

Tell me of this accident, the doctor said.

My brother got shot in the chest with a rifle.

And when did this happen?

Two days ago.

Does he speak?

Sir?

Does he speak? Is he awake?

Yessir. He's awake. He never did talk much.

Yes, said the doctor. Of course. He lit a cigarette and smoked quietly on the road south. He said that the car had a radio and that Billy could play it if he wished but Billy thought that the doctor would play it himself if he wanted to hear it. After a while the doctor did so. They listened to american hillbilly music coming out of Acuña on the Texas border and the doctor drove and smoked in silence and the hot eyes of cattle feeding in the bar ditches at the side of the road floated up in the carlights and everywhere the desert stretched away in the dark beyond.

They turned up the ejido road through the river loam and the pale shapes of the cottonwood trunks passing in the lights and lumbered over the wooden bridge and up the hill and into the compound. The ejido dogs crossed back and forth in the lights howling. Billy pointed their way and they drove up past the darkened doors of the sleeping communals and halted before the dim yellow light where his brother lay within among his offerings like some feastday icon. The doctor shut off the engine and the lights and reached for the bag but Billy had already taken it to carry. He nodded and stepped out of the car and adjusted his hat and entered the house with Billy behind him.

The Muñoz woman had already come from the other room and she stood in the frail light of the votive candle in the only dress Billy had ever seen her in and wished the doctor a good evening. The doctor handed her his hat and then unbuttoned his coat and slipped it from his shoulders and held it up and turned it and reached his glasses in their case from the inside pocket. Then he handed the coat to the woman and removed his cufflinks left and right and put them in his trouser pocket and turned up his starched white shirtsleeves two turns each and sat on the low pallet and took the glasses from their case and put them on and looked at Boyd. He placed one hand on Boyd's forehead. Cómo estás? he said. Cómo te sientes?

Nunca mejor, wheezed Boyd.

The doctor smiled. He turned to the woman. Hiérvame algo de agua, he said. Then he took from his pocket a small nickel-plated flashlight and leaned over Boyd. Boyd closed his eyes but the doctor pulled down the lower lid of each eye in turn and examined them. He waved the light slowly back and forth across the pupils and looked in. Boyd tried to turn his head away but the doctor had placed his hand alongside his cheek. Véame, he said.

He pulled back the blanket. Something small scurried away over the muslin. Boyd was wearing one of the white cotton jumpers the workers in the field wore and it had neither collar nor buttons. The doctor pushed it up and pulled Boyd's right elbow down from the sleeve and pulled it over his head and then very carefully pulled the garment down off of Boyd's left arm and handed it to Billy without even looking at him. Boyd lay wrapped in cotton sheeting and his wound had bled through the winding and the blood had dried and blackened. The doctor slid the flat of his hand up under the wrappings and placed his hand on Boyd's chest. Respire, he said. Respire profundo. Boyd breathed but his breathing was shallow and labored. The doctor slid his hand to the left side of his chest near to the dark stains in the sheeting and told him to breathe again. He bent and unsnapped the clasps on his bag and took out his stethoscope and hung it around his neck and he took out a pair of spade-ended scissors and cut through the filthy windings and lifted back the severed ends all stiff with blood. He placed his fingers on Boyd's naked chest and tapped his left middle finger with his right and listened. He moved his hand and thumped again. He moved his hand down to Boyd's caved and sallow abdomen and probed gently with his fingers. He watched the boy's face.

Tienes muchos amigos, he said. No?

Cómo? wheezed Boyd.

Tantos regalos.

He lifted the earpieces of the stethoscope into place and put the cone on Boyd's chest and listened. He moved it from the right to the left. Respire profundo, he said. Por la boca. Otra vez. Bueno. He placed the cone over Boyd's heart and listened. He listened with his eyes closed.

Billy, Boyd wheezed.

Shh, said the doctor. He put his fingers to his lips. No habla.

He dropped the earpieces of the stethoscope down about his neck and he lifted by its chain a gold casewatch from his waistcoat pocket and snapped it open with his thumb. He sat with two fingers pressed to the side of Boyd's neck beneath his jaw and he tilted the white porcelained face of the watch toward the votive lamp and sat watching quietly while the needlethin sweepsecond hand sectored the dial with its small black roman numbers.

Cuándo puedo yo hablar? Boyd whispered.

The doctor smiled. Ahora si quieres, he said.

Billy?

Yeah.

You dont have to stay.

I'm all right.

You dont have to stay if you dont want. It's all right.

I aint goin nowheres.

The doctor slid the watch back into his waistcoat. Saca la lengua, he said.

He examined Boyd's tongue and he put his finger inside Boyd's mouth and felt the inner face of his cheek. Then he bent and picked up the bag and set it on the pallet beside him and opened the bag and tilted it slightly toward the light. The bag was of heavy pebbled leather dyed black and it was scuffed and worn at the corners and the leather there and along the edges had gone brown again. The brass catches were worn from eighty years of use for his father had carried it before him. He took out a bloodpressure cuff and wrapped it around Boyd's thin upper arm and pumped the contrivance with the bulb. He placed the cone of the stethoscope in the crook of Boyd's arm and listened. He watched the needle drop and watched it bounce. In

the panes of his antique eyeglasses the thin and upright flame
of the votive lamp stood centered. Very small, very steadfast.
Like the light of holy inquiry burning in his aging eyes. He
unwound the cloth and turned to Billy.

Hay una mesa chica en la casa? O una silla?

Hay una silla.

Bueno. Tráigala. Y tráigame una contenidor de agua. Una
bota o cualquiera cosa que tenga.

Sí señor.

Y traiga un vaso de agua potable.

Yessir.

Él debe tomar agua. Me entiendes?

Yessir.

Y deja abierta la puerta. Necesitamos aire.

Yessir. I will.

He came back carrying the chair upside down over his arm
by the rung and he had a clay olla of water in one hand and
a cup of wellwater in the other. The doctor had risen and he
had donned a white apron and he was holding a towel and a
bar of darklooking soap. Bueno, he said. He folded the soap
in the towel and stuck it beneath his arm and took the chair
from Billy carefully and righted it and set it in the floor and
turned it slightly in the place he wished for it to go. He took
the olla from Billy and set it on the chair and he bent and sorted
through his bag and came up with a bent glass straw and stood
it in the cup Billy was holding. He said for him to give his
brother the water to drink. He said for him to see that he drank
slowly.

Yessir, Billy said.

Bueno, said the doctor. He took the towel from under his
arm and rolled his sleeves up each another turn. He looked
down at Billy.

No te preocupes, he said.

Yessir, said Billy. I'll try.

The doctor nodded and turned and left to go wash his hands.
Billy sat on the pallet and leaned forward and held the cup and

the straw for Boyd to drink. I can pull these covers up, he said. Are you cold? You aint cold are you?

I aint cold.

Here you go.

Boyd drank.

Dont drink too fast, Billy said. He tilted the cup. You looked like one of these dirtfarmers in that rig.

Boyd drank deeply through the straw and then turned away coughing.

Dont drink so fast.

He lay getting his breath. He drank again. Billy took the cup away and waited and then offered it again. The glass pipe rattled and sucked. He tilted the cup. When Boyd had drunk all the water he lay getting his breath and he looked up at Billy. There's worse things to look like, he said.

Billy set the cup on the chair. I didnt take much care of you did I? he said.

Boyd didnt answer.

The doctor says you're goin to be all right.

Boyd lay breathing shallowly, his head back. He stared at the dark vigas of the ceiling overhead.

He says you're goin to be good as new.

I didnt hear him say it, Boyd said.

When the doctor came back Billy picked up the cup and rose and stood holding it. The doctor was drying his hands. Él tenía sed, verdad?

Yessir, Billy said.

The woman came through the door carrying a pail of steaming water. Billy went to her and took the bucket by the bail and the doctor gestured for him to place it on the hearth. He folded the towel and laid it by his bag and laid the soap on top of it and sat. Bueno, he said. Bueno. He turned to Billy. Ayúdame, he said.

Together they turned Boyd on his side. Boyd gasped and clutched about in the air with one hand. He seized Billy's shoulder.

Easy pardner, Billy said. I know it hurts.

No you dont, wheezed Boyd.

Está bien, said the doctor. Está bien así.

He gently pulled away the stained and blackened sheeting from Boyd's chest and lifted it free and handed it up to the woman. He left the black and weedy poultices in place, the one on his chest and the larger one behind his shoulder. He leaned over the boy and pressed the poultices gently each in turn to see if anything should run from beneath them and he tested the air tentatively with his nose for any hint of rot. Bueno, he said. Bueno. He touched gently the area under Boyd's arm between the poultices where the skin was blue and swollenlooking.

La entrada es en el pecho, no?

Sí, said Billy.

He nodded and took up the towel and soap and dipped the towel in the olla of water and soaped it and set about cleaning Boyd's back and chest, washing carefully around the poultices and under his arm. He rinsed the towel in the olla and squeezed it out and bent and wiped away the soap. The towel where he turned it was dark with grime. No estás demasiado frío? he said. Estás cómodo? Bueno. Bueno.

When he was done he laid the towel by and set the olla in the floor and leaned and took from his bag a folded towel which he laid on the chair and opened carefully with just his fingertips. Inside was a second towel cured in the autoclave and done up in a bundle fastened with tape. He gently pried loose and lifted away the tape and holding the edges delicately between thumb and finger he spread the towel open upon the chair seat. Inside were gauze squares and squares of muslin and cottonballs. Small folded towels. Rolls of cloth bandage. He lifted his hands away without touching anything and he took two small enameled pans nested together from his bag and one he laid near the bag and the other he leaned and dipped partly full of hot water from the bucket and then conveyed it carefully in both hands to the chair and set it at the edge of the chair away from the bandages. He selected from their fitted compartments in his case his tools of nickel steel. Sharpnosed scissors and forceps and hemostats some dozen in number. Boyd watched. Billy watched. He dropped the instruments into the pan and he took from the bag a small red bulb syringe and placed that in the pan and he took out a small tin of bismuth and he took out two small sticks of silver nitrate and unwrapped them from out of their foil coverings and laid them on the towel beside the pan. Then he took out a bottle of iodine and loosed the cap and passed the bottle up to the woman and he held his hands over the pan and instructed her to pour the iodine over his hands. She stepped forward and took the cap from the bottle.

Ándale, he said.

She poured.

Más, he said. Un poquito más.

Because the outer door was open the flame in the glass fluttered and twisted and the little light that it afforded waxed and waned and threatened to expire entirely. The three of them bent over the poor pallet where the boy lay looked like ritual assassins. Bastante, the doctor said. Bueno. He held up his dripping hands. They were dyed a rusty brown. The iodine moved in the pan like marbling blood. He nodded to the woman. Ponga el resto en el agua, he said.

She poured the remainder of the iodine into the pan and the doctor tested the water with one finger and then quickly fished a hemostat from the pan and with the hemostat he took up a packet of the muslin squares and dipped them and held them up to drain. He turned to the woman again. Bueno, he said. Quita la cataplasma.

She put one hand to her mouth. She looked at Boyd and she looked at the doctor.

Ándale pues, he said. Está bien.

She blessed herself and bent and reached and took hold of the rag that bound the poultice and lifted it and slid her thumb beneath the poultice and pulled it away. It was of matted weeds and dark with blood and it came away unwillingly. Like something that had been feeding there. She stepped back and folded it from sight in the dirty sheeting. Boyd lay in the flickering light of the votive candle with a small round hole a few inches above and to the left of his left nipple. The wound was dry and crusted and palelooking. The doctor bent and swabbed it carefully with the cotton. The iodine stained Boyd's skin. Blood welled slowly in the hole and a thin line of it ran across Boyd's chest. The doctor laid a clean gauze square over the wound. They watched it slowly darken with blood. The doctor looked up at the woman.

La otra? she said.

Sí. Por favor.

She leaned and freed the poultice from Boyd's back with her thumb and lifted it away. Larger, blacker, uglier. Beneath it was a ragged hole that yawned redly. About it the flesh was crusted with scale and blackened blood. The doctor placed a sheaf of the gauze squares over the wound and placed a square of muslin over them and pressed upon it with the tips of his fingers and held it there. Slowly the cloth darkened. The doctor placed more patches. A thin trickle of blood ran down Boyd's back. The doctor swabbed it up and pressed again with the tips of his fingers against the wound.

When the bleeding had stopped he took a cloth and dipped it in the iodine solution in the pan and while he held the packing against the wound in the boy's back he set to cleaning closely about both wounds. He dropped the soiled swabs in the dry tray beside him and when he was done he pushed his glasses up on the bridge of his nose with the back of his wrist and looked at Billy.

Take his hand, he said.

Mánde?

Take his hand.

No sé si me va permitir.

Él te permite.

He sat on the edge of the pallet and took hold of Boyd's hand and Boyd clasped it in his grip.

Do your damndest, Boyd whispered.

Qué dice?

Nada, said Billy. Ándale.

The doctor took a sterile cloth and wrapped it around the little flashlight and turned the flashlight on and picked it up and put it in his mouth. Then he dropped the cloth into the pan with the swabs and leaned and took a hemostat from the pan and bent over Boyd and gently lifted away the pads from the exit wound and trained his light upon it. The blood was already beginning to well anew and he placed the hemostat in the wound and snapped it shut.

Boyd bowed and threw his head back but he did not cry out. The doctor took another hemostat from the pan and he dabbed up the blood with a cloth patch and studied the wound with the light and then clamped again. The tendons in Boyd's neck shone taut in the lamplight. The doctor gripped the flashlight in his teeth. Unos pocos minutos más, he said. Unos pocos minutos.

He placed two more hemostats and then he took the red bulb syringe from the pan and filled it with the solution and he instructed the woman to take the towel and hold it against the boy's back. Then he slowly flooded the wound. He cleaned the wound with a swab and flooded it again washing out clots of blood and bits of matter. He reached into the pan with his hand and brought up a hemostat and clamped it in place.

Pobrecito, said the woman.

Unos pocos minutos más, said the doctor.

He flooded the wound out once again with the syringe and he took up one of the sticks of silver nitrate and with a muslin swab held in a hemostat in one hand he cleaned away clots and debris while with the other he cauterized with the silver nitrate. The silver nitrate left pale gray tracks in the tissue. He clamped one more hemostat and again flooded the wound. The woman doubled the towel against Boyd's back and held it. With the forceps the doctor picked out something small from the wound and held it to the light. It was about the size of a grain of wheat and he held it and turned it in the small cone of light.

Qué es eso? Billy said.

The doctor leaned with the flashlight in his teeth so that the boy could see better. Plomo, he said. But it was a small chip flaked off from Boyd's sixth rib and he was referring to the faint metal coloring along the conchoidal edge of the bone. He laid it on the towel together with the forceps and with his forefinger he felt along Boyd's ribs from front to back. He watched Boyd's face while he did so. Te duele? he said. Allá? Allá? Boyd lay with his face turned away. He sounded as if he could hardly breathe.

The doctor took a pair of small sharpnosed scissors from the pan and glanced at Billy and then began to snip away the dead tissue along the edges of the wound. Billy reached and took Boyd's hand in both of his.

Le interesa el perro, the doctor said.

Billy looked toward the door. The dog sat watching them. Git, he said.

Está bien, the doctor said. No lo molesta. Es de su hermano, no?

Sí.

The doctor nodded.

When he was done he instructed the woman to hold the towel beneath the wound in the boy's chest and then he flooded and cleaned it also. He flooded it again and he probed it with a swab. Finally he sat back and took the flashlight from his mouth and laid it on the towel and looked at Billy.

Es un muchacho muy valiente, he said.

Es grave? said Billy.

Es grave, the doctor said. Pero no es muy grave.

Qué sería muy grave?

The doctor adjusted his spectacles, pushing them back again with his wrist. It had grown cold in the room. You could see very faintly the doctor's breath plume and lapse in the lapsing light. A light bead of sweat lay across his forehead. He made the sign of the cross in the air before him. Eso, he said. Eso es muy grave.

He reached and took up the flashlight again, holding it in one of the muslin squares. He put it in his teeth and took up the bulb and refilled it and laid it by and then slowly unclamped the first of the hemostats that lay in a circle of hardware about the wound in Boyd's back. He drew it away very slowly. Then he unclamped the next.

He took up the bulb and gently washed the wound and swabbed it and took up the silver nitrate stick and gently touched it in the wound. He worked from the top of the wound downward. When he had removed the last hemostat and dropped it into the pan he sat for a moment with both hands over Boyd's back as if exhorting him to heal. Then he took up the tin of bismuth and unscrewed the lid and held it over the wounds and shook the white powder over them.

He laid gauze squares on the wounds and over the wound in the boy's back he placed a small clean towel from among his sterile dressings and he taped them down and then he and Billy eased Boyd up and the doctor quickly wrapped him about with a roll of cloth bandaging, passing the roll under his arms, until he reached the end of it. He fastened the end with two small steel clamps and they pulled Boyd's jumper back over him and eased him down again. His head lolled and he sucked a long rasping breath.

Fué muy afortunado, the doctor said.

Cómo?

Que no se le han punzando los pulmones. Que no se le ha quebrado la gran arteria cual era muy cerca de la dirección de la bala. Pero sobre todo que no hay ni gran infección. Muy afortunado.

He wrapped his instruments in the towel and placed them in his bag and he emptied the basins into the bucket and swabbed them out and put them away and closed the bag. He rinsed and dried his hands and stood and took his cufflinks from his pocket and rolled down his sleeves and fastened them. He told the woman that he would return the following day and change the dressings and that he would leave the supplies with her and show her how he wished it to be done. He said that the boy must drink plenty of water. That they must keep him warm. Then he handed Billy his bag and turned and the woman helped him on with his coat and he took his hat and thanked her for her help and ducked out through the low door.

Billy followed him out with the bag and intercepted the doctor coming around to the front of the car with the crank. He handed him the bag and took the crank from him. Permítame, he said.

He bent in the dark and found the slot in the radiator grill with his fingers and fitted the crank and pushed it into the socket. Then he stood and swung the crank. The motor started and the doctor nodded. Bueno, he said. He stepped back along the fender and idled down the throttle and turned and took the crankhandle from Billy and bent and stowed it under the seat.

Gracias, he said.

A usted.

The doctor nodded. He looked toward the doorway where the woman stood and he looked again at Billy. He took a cigarette from his pocket and put it in his mouth.

Se queda con su hermano, he said.

Sí. Acepte el caballo, por favor.

The doctor said that he would not. He said that he would send his mozo with the horse in the morning. He looked at the sky to the east where the first gray light was shaping out the roofline of the hacienda from the accommodate darkness. Ya es de mañana, he said. Viene la madrugada.

Yes, said Billy.

Stay with your brother. I will send the horse.

Then he climbed into the car and pulled shut the door and switched on the lights. There was nothing to see yet the ejiditarios had come to their doorways all down the wall of dwellings, men and women pale in the lights, pale in their clothes of unbleached cotton, children clutching at their knees and all of them watching while the car trundled slowly past and swung around in the compound and went out and down the road with the dogs running alongside howling and leaning to nip at the softly rumpling tires where they turned on the clay.

* * *

WHEN BOYD AWOKE late in the morning Billy was sitting there and when he woke midday and when he woke again in the evening he was there. He sat nodding and tottering on into the twilight and he was surprised to hear his name called.

Billy?

He opened his eyes. He leaned forward.

I dont have no water.

Let me get it. Where's the glass?

Right here. Billy?

What?

You got to go to Namiquipa.

I aint goin nowheres.

She'll think we just ditched her.

I caint leave you.

I'll be all right.

I caint go off down there and leave you.

Yeah you can.

You need somebody to look after you.

Listen, Boyd said. I've done got over all that. Go on like I asked you. You was worried about the horse anyways.

The mozo arrived at noon the day following riding a burro and leading Niño on a rope halter. The workers were in the fields and he rode across the bridge and up past the row of their habitations calling out as he went for señor Páramo. Billy went out and the mozo halted the burro and nodded to him. Su caballo, he said.

He looked at the horse. The horse had been fed and curried and watered and rested and looked another horse altogether and he told the mozo so. The mozo nodded easily and undallied the end of the halter rope from the horn of his saddle and slid from the burro.

Por qué no montaba el caballo? Billy said.

The mozo shrugged. He said that it was not his horse to ride.

Quiere montarlo?

He shrugged again. He stood with the halter rope.

Billy stepped to the horse and unlooped the bridlereins from the saddlehorn where they'd been hung and bridled the horse and let the reins fall and slid the halter off Niño's neck.

Ándale, he said.

The mozo coiled the rope and hung it over the horn of the burro's saddle and walked around the horse and patted him and took up the reins and stepped into the stirrup and swung up. He turned the horse and rode out down the paseo between the row houses and put the horse into a trot and rode up the hill past the hacienda and turned there for he would not take the horse out of sight. He backed the horse and turned it and rode a few figure eights and then galloped the horse down the hill and stopped it in a sliding squat before the door and stepped down all in one motion.

Le gusta? said Billy.

Claro que sí, said the mozo. He leaned and put the flat of his hand on the horse's neck and then nodded and turned and climbed aboard the burro and rode out down the paseo without looking back.

IT WAS ALMOST DARK when he left. The Muñoz woman tried to have him wait until morning but he would not. The doctor had arrived in the late afternoon and he had left the dressings for the woman and a package of epsom salts and the woman had fixed Boyd a tea made from manzanilla and árnica and the root of the golondrina bush. She'd put up provisions for Billy in an old canvas moral and he slung it over the horn of the saddle and mounted up and turned the horse and looked down at her.

Dónde está la pistola? he said.

She said that it was under the pillow beneath his brother's head. He nodded. He looked out down the road toward the bridge and the river and he looked at her again. He asked her if any men had been to the ejido.

Sí, she said. Dos veces.

He nodded again. Es peligroso para ustedes.

She shrugged. She said that life was dangerous. She said that for a man of the people there was no choice.

He smiled. Mi hermano es hombre de la gente?

Sí, she said. Claro.

He rode south along the road through the riverside cottonwoods, riding through the town of Mata Ortíz and riding the moon up out of the west to its cool meridian before he turned off and put up for the remainder of the night in a grove of trees he'd skylighted from the road. He rolled himself in his serape and hung his hat over the tops of his standing boots and did not wake till daylight.

He rode all day the day following. Few cars passed and he saw no riders. In the evening the truck that had carried his brother to San Diego came lumbering down the road from the north in a slow uncoiling of road dust and ground to a stop. The workers on the bed of the truck waved and called out to him and he rode up and pushed his hat back on his head and held up his hand to them. They gathered along the edge of the truckbed and held out their hands and he leaned from the horse and shook hands with them every man. They said that it was dangerous for him to be on the road. They did not ask about Boyd and when he began to tell them they waved away his words for they had been to see him that very day. They said that he had eaten and that he'd drunk a small glass of pulque for the vigor in it and that all signs were of the most affirmative nature. They said that only the hand of the Virgin could have sustained him through such a terrible wound. Herida tan grave, they said. Tan horrible. Herida tan fea.

They spoke of his brother lying with the pistol under his pillow and spoke in a high whisper. Tan joven, they said. Tan valiente. Y peligroso por todo eso. Como el tigre herido en su cueva.

Billy looked at them. He looked out across the cooling country to the west, the long bands of shadow. Doves were calling from the acacias. The workers believed that his brother had killed the

manco in a gunfight in the streets of Boquilla y Anexas. That
the manco had fired upon him without provocation and what
folly for the manco who had not reckoned upon the great heart
of the güerito. They pressed him for details. How the güerito
had risen from his blood in the dust to draw his pistol and shoot
the manco dead from his horse. They addressed Billy with great
reverence and they asked him how it was that he and his brother
had set out upon their path of justice.

He scanned their faces. What he saw in those eyes was very
moving to him. The driver and the two other men in the cab of
the truck had got down and were standing along the bed of the
truck at the rear. All waited to see what he would say. In the
end he told them that the accounts of the conflict were greatly
exaggerated and that his brother was only fifteen years old and
that he himself was to blame for he should have cared better for
his brother. He should not have carried him off to a strange
country to be shot down in the street like a dog. They only
shook their heads and repeated among themselves Boyd's age.
Quince años, they said. Que guapo. Que joven tan enforzado.
In the end he thanked them for their care of his brother and
touched the brim of his hat at which they all crowded again
with their hands outstretched and he shook their hands again
and the hands of the driver and the other two men standing in
the road and then reined the horse around and rode past the
truck and out along the road south. He heard the truckdoors
slam behind him and heard the driver put the truck in gear and
they rumbled slowly past him in the augmenting dust. The
workers on the bed of the truck waved and some took off their
hats and then one of them stood and steadied himself by one
hand on the shoulder of his companion and raised one fist in the
air and shouted to him. Hay justicia en el mundo, he called.
Then they all rode on.

He woke that night with the ground trembling beneath him
and he sat up and looked for the horse. The horse stood with
its head raised against the desert nightsky looking toward the
west. A train was going downcountry, the pale yellow cone of

the headlight boring slowly and sedately down the desert and the distant clatter of the wheeltrucks outlandish and mechanical in that dark waste of silence. Finally the small square windowlight of the caboose trailing after. It passed and left only the faint pale track of boilersmoke hanging over the desert and then came the long lonesome whistle echoing across the country where it called for the crossing at Las Varas.

He rode into Boquilla at noon with the shotgun across the pommel of the saddle. There was no one about. He took the road south to Santa Ana de Babícora. Towards dark he began to come upon riders riding north toward Boquilla, young men and boys with their black hair slicked down on their skulls and their boots polished and the cheap cotton shirts they wore that had been pressed with hot bricks. It was Saturday night and they were going to a dance. They nodded gravely, mounted on burros or on the little distaff mules from the mines. He nodded back, his eyes watching every movement, the shotgun upright against him with the buttstock cradled against his inner thigh. The good horse he rode flaring its nostrils at them. When he rode through La Pinta on the high juniper plain above the Santa María River Valley the moon was up and when he rode into Santa Ana de Babícora it was midnight and the town was dark and empty. He watered the horse in the alameda and took the road west to Namiquipa. An hour's ride he came to a small stream that was part of the headwaters of the Santa María and turned the horse off down out of the road and hobbled him in the river grass and rolled himself into his serape and slept in dreamless exhaustion.

When he woke the sun was hours high. He walked down to the creek carrying his boots and stood in the water and bent and washed his face. When he raised up and looked for the horse the horse was standing looking toward the road. In a few minutes a rider came along. Coming down the road on the horse his mother used to ride was the girl wearing a new dress of blue cotton and a small straw hat with a green ribbon that hung down her back. Billy watched her pass and when she was out of sight he sat in the grass and studied his boots standing there and the slow passing of the small river and the tops of the grass that bent and recovered constantly in the morning breeze. Then he reached for the boots and pulled them on and stood and walked up and bridled and saddled the horse and mounted up and rode out into the road and set out behind her.

When she heard the horse on the road she put her hand on top of her hat and turned and looked back. Then she stopped. He slowed the horse and rode up to her. She fixed him with her dark eyes.

Está muerto? she said. Está muerto?

No.

No me mienta.

Le juro por Dios.

Gracias a Dios. Gracias a Dios. She slid from the horse and dropped the reins and knelt in her new clothes in the dry rutted clay of the road and blessed herself and closed her eyes and folded her hands to pray.

An hour later when they rode back through Santa Ana de Babícora she'd still hardly spoken. It was almost noon and they rode up the one mud street past the lowslung rows of slumped mud buildings and the half dozen painted trees that composed the alameda and on across the upland desert plain again. He saw nothing that looked like a tienda in the town and he'd nothing with which to buy anything if there had been one. She rode a sedate dozen paces behind him and he looked back at her once or twice but she did not smile nor acknowledge him in any way and after a while he didn't look anymore. He knew she'd not left her house without provisions but she didnt mention it and neither did he. A little ways north of the town she spoke behind him and he stopped and turned the horse in the road.

Tienes hambre? she said.

He thumbed his hat back and looked at her. I could eat the runnin gears of a bull moose, he said.

Mánde?

They ate in a grove of acacia by the roadside. She spread her serape and laid out tortillas in a cloth and tamales in their corded wraps of cornhusk and a small jar of frijoles from which she unscrewed the lid and in which she stood a wooden spoon. She opened a cloth containing four empanadas. Two ears of cold corn dusted with red chile powder. The quarter part of a small wheel of goatcheese.

She sat with her legs tucked under her, her head turned for the brim of the hat to shade her face. They ate. When he asked her didnt she want to know about Boyd she said she already knew. He watched her. She seemed fragilely wrapped in her clothing. On her left wrist there was a blue discoloration. Other than that her skin was so perfect it appeared oddly false. As if it had been painted on.

Tienes miedo de los hombres, he said.

Cuáles hombres?

Todos los hombres.

She turned and looked at him. She looked down. He thought that she was reflecting upon the question but she only brushed an escarabajo from the serape and reached and took up one of the empanadas and bit delicately into it.

Y quizás tienes razón, he said.

Quizás.

She looked off to where the horses stood in the roadside grass, their tails whisking. He thought she would say no more but she began to talk about her family. She said that her grandmother had been widowed by the revolution and married again and was widowed again within the year and married a third time and was a third time widowed and wed no more although there were opportunities enough for her to do so as she was a great beauty and not yet twenty years of age when the last husband fell as detailed by his own uncle at Torreón with one hand over his breast in a gesture of fidelity sworn, clutching the rifleball to him like a gift, the sword and pistol he carried falling away behind him useless in the palmettos, in the sand, the riderless horse stepping about in the melee of shot and shell and the cries of men, trotting off with the stirrups flapping, coming back, wandering in silhouette with others of its kind among the bodies of the dead on that senseless plain while the dark drew down around them all about and small birds driven from their arbors in the thorns returned and flitted about and chittered and the moon rose blind and white in the east and the little jackal wolves came trotting that would eat the dead from out of their clothes.

She said that her grandmother was skeptical of many things in this world and of none more than men. She said that in every trade save war men of talent and vigor prosper. In war they die. Her grandmother spoke to her often of men and she spoke with great earnestness and she said that rash men were a great temptation to women and this was simply a misfortune like others and there was little that could be done to remedy it. She said that to be a woman was to live a life of difficulty and heartbreak and those who said otherwise simply had no wish to face the facts. And she said that since this was so nor could it be altered one was better to follow one's heart in joy and in misery than simply to seek comfort for there was none. To seek it was only to welcome in the misery and to know little else. She said that these were things all women knew yet seldom spoke of. Lastly she said that if women were drawn to rash men it was only that in their secret hearts they knew that a man who would not kill for them was of no use at all.

She had finished eating. She sat with her hands folded in her lap and the things she'd said sorted oddly with her composure. The road was empty, the country silent. He asked her if she thought that Boyd would kill a man. She turned and studied him. As if he were someone for whom words must be weighed so as to accommodate their understanding. Finally she said that the word was abroad in the country. That all the world knew that the güerito had killed the gerente from Las Varitas. The man who had betrayed Socorro Rivera and sold out his own people to the Guardia Blanca of La Babícora.

Billy listened to all this and when she was done he said that the manco had fallen from his horse and broken his back and that he himself had seen it happen.

He waited. After a while she looked up.

Quieres algo más? she said.

No. Gracias.

She began to pack up the remains of their picnic. He watched her but he made no move to help. He rose and she folded the serape and rolled the remainder of the provisions in it and retied it with the cords.

No sabes nada de mi hermano, he said.

Quizás, she said.

She stood with the rolled serape over her shoulder.

Por qué no me contesta? he said.

She looked up at him. She said that she had answered him. She said that in every family there is one who is different and the others believe that they know that person but they do not know that person. She said that she herself was such a one and knew whereof she spoke. Then she turned and walked out to where the horses were grazing in the dusty roadside weeds and tied the serape on behind the cantle and tightened the cinch and stood up into the saddle.

He mounted up and rode the horse past her into the road. Then he stopped and looked back. He said that there were things about his brother that only his family could know and that as his family was dead there was no one who knew save he. Every small thing. Any time that he was sick as a child or the day he was bitten by a scorpion and thought he was going to die or any of his life in another part of the country that even Boyd remembered little of or none at all including his grandmother and his twin sister dead and buried in that long ago in a place he'd likely never see again.

Sabías que él tenía una gemela? he said. Que murió cuando tenía cinco años?

She said that she did not know that Boyd had once had a twin sister or that she died but that it was not important for now he had another. Then she put the horse forward and went past him and into the road.

An hour later they overtook three young girls afoot. Two of

them carried a basket between them with a cloth over it. They were on their way to the pueblo of Soto Maynez and they had yet a ways to go. They looked back when they heard the riders on the road behind them and they huddled together laughing and when the riders passed they pushed one another to the verge of the road and looked up with their quick dark eyes and laughed behind their hands. Billy touched his hat and rode on but the girl stopped and walked the horse beside them and when he looked back she was talking to them. They were little younger than she but she was calling them to task in that same low flat voice. Finally they stopped and stood back against the roadside chaparral but here she halted the horse entirely and continued until she was done. Then she turned and put the horse forward and did not look back.

They rode all day. It was dark when they entered La Boquilla and he rode through the town as he had come with the shotgun upright before him. When they passed the spot where the manco had fallen she made the sign of the cross and kissed her fingers. Then they rode on. The sparse trunks of the painted alameda trees stood pale as bone in the light from the windows. Some windows of glass but mostly oiled butcherpaper tacked up in frames and behind them neither movement nor shadow but only those sallow squares like parchments or old barren maps long weathered of any trace of their terrains or routes upon them. On the outskirts of the settlement there was a fire burning just off the roadside and they slowed and rode past cautiously but the fire appeared to be only a trashfire and there was no one about and they rode on into the dark country to the west.

That night they camped in a swale at the edge of the lake and shared the last of the provisions she'd brought. When he asked her would she not have been afraid to ride through this country by herself at night she said that there was no remedy for it and that one must put oneself in the care of God.

He asked if God always looked after her and she studied the heart of the fire for a long time where the coals breathed bright and dull and bright again in the wind from the lake. At last she said that God looked after everything and that one could no more evade his care than evade his judgment. She said that even the wicked could not escape his love. He watched her. He said that he himself had no such idea of God and that he'd pretty much given up praying to Him and she nodded without taking her eyes from the fire and said that she knew that.

She took her blanket and went off down by the lake. He watched her go and then shucked off his boots and rolled his serape about him and fell into a troubled sleep. He woke some-time in the night or in the early morning and turned and looked at the fire to see how long he'd slept but the fire was all but cold on the ground. He looked to the east to see if there were any trace of dawn graying over the country but there was only the darkness and the stars. He prodded the ashes with a stick. The few red coals that turned up in the fire's black heart seemed secret and improbable. Like the eyes of things disturbed that had best been left alone. He rose and walked down to the lake with the serape about his shoulders and he looked at the stars in the lake. The wind had died and the water lay black and still. It lay like a hole in that high desert world down into which the stars were drowning. Something had woke him and he thought perhaps he'd heard riders on the road and that they'd seen his fire but there was no fire to see and then he thought perhaps the girl had risen and come to the fire and stood over him where he slept and he remembered tasting rain on his face but there was no rain nor had there been and then he remembered his dream. In the dream he was in another country that was not this country and the girl who knelt by him was not this girl. They knelt in the rain in a darkened city and he held his dying brother in his arms but he could not see his face and he could not say his name. Somewhere among the black and dripping streets a dog howled. That was all. He looked out at the lake where there was no wind but only the dark stillness and the stars and yet he felt a cold wind pass. He crouched in the sedge by the lake and he knew he feared the world to come for in it were already written certainties no man would wish for. He saw pass as in a slow tapestry unrolled images of things seen and unseen. He saw the shewolf dead in the mountains and the hawk's blood on the stone and he saw a glass hearse with black drapes pass in a street carried on poles by mozos. He saw the castaway bow floating on the cold waters of the Bavispe like a dead serpent and the solitary sexton in the ruins of the town where the terremoto had passed and the hermit in the broken transept of the church at Caborca. He saw rainwater dripping from a lightbulb screwed into the sheetiron wall of a warehouse. He saw a goat with golden horns tethered in a field of mud.

Lastly he saw his brother standing in a place where he could not reach him, windowed away in some world where he could never go. When he saw him there he knew that he had seen him so in dreams before and he knew that his brother would smile at him and he waited for him to do so, a smile which he had evoked and to which he could find no meaning to ascribe and he wondered if what at last he'd come to was that he could no longer tell that which had passed from all that was but a seeming. He must have knelt there a long time because the sky in the east did grow gray with dawn and the stars sank at last to ash in the paling lake and birds began to call from the far shore and the world to appear again once more.

They rode out early with nothing to eat save the last few tortillas dried and hardening at the edges. She rode behind him and they did not speak and in this manner they rode at noon across the wooden river bridge and into Las Varas.

There were few people about. They bought beans and tortillas at a small tienda and they bought four tamales from an old woman who sold them in the street out of a steel oildrum sashed up in a wooden frame with castiron wheels from off an orecart. The girl paid the woman and they sat in a stack of piñon firewood behind a store and ate in silence. The tamales smelled and tasted of charcoal. While they were eating a man approached them and smiled and nodded. Billy looked at the girl, she looked at him. He looked at the horse and at the stock of the shotgun jutting from the boot under the saddle.

No me recuerdas, the man said.

Billy looked at him again. He looked at his boots. It was the arriero last seen on the steps of the opera caravan in the roadside grove south of San Diego.

Le conozco, Billy said. Cómo le va?

Bien. He looked at the girl. Dónde está su hermano?

Ya está en San Diego.

The arriero nodded sagely. As if he understood some situation.

Dónde está la caravana? said Billy.

He said he did not know. He said that they had waited by the side of the road but that no one had ever returned.

Cómo no?

The arriero shrugged. He made a chopping motion with the heel of his hand out through the air. Se fué, he said.

Con el dinero.

Claro.

He said that they'd been left without resources or any means to travel. At the time of his own departure the dueña had sold all the mules save one and bickering had broken out. When Billy asked what she would do he shrugged again. He looked away down the street. He looked at Billy. He asked him if he could spare him a few pesos so that he could get something to eat.

Billy said that he had no money but the girl had already risen and walked out to the horse and when she returned she gave the arriero some coins and he thanked her a number of times and bowed and touched his hat and put the coins in his pocket and wished them a good voyage and turned and went off down the street and disappeared into the sole cantina in that upland pueblo.

Pobrecito, the girl said.

Billy spat into the dry grass. He said that the arriero was probably lying and besides he was only a drunk and she should not have given him money. Then he got up and walked out to where the horses were standing and buckled the latigo and took up the reins and mounted up and rode out up through the town toward the railroad tracks and the road north without even looking back to see if she would follow.

In the three days' riding that took them to San Diego she spoke hardly at all. The last night she had wanted to keep riding on in the dark to reach the ejido but he would not. They camped on the river some miles south of Mata Ortíz and he built a fire of driftwood on a gravel bar in the river and she cooked the last of the dried beans and tortillas which was all the rations they'd had to eat since they left Las Varas. They ate seated across from each other while the fire burned down to a frail basket of coals and the moon rose in the east and overhead very high and very faint they could hear the calls of birds moving south and they could see them trail in slender cipherings across the deeply smoldering western rim and into the dusk and the darkness beyond.

Las grullas llegan, she said.

He watched them. The cranes were moving south and he watched their thin echelons trail along those unseen corridors writ in their blood a hundred thousand years. He watched them until they were gone and the last thin fluted cry like a child's horn floated away on the night's onset and then she rose and took her serape and walked off down the gravel bar and vanished among the cottonwoods.

They rode across the plankwood bridge and up to the old hacienda at noon the day following. People stood all along in the doorways of the domicilios who should have been in the fields and he realized that it was some feastday of the calendar. He rode past her and pulled the horse up in front of the Muñoz door and dismounted and dropped the reins and pulled off his hat and ducked and entered the low doorway.

Boyd was sitting on the pallet with his back against the wall. The flame of the votive candle heeled about in the glass above his head and swathed as he was in his wraps of sheeting he looked like someone sat suddenly upright at his own vigil. The mute dog had been lying down and it stood and moved against him. Dónde estabas? Boyd said. He wasnt talking to his brother.

He was talking to the girl who came smiling through the doorway behind him.

THE NEXT DAY he rode out down the river and he was gone all day. High thin skeins of wildfowl were moving downcountry and leaves were falling in the river, willow and cottonwood, coiling and turning in the current. Their shadows where they skated over the river stones looked like writing. It was dark when he returned, riding the horse up through the smoke of the cookfires from pool to pool of light like a mounted sentry posted to patrol the watchfires of a camp. In the days to follow he worked with the herders, driving sheep down from the hills and through the high vaulted gate of the compound where the animals milled and climbed against each other and the esquiladores stood at the ready with their shears. They drove the sheep half a dozen at a time into the highceilinged and ruinous storeroom and the esquiladores stood them between their knees and clipped them by hand and young boys gathered the wool up from off the raincupped boards of the floor and stamped it into the long cotton bags with their feet.

It was cool in the evening and he would sit by the fire and drink coffee with the ejiditarios while the dogs of the compound moved from fire to fire scavenging for scraps. By now Boyd was riding out in the evening, sitting the horse stiffly and riding at a walk with the girl riding Niño close beside him. He'd lost his hat in the fray on the river and he wore an old straw hat they'd found for him and a shirt made from striped ticking. After they'd come back Billy would walk out to where the horses were hobbled below the domicilios and ride Niño bareback down to the river and wade the horse out into the darkening shallows where he'd seen the naked dueña at her bath and the horse would drink and raise its dripping muzzle and they would listen together to the river passing and to the sound of ducks somewhere on the water and sometimes the high thin cranking of the flights of cranes still passing south a mile above the river. He

rode down the far bank in the twilight and he could see in the
river loam among the cottonwoods the tracks of the horses where
Boyd had passed and he followed the tracks to see where they
had gone and he tried to guess the thoughts of the rider who
had made them. When he walked back up to the compound it
was late and he entered the low door and sat on the pallet where
his brother lay sleeping.

Boyd, he said.

His brother woke and turned and lay in the pale candlelight
and looked up at him. It was warm in the room from the day's
heat seeping back out of the mud walls and Boyd was naked to
the waist. He'd taken the wrapping from about his chest and he
was paler than his brother could ever remember and so thin
with the rack of his ribs stark against the pale skin and when he
turned in the reddish light Billy could see the hole in his chest
for just a moment and he turned his eyes away like a man
unwittingly made privy to some secret thing to which he was
in no way entitled, for which he was in no way prepared. Boyd
pulled the muslin cover up and lay back and looked at him. His
long pale uncut hair all about him and his face so thin. What is
it? he said.

Talk to me.

Go to bed.

I need for you to talk to me.

It's okay. Everthing's okay.

No it aint.

You just worry about stuff. I'm all right.

I know you are, said Billy. But I aint.

THREE DAYS LATER when he woke in the morning and walked
out they were gone. He walked out to the end of the row and
looked down toward the river. His father's horse standing in the
field raised its head and looked at him and looked out down the
road toward the river and the river bridge and the road beyond.

He got his things from the house and saddled the horse and

rode out. He said goodbye to no one. He sat the horse in the road beyond the river cottonwoods and he looked off downcountry at the mountains and he looked to the west where thunderheads were standing sheared off from the thin dark horizon and he looked at the deep cyanic sky taut and vaulted over the whole of Mexico where the antique world clung to the stones and to the spores of living things and dwelt in the blood of men. He turned the horse and set out along the road south, shadowless in the gray day, riding with the shotgun unscabbarded across the bow of the saddle. For the enmity of the world was newly plain to him that day and cold and inameliorate as it must be to all who have no longer cause except themselves to stand against it.

He looked for them for weeks but he found only shadow and rumor. He found the little heartshaped milagro in the watch-pocket of his jeans and he hooked it out with his forefinger and held it in the palm of his hand and he studied it long and long. He rode as far south as Cuauhtémoc. He rode north again to Namiquipa but could find no one who owned to know the girl and he rode as far west as La Norteña and the watershed and he grew thin and gaunted in his travels and pale with the dust of the road but he never saw them again. He sat the horse at dawn in the crossroads at Buenaventura and watched waterfowl trailing over the river and the lonely lagunas, the dark liquid movement of their wings against the red sunrise. He passed back north through the small mud hamlets of the mesa, through Alamo and Galeana, settlements through which he'd passed before and where his return was remarked upon by the poblanos so that his own journeying began to take upon itself the shape of a tale. It was cold at night on the high plains in these early days of December and he had little to keep him warm. When he rode once more into Casas Grandes he'd not eaten in two days and it was past midnight and a cold rain falling.

He rapped long at the zaguán gates. Toward the rear of the house a dog barked. Finally a light came on.

When the mozo opened the gate and looked out to see him

standing there in the rain holding the horse he did not seem surprised. He asked after his brother and Billy said that his brother had recovered from his wounds but that he had disappeared and he apologized for the hour but wished to know if he might see the doctor. The mozo said that the hour was of no consequence for the doctor was dead.

He didnt ask the mozo when had the doctor died or of what cause. He stood with his hat and held it in both hands before him. Lo siento, he said.

The mozo nodded. They stood there in silence and then the boy put on his hat and turned and put one foot into the stirrup and stood up into the saddle and sat the dark wet horse and looked down at the mozo. He said that the doctor had been a good man and he looked off down the street toward the lights of the town and he looked again at the mozo.

Nadie sabe lo que le espera en este mundo, said the mozo.

De veras, the boy said.

He nodded and touched his hat and turned and rode back down the darkened street.

IV

H E CROSSED THE BORDER at Columbus New Mexico. The guard in the gateshack studied him briefly and waved him through. As if he saw his like too often these days to be in doubt about him. Billy halted the horse anyway. I'm an American, he said, if I dont look like it.

You look like you might of left some bacon down there, the guard said.

I aint come back rich, that's for sure.

I guess you come back to sign up.

I reckon. If I can find a outfit that'll have me.

You neednt to worry about that. You aint got flat feet have you?

Flat feet?

Yeah. You got flat feet they wont take you.

What the hell are you talkin about?

Talkin about the army.

Army?

Yeah. The army. How long you been gone anyways?

I dont have no idea. I dont even know what month this is.

You dont know what's happened?

No. What's happened?

Hell fire, boy. This country's at war.

He took the long straight clay road north to Deming. The day was cold and he wore the blanket over his shoulders. The knees were out of his trousers and his boots were falling apart. The pockets which had hung by threads from his shirt he'd long ago torn off and thrown away and the back of the shirt where it had separated was sewn with agave and the collar of his jacket had separated and the shredded facing stood about his neck like some tawdry sort of lace and gave him the improbable look of a ruined dandy. The few cars that passed gave him all the berth that narrow road afforded and the people looked back at him through the rolling dust as if he were a thing wholly alien in that landscape. Something from an older time of which they'd only heard. Something of which they'd read. He rode all day and he crossed in the evening through the low foothills of the Florida Mountains and he rode on across the upland plain into the dusk and into the dark. In that dark he passed a file of five horsemen riding south back the way he'd come and he spoke to them in spanish and wished them a good evening and they spoke back to him each one in their soft voices as they passed. As if the closeness of the dark and the straitness of the way had made of them confederates. Or as if only there would confederates be found.

He rode into Deming at midnight and rode the main street from one end to the other. The horse's shoeless hooves clapping dully on the blacktop in the silence. It was bitter cold. Nothing was open. He spent the night in the bus station at the corner of Spruce and Gold, sleeping on the tile floor wrapped in the filthy serape with his warbag for a pillow and the stained and filthy hat over his face. The sweatblackened saddle stood against the wall along with the shotgun in its scabbard. He slept with his boots on and he got up twice in the night and went out to see about his horse where he'd left it tethered to a lampstandard by the catchrope.

In the morning when the cafe opened he went up to the counter and asked the woman where you went to join the army. She said that the recruiting office was at the armory on South Silver Street but she didnt think they'd be open this early.

Thank you mam, he said.

You want some coffee?

No mam. I aint got no money.

Set down, she said.

Yes mam.

He sat on one of the stools and she brought him a cup of coffee in a white china mug. He thanked her and sat drinking it. After a while she came from the grill and set a plate of eggs and bacon in front of him and a plate of toast.

Dont tell nobody where you got it, she said.

The recruiting office was closed when he got there and he was waiting on the steps with two boys from Deming and a third from an outlying ranch when the sergeant arrived and unlocked the door.

They stood in front of his desk. He studied them.

Which one of you all aint eighteen, he said.

No one answered.

They's usually about one in four and I see four recruits in front of me.

I aint but seventeen, Billy said.

The sergeant nodded. Well, he said. You'll have to get your mama to sign for you.

I dont have no mama. She's dead.

What about your daddy?

He's dead too.

Well you'll have to get your next of kin. Uncle or whatever. He'll need to get a notarized statement.

I dont have no next of kin. I just got a brother and he's youngern me.

Where do you work at?

I dont work nowheres.

The sergeant leaned back in his chair. Where are you from? he said.

From over towards Cloverdale.

You got to have some kin.

Not that I know of I dont.

The sergeant tapped his pencil on the desk. He looked out the window. He looked at the other boys.

You all want to join the army? he said.

They looked at one another. Yessir, they said.

You dont sound real sure.

Yessir, they said.

He shook his head and swiveled his chair and rolled a printed form into his typewriter.

I want to join the cavalry, the boy from the ranch said. My daddy was in the cavalry in the last war.

Well son you just tell em when you get to Fort Bliss that that's what you want to do.

Yessir. Do I need to take my saddle with me?

You dont need to take a thing in the world. They're goin to look after you like your own mother.

Yessir.

He took their names and dates of birth and next of kin and their addresses one by one and he signed four mealvouchers and gave them to them and he gave them directions to the doctor's office where they were to get their physical examinations and he gave them the forms for that.

You all should be done and back here right after dinner, he said.

What about me? Billy said.

Just wait here. The rest of you all take off now. I'll see you back here this afternoon.

When they'd left the sergeant handed Billy his forms and his voucher.

You look there at the bottom of that second sheet, he said. That's a parental consent form. If you want to join this man's army you better bring it back with your mama's signature on it. If she has to come down from heaven to do it I dont have a problem in the world with that. You understand what I'm tellin you?

Yessir. I guess you want me to sign my dead mama's name on that piece of paper.

I didnt say that. Did you hear me say that?

No sir.

Go on then. I'll see you back here after dinner.

Yessir.

He turned and went out. There were people standing in the door behind him and they stood aside to let him pass.

Parham, the sergeant said.

He turned. Yessir, he said.

You come back here this afternoon now, you hear?

Yessir.

You aint got noplace else to go.

He walked across the street and untied his horse and mounted up and rode back up Silver Street and up West Spruce, holding the papers in his hand. All the streets east and west were trees, north and south minerals. He tied his horse in front of the Manhattan Cafe cattycorner from the bus station. Next to it was the Victoria Land and Cattle Company and two men in the narrowbrimmed hats and walkingheel boots that landowners wore were standing on the sidewalk talking. They looked at him when he passed and he nodded but they didnt nod back.

He slid into the booth and laid the papers on the table and looked at the menu. When the waitress came he started to order the plate lunch but she said that lunch didnt start till eleven oclock. She said he could get breakfast.

I've done eat one breakfast today.

Well we dont have no city ordinance about how many breakfasts you can eat.

How big of a breakfast can I get?

How big of a one can you eat?

I've got a mealticket from the recruitin office.

I know it. I see it layin yonder.

Can I get four eggs?

You just tell me how you want em.

She brought the breakfast on an oblong crockery platter with the four eggs over medium and a slice of fried ham and grits with butter and she brought a plate of biscuits and a small bowl of gravy.

You want anything else you let me know, she said.

All right.

You want a sweetroll?

Yes mam.

You need some more coffee?

Yes mam.

He looked up at her. She was about forty years old and she had black hair and bad teeth. She grinned at him. I like to see a man eat, she said.

Well, he said. You're lookin at one I believe ought to meet your requirements.

When he was done eating he sat drinking coffee and studying the form his mother was supposed to sign. He sat studying it and thinking about it and after a while he asked the waitress if she could bring him a fountainpen.

She brought it and handed it to him. Dont carry it off, she said. It aint mine.

I wont.

She left to go back to the counter and he bent over the form and wrote on the line Louisa May Parham. His mother's name was Carolyn.

When he walked out the other three boys were coming up the sidewalk toward the cafe. They were talking together like they'd all been friends forever. When they saw him they stopped talking and he spoke to them and asked them how they were doing and they said they were doing all right and entered the cafe.

The doctor's name was Moir and his office was out on West Pine. By the time he got there there were half a dozen people waiting, mostly young men and boys sitting holding their recruiting forms. He gave his name to the nurse at the desk and sat in a chair and waited along with the others.

When the nurse finally called his name he was asleep and he jerked awake and looked around and he didnt know where he was.

Parham, she said again.

He stood up. That's me, he said.

The nurse handed him a form and he stood in the hallway

while she held a card over his eye and told him to read the chart on the wall. He read it to the bottom letter and she tested the other eye.

You got good eyes, she said.

Yes mam, he said. I always did.

Well I guess so, she said. You dont normally start out with bad ones and they get better.

When he went into the doctor's office the doctor had him sit in a chair and he looked in his eyes with a flashlight and he put a cold instrument in his ear and looked in there. He told him to unbutton his shirt.

You came here horseback, he said.

Yessir.

Where did you come from.

Mexico.

I see. Have you got any history of disease in your family?

No sir. They're all dead.

I see, the doctor said.

He put the cool cone of the stethoscope against the boy's chest and listened. He thumped his chest with the tips of his fingers. He put the stethoscope to his chest again and listened with his eyes closed. He sat up and took the tubes from his ears and leaned back in his chair. You've got a heartmurmur, he said.

What does that mean?

It means you wont be joining the army.

He worked for a stable out on the highway for ten days and slept in a stall until he had money for clothes and for the busfare to El Paso and he left the horse with the owner of the lot and set out east in a new duckingcloth workcoat and a new blue shirt with pearl buttons.

It was a cold and blustery day in El Paso. He found the recruiting office and the clerk filled out the same forms over again and he stood in line with a number of men and they undressed and put their clothes in a basket and were given a brass chit with a number on it and then they stood in line naked holding their papers.

When he reached the examining station he handed the doctor his medical form and the doctor looked in his mouth and into his ears. Then he put the stethoscope to his chest. He told him to turn around and he put the stethoscope to his back and listened. Then he listened to his chest again. Then he picked up a stamp from the desk and stamped Billy's form and signed it and picked up the form and handed it to him.

I cant pass you, he said.

What's wrong with me.

You've got an irregularity in your heartbeat.

There aint nothin wrong with my heart.

Yes there is.

Will I die?

Sometime. It's probably not all that serious. But it will keep you out of the army.

You could pass me if you wanted to.

I could. But I wont. They'd find it somewhere down the line anyway. Sooner or later.

It was not yet noon when he walked out and down San Antonio Street. He went down South El Paso Street to the Splendid Cafe and ate the plate lunch and walked back to the bus station and he was in Deming again before dark.

In the morning when he walked up the barn bay Mr Chandler was sorting through tack in the saddleroom. He looked up. Well, he said. Did you get in the army?

No sir, I didnt. They turned me down.

Well I'm sorry to hear it.

Yessir. I am too.

What do you aim to do?

I'm goin to try em in Albuquerque.

Son they got a awful lot of recruitin offices set up all over the country. A man could make a career out of it.

I know it. I'm goin to try it one more time.

He worked on to the end of the week and drew his pay and took the bus out on Sunday morning. He was all day on the road. Night set in just north of Socorro and the sky was filled with flights of waterfowl circling and dropping in to the river marshlands east of the highway. He watched with his face to the cold and darkening glass of the window. He listened for their cries but he could not hear them above the drone of the bus.

He slept at the YMCA and he was at the recruiting office when they opened in the morning and he was on the bus south again before noon. He'd asked the doctor if there was any medicine he could take but the doctor said that there was not. He asked if there was something you could take that would make it run all right just for a while.

Where are you from, the doctor said.

Cloverdale New Mexico.

How many different recruiting offices have you tried to enlist at?

This makes the third one.

Son, even if we did have a deaf doctor we wouldnt put him to listening to recruits with a stethoscope. I think you need to just go on home.

I dont have one to go to.

I thought you said you were from somethingdale. Where was it?

Cloverdale.

Cloverdale.

I was but I aint no more. I dont have anyplace to go. I think I need to be in the army. If I'm goin to die anyways why not use me? I aint afraid.

I wish I could, the doctor said. But I cant. It's not up to me. I have to follow regulations like everybody else. We turn away good men every day.

Yessir.

Who told you you were going to die?

I dont know. They never told me I wasnt goin to.

Well, the doctor said. They couldnt very well tell you that even if you had a heart like a horse. Could they?

No sir. I reckon not.

Go on now.

Sir?

Go on now.

When the bus pulled into the lot behind the bus station at Deming it was three oclock in the morning. He walked out to Chandler's and went to the saddleroom and got his saddle and went to the stall and led Niño out into the bay and threw the saddleblanket over him. It was very cold. The barn was oak batboards and he could see the horse's breath pass across the slats lit from the single yellow bulb outside. The groom Ruiz came and stood in the door with his blanket around his shoulders. He watched while Billy saddled the horse. He asked him if he had succeeded in joining the army.

No, Billy said.

Lo siento.

Yo también.

Adónde va?

No sé.

Regresa a Mexico?

No.

Ruiz nodded. Buen viaje, he said.

Gracias.

He led the horse out down the barn bay and through the door and mounted up and rode out.

He rode through the town and took the old road south to Hermanas and Hachita. The horse was newly shod and in good plight from the grain it had been fed on and he rode the sun up and he rode all day and rode it down again and rode on into the night. He slept on the high plain wrapped in his blanket and rose shivering before dawn and rode on again. He quit the road just west of Hachita and rode through the foothills of the Little Hatchet Mountains and struck the railroad coming out of the Phelps Dodge smelter to the south and crossed the tracks and reached the shallow salt lake at sunset.

There was water standing in the flats as far as he could see and the sunset on the water had turned it to a lake of blood. He tried to put the horse forward but the horse could not see across the lake and balked and would not go. He turned and rode south along the flats. Gillespie Mountain lay covered in snow and beyond that the Animas Peaks standing in the last of that day's sun with the snow lying red in the rincons. And far to the south the pale and ancient cordilleras of Mexico impounding the visible world. He came to the remnants of an old fence and dismounted and twisted out the staples from some of the spindly posts and made a fire and sat with his boots crossed before him staring into it. The horse stood in the dark at the edge of the fire and gazed bleakly at the barren salt ground. It's your own doin, the boy said. I got no sympathy for you.

They crossed the flat shallow lake in the morning and before noon they struck the old Playas road and followed it west into the mountains. There was snow in the pass and not a track in it. They rode down into the beautiful Animas Valley and took the road south from Animas and reached the Sanders ranch about two hours past nightfall.

He called from the gate and the girl came out on the porch. It's Billy Parham, he called.

Who?

Billy Parham.

Come up Billy Parham, she called.

When he entered the parlor Mr Sanders stood. He was older, smaller, more frail. Get in this house, he said.

I'm awful dirty to come in.

You come on in. We thought you'd died.

No sir. Not yet I aint.

The old man shook his hand and held it. He was looking past him toward the door. Where's that Boyd at? he said.

They ate in the diningroom. The girl served them and then sat down. They ate roast beef and potatoes and beans and the girl passed him a bread dish covered with a linen cloth and he took a piece of cornbread and buttered it. This is awful good, he said.

She's a good cook, the old man said. I hope she dont decide

to get married and quit me. If I had to cook for myself the cats'd leave.

Oh Grandaddy, the girl said.

They wanted to put Miller four-F too, the old man said. On account of his leg. They took him up at Albuquerque. They run em through up there I reckon in wholesale lots.

They didnt me. Are they goin to put him in the cavalry?

I dont think so. I dont think they're even goin to have one.

He looked out across the table, chewing slowly. In the yellow light of the pressed glass chandelier the old photographs and portraits above the sideboard seemed like artifacts salvaged from some ancient removal. Even the old man seemed distant from them. From the sepia-tinted buildings, the old shake roofs. The people on horseback. Men sitting among cardboard cactus in a photographer's studio in suits and ties with the legs of their breeches stogged into their boottops and rifles standing upright before them. The antique dresses of the women. The wary or haunted cast to their eyes. Like people photographed at gunpoint.

That's John Slaughter in that picture at the end yonder.

Which one?

That last one on the top right under Miller's certificate. That was took in front of his house.

Who's the indian girl?

That's Apache May. They brought her back from a indian camp they raided, bunch of Apaches been stealin cattle. Eighteen ninety-five or six, somewheres in there. He may have killed some of em. He come back with her, she was just a little thing. She was wearin a dress made from an election poster and he took her and raised her as his own. He was just crazy about her. She died in a fire not long after that picture was took.

Did you know him?

I did. I worked for him at one time.

Did you ever kill a indian?

No. I come near it a time or two. Some that worked for me. Who is that on the mule?

That's James Autry. He didnt care what he rode.

Who's that with the lion on the packhorse?

The old man shook his head. I know his name, he said. But I cant say it.

He drained his coffee and rose and got his cigarettes and an ashtray from the sideboard. The ashtray was from the Chicago World's Fair and it was cast from potmetal and it said 1833–1933. It said A Century of Progress. Let's go in here, he said.

They went in the parlor. There was a paneled oak pumporgan against the wall where they passed through from the diningroom. A lace throw on top of it. A framed handtinted portrait of the old man's wife as a young woman.

That thing dont play, the old man said. Aint nobody to play it noway.

My grandmama used to play one, Billy said. In the church.

Women used to play music. Anymore you just turn on a victrola.

He bent and opened the stove door with the poker and poked the fire up and put another split log in and shut the door.

They sat and the old man told him stories about rawhiding cattle in Mexico as a young man and about Villa's raid on Columbus New Mexico in nineteen sixteen and about sheriff's posses tracking badmen down into the bootheel as they fled toward the border and about the drought and die-up of eighty-six and trailing north the corriente cattle that they'd bought for next to nothing up out of that stricken ground across the high parched plains. Cattle so poor the old man said that at evening crossing before the sun where it burned upon the western desert shore you could all but see through them.

What do you aim to do? he said.

I dont know. Try and hire on somewheres I reckon.

We're about shut down here altogether.

Yessir. I wasnt askin.

This war, the old man said. There's no way to calculate what's to come.

No sir. I dont reckon there is.

The old man tried to get him to stay the night but he would not. They stood on the porch. It was cold and the prairie all about lay in a deep silence. The horse nickered at them from the gate.

You'd do just as well to start fresh in the mornin, the old man said.

I know it. I just need to get on.

Well.

I like ridin of a night anyways.

Yes, the old man said. I always did. You take care, son.

Yessir. I will. Thank you.

HE CAMPED THAT NIGHT on the broad Animas Plain and the wind blew in the grass and he slept on the ground wrapped in the serape and in the wool blanket the old man had given him. He built a small fire but he had little wood and the fire died in the night and he woke and watched the winter stars slip their hold and race to their deaths in the darkness. He could hear the horse step in its hobbles and hear the grass rip softly in the horse's mouth and hear it breathing or the toss of its tail and he saw far to the south beyond the Hatchet Mountains the flare of lightning over Mexico and he knew that he would not be buried in this valley but in some distant place among strangers and he looked out to where the grass was running in the wind under the cold starlight as if it were the earth itself hurtling headlong and he said softly before he slept again that the one thing he knew of all things claimed to be known was that there was no certainty to any of it. Not just the coming of war. Anything at all.

He went to work for the Hashknives except that it wasnt the Hashknives any more. They sent him out to a linecamp on the Little Colorado. In three months he saw three other human beings. When he got paid in March he went to the post office in Winslow and sent a money order to Mr Sanders for the twenty dollars he owed him and he went to a bar on First Street and sat on a stool and pushed back his hat with his thumb and ordered a beer.

What kind of beer you want? the barman said.

Just any kind. It dont matter.

You aint old enough to drink beer.

Then why did you ask me what kind I wanted?

It dont matter cause I aint servin you.

What kind is he drinkin?

The man down the bar that he'd nodded to studied him. This is a draft, son, he said. Just tell em you want a draft.

Yessir. Thank you.

Dont mention it.

He walked up the street and went in the next bar and sat on a stool. The barman wandered down and stood before him.

Give me a draft.

He went back down the bar and pulled the beer into a round glass mug and came back and set it on the bar. Billy put a dollar on the bar and the barman went to the cash register and rang it up and came back and clapped down seventy-five cents.

Where you from? he said.

Down around Cloverdale. I been workin for the Hashknives.

There aint no Hashknives. Babbitts sold it.

Yeah. I know it.

Sold it to a sheepherder.

Yeah.

What do you think of that?

I dont know.

Well I do.

Billy looked down the bar. It was empty save for a soldier who looked drunk. The soldier was watching him.

They never sold him the brand though, did they? the barman said.

No.

No. So there aint no Hashknives.

You want to flip for the jukebox? the soldier said.

Billy looked at him. No, he said. I wouldnt care to.

Set there then.

I aim to.

Is there somethin wrong with that beer? the barman said.

No. I dont reckon. Do you get a lot of complaints?

I just noticed you aint drinkin it is all.

Billy looked at the beer. He looked down the length of the bar. The soldier had turned slightly and was sitting with one hand on his knee. As if he might be deciding whether or not to get up.

I just thought there might be somethin wrong with it, the barman said.

Well I dont reckon there is, Billy said. But if there is I'll let you know.

You got a cigarette? the soldier said.

I dont smoke.

You dont smoke.

No.

The barman fished a pack of Lucky Strikes from his shirtpocket and palmed them onto the bar and slid them down to the soldier. There you go, soldier, he said.

Thanks, the soldier said. He shook a cigarette upright in the pack and pulled it free with his mouth and took a lighter from his pocket and lit the cigarette and put the lighter on the bar and slid the pack of cigarettes back to the barman. What's that in your pocket? he said.

Who are you talkin to? said Billy.

The soldier blew smoke down the bar. Talkin to you, he said.

Well, said Billy. I reckon its my business what I got in my pocket.

The soldier didnt answer. He sat smoking. The barman reached and got the cigarettes from the bar and took one and lit it and put the pack back in his shirtpocket. He stood leaning against the backbar with his arms crossed and the smoldering cigarette in his fingers. No one spoke. They seemed to be waiting for someone to arrive.

Do you know how old I am? the barman said.

Billy looked at him. No, he said. How would I know how old you are?

I'll be thirty-eight years old in June. June fourteenth.

Billy didnt answer.

That's how come I aint in uniform.

Billy looked at the soldier. The soldier sat smoking.

I tried to enlist, the barman said. Tried to lie about my age but they wasnt havin none of it.

He dont care, the soldier said. Uniform dont mean nothin to him.

The barman pulled on his cigarette and blew smoke toward the bar. I'll bet it'd mean somethin if it had that risin sun on the collar and they was comin down Second Street about ten abreast. I bet it'd mean somethin then.

Billy picked up the beermug and drank it dry and set it back on the bar and stood up and pulled his hat forward and looked a last time at the soldier and turned and went out into the street.

He worked another nine months for Aja and when he left he had a packhorse that he'd traded for and a regular bedroll and soogan and an old singleshot 32 caliber Stevens rifle. He rode south across the high plains west of Socorro and he rode through Magdalena and across the plains of Saint Augustine. When he rode into Silver City it was snowing and he checked into the Palace Hotel and sat in the room and watched the snow falling in the street. There was no one about. He went out after a while and walked down Bullard Street to the feed store but it was closed. He found a grocery store and bought six boxes of breakfast cereal and came back and fed them to the horses and put the horses in the yard behind the hotel and got his supper in the hotel diningroom and went up and went to bed. When he came down in the morning he was the only one at breakfast and when he went out to try and buy some clothes all the shops were closed. It was gray and cold in the streets and a mean wind blew out of the north and there was no one about. He tried the door of the drugstore because there was a light on inside but it was closed too. When he got back to the hotel he asked the clerk if today was Sunday and the clerk said it was Friday.

He looked out at the street. There aint no stores open, he said.

It's Christmas day, the clerk said. Aint no stores open on Christmas day.

He drifted into the north Texas panhandle and he worked out most of the following year for the Matadors and he worked for the T Diamond. He drifted south and he worked small spreads some no more than a week. By the spring of the third year of the war there was hardly a ranch house in all of that country that did not have a gold star in the window. He worked until March on a small ranch out of Magdalena New Mexico and then one day he got his pay and saddled his horse and tied his bedroll onto the packhorse and rode south again. He crossed the last blacktop highway just east of Steins and two days later rode up to the SK Bar gate. It was a cool spring day and the old man was sitting on the porch in his rocker with his hat on and a bible in his lap. He'd bent forward to see if he could tell who it was. As if the extra foot of proximity might bring the rider into focus. He looked older and more frail, much reduced from his former self in the two years since he'd seen him. Billy called his name and the old man said for him to get down and he did. When he got to the foot of the steps he stopped with one hand on the paintflaked baluster and looked up at the old man. The old man sat with the bible closed over one finger to mark its place. Is that you, Parham? he said.

Yessir. Billy.

He walked up the steps and took off his hat and shook hands with the old man. The old man's eyes had faded to a paler blue. He held Billy's hand a long time. Bless your heart, he said. I've thought about you a thousand times. Set down here where we can visit.

He pulled up one of the old canebottomed chairs and sat and

put his hat over his knee and looked out over the pasturelands toward the mountains and he looked at the old man.

I reckon you knew about Miller, the old man said.

No sir. I've not had much news.

He was killed on Kwajalein Atoll.

I'm awful sorry to hear that.

We've had it pretty rough here. Pretty rough.

They sat. There was a breeze coming up the country. A pot of asparagus fern hanging from the porch eaves at the corner swung gently and its shadow oscillated over the boards of the porch slow and random and uncentered.

Are you doin all right? Billy said.

Oh I'm all right. I had a operation for cataracts back in the fall but I'm makin it. Leona went off and got married on me. Now her husband's shipped out and she's livin in Roswell I dont know what for. Got a job. I tried to reason with her but you know how that goes.

Yessir.

By rights I got no business bein here atall.

I hope you live forever.

Dont wish that on me.

He'd leaned back and closed the bible shut. That rain is comin this way, he said.

Yessir. I believe it is.

Can you smell it?

Yessir.

I always loved that smell.

They sat. After a while Billy said: Can you smell it?

No.

They sat.

What do you hear from that Boyd? the old man said.

I aint heard nothin. He never come back from Mexico. Or if he did I never heard it.

The old man didnt speak for a long time. He watched the darkening country to the south.

I seen it rain on a blacktop road in Arizona one time, he said. It rained on one side of the white line for a good half mile and the other side bone dry. Right down the centerline.

I can believe that, Billy said. I've seen it rain thataway.

It was a peculiar thing to see.

I seen it thunder in a snowstorm one time, Billy said. Thunder and lightnin. You couldnt see the lightnin. Just everthing would light up all around you, white as cotton.

I had a Mexican one time to tell me that, the old man said. I didnt know whether to believe him or not.

It was in Mexico was where I seen it.

Maybe they dont have it in this country.

Billy smiled. He crossed his boots on the boards of the porch in front of him and watched the country.

I like them boots, the old man said.

I bought em in Albuquerque.

They look to be good'ns.

I hope they are. I give enough for em.

Everthing's higher than a cat's back with the war and all. What all you can even find to buy.

Doves were coming in and crossing the pasture toward the stockpond west of the house.

You aint got married on us have you? the old man said.

No sir.

People hate to see a man single. I dont know what there is about it. They used to pester me about gettin married again and I was near sixty when my wife died. My sister in law primarily. I'd done already had the best woman ever was. Aint nobody goin to be that lucky twice runnin.

No sir. Most likely not.

I remember old Uncle Bud Langford used to tell people, said: It would take one hell of a wife to beat no wife at all. Course then he was never married, neither. So I dont know how he would know.

I guess I've got to say that I dont understand the first thing about em.

What's that.

Women.

Well, said the old man. At least you aint took to lyin.

There wouldnt be no use in it.

Why dont you put your horses up fore your plunder gets wet out yonder.

I reckon I'd best be gettin on.

You aint goin to ride off in the rain. We're fixin to eat supper here in just a few minutes. I got a Mexican woman cooks for me.

Well. I probably need to move while the spirit's on me.

Just stay and take supper. Hell, you just got here.

When he came back from the barn the wind was blowing harder but it still had not begun to rain.

I remember that horse, the old man said. That was your daddy's horse.

Yessir.

He bought it off a Mexican. He claimed the horse when he bought it didnt know a word of english.

The old man pushed himself up from his rocker and clutched the bible under his arm. Even gettin up out of a chair gets to be work. You wouldnt believe that, would you?

Do you think horses understand what people say?

I aint sure most people do. Let's go in. She's done hollered twice.

He was up in the morning before daybreak and he went through the dark house to the kitchen where there was a light. The woman was sitting at the kitchen table listening to an old wooden radio shaped like a bishop's hat. She was listening to a station out of Ciudad Juárez and when he stood in the door she turned it off and looked at him.

Está bien, he said. No tiene que apagarlo.

She shrugged and rose. She said that it was over anyway. She asked him if he would like his breakfast and he said that he would.

While she was fixing it he walked out to the barn and brushed the horses and cleaned their hooves and then saddled Niño and left the latigo loose and he strapped the old visalia packframe onto his bedhorse and tied on his soogan and went back to the house. She got his breakfast out of the oven and set it on the table. She'd cooked eggs and ham and flour tortillas and beans and she set it in front of him and poured his coffee.

Quiere crema? she said.

No gracias. Hay salsa?

She set the salsa at his elbow in a small lavastone molcajete.

Gracias.

He thought that she would leave but she didnt. She stood watching him eat.

Es pariente del señor Sanders? she said.

No. Él era amigo de mi padre.

He looked up at her. Siéntate, he said. Puede sentarse.

She made a little motion with her hand. He didnt know what it meant. She stood as before.

Su salud no es buena, he said.

She said that it was not. She said that he had had trouble with his eyes and that he was very sad over his nephew who was killed in the war. Conoció a su sobrino? she said.

Sí. Y usted?

She said that she had not known the nephew. She said that when she came to work here the nephew was already dead. She said that she had seen his picture and that he was very handsome.

He ate the last of the eggs and wiped the plate with the tortilla and ate the tortilla and drank the last of the coffee and wiped his mouth and looked up and thanked her.

Tiene que hacer un viaje largo? she said.

He rose and put the napkin on the table and took his hat up from the other chair and put it on. He said that he did indeed have a long journey. He said he did not know what the end of his journey would look like or whether he would know it when he got there and he asked her in spanish to pray for him but she said she had already decided to do so before he even asked.

*   *   *

HE SIGNED the horses through the Mexican customs at Berendo and folded the stamped entry papers into his saddlebag and gave the aduanero a silver dollar. The aduanero saluted him gravely and addressed him as caballero and he rode south into old Mexico, State of Chihuahua. He'd last passed through this port of entry seven years ago when he was thirteen and his father rode the horse he now rode and they had taken delivery of eight hundred head of cattle from two Americans rawhiding the back acres of an abandoned ranch in the mountains to the west of Ascensión. At that time there had been a cafe here but now there was none. He rode down the little mud street and bought three tacos from a woman sitting beside a charcoal brazier in the dust of the roadside and ate them as he went.

Two days' riding brought him at evening to the town of Janos, or to the lights thereof sited on the darkening plain below him. He sat the horse in the old rutted wagonroad and looked off toward the western sierras black against the bloodred drop of the sky. Beyond lay the Bavispe River country and the high Pilares with the snow still clinging in the northern rincons and the nights still cold up there on the alto plano where he had ridden another horse in another time long ago.

He approached from the east in the dark, riding past one of the crumbling mud towers of the ancient walled town and riding slowly through a settlement composed wholly of mud and in ruins a hundred years. He rode past the tall mud church and past the old green spanish bells hung from their trestlepole in the yard and past the open doors of the houses where men sat smoking quietly. Behind them in the yellow light of the oil lamps the women moved at their tasks. Over the town hung a haze of charcoal smoke and from somewhere in those dusky warrens music was playing.

He followed the sound down the narrow mud corridors and hove up at last before a door nailed up out of raw pine boards crusted with dried rosin and hung on bullhide hinges. The room he entered was but one more in the row of cribs inhabited or abandoned that lined either side of the little street. When he entered the music ceased and the musicians turned and looked at him. There were several tables in the room and all had ornately turned legs that were stained with mud as if they'd stood outside in the rain. At one of the tables sat four men with glasses and a bottle. Along the back wall was an ornate Brunswick bar brought here from God knew where and on the shelves of the carved and dusty backbar there were half a dozen bottles, some with labels, some without.

Está abierto? he said.

One of the men pushed back his chair on the clay floor and stood. He was very tall and when he stood his head vanished into the darkness above the single shaded bulb that hung over the table. Sí, caballero, he said. Cómo no?

He went to the bar and took down an apron from a nail and tied it about his waist and stood before the dimly lit carved mahogany with his hands crossed before him. He looked like a butcher standing in a church. Billy nodded at the other three men at the table and wished them a good evening but none spoke back. The musicians rose with their instruments and filed out into the street.

He pushed his hat back slightly on his head and crossed the room and put his hands on the bar and studied the bottles on the back wall.

Déme un Waterfills y Frazier, he said.

The barman held up one finger. As if agreeing with the wisdom of this choice. He reached and took down a tumbler from among a varied collection and righted it on the bar and reached down the whiskey and poured the glass half full.

Agua? he said.

No gracias. Tome algo para usted.

The barman thanked him and reached down another tumbler and poured it and set the bottle on the bar. On the dust of the bottle his hand had left an imprint visible in the sallow glare from the lamp. Billy held up his glass and looked at the barman across the rim of it. Salud, he said.

Salud, said the barman. They drank. Billy set his glass down and gestured at it with a circling motion of his finger that included the barman's glass also. He turned and looked at the three men sitting on the table. Y sus amigos también, he said.

Bueno, said the barman. Cómo no.

He crossed the room in his apron with the bottle and poured their glasses and they toasted his health and he raised his own glass and they drank. The barman returned to the bar where he stood uncertainly, glass and bottle in hand. Billy set his glass on the bar. Finally a voice from the table spoke to ask that he join them. He picked up the glass and turned and thanked them. He did not know who had spoken.

When he pulled back the chair which the barman had earlier vacated and sat in it and looked up he could see that the oldest of the three men was very drunk. He wore a sweatstained guayabera and he slouched in his chair with his chin resting in the open collar of it. The black eyes in their redrimmed cups were sullen and depthless. Like lead slag poured into borings to seal away something virulent or predacious. In the slow shuttering of the lids an overlong interval. It was the younger man on his right who spoke. He said that it was a long distance between drinks of whiskey for a traveler in this country.

Billy nodded. He looked at the bottle standing on their table. It was slightly yellow, slightly misshapen. There was no stopper to it nor label and it held a thin lees of fluid, a thin sediment. A thinly curved agave worm. Tomamos mescal, the man said. He leaned back in his chair and called to the barman. Venga, he called. Siéntate con nosotros.

The barman set the whiskey bottle on the bar but Billy said for him to bring it. He untied his apron and took it off and hung it back on the nail and came over with the bottle. Billy waved at the glasses on the table. Otra vez, he said.

Otra vez, said the barman. He poured the glasses round.

When he had filled all save the glass of the man who was drunk he hesitated for the prior pouring yet stood before him. The younger man touched his elbow. Alfonso, he said. Tome.

Alfonso drank not. He stared leadenly at the pale newcomer. He seemed not so much reduced by drink as restored to some atavistic state once lost to him. The younger man looked across the table at the American. Es un hombre muy serio, he said.

The barman stood the bottle before them and dragged a chair across from a nearby table and sat. All raised their glasses. They would have drunk except that Alfonso chose that moment to speak. Quién es, joven? he said.

They paused. They looked at Billy. Billy lifted his glass and drank and sat the empty glass down and looked across the table at those eyes again.

Un hombre, he said. No más.

Americano.

Claro. Americano.

Es vaquero?

Sí. Vaquero.

The drunk man did not move. His eyes did not move. He could have been speaking to himself.

Tome, Alfonso, said the younger man. He raised his own glass and looked around the table. The others raised their glasses. All drank.

Y usted? said Billy.

The drunk man did not answer. His wet red underlip hung loosely away from the perfect white teeth. He seemed not to have heard.

Es soldado? he said.

Soldado no.

The younger man said that the drunk man had been a soldier in the revolution and that he had fought at Torreón and at Zacatecas and that he had been wounded many times. Billy looked at the drunk man. The opaque black of his eyes. The younger man said that he had received three bullets in the chest at Zacatecas and lain in the dirt of the streets in darkness and

cold while the dogs drank his blood. He said that the holes were
there in the patriot's chest for all to see.

Otra vez, said Billy. The barman leaned forward with the
bottle and poured.

When all the glasses were filled the younger man raised his
glass and offered a toast to the revolution. They drank. They
set their glasses down and wiped their mouths with the backs
of their hands and looked at the drunk man. Por qué viene aquí?
the drunk man said.

They looked at Billy.

Aquí? said Billy.

But the drunk man did not respond to questions, he only
asked them. The younger man leaned slightly forward. En este
país, he whispered.

En este país, said Billy. They waited. He leaned forward and
reached across the table and took the drunk man's glass of mescal
and slung its contents out across the room and set the glass back
on the table. No one moved. He gestured to the barman. Otra
vez, he said.

The barman reached slowly for the bottle and slowly poured
the glasses once again. He set the bottle down and wiped his
hand on the knee of his trousers. Billy picked up his glass and
held it before him. He said that he was in their country to find
his brother. He said that his brother was a little crazy and he
should not have abandoned him but he did.

They sat holding their glasses. They looked at the drunk
man. Tome, Alfonso, said the younger man. He gestured with
his glass. The barman raised his own glass and drank and set
the empty glass on the table again and leaned back. Like a player
who has moved his piece and sits back to await the results. He
looked across the table at the youngest man who sat slightly
apart with his hat down over his forehead and his full glass in
both hands before him like an offering. Who'd so far said no
word at all. The whole room had begun to hum very slightly.

The ends of all ceremony are but to avert bloodshed. But
the drunk man by his condition inhabited a twilight state of

responsibility and to this the man at his side made silent appeal. He smiled and shrugged and raised his glass to the norteamericano and drank. When he set his glass down again the drunk man stirred. He leaned slowly forward and reached for his glass and the younger man smiled and raised his glass again as if to welcome him back from his morbidities. But the drunk man clutched the glass and then slowly held it out to the side of the table and poured the whiskey on the floor and set the glass back upon the table once more. Then he reached unsteadily for the bottle of mescal and turned it up and poured the oily yellow fuel into his glass and set the bottle back on the table with the sediment and the worm coiling slowly clockwise in the glass floor of it. Then he leaned back as before.

The younger man looked at Billy. Outside in the darkened town a dog barked.

No le gusta el whiskey? Billy said.

The drunk man did not answer. The glass of mescal sat as it had sat when Billy first entered the bar.

Es el sello, said the younger man.

El sello?

Sí.

He said that he objected to the seal which was the seal of an oppressive government. He said that he would not drink from such a bottle. That it was a matter of honor.

Billy looked at the drunk man.

Es mentira, the drunk man said.

Mentira? said Billy.

Sí. Mentira.

Billy looked at the younger man. He asked him what it was that was a lie but the younger man told him not to preoccupy himself. Nada es mentira, he said.

No es cuestión de ningún sello, the drunk man said.

He spoke slowly but not without facility. He had turned and addressed his statement to the younger man beside him. Then he turned back and continued to stare at Billy. Billy made a

circle with his finger. Otra vez, he said. The barman reached
and took up the bottle.

You want to drink that stinkin catpiss in favor of good american whiskey, Billy said, you be my guest.

Mánde? said the drunk man.

The barman sat uncertainly. Then he leaned and poured the
empty glasses and picked up the cork and pushed it back into
the bottle. Billy raised his glass. Salud, he said. He drank. All
drank. Save for the drunk man. Out in the street the old spanish
bells rang once, rang twice. The drunk leaned forward. He
reached past the glass of mescal standing before him and seized
the bottle of mescal again. He picked it up and poured Billy's
glass full with a slight circular movement of his hand. As if the
small tumbler must be filled in some prescribed fashion. Then
he tipped the bottle up and set it on the table and leaned back.

The barman and the two younger men sat holding their
glasses. Billy sat looking at the mescal. He leaned back in the
chair. He looked toward the door. He could see Niño standing
in the street. The musicians who had fled were already playing
again somewhere in another street, another taverna. Or perhaps
it was other musicians. He reached and took up the mescal and
held it to the light. A smokelike sediment curled in the glass.
Small bits of debris. No one moved. He tilted the glass and
drank.

Salud, called the younger man. They drank. The barman
drank. They clapped their empty tumblers on the table and
they smiled around. Then Billy leaned to one side and spat the
mescal in the floor.

In the ensuing silence the pueblo itself seemed to have been
sucked up by the desert round. There was no sound anywhere.
The drunk man sat stilled in the act of reaching for his glass.
The younger man lowered his eyes. In the shadow of the lamp
his eyes even looked closed and may have been. The drunk man
balled his reaching hand and lowered it to the table. Billy circled
one finger in the air slowly. Otra vez, he said.

The barman looked at Billy. He looked at the leaden-eyed patriot sitting with his fist upright beside his glass. Era demasiado fuerte para él, he said. Demasiado fuerte.

Billy didnt take his eyes from the drunk man. Más mentiras, he said. He said that it was not at all the case that the mescal was too strong for him as the barman claimed.

They sat looking at the mescal bottle. At the black half moon of the bottle's shadow beside the bottle. When the drunk man did not move or speak Billy reached across the table for the whiskey bottle and poured the glasses round once more and set the bottle back on the table. Then he pushed back his chair and stood.

The drunk man placed both hands on the edge of the table.

The man who had so far not spoken at all said in english that if he reached for his billfold the man would shoot him.

I dont doubt that for a minute, Billy said. He spoke to the bartender without taking his eyes from the man across the table. Cuánto debo? he said.

Cinco dolares? said the barman.

He reached into his shirtpocket with two fingers and took out his money and dealt it open with his thumb and slid loose a five-dollar bill and laid it on the table. He looked at the man who'd spoken to him in english. Will he shoot me in the back? he said.

The man looked up at him from under his hatbrim and smiled. No, he said. I dont think so.

Billy touched the brim of his hat and nodded to the men at the table. Caballeros, he said. And turned to start for the door leaving his filled glass on the table.

If he calls to you do not turn around, the young man said.

He did not stop and he did not turn and he'd very nearly reached the door when the man did call. Joven, he said.

He stopped. The horses out in the street raised their heads and looked at him. He looked at the distance to the door which was no more than his own length. Walk, he said. Just walk. But he didnt walk. He turned around.

The drunk man had not moved. He sat in his chair and the

young man who spoke english had risen and stood beside him with one hand on his shoulder. They looked to be posed for some album of outlawry.

Me llama embustero? said the drunk man.

No, he said.

Embustero? He clawed at his shirt and ripped it open. It was fastened with snaps and it opened easily and with no sound. As if perhaps the snaps were worn and loose from just such demonstrations in the past. He sat holding his shirt wide open as if to invite again the trinity of rifleballs whose imprint lay upon his smooth and hairless chest just over his heart in so perfect an isoscelian stigmata. No one at the table moved. None looked at the patriot nor at his scars for they had seen it all before. They watched the güero where he stood framed in the door. They did not move and there was no sound and he listened for something in the town that would tell him that it was not also listening for he had a sense that some part of his arrival in this place was not only known but ordained and he listened for the musicians who had fled upon his even entering these premises and who themselves perhaps were listening to the silence from somewhere in those cratered mud precincts and he listened for any sound at all other than the dull thud of his heart dragging the blood through the small dark corridors of his corporeal life in its slow hydraulic tolling. He looked at the man who'd warned him not to turn but that was all the warning that man had. What he saw was that the only manifest artifact of the history of this negligible republic where he now seemed about to die that had the least authority or meaning or claim to substance was seated here before him in the sallow light of this cantina and all else from men's lips or from men's pens would require that it be beat out hot all over again upon the anvil of its own enactment before it could even qualify as a lie. Then it all passed. He took off his hat and stood. Then for better or for worse he put it on again and turned and walked out the door and untied the horses and mounted up and rode out down the narrow street leading the packhorse and he did not look back.

* * *

HE'D NOT GOT CLEAR of the town before a drop of rain the size of a middle taw landed in the brim of his hat. Then another. He looked up into a cloudless sky. The visible planets burning in the east. There was no wind nor smell of rain in the air yet the drops fell the more. The horse wanted to stop in the road and the rider looked back at the dark town. The few small window squares of dim and reddish light. The smack of the rain falling on the hard clay of the road sounded like horses somewhere in the darkness crossing a bridge. He was beginning to feel drunk. He halted the horse and then turned and rode back.

He rode the horse through the first door he came to, dropping the packhorse's rope and leaning low along his horse's neck to clear the doorbeam. Inside he sat the animal in the selfsame rain and he looked up to see the selfsame stars above him. He reined the horse about and rode out again and entered another doorway and at once the muted clatter of the raindrops on the crown of his hat ceased. He got down and stomped about in the dark to see what was underfoot. He went out and brought in the pack-horse and untied the diamondhitch and pulled his soogan off onto the ground and unbuckled and pulled down the packframe and hobbled the animal and drove it back out into the rain. Then he pulled loose the latigo on his saddlehorse and pulled off the saddle and saddlebags and stood the saddle against the wall and knelt down and felt out the ropes on the soogan and untied and unrolled it and sat and pulled off his boots. He was feeling drunker. He took off his hat and lay down. The horse walked past his head and stood looking out the door. Dont you step on me damn you, he said.

When he woke in the morning the rain had stopped and it was full daylight. He felt awful. He'd risen sometime in the night and staggered out to vomit and he remembered casting about with his weeping eyes for some sign of the horses and then staggering in again. He might not have remembered it except that when he sat up and looked around for his boots they were on his feet. He picked up his hat and put it on and looked toward the door. Several children who had been crouched there watching him stood up and backed away.

Dónde están los caballos? he said.

They said that the horses were eating.

He stood too fast and leaned against the doorjamb holding his eyes. He was afire with thirst. He raised his head again and stepped out through the door and looked at the children. They were pointing down the road.

He walked out past the last of the row of low mud dwellings with the children following behind and walked the horses down in a grassy field on the south side of the town where a small stream crossed the road. He stood holding Niño's reins. The children watched.

Quieres montar? he said.

They looked at one another. The youngest was a boy of about five and he held both arms straight up in the air and stood waiting. Billy picked him up and set him astride the horse and then the little girl and lastly the oldest boy. He told the oldest boy to hold on to the younger ones and the boy nodded and he picked up the reins again and the packhorse's trailing rope and led both horses back up toward the road.

A woman was coming along from the town. When the children saw her they whispered among themselves. She was carrying a blue pail with a cloth over it. She stood by the side of the road holding the pail by the bailwire in both hands before her. Then she started down through the field towards them.

Billy touched his hat and wished her a good morning. She stopped and stood holding the pail. She said that she had been looking for him. She said that she knew he'd not gone far because his bed and his saddle were where he'd left them. She said that the children had told her that there was a horseman asleep in the caídas at the edge of town who was sick and she had brought him some menudo hot from the fire and if he would eat it he would then have strength for his journey.

She bent and set the pail on the ground and lifted away the cloth and handed the cloth to him. He stood holding it and looking down at the pail. Inside sat a bowl of speckled tinware covered with a saucer and beside the bowl were wedged some folded tortillas. He looked at her.

Ándale, she said. She gestured toward the pail.

Y usted?

Ya comí.

He looked at the children aligned upon the horse's back. He handed up the reins and the catchrope to the boy.

Toma un paseo, he said.

The boy reached forward and took the reins and he handed the end of the catchrope to the girl and then handed the half rein over the girl's head and booted the horse forward. Billy looked at the woman. Es muy amable, he said. She said for him to eat before it grew cold.

He squatted on the ground and tried to lift out the bowl but it was too hot. Con permiso, she said. She reached down and took the bowl from the pail and lifted off the saucer and set the bowl in the saucer and handed it to him. Then she reached down and took out a spoon and handed him that.

Gracias, he said.

She knelt in the grass opposite to watch him eat. The ribbons of tripe swam in the clear and oily broth like slow planarians. He said that he was not really sick but only somewhat crudo from his night in the tavern. She said that she understood and that it was of no consequence and that sickness had no way to know who'd caused it thanks be to God for all of us.

He took a tortilla from the pail and tore it and refolded it and dipped it in the broth. He spooned up a piece of tripe and it sloughed from the spoon and he cut it in two against the side of the bowl with the edge of the spoon. The menudo was hot and rich with spice. He ate. She watched.

The children rode up on the horse behind him and sat waiting. He looked up at them and made a circling motion with his finger and they set off again. He looked at the woman.

Son suyos?

She shook her head. She said that they were not.

He nodded. He watched them go. The bowl had cooled somewhat and he took it by the rim and tipped it up and drank from it and took a bite of the tortilla. Muy sabroso, he said.

She said that she had had a son but that he was dead twenty years.

He looked at her. He thought that she did not look old enough to have had a child twenty years ago but then she seemed no particular age at all. He said that she must have been very young and she said that she had indeed been very young but that the grief of the young is greatly undervalued. She put one hand to her chest. She said that the child lived in her soul.

He looked out across the field. The children sat astride the horse at the edge of the river and the boy seemed to be waiting for the horse to drink. The horse stood waiting for whatever next thing might be required of it. He drained the last of the menudo and folded the last quadrant of the tortilla and wiped the bowl with it and ate it and set bowl and spoon and saucer back in the bucket and looked at the woman.

Cuánto le debo, señora, he said.

Señorita, she said. Nada.

He took the folded bills from his shirtpocket. Para los niños.

Niños no tengo.

Para los nietos.

She laughed and shook her head. Nietos tampoco, she said.

He sat holding the money.

Es para el camino, she said.

Bueno. Gracias.

Déme su mano.

Cómo?

Su mano.

He gave her his hand and she took it and turned it palm up and held it in hers and studied it.

Cuántos años tiene? she said.

He said that he was twenty.

Tan joven. She traced his palm with the tip of her finger. She pursed her lips. Hay ladrónes aquí, she said.

En mi palma?

She leaned back and closed her eyes and laughed. She laughed with an easy enthusiasm. Me lleva Judas, she said. No. She shook her head. She had on only a thin flowered shift and her breasts swung inside the cloth. Her teeth were white and perfect. Her legs bare and brown.

Dónde pues? he said.

She caught her lower lip with her teeth and studied him with her dark eyes. Aquí, she said. En este pueblo.

Hay ladrónes en todos lados, he said.

She shook her head. She said that in Mexico there were villages where robbers lived and villages where they did not. She said that it was a reasonable arrangement.

He asked her if she was a robber and she laughed again. Ay, she said. Dios mio, que hombre. She looked at him. Quizás, she said.

He asked her what sorts of things she would steal if she were a robber but she only smiled and turned his hand in hers and studied it.

Qué ve? he said.

El mundo.

El mundo?

El mundo según usted.

Es gitana?

Quizás sí. Quizás no.

She placed her other hand over his. She looked out across the field where the children were riding.

Qué vio? he said.

Nada. No vi nada.

Es mentira.

Sí.

He asked her why she would not tell what she had seen but she only smiled and shook her head. He asked if there were no good news at all and she became more serious and nodded yes and she turned his palm up again. She said that he would live a long life. She traced the line where it circled under the base of his thumb.

Con mucha tristeza, he said.

Bastante, she said. She said that there was no life without sadness.

Pero usted ha visto algo malo, he said. Qué es?

She said that whatever she had seen could not be helped be it good or bad and that he would come to know it all in God's good time. She studied him with her head slightly cocked. As if there were some question he must ask if only he were quick enough to ask it but he did not know what it was and the moment was fast passing.

Qué novedades tiene de mi hermano, he said.

Cuál hermano?

He smiled. He said that he had but one brother.

She uncovered his hand and held it. She did not look at it. Es mentira, she said. Tiene dos.

He shook his head.

Mentira tras mentira, she said. She bent to study his palm.

Qué ve? he said.

Veo dos hermanos. Uno ha muerto.

He said that he had a sister who had died but she shook her head. Hermano, she said. Uno que vive, uno que ha muerto.

Cuál es cual?

No sabes?

No.

Ni yo tampoco.

She let go his hand and rose and took up the bucket. She looked again across the field at the children and the horse. She said that he had perhaps been fortunate in the night for the rain may have kept those indoors who might otherwise have been abroad but she said that the rain which befriends can also betray one. She said also that while the rain fell by the will of God evil chose its own hour and that those whom it sought out were perhaps not entirely lacking of some certain darkness in themselves. She said that the heart betrayed itself and the wicked often had eyes to see that which was hidden from the good.

Y sus ojos?

She tossed her head, her black hair flowed about her shoulders. She said that she had seen nothing. She said that it was only a game. Then she turned and walked across the field and up toward the road.

He rode south all day and in the evening he passed through the town of Casas Grandes and set out south along the road that he'd first ridden with his brother three years before, out past the darkening ruins in the dusk, past the ancient ballcourts where the nighthawks were hunting yet. The day following he reached the hacienda at San Diego and sat the horse in the old cottonwoods by the river. Then he rode the horse across the board bridge and up to the domicilios.

The Muñoz house stood empty. He walked through the rooms. There were no furnishings of any kind. In the niche where the Virgin had stood nothing but a gray scale of old candlewax pooled on the dusty plaster.

He stood in the door, then he walked out and mounted up and rode up to the compound and through the gates.

In the courtyard an old man who sat weaving baskets told him that they were gone. He asked the old man if he knew where they had gone but the old man seemed not to have a clear understanding of the idea of destination. He gestured widely at the world. The rider sat the horse and looked about the courtyard. The old touring car. The ruining buildings. A hen turkey roosting in a sashless window. The old man had bent again to his basket and he wished him a good day and turned the horse and leading the packhorse rode out through the tall arched gate and past the tenants' quarters and down the hill to the river and across the bridge again.

Two days later he rode through Las Varas and turned east toward La Boquilla on the road where he and his brother had first seen their father's horse come up from the lake into the road wet and dripping. There'd been no rain in the high country and the road was dusty underfoot. A dry wind blowing down from the north. On the distant plain beyond the lake the dust blowing out of Babícora as if it were afire. In the evening the big red Waco plane came in from the west and circled and dropped among the trees.

He camped on the plain and made a small fire that seethed in the wind like a forgefire and swallowed up his meager hoard of sticks and limbs. He watched it burn and watched it burn. The rags of flame that fled downcountry broke and vanished like a shout in the darkness. The next day he rode through Babícora and Santa Ana de Babícora and took the road north to Namiquipa.

The town was little more than a mining camp sited on a bluff above the river and he staked his horses below the town to the east in a grove of river willows and bathed in the river and washed his clothes. In the morning when he rode up into the town he encountered a wedding party coming along the road. A common wood carreta hung with bunting. A tarp of manta tied over a rickety bowframe of willow poles to keep the bride from the sun. The cart was drawn by a single small mule, gray and shambling, the bride sat alone in the cart holding a parasol open beneath the teetering canopy. In the road beside her walked a company of men in suits of black or suits of gray that had perhaps once been black and as they passed the bride turned and looked at him sitting the horse by the roadside like some pale witness of ill omen and she blessed herself and turned away again and they went on. He would see the cart again in the village. The wedding was not till after noon and they had ridden in so early solely to take advantage of the dustless condition of the road at that hour.

He followed them down into the town and he rode his horse through the small dusty streets. No one was about. He leaned from his horse and rapped at a random door and sat listening. No one came. He shucked his boot backwards out of the stirrup and kicked at the door by way of knocking louder but the door was imperfectly latched and it swung slowly open into the low darkness.

Hola, he called.

No one answered. He looked out down the narrow street. He looked in through the top of the door. Against the far wall of the hovel a candle burned in a dish and lying on a trestle with wildflowers from the mountains about him lay an old man dressed in his burial suit.

He got down and dropped the reins and stepped through the low door and doffed his hat. The old man had his hands composed upon his chest and he had no shoes on and his bare feet had been tied together at the toes with twine so that they would not lie asplay. Billy called softly into the darkness of the house but that room was all the house there was. Four empty chairs stood against one wall. A fine dust lay over everything. High in the rear wall was one small window and he crossed the room and looked out into the patio behind the house. An old horse-drawn hearse stood with the wagonshafts tilted back against the box. In an open shed at the far side of the enclosure stood a raw wood coffin on sawhorses made from pine poles. The lid of the coffin leaned against the wall of the shed. The coffin and the lid had been blacked on the outside but the inside of the box was raw new wood and no cloth or any lining to it.

He turned and looked at the old man on his coolingboard. The old man had a moustache and his moustache and his hair were silver gray. The hands crossed at his chest were broad and sturdy. His nails had not been cleaned. His skin was dark and dusty, his bare feet square and knotty. The suit he wore seemed small for him and was of a cut no longer seen even in that country and the old man had most likely had it all his life.

He picked up a small yellow flower in shape like a daisy and which he'd seen grow by the roadside and he looked at the flower and at the old man. In the room the smell of wax, a faint hint of rot. A frail afterscent of burnt copal. Qué novedades ahora viejo? he said. He put the flower in the buttonhole of his shirtpocket and went out and pulled the door shut behind him.

NONE IN THAT TOWN knew what had become of the girl. Her mother had moved away. Her sister had gone to Mexico years since, who knew what happened to such girls? In the afternoon the wedding party came up the street with the bride and groom sitting on the box of the covered carreta. They passed slowly, accompanied by drum and cornet, the cart creaking, the bride in her veil of white, the groom in black. Their smiles like grimaces, terror in their eyes. In appearance they were like certain folk figures of that country who dance together with their own pale bones painted on their costumes. The cart in its slow creaking like that which fords the dreams of the paisano in his weary sleep, passing slowly from left to right through the irrestorable night for which alone he labors, dying away toward the dawn in a faint rattle, a tenuous dread.

In the evening they carried the old man up from the dead-house and interred him in the cemetery among the tilted weathered boards that passed for tombstones in that austere upland country. No one questioned the right of the güero to be among the mourners and he nodded silently to them and entered the low house where a table had been laid with much of the best that the country had to offer. While he was standing against the wall eating tamales a woman came up to him and said to him that the girl would not be so easy to find as she was a notorious bandida and that many people were looking for her. She said it was rumored that at La Babícora they had put a price on her head. She said that some believed that the girl made gifts of silver and jewels to the poor and others believed that she was a witch or demon. It was also possible that the girl was dead although it was certainly not true that she had been killed at Ignacio Zaragosa.

He studied her. She was just a young woman of the campo.

Dressed in a poor black shift of cotton imperfectly mordant, imperfectly dyed. The blacking of it had left dark rings at her wrists.

Y por qué me dice esto pues? he said.

She stood with her upper lip in her lower teeth. Finally she said that it was because she knew who he was.

Y quién soy? he said.

She said that he was the brother of the güerito.

He lowered his foot from the wall behind him and looked at her and he looked beyond her at the dark mourners who filed past and foraged from the board like those same figures of death at the feast and he looked at her again. He asked her if she knew where he could find his brother.

She didnt answer. The movement of figures in the room slowed, the low mutterings of the condolent died to a whisper. The mourners wished one another that they profit from their meal and then all of it ground away in the history of its own repetition and he could hear those antecedent ceremonies dropping somewhere like wooden blocks into their slots. Like tumblers in a lock or like the wooden gearteeth in old machinery slipping one by one into the mortices cut in the cogwheel rolling up to meet them. No sabe? she said.

No.

She put her hand forefinger first against her mouth. Almost in such a gesture as to admonish one to silence. She held her hand out as if she might touch him. She said that his brother's bones lay in the cemetery at San Buenaventura.

It was dark when he went out and untied the horse and mounted up. He rode out past the sallow waxen windowlights and took the road south the way he'd come. Beyond the first rise the town vanished behind him and the stars swarmed everywhere in the blackness overhead and there was no sound at all in the night save the steady clop of the hooves in the road, the faint creak of leather, the breath of the horses.

He rode that country for weeks making inquiry of anyone willing to be inquired of. In a bodega in the mountain town of

Temosachic he first heard lines from that corrido in which the young güero comes down from the north. Pelo tan rubio. Pistola en mano. Qué buscas joven? Que te levantas tan temprano. He asked the corridero who was this joven of which he sang but he only said that it was a youth who sought justice as the song told and that he had been dead many years. The corridero held the fretted neck of his instrument with one hand and raised his glass from the table and toasted silently his inquisitor and toasted aloud the memory of all just men in the world for as it was sung in the corrido theirs was a bloodfilled road and the deeds of their lives were writ in that blood which was the world's heart's blood and he said that serious men sang their song and their song only.

Late April in the town of Madera he stabled his horse and went afoot through a fair in the field beyond the railtracks. It was cold in that mountain town and the air was filled with the smoke of piñon wood and the smell of pitch from the sawmill. In the field the lights were strung overhead and barkers called out their nostrums or called out the wonders hid within the shabby stenciled pitchtents staked with guyropes in the trampled grass. He bought a cup of cider from a vendor and watched the faces of the townsfolk, the faces dark and serious, the black eyes that seemed on the point of ignition beneath the feria lights. The girls that passed holding hands. The naive boldness of their glances. He stood before a painted caravan where a man in a red and gilded pulpit chanted to a gathering of men. A wheel with the figures from the lotería was fastened to the wall of the caravan and a girl in a red sheath and a black and silver bolero jacket stood on a wood platform ready to turn the wheel. The man in the pulpit turned to the girl and held out his cane and the girl smiled and pulled down on the side of the wheel and set it clacking. All faces turned to watch. The nails in the rim of the wheel went ratcheting over the leather pawl and the wheel slowed and came to a stop and the woman turned to the crowd and smiled. The pitchman held up his cane again and named the fading figure on the wheel whose turn had come.

La sirena, he cried.

No one moved.

Alguien?

He surveyed the crowd. They stood within a makeshift cuadra of rope. He held the cane out over them as if to ordain them into some sort of collective. The cane was black enamel and the silver head of it was in the form of a bust that may have been a likeness of the pitchman himself.

Otra vez, he cried.

His eyes swept over them. They swept over Billy where he stood alone at the edge of the crowd and they swept back. The wheel clacked and spun on its slightly eccentric track, the figures wheeled into a blur. The leather stop chattered.

A small toothless man sidled up to him and tugged at his shirt. He fanned before him the deck of cards. On the backs a pattern of arcane symbols woven into a damascene. Tome, he said. Pronto, pronto.

Cuánto?

Está libre. Tome.

He took a peso coin from his pocket and tried to hand it to the man but the man shook his head. He looked toward the wheel. The wheel slapped slowly.

Nada, nada, he said. Tenga prisa.

The wheel slapped, slapped. He took a card.

Espere, cried the pitchman. Espere...

The wheel turned a last soft click and stopped.

La calavera, cried the pitchman.

He turned over his card. Printed on it was the calavera.

Alguien? cried the pitchman. In the crowd they looked from one to the other.

The small man at his side seized his elbow. Lo tiene, he hissed. Lo tiene.

Qué gano?

The man shook his head impatiently. He tried to hold up his hand that held the card. He said that he would get to see.

Ver que?

Adentro, hissed the man. Adentro. He reached and snatched

the card from his grip and held it aloft. Aquí, he called. Aquí
tenemos la calavera.

The pitchman swept his cane in a slow acceleration over the
heads of the crowd and then suddenly pointed the silver cap
toward Billy and the shill.

Tenemos ganador, he cried. Adelante, adelante.

Venga, wheezed the shill. He tugged at Billy's elbow. But
Billy had already seen bleeding through the garish paintwork
old lettering from a prior life and he recognized the caravan of
the traveling opera company that he'd seen standing with its
gilded wheelspokes in the smoky courtyard of the hacienda at
San Diego when he and Boyd had first ridden through the gates
there in that long ago and the caravan he'd seen stranded by the
roadside while the beautiful diva sat beneath her awning and
waited for men and horses to return who would not return ever.
He pushed the shill's hand from his sleeve. No quiero ver, he
said.

Sí, sí, slurred the shill. Es un espectáculo. Nunca ha visto
nada como esto.

He seized the shill's thin wrist and held it. Oiga, hombre, he
said. No quiero verlo, me entiende?

The shill shrank in his grip, he cast a despairing look back
over his shoulder toward the pitchman who stood waiting with
his cane resting across the rostrum before him. All had turned
to see the winner at the outermost reach of the lights. The
woman by the wheel stood coquettishly, her forefinger twisted
into the dimple in her cheek. The pitchman raised his cane and
made with it a sweeping motion. Adelante, he cried. Qué pasó?

He pushed the shill from him and released his wrist but the
shill far from being cast down only crept to his side and plucking
with small motions of his fingers at his clothes began to whisper
at his ear of the attractions of the spectacle within the caravan.
The pitchman called out to him again. He said that everyone
was waiting. But Billy had already turned to go and the pitchman called after him a last time and made some comment to the
crowd which set them laughing and trying to see over their

shoulders. The shill stood forlornly with the barata in his hands but the pitchman said that there would be no third assay with the wheel but rather the woman who turned the wheel would make a selection herself as to who should enter free. She smiled and scanned the faces with her painted eyes and pointed out a young boy at the forefront of the crowd but the pitchman said that he was too young and that it would not be permitted and the woman made a pout and said that all the same he was muy guapo and then she selected a brownskinned peon who stood stiffly before her in what may have been rented clothes and came down the steps and took him by the hand and the pitchman held up a roll of tickets in his fist and the men pressed forward to purchase them.

He walked out beyond the strung lights and crossed the field to where he'd left his horse and he paid the establero and led Niño clear of the other animals and mounted up. He looked back at the haze of the carnival lights burning in the crisp and smoky air and then rode out across the railtracks and took the road south out of Madera toward Temosachic.

A week later he rode again through Babícora in the early morning dark. Cool and quiet. No dogs. The hoofclop of the horses. The blue moonshadow of the horses and the rider passing slant along the street in a constant headlong falling. The road north had been freshly graded with a fresno and he rode along the selvedge through the soft dirt of the endspill. Dark junipers out on the plain islanded in the dawn. Dark cattle. A white sun rising.

He watered the horses at a grassy ciénega where ancient cottonwoods stood in an elfin round and rolled himself into his soogan and slept. When he woke a man was sitting a horse watching him. He sat up. The man smiled. Te conozco, he said.

Billy reached and got his hat and put it on. Yeah, he said. And I know you.

Mánde?

Dónde está su compañero?

The man lifted one hand from the pommel in a vague gesture.
Se murió, he said. Dónde está la muchacha?

Lo mismo.

The man smiled. He said that God's ways were strange ones.

Tiene razón.

Y su hermano?

No sé. Muerto también, tal vez.

Tantos, said the man.

Billy looked toward where the horses were grazing. He'd
been sleeping with his head on the mochila where his pistol was
buckled away. The man's eyes followed his where they looked.
He said for every man that death selects another is reprieved
and he smiled in a conspiratorial manner. As one met with
another of his kind. He leaned forward with his hands squared
on the pommel of his saddle and spat.

Qué piensa? he said.

Billy wasnt sure what it was that he was being asked. He said
men die.

The man sat his horse and weighed this soberly. As if there
might be some deeper substrate to this reflection with which he
must reckon. He said that men believe death's elections to be a
thing inscrutable yet every act invites the act which follows and
to the extent that men put one foot before the other they are
accomplices in their own deaths as in all such facts of destiny.
He said that moreover it could not be otherwise that men's ends
are dictated at their birth and that they will seek their deaths in
the face of every obstacle. He said that both views were one
view and that while men may meet with death in strange and
obscure places which they might well have avoided it was more
correct to say that no matter how hidden or crooked the path to
their destruction yet they would seek it out. He smiled. He
spoke as one who seemed to understand that death was the
condition of existence and life but an emanation thereof.

Qué piensa usted? he said. Billy said that he had no opinion
beyond the one he'd given. He said that whether a man's life
was writ in a book someplace or whether it took its form day

by day was one and the same for it had but one reality and that was the living of it. He said that while it was true that men shape their own lives it was also true that they could have no shape other for what then would that shape be?

Bien dicho, the man said. He looked across the country. He said that he could read men's thoughts. Billy didnt point out to him that he'd already asked him twice for his. He asked the man could he tell what he was thinking now but the man only said that their thoughts were one and the same. Then he said he harbored no grudge toward any man over a woman for they were only property afoot to be confiscated and that it was no more than a game and not to be taken seriously by real men. He said that he had no very high opinion of men who killed over whores. In any case, he said, the bitch was dead, the world rolled on.

He smiled again. He had something in his mouth and he rolled it to one side and sucked at his teeth and rolled it back. He touched his hat.

Bueno, he said. El camino espera.

He touched his hat again and roweled the horse and sawed it around until its eyes rolled and it squatted and stamped and then went trotting out through the trees and into the road where it soon disappeared from sight. Billy unbuckled the mochila and took out the pistol and thumbed open the gate and turned the cylinder and checked the chambers and then lowered the hammer with his thumb and sat for a long time listening and waiting.

On the fifteenth of May by the first newspaper he'd seen in seven weeks he rode again into Casas Grandes and stabled his horse and took a room at the Camino Recto Hotel. He rose in the morning and walked down the tiled hallway to the bath. When he came back he stood in the window where the morning light fell slant upon the raw cords in the worn carpet underfoot and listened to a girl singing in the garden below. She was sitting on a cloth of white canvas and piled on the canvas were nueces or pecans some bushels in quantity. She sat with a flat stone in the crook of her knees and she was breaking the pecans with a stone mano and as she worked she sang. Leaning forward with her dark hair veiled about her hands she worked and sang. She sang:

> Pueblo de Bachiniva
> Abril era el mes
> Jinetes armados
> Llegaron los seis

She crushed the hulls between the stones, she separated out the meats and dropped them in a jar at her side.

> Si tenía miedo
> No se le veía en su cara
> Cuantos vayan llegando
> El güerito les espera

Splitting out with her fineboned fingers the meat from the hulls, the delicate fissured hemispheres in which is writ we must believe each feature of the tree which bore them, each feature of the tree they'd come to bear. Then she sang the same two verses over. He buttoned his shirt and got his hat and went down the stairs and out into the courtyard. When she saw him coming across the cobbles she stopped singing. He touched his hat and wished her a good day. She looked up and smiled. She was a girl of perhaps sixteen. She was very beautiful. He asked her if she knew any more verses of the corrido which she sang but she did not. She said that it was an old corrido. She said that it was very sad and that at the end the güerito and his novia die in each other's arms for they have no more ammunition. She said that at the end the patrón's men ride away and the people come from the town and carry the güerito and his novia to a secret place and bury them there and the little birds flew away but that she did not remember all the words and anyway she was embarrassed that he had been listening to her sing. He smiled. He told her that she had a pretty voice and she turned away and clucked her tongue.

He stood looking out across the courtyard toward the mountains to the west. The girl watched him.

Déme su mano, she said.

Mánde?

Déme su mano. She held out her own hand in a fist before her. He squatted on his bootheels and held out his hand and she gave him a handful of the shelled pecans and then closed his hand with hers and looked about as if it were some secret gift and someone might see. Ándale pues, she said. He thanked her and stood and walked back across the courtyard and up to his room but when he looked from the window again she was gone.

Days to come he rode up through the high country of the Babícora. He'd build his fire in some sheltered swale and at night sometimes he'd walk out over the grasslands and lie on the ground in the world's silence and study the burning firmament above him. Walking back to the fire those nights he often thought about Boyd, thought of him sitting by night at just such a fire in just such country. The fire in the bajada no more than a glow, hid in the ground like some secret glimpse of the earth's burning core broke through into the darkness. He seemed to himself a person with no prior life. As if he had died in some way years ago and was ever after some other being who had no history, who had no ponderable life to come.

He saw in his riding occasional parties of vaqueros crossing the high grasslands, sometimes mounted on mules for their good footing in the mountains, sometimes driving beeves before them. It was cold in the mountains at night but they seemed thinly dressed and had only their serapes in which to sleep. They were called mascareñas for the whitefaced cattle bred on the Babícora and they were called agringados because they worked for the white man. They crossed in silent defile over the talus slopes and rode up through the passes toward the high grassy vegas, sitting their horses with their easy formality, the low sun catching the tin cups tied to their saddlehorns. He saw their fires burning on the mountain at night but never did he go to them.

On a certain evening just before dark he entered into a road and turned and followed it west. The red sun that burned in the broad gap of the mountains before him sloughed out of its form and was slowly sucked away to light all the sky in a deep red afterflash. When darkness had come there stood in the distance on the plain the single yellow light from a dwelling and he rode on until he came to a small weatherboard cabin and sat the horse before it and called out.

A man came to the door and stepped out onto the gallery. Quién es? he said.

Un viajero.

Cuántos son ustedes?

Yo sólo.

Bueno, the man said. Desmonte. Pásale.

He stepped down and tied the bridlereins about the porch post and mounted the steps and removed his hat. The man held the door for him and he entered and the man followed and shut the door and nodded toward the fire.

They sat and drank coffee. The man's name was Quijada and he was a Yaqui indian from western Sonora and he was the same gerente of the Nahuerichic division of the Babícora who'd told Boyd to cut their horses out of the remuda and take them. He'd seen the lone güero riding in the mountains and told the alguacil not to molest him. He told his guest that he knew who he was and why he'd come. Then he leaned back in his chair. He raised the cup to his lips and drank and watched the fire.

You're the man give us back our horses, Billy said.

He nodded. He leaned forward and he looked at Billy and then he sat looking into the fire. The thick handleless porcelain cup from which he drank looked like a chemist's mortar and he sat with his elbows on his knees and held it before him in both hands and Billy thought that he would say something more but he did not. Billy drank from his cup and sat holding it. The fire ticked. Outside in the world all was silence. Is my brother dead? he said.

Yes.

He was killed in Ignacio Zaragosa?

No. In San Lorenzo.

The girl too?

No. When they took her away she was covered in blood and she was falling down and so it was natural that people thought that she had been shot but it was not so.

What became of her?

I dont know. Perhaps she went back to her family. She was very young.

I asked about her in Namiquipa. They didnt know what had become of her.

They would not tell you in Namiquipa.

Where is my brother buried?

He is buried at Buenaventura.

Is there a stone?

There is a board. He was very popular with the people. He was a popular figure.

He didnt kill the manco in La Boquilla.

I know.

I was there.

Yes. He killed two men in Galeana. No one knows why. They did not even work for the latifundio. But the brother of one was a friend to Pedro Lopéz.

The alguacil.

The alguacil. Yes.

He'd seen him once in the mountains, he and his henchmen, the three of them descending a ridgeline in the twilight. The alguacil carried a short sword in a beltscabbard and he answered to no one. Quijada leaned back and sat with his boots crossed before him. The cup in his lap. Both watched the fire. As if some work were there annealing. Quijada raised his cup as if to drink. Then he lowered it again.

There is the latifundio of Babícora, he said. With all the wealth and power of Mr Hearst to call upon. And there are the campesinos in their rags. Which do you believe will prevail?

I dont know.

His days are numbered.

Mr Hearst?

Yes.

Why do you work for the Babícora?

Because they pay me.

Who was Socorro Rivera?

Quijada tapped the rim of his cup softly with the gold band on his finger. Socorro Rivera tried to organize the workers against the latifundio. He was killed at the paraje of Las Varitas by the Guardias Blancas five years ago along with two other men. Crecencio Macías and Manuel Jiménez.

Billy nodded.

The soul of Mexico is very old, said Quijada. Whoever claims to know it is either a liar or a fool. Or both. Now that the yankees have again betrayed them the Mexicans are eager to reclaim their indian blood. But we do not want them. Most particularly the Yaqui. The Yaqui have long memories.

I believe you. Did you ever see my brother again after we left with the horses?

No.

How do you know about him?

He was a hunted man. Where would you go? Inevitably he was taken in by Casares. You go to the enemy of your enemies.

He was only fifteen. Sixteen, I guess.

All the better.

They didnt take very good care of him, did they?

He didnt want to be taken care of. He wanted to shoot people. What makes one a good enemy also makes one a good friend.

Yet you work for Mr Hearst?

Yes.

He turned and looked at Billy. I am not a Mexican, he said. I dont have these loyalties. These obligations. I have others.

Would you have shot him yourself?

Your brother?

Yes.

If it had come to that. Yes.

Maybe I ought not to be drinkin your coffee.

Maybe not.

They sat for a long time. Finally Quijada leaned forward and studied his cup. He should have gone home, he said.

Yes.

Why didnt he?

I dont know. Maybe the girl.

The girl would not have gone with him?

I suppose she would have. He didnt rightly have a home to go to.

Maybe you are the one who should have cared for him better.

He wasnt easy to care for. You said it yourself.

Yes.

What does the corrido say?

Quijada shook his head. The corrido tells all and it tells nothing. I heard the tale of the güerito years ago. Before your brother was even born.

You dont think it tells about him?

Yes, it tells about him. It tells what it wishes to tell. It tells what makes the story run. The corrido is the poor man's history. It does not owe its allegiance to the truths of history but to the truths of men. It tells the tale of that solitary man who is all men. It believes that where two men meet one of two things can occur and nothing else. In the one case a lie is born and in the other death.

That sounds like death is the truth.

Yes. It sounds like death is the truth. He looked at Billy. Even if the güerito in the song is your brother he is no longer your brother. He cannot be reclaimed.

I aim to take him back with me.

It will not be permitted.

Who would I go to?

There is no one to go to.

Who would I go to if there was someone?

You could apply to God. Otherwise there is no one.

Billy shook his head. He sat regarding his own dark visage

where it yawed in the white ring of the cup. After a while he looked up. He looked into the fire. Do you believe in God? he said.

Quijada shrugged. On godly days, he said.

No one can tell you what your life is goin to be, can they?

No.

It's never like what you expected.

Quijada nodded. If people knew the story of their lives how many would then elect to live them? People speak about what is in store. But there is nothing in store. The day is made of what has come before. The world itself must be surprised at the shape of that which appears. Perhaps even God.

We come down here to get our horses. Me and my brother. I dont think he even cared about the horses, but I was too dumb to see it. I didnt know nothin about him. I thought I did. I think he knew a lot more about me. I'd like to take him back and bury him in his own country.

Quijada drained his cup and sat holding it in his lap.

I take it you dont think that's such a good idea.

I think you may have some problems.

But that aint all you think.

No.

You think he belongs where he's at.

I think the dead have no nationality.

No. But their kin do.

Quijada didnt answer. After a long time he stirred. He leaned forward. He turned the white porcelain bowl up and held it in the palm of his hand and regarded it. The world has no name, he said. The names of the cerros and the sierras and the deserts exist only on maps. We name them that we do not lose our way. Yet it was because the way was lost to us already that we have made those names. The world cannot be lost. We are the ones. And it is because these names and these coordinates are our own naming that they cannot save us. That they cannot find for us the way again. Your brother is in that place which the world has chosen for him. He is where he is supposed to be. And yet the place he has found is also of his own choosing. That is a piece of luck not to be despised.

GRAY SKY, gray land. All day he slouched north on the wet and slouching horse through the sandy muck of the upcountry roads. The rain went harrying over the road before him in the gusts of wind and rattled over his slicker and the hooftracks oozed shut behind him. In the evening he heard again the cranes overhead, passing high above the overcast, balancing beneath them the bight of the earth's curve, earth's weather. Their metal eyes grooved to the pathways which God has chosen for them to follow. Their hearts in flood.

He rode into the town of San Buenaventura in the evening and he rode through pools of standing water past the alameda with its whitepainted treetrunks and the old white church and out along the old road to Gallego. The rain had stopped and rain dripped from the alameda trees and dripped from the high canales in the mudwalled houses he passed. The road led up through the low hills to the east of the town and set in a bench of land there a mile or so above the town lay the cemetery.

He turned off and slogged out along the muddy lane and halted his horse before the wooden gates. The cemetery was a large and wild enclosure set in a field filled with loose stones and brambles and surrounded by a low mud wall already then in ruins. He halted and looked out over this desolation. He turned and looked back at the packhorse and he looked at the gray scud of clouds and at the evening light failing in the west. A wind was blowing down from the gap in the mountains and he stepped down and dropped the reins and passed through the gate and started out across the rough cobbled field. A raven flew up out of the bracken and parried away on the wind croaking thinly. The red sandstone dolmens that stood upright among the low tablets and crosses on that wild heath looked like the distant ruins of some classic enclave ringed about by the blue mountains, the closer hills.

Most of the graves were no more than cairns of rock without marker of any kind. Some held a simple wooden cross composed of two slats nailed together or twisted together with wire. The cobbled rocks everywhere underfoot were the scattered remains of these cairns and ignoring the red stone steles this place looked the burial of some aftermath of battle. Other than the wind in the wild rough grass there was no sound at all. He walked out along a narrow and uncertain footpath winding among the graves, among the slabs and sepulchre tablets blacked over with lichen. In the middle distance a red stone pillar in the shape of a pollarded treetrunk.

His brother was buried against the southmost wall under a board cross in which had been burned with a hot nail the words Fall el 24 de febrero 1943 sus hermanos en armas dedican este recuerdo D E P. A ring of rusted wire that once had been a wreath leaned against the board. There was no name.

He squatted and took off his hat. Off to the south a pile of trash was smoldering in the damp and a black smoke rose into the dark overcast. The desolation of that place was a thing exquisite.

It was dark when he rode back into Buenaventura. He dismounted before the church door and walked in and took off his hat. At the altar a few small candles burned and in that half fugitive light knelt a solitary figure bent at prayer. He walked up the aisle. There were loose tiles in the floor that rocked and clicked under his boots. He bent and touched the kneeling figure on the arm. Señora, he said.

She raised her head, a dark seamed face faintly visible in the darker folds of her rebozo.

Dónde está el sepulturero?

Muerto.

Quién está encargado del cementerio?

Dios.

Dónde está el sacerdote.

Se fué.

He looked about at the dim interior of the church. The woman seemed to be waiting for further questions but he could think of none to put.

Qué quiere, joven? she said.

Nada. Está bien. He looked down at her. Por quién está orando? he said.

She said that she only prayed. She said that she left it to God as to how the prayers should be apportioned. She prayed for all. She would pray for him.

Gracias.

No puedo hacerlo de otro modo.

He nodded. He knew her well enough, this old woman of Mexico, her sons long dead in that blood and violence which her prayers and her prostrations seemed powerless to appease. Her frail form was a constant in that land, her silent anguishings. Beyond the church walls the night harbored a millennial dread panoplied in feathers and the scales of royal fish and if it yet fed upon the children still who could say what worse wastes of war and torment and despair the old woman's constancy might not have stayed, what direr histories yet against which could be counted at last nothing more than her small figure bent and mumbling, her crone's hands clutching her beads of fruitseed. Unmoving, austere, implacable. Before just such a God.

When he rode out the next morning early the rain had stopped but the day had not cleared and the landscape lay gray under a gray sky. To the south the raw peaks of the Sierra del Nido loomed out of the clouds and closed away again. He dismounted at the wooden gate and hobbled the packhorse and untied the spade and mounted up again and rode out down the footpath among the cobbled rocks with the spade over his shoulder.

When he reached the gravesite he stood down and chucked the spade in the ground and took his gloves from the saddlebag and looked at the gray skies and finally he unsaddled the horse and hobbled it and left it to graze among the stones. Then he turned and squatted and rocked the fragile wooden cross loose in its clutch of rocks and lifted it away. The spade was a primitive thing helved in a long paloverde pole and the tang bore the marks where it had been beaten out over a pritchel and the seam rudely welded shut at the forge. He hefted it in his hand and looked again at the sky and bent and began to shovel away the cairn of loose rock over his brother's grave.

He was a long time at his work. He'd taken off his hat and after a while he took off his shirt and laid it across the wall. By what he reckoned to be noon he'd dug down some three feet and he stood the shovel in the dirt and walked back to where he'd left the saddle and the bags and he got out his lunch of beans wrapped in tortillas and sat in the grass eating and drinking water from the canvascovered zinc bottle. There had been no one along the road all morning except for a solitary bus, grinding slowly up the grade and on through the gap toward Gallego to the east.

In the afternoon three dogs appeared and sat down among the stones to watch him. He bent to pick up a rock but they ducked and vanished among the bracken. Later a car came out the cemetery road and stopped at the gate and two women came out along the path and went on to the far west corner of the burial ground. After a while they came back. The man who had driven them sat on the wall and smoked and watched Billy but he did not speak. Billy dug on.

Midafternoon the blade struck the box. He'd thought maybe there would be none. He dug on. By the time he had the top of the box dug clear there was little left of the day. He dug down along the side and felt along the wood for handles but he couldnt find any. He dug on until he had one end of the box clear and by then it was growing dark. He stood the spade in the loose dirt and went to get Niño.

He saddled the horse and led him back to the grave and took down the catchrope and doubled and dallied it and then worked the free end around the box, forcing it along the wood with the blade of the shovel. Then he pitched the shovel to one side and climbed out and untracted the horse and led him slowly forward.

The rope grew taut. He looked back. Then he eased the horse forward again. There was a muffled explosion of wood in the hole and the rope went slack. The horse stopped.

He walked back. The box had collapsed and he could see Boyd's bones in their burial clothes through the broken boards. He sat down in the dirt. The sun had set and it was growing dark. The horse stood at the end of the rope waiting. He felt suddenly cold and he got up and walked over to the wall and got his shirt and pulled it on and came back and stood.

You could just shovel the dirt back in, he said. It wouldnt take a hour.

He walked over to the saddlebags and got out his matches and came back and lit one and held it out over the grave. The box was badly caved. A musty cellar odor rose from the dark ground. He shook out the match and walked over to the horse and unhitched the rope and came back coiling it in his hand and he stood with the coiled rope in the blue and windless dusk and looked off to the north where under the overcast the earliest stars were burning. Well, he said. You could do that.

He worked the end of the rope loose from the coffinbox and laid the rope by on the mound of loose dirt. Then he took up the spade and with the blade of it he split away a long sliver of wood from one of the broken boards and knocked the dirt loose from it against the box and struck a match and got it lit and stood it slantwise in the ground. Finally he climbed down into the grave and by that pale and fluttering light he began to pry apart the boards with the spade and cast them out until the remains of his brother lay wholly to sight, composed on a pallet of rotting rags, lost in his clothes as always.

He rode the horse back out through the gate and got down and skylighted the packhorse off to the south and remounted and rode out and brought the animal back and led it through the gates and back to the grave. He dismounted and untied the bedroll and unrolled it on the ground and pulled loose the tarp and spread it out. It was a windless night and his cryptboard taper was still burning at the side of the grave. He climbed down into the excavation and gathered his brother up in his arms and lifted him out. He weighed nothing. He composed the bones upon the soogan and folded them away and tied the bundle shut at the ends with lengths of pigginstring while the horse stood watching. Over on the gravel highway he could hear the whine of a truck on the grade and the lights came up and swept slowly across the desert and over the bleak headlands and then the truck passed on in its pale wake of dust and ground on toward the east.

By the time he'd filled the grave back in it was close to midnight. He trod down the dirt with his boots and then shoveled the loose rocks back over the top and lastly he took the cross from where he'd leaned it against the wall and stood it in the rocks and piled rocks about it to support it. The wooden torch had long since burned out and he took the charred end of it up and threw it across the wall. Then he threw the spade after it.

He lifted Boyd and laid him across the wooden packframe and he rolled up the blankets from his bedroll and laid them across the horse's haunches and tied everything down. Then he walked over and picked up his hat and put it on and picked up the waterbottle and hung it by its strap over the saddlehorn and mounted up and turned the horse. He sat there for a minute taking a last look around. Then he got down again. He walked over to the grave and pulled the wooden cross loose from the cobbles and carried it back to the packhorse and tied it down on the leftside forks of the packtree and then mounted up again and leading the packhorse rode out through the cemetery and through the gate and down the road. When he reached the highway he crossed it and struck out crosscountry toward the watershed of the Santa María, keeping the polestar to his right, looking back from time to time to see how rode the canvas that held his brother's remains. The little desert foxes barking. The old gods of that country tracing his progress over the darkened ground. Perhaps logging his name into their ancient daybook of vanities.

In two nights' riding he passed the lights of Casas Grandes off to the west, the small city receding away behind him on the plain. He crossed the old road coming down from Guzmán and Sabinal and struck the Casas Grandes River and took the trail north along the river bank. In the early morning hours and before it was quite light he passed through the pueblo of Corralitos, half abandoned, half in ruins. The houses of the town loopholed against the vanished Apaches. The naked slagheaps dark and volcanic against the skyline. He crossed the railroad tracks and an hour north of the town in the gray dawn four horsemen sallied forth from a grove of trees and halted their mounts in the track before him.

He reined the horse. The riders sat silently. The dark animals they rode raised their noses as if to search him out on the air. Beyond the trees the bright flat shape of the river lay like a knife. He studied the men. He'd not seen them move yet they seemed closer. They sat divided before him on the track two and two.

Qué tiene allá? they said.

Los huesos de mi hermano.

They sat in silence. One of the riders detached himself and rode forward. He crossed the track in his riding forward and then crossed it back. Riding erect, archly. As if at some sinister dressage. He halted the horse almost within armreach and he leaned forward with his forearms crossed on the pommel of his saddle.

Huesos? he said.

Sí.

The new light in the east was behind him and his face was a shadow under the shape of his hat. The other riders were darker figures yet. The rider sat upright in the saddle and looked back towards them. Then he turned to Billy again.

Abralo, he said.

No.

No?

They sat. There was a flash of white beneath his hat as if he'd smiled. What he'd done was to seize his horse's reins in his teeth. The next flash was a knife that had come from somewhere in his clothing and caught the light in turning for just a moment like a fish deep in a river. Billy dropped down from the offside of his horse. The bandolero caught up the packhorse's leadrope but the packhorse balked and squatted on its haunches and the man booted his horse forward and made a pass at the hitchropes with his knife while the packhorse sawed about on the end of the lead. Some among his companions laughed and the man swore and he hauled the packhorse forward and dallied the leadrope to his saddlehorn again and reached and cut the ropes and pulled the soogan of bones to the ground.

Billy was trying to undo the tie on the flap of the saddlebag to get to his pistol but Niño turned and stamped and backed away sawing his head. The bandolero undallied and cast off the leadrope and stepped down. The packhorse turned and went trotting. The man bent above the shrouded form on the ground and unseamed with a single long pass of the knife ropes and soogan all from end to end and kicked aside the coverings to reveal in the graying light Boyd's poor form in the loosely fitting coat with his hands crossed at his chest, the withered hands with the bones imprinted in the leather skin, lying there with his caven face turned up and clutching himself like some fragile being fraught with cold in that indifferent dawn.

You son of a bitch, said Billy. You son of a bitch.

Es un engaño? said the man. Es un engaño?

He kicked at the poor desiccated thing. He turned with the knife.

Dónde está el dinero?

Las alforjas, called out one of the riders. Billy had swung under Niño's neck and he reached again for the flap of the saddlebag on the horse's offside. The bandolero cut open the bedroll under his feet and kicked it apart and trod in it with his boots and turned and then reached and seized Niño's bridle-reins. But the horse must have begun to see the loosening of some demoniac among them for he reared and backed and in his backing trod among the bones and he reared again and pawed and the bandolero was snatched off balance and one forehoof caught his belt and ripped it from him and tore open the front of his trousers. He scrambled from under the horse and swore wildly and made a grab again for the swinging reins and the men behind him laughed and before anyone would have thought of such a thing occurring he plunged his knife into the horse's chest.

The horse stopped and stood quivering. The point of the blade had bedded itself in the animal's breastbone and the bandolero stepped back and threw out his hands.

Goddamn you to hell, Billy said. He held the trembling horse by the throatlatch and took hold of the handle of the knife and pulled the blade from the horse's chest and flung it away. Blood welled, blood ran down the front of the horse. He snatched off his hat and pushed it against the wound and looked wildly back at the mounted men. They sat their horses as before. One of them leaned and spat and jerked his chin at the others. Vámonos, he said.

The bandolero was demanding that Billy go fetch the knife. Billy didnt answer. He held his hat against the horse's chest and tried once more to reach back and unfasten the saddlebag pocket but he could not reach it. The bandolero reached and got hold of the tiestraps and pulled down the saddlebags onto the ground and dragged them from under the horse.

Vámonos, called the rider.

But the bandolero had already found the pistol and he held it up to show to them. He dumped the bags out and kicked Billy's possibles over the ground, his spare clothes, his razor. He picked up a shirt and held it up and then draped it across his shoulder and he cocked the pistol and spun the cylinder and let the hammer down again. He stepped across the wreckage of the bones unshrouded from out of the soogan and cocked the pistol and put it to Billy's head and demanded his money. Billy could feel his hat going warm and sticky with blood where he held it to the horse's chest. The blood was seeping through the felt and running on his arm. You go to hell, he said.

Vámonos, called the rider. He turned his horse

The man with the pistol looked at them. Tengo que encontrar mi cuchillo, he called.

He uncocked the pistol and went to shove it in his belt but he had no belt. He turned and looked upriver where the day was coming beyond the brambly river breaks. The breath of the standing horses plumed and vanished. The leader told him to get his horse. He said that he did not need his knife and that he had killed a good horse for no reason.

Then they were gone. Billy stood holding the crushed and bloodsogged hat and he heard the horses crossing the river upstream and then he just heard the river and the first birds that were waking in that country and his own breath and the labored breathing of the horse. He put his arm around the horse's neck and held it and he could feel it trembling and feel it lean against him and he was afraid that it would die and he could feel in the horse's breast a despair much like his own.

He wrung the blood from the hat and wiped his hand on his trousers and unbuckled and pulled down the saddle and left it lying where it fell in the track along with the other wreckage there and he led the horse slowly out through the trees and across a gravel bar and into the river. The water was cold running into his boots and he talked to the horse and bent and lifted a hatful of water and poured it over the animal's chest. The horse steamed in the cold and its breathing had begun to suck and rattle and it sounded all wrong. He put the palm of his hand over the hole but the blood ran between his fingers. He stripped off his shirt and folded it and pushed it against the animal's chest but the shirt soon filled with blood and still the blood ran.

He'd let the reins trail in the river and he patted the horse and spoke to it and left it standing there while he waded to the river bank and clawed up a handful of wet clay from under the roots of the willows. He came back and plastered the clay over the wound and troweled it down with the flat of his hand. He rinsed out the shirt and wrung the water from it and folded it over the plaster of mud and waited in the gray light with the steam rising off the river. He didnt know if the blood would ever stop running but it did and in the first pale reach of sunlight across the eastern plain the gray landscape seemed to hush and the birds to hush and in the new sun the peaks of the distant mountains to the west beyond the wild Bavispe country rose out of the dawn like a dream of the world. The horse turned and laid its long bony face upon his shoulder.

He led the animal ashore and up into the track and turned it to face the light. He looked in its mouth for blood but there was none that he could see. Old Niño, he said. Old Niño. He left the saddle and the saddlebags where they'd fallen. The trampled bedrolls. The body of his brother awry in its wrappings with one yellow forearm outflung. He walked the horse slowly at his elbow and held the mudstained shirt against its chest. His boots sloshed with river water and he was very cold. They walked up the track and into a grove of wild mahogany where he'd be partly hid from sight of any parties passing along the river and then he went back and got the saddle and the saddlebags and the bedroll. Lastly he went to fetch the remains of his brother.

The bones seemed held together only by the dry outer covering of hide and by their integuments but they were of a piece and nothing scattered. He knelt in the road and refolded the weightless arms and wrapped the soogan about and sorted the ropes and tied the ends to make the severed pieces do. By the time he had all this done the sun was well up and he gathered the bones in his arms and carried them up into the trees and laid them on the ground. Lastly he walked back out to the river and washed and wrung out his hat and filled it with river water and carried it back to the horse to see if it would drink. The horse would not. It was lying in the leaves and the shirt was lying in the leaves and the clay compress had begun to break away and blood was running from the wound again and pooling darkly in the little jagged cups of the dry mahogany leaves and the horse would not raise its head.

He walked out and looked for the packhorse but he couldnt see it. He went to the river and squatted and rinsed out the shirt and put it on and he got a fresh handful of clay from under the willows and carried it back and caked the new mud over the old and sat shivering in the leaves watching the horse. After a while he went back out and down the track to hunt for the other horse.

He couldnt find it. When he came back up the river he picked up the waterbottle where it lay by the side of the trail and he picked up his cup and his razor and walked back up to the trees. The horse was shivering in the leaves and he pulled one of the blankets from the bedroll and spread it over the horse and sat with his hand on the horse's shoulder and after a while he fell asleep.

He woke with a start from some half desperate dream. He bent over the horse where it lay quietly breathing among the leaves and he looked at the sun to see how far the day had got to. His shirt was almost dry on him and he unbuttoned the pocket and took out his money and spread it out to dry. Then he got the box of wood matches out of the saddlebags and spread them also. He walked out down the track to the spot where the ambuscade had occurred and cast about in the trackside chaparral until he found the knife. It was an oldfashioned dirk ground down out of a cheap military knife with an edge honed into both sides of the blade. He wiped it on his trousers and went back and put the knife with his other plunder. Then he walked out to where he'd left Boyd. A column of red ants had found the bones and he squatted in the leaves and studied them and then rose and trod them into the dirt and picked up the soogan and carried it out and lodged it in the fork of one of the trees and walked back and sat beside the horse.

No one passed the day long. In the afternoon he went once more to look for the other horse. He thought maybe it had gone upriver or that the highwaymen had taken it but in any case he never saw it again. By dark the matches had dried and he built a fire and put some beans to boil and sat by the fire and listened to the river passing in the dark. The cottoncolored moon that had stood in the daysky to the east rose overhead and he lay in his blankets and watched to see if any birds might cross before it on their way upriver north but if they did he did not see them and after a while he slept.

In the night as he slept Boyd came to him and squatted by the deep embers of the fire as he'd done times by the hundreds and smiled his soft smile that was not quite cynical and he took off his hat and held it before him and looked down into it. In the dream he knew that Boyd was dead and that the subject of his being so must be approached with a certain caution for that which was circumspect in life must be doubly so in death and he'd no way to know what word or gesture might subtract him back again into that nothingness out of which he'd come. When finally he did ask him what it was like to be dead Boyd only smiled and looked away and would not answer. They spoke of other things and he tried not to wake from the dream but the ghost dimmed and faded and he woke and lay looking up at the stars through the bramblework of the treelimbs and he tried to think of what that place could be where Boyd was but Boyd was dead and wasted in his bones wrapped in the soogan upriver in the trees and he turned his face to the ground and wept.

He was asleep in the morning when he heard the shouts of arrieros and the crack of whips and a wild singing in the woods downriver. He pulled on his boots and walked out to where the horse lay in the leaves. Its side rose and fell beneath the blanket that he had feared would be stiff and cold and it turned up one eye to him as he knelt over it. An eye in which lay cupped the sky and arching trees and his own nearing face. He placed one hand over the animal's chest where the mud had caked and dried and broken. The hair was stiff and bristly with dried blood. He stroked the muscled shoulder and spoke to the horse and the horse exhaled slowly through its nose.

He fetched water again in his hat but the horse could not drink without rising. He sat and wet its mouth with his hand and listened to the arrieros on the track drawing nearer and after a while he rose and walked out and stood waiting for them.

They appeared out of the trees driving a team of six yoked oxen and they wore costumes such as he'd never seen before. Indians or gypsies perhaps by the bright colors of the shirts and the sashes that they wore. They drove the oxen with jerkline and jockeystick and the oxen labored and swayed in the traces and their breath steamed in the morning cold. Behind them on a handmade float built from green lumber and carried on old truckaxles was an airplane. It was of some ancient vintage and it was disassembled and the wings tied down with ropes alongside the fuselage. The rudder in the vertical stabilizer swung back and forth in small erratic movements with the jostling of the float as if to make corrections in their course and the oxen swayed heavily in their harness and the mismatched rubber tires rumbled softly over the stones and through the weeds on either side of the narrow track.

The drovers when they saw him raised their hands in greeting and cried out. Almost as if they'd been expecting to come upon him soon or late. They wore necklaces and silver bracelets and some wore hooplets of gold in their ears and they called out to him and pointed along the narrow road upstream in the river's bend to a grassy flat where they would stop and rendezvous. The airplane was little more than a skeleton with sunbleached shreds of linen the color of stewed rhubarb clinging to the steambent ashwood ribs and stays and inside you could see the wires and cables that ran aft to the rudder and elevators and the cracked and curled and sunblacked leather of the seats and in their tarnished nickel bezels the glass of instrument dials glaucous and clouded from the pumicing of the desert sands. The wingstruts were tied in bundles alongside and the blades of the propellor were bent back along the cowling and the landingstruts were bent beneath the fuselage.

They passed on and halted in the flat and they left the youngest among them to tend the animals and then they came back down the track rolling cigarettes and passing among them an esclarajo made from a 50 caliber shellcasing in which burned a bit of tow. They were gypsies from Durango and the first thing that they asked him was what was the matter with the horse.

He told them that the horse was wounded and that he thought its condition was serious. One of them asked him when this had occurred and he said that it was the day before. He sent one of the younger men back to the float and in a few minutes he returned with an old canvas musette bag. Then they all walked up through the trees to look at the horse.

The gypsy knelt in the leaves and looked first into the animal's eyes. Then he pinched away the cracked mud from its chest and looked at the wound. He looked up at Billy.

Herida de cuchillo, said Billy.

The gypsy's expression did not change and he did not take his eyes from Billy. Billy looked at the other men. They were squatting on their haunches about the horse. He thought that if the horse died they might eat it. He said that the horse had been attacked by a lunatic one of four among a band of robbers. The man nodded. He passed his hand across the underside of his chin. He did not look at the horse again. He asked Billy if he wanted to sell the horse and Billy knew for the first time that the horse would live.

They squatted there, all watching him. He looked at the drover. He said that the horse had belonged to his father and that he could not part with him and the man nodded and opened the bag.

Porfirio, he said. Tráigame agua.

He looked down through the trees toward Billy's camp where a thin wisp of smoke stood in the morning air motionless as rope. He called after the man to put the water to boil and then looked at Billy again. Con su permiso, he said.

Por supuesto.

Ladrónes.

Sí. Ladrónes.

The drover looked down at the horse. He gestured with his chin out toward the tree where Boyd's bones were lodged in their trussings.

Qué tiene allá? he said.

Los huesos de mi hermano.

Huesos, said the gypsy. He turned and looked toward the river where his man had gone with the bucket. The other three men crouched waiting. Rafael, he said. Leña. He turned to Billy and smiled. He looked about at the little grove of trees and he put the flat of his hand to his cheek in a curious gesture such as a man might make who remembers he has forgotten something. He wore on one forefinger an ornate ring of gold and jewels and he wore a golden rope about his throat. He smiled again and gestured toward the fire that they proceed there.

They collected wood and built back the fire and they fetched rocks to make a trivet and there they set the bucket to boil. Soaking in the pail were several handfuls of small green leaves and the waterbearer had covered the bucket with what looked to be an old brass cymbal and all sat about the fire and watched the bucket and after a while it began to steam among the flames.

The one called Rafael lifted the cover with a stick and laid the cover by and stirred the green froth within and then put the cover back again. A pale green tea ran down the sides of the bucket and hissed in the fire. The chief of the drovers sat rolling a cigarette. He passed the cloth pouch on to the man beside him and he leaned and took a burning branch from the fire and with his head cocked to one side lit the cigarette and then put the branch back in the fire. Billy asked him if he himself was not afraid of robbers in that country but the man only said that the robbers were loath to molest the gitanos for they also were men of the road.

Y adónde van con el aeroplano? said Billy.

The gypsy gestured with his chin. Al norte, he said.

They smoked. The bucket steamed. The gypsy smiled.

Con respecto al aeroplano, he said, hay tres historias. Cuál quiere oír?

Billy smiled. He said that he wished to hear the true history.

The gypsy pursed his lips. He seemed to be considering the plausibility of this. Finally he said that it was necessary to state that there were two such airplanes, both of them flown by young Americans, both lost in the mountains in the calamitous summer of nineteen fifteen.

He drew deeply upon the cigarette and blew the smoke toward the fire. Certain facts were known, he said. There was common ground and there one could begin. This airplane had sat in the high desert mountains of Sonora and the wind and the blowing sand had flayed it of its fabric and passing indians had pried away and carried off the brass inspection plate from the instrument panel for amulet and there it had languished on in that wild upcountry lost and unclaimed and indeed unclaimable for nearly thirty years. Thus far all was a single history. Whether there be two planes or one. Whichever plane was spoken of it was the same.

He drew carefully at the stub of the cigarette between his thumb and forefinger, one dark eye asquint against the smoke rising past his nose in the motionless air. Finally Billy asked him whether it made any difference which plane it was since there was no difference to be spoken of. The gypsy nodded. He seemed to approve of the question although he did not answer it. He said that the father of the dead pilot had contracted for the removal of the airplane to a place on the border just east of Palomas. He had sent his agent to the town of Madera—pueblo que conoce—and this agent was himself such a man as might ask just such a question.

He smiled. He smoked the last of the cigarette to an ash and let the ash fall into the fire and blew the smoke slowly after. He licked his thumb and wiped it on the knee of his trousers. He said that for men of the road the reality of things was always of consequence. He said that the strategist did not confuse his devices with the reality of the world for then what would become of him? El mentiroso debe primero saber la verdad, he said. De acuerdo?

He nodded toward the fire. The watercarrier rose and jostled the coals with a stick and fed more wood under the pail and returned to his place again. The gypsy waited till he was done. Then he continued. He spoke of the identity of the little canvas biplane as having no meaning except in its history and he said that since this tattered artifact was known to have a sister in the same condition the question of identity had indeed been raised. He said that men assume the truth of a thing to reside in that thing without regard to the opinions of those beholding it while that which is fraudulent is held to be so no matter how closely it might duplicate the required appearance. If the airplane which their client has paid to be freighted out of the wilderness and brought to the border were in fact not the machine in which the son has died then its close resemblance to that machine is hardly a thing in its favor but is rather one more twist in the warp of the world for the deceiving of men. Where then is the truth of this? The reverence attached to the artifacts of history is a thing men feel. One could even say that what endows any thing with significance is solely the history in which it has participated. Yet wherein does that history lie?

The gypsy looked away upriver to where the airplane sat beyond the trees. He seemed to ponder its shape there. As if were contained in that primitive construction some yet uncoded clue to the campaigns of the revolution, the strategies of Angeles, the tactics of Villa. Y por qué lo quiere el cliente? he said. Que despues de todo no es nada más que el ataúd de su hijo?

No one answered. After a while the gypsy continued. He said that he'd thought at one time that the client wished simply to have the aircraft as a memento. He whose son's bones were themselves long scattered on the sierra. Now his thought was different. He said that as long as the airplane remained in the mountains then its history was of a piece. Suspended in time. Its presence on the mountain was its whole story frozen in a single image for all to contemplate. The client thought and he thought rightly that could he remove that wreckage from where it lay year after year in rain and snow and sun then and then only could he bleed it of its power to commandeer his dreams. The gypsy gestured with one hand in a slow suave gesture. La historia del hijo termina en las montañas, he said. Y por allá queda la realidad de él.

He shook his head. He said that simple tasks often prove most difficult. He said that in any case this gift from the mountains had no real power to quiet an old man's heart because once more its journey would be stayed and nothing would be changed. And the identity of the airplane would be brought into question which in the mountains was no question at all. It was forcing a decision. It was a difficult matter. And as is so often the case God had finally taken a hand and decided things himself. For ultimately both airplanes were carried down from the mountain and one was in the Río Papigochic and the other was before them. Como lo ve.

They waited. Rafael rose again and prodded the fire and he lifted the lid from the pail and stirred the steaming soup within and re-covered it. The gypsy in the meantime had rolled another cigarette and lit it. He considered how to continue.

Town of Madera. A stained and whimsical map printed on poor paper already severing at the folds. A canvas bankbag full of silver pesos. Two men met almost by chance neither of whom would ever trust the other. The gypsy thinned his lips in what would not quite pass for a smile. He said that where expectations are few disappointments are rare. They had gone into the mountains in the fall two years ago and they had built a sled from the limbs of trees and by this conveyance had brought the wreckage to the rim of the great gorge of the Papigochic River. There with rope and windlass they would lower the thing to the river and there build a raft by which to ferry it carcass and wings and struts all down to the bridge on the Mesa Tres Ríos road and from there overland to the border west of Palomas. Snow drove them from the high country before they ever reached the river.

The other men about that pale dayfire seemed to attend his words closely. As if they themselves were only recent conscriptees to this enterprise. The gypsy spoke slowly. He described to them the nature of the country where the airplane had gone down. The wildness of it and the high grassy vegas and the deep barrancas where the days were polar in their brevity, barrancas in the floor of which great rivers looked no more than bits of string. They quit the country and returned again in the spring. They had no money left. A seeress tried to warn them back. One of their own. He had weighed the woman's words, but he knew what she did not. That if a dream can tell the future it can also thwart that future. For God will not permit that we shall know what is to come. He is bound to no one that the world unfold just so upon its course and those who by some sorcery or by some dream might come to pierce the veil that lies so darkly over all that is before them may serve by just that vision to cause that God should wrench the world from its heading and set it upon another course altogether and then where stands the sorcerer? Where the dreamer and his dream? He paused that all might contemplate this. That he might contemplate it himself. Then he continued. He spoke of the cold in the mountains at that season. He populated the terrain for them with certain birds and animals. Parrots. Tigers. Men of another time living in the caves of that country so remote that the world had overlooked to kill them. The Tarahumara standing half naked along the sheer rock wall of the void while the fuselage and the wingstructure of the broken plane dangled in the blue and grew small and turned slowly in the deepening gulf of the barranca silent and chimeless and far below them the shapes of vultures in slow spirals like bits of ash in an updraft.

He spoke of the rapids in the river and the great rocks that stood in the gorge and the rain in the mountains in the night and the way the river went howling through the narrows like a train and at night the rain which had fallen for miles into that ultimate sundering of the earth's rind hissed in their driftwood fires and the solid rock about them through which the water roared would shudder like a woman and if they spoke to one another no words formed in the air for the awful noise in that nether world.

They passed nine days in the gorge while the rain fell and the river rose until at last they were socketed high in a rocky crevice like refugent woodmice seven of them without food or fire and the whole gorge trembling as if the world itself were like to cleave beneath them and swallow up all and they posted watches in the night until he himself asked what it was they watched for? What do if it came?

The brass cymbal over the bucket rose slightly along one edge and a green froth belched forth and ran down the side of the bucket and the cymbal fell again soundlessly. The gitano reached and tipped the end of ash from his cigarette thoughtfully into the coals.

Nueve días. Nueve noches. Sin comida. Sin fuego. Sin nada. The river rose and they tied the raft with the windlass ropes and then with vines and the river rose and ate away the raft by pole and by plank and nothing to be done for it and the rain fell. First the wings were swept away. They hung he and his men from the rocks in the howling darkness like beleaguered apes and screamed mutely to one another in the maelstrom and his primo Macio descended to secure the fuselage although what use it could be without the wings none knew and Macio himself was nearly swept away and lost. On the morning of the tenth day the rain ceased. They made their way along the rocks in the wet gray dawn but all sign of their enterprise had vanished in the flood as if it had never been at all. The river continued to rise and on the morning of the day following while they sat staring at the hypnotic flume below them a drowned man shot out of the cataract upriver like a pale enormous fish and circled once facedown in the froth of the eddywater beneath them as if he were looking for something on the river's floor and then he was sucked away downriver to continue his journey. He'd come already a long way in his travels by the look of him for his clothes were gone and much of his skin and all but the faintest nap of hair upon his skull all scrubbed away by his passage over the river rocks. In his circling in the froth he moved all loosely and disjointed as if there were no bones to him. Some incubus or mannequin. But when he passed beneath them they could see revealed in him that of which men were made that had better been kept from them. They could see bones and ligaments and they could see the tables of his smallribs and through the leached and abraded skin the darker shapes of organs within. He circled and gathered speed and then exited in the roaring flume as if he had pressing work downriver.

The gypsy blew softly through his teeth. He studied the fire.

Y entonces qué? said Billy.

He shook his head. As if the recollection of these things were a trial to him. Ultimately they had climbed out of the gorge and made their way out of the mountains as far as Sahuaripa and there they had waited until at last a truck came droning down the all but impassable road from Divisaderos and they rode in the bed of this truck for four days, sitting with shovels across their knees, shapeless with mud, climbing down times uncounted to dig and pitch in the muck like convicts while the driver shouted at them from the cab and then groaning on again. To Bacanora. To Tonichi. North again out of Nuri to San Nicolás and Yécora and on through the mountains to Temosachic and Madera where the man with whom they had first contracted would demand the return of the monies advanced them.

The gypsy pitched the stub of his cigarette into the fire and crossed his boots before him and drew them to him in his hands and sat leaning forward studying the flames. Billy asked him if the airplane had ever been found and he said that it had not for indeed there was nothing to find. Billy then asked him why they had returned to Madera at all and the man weighed this question. Finally he said that he did not believe that it was by chance that he had first met this man and been hired to go into the mountains nor was it chance that sent the rains and flooded the Papigochic. They sat. The tender of the pail rose a third time and stirred it and set it by to cool. Billy looked at the solemn faces about the fire. The bones beneath the olive skin. World wanderers. They squatted lightly there in that ring in the wood, at once vigilant and unconstrained. They stood in no proprietary relationship to anything, scarcely even to the space they occupied. Out of their anterior lives they had arrived at the same understanding as their fathers before them. That movement itself is a form of property. He looked at them and he said that the airplane they now freighted north along the road was then some other airplane.

The black eyes all shifted to the leader of their small clan. He sat for a long time. It was very quiet. Out on the road one of the oxen began to piss loudly. Finally he shaped his mouth and said that he believed that fate had intervened in the matter for its own good reasons. He said that fate might enter into the affairs of men in order to contravene them or set them at naught but to say that fate could deny the true and uphold the false would seem to be a contradictory view of things. To speak of a will in the world that ran counter to one's own was one thing. To speak of such a will that ran counter to the truth was quite another, for then all was rendered senseless. Billy then asked him if it was his notion that the false plane had been swept away by God in order to single out the true and the gypsy said that it was not. When Billy said that he had understood him to say that it was God who had ultimately made the decision concerning the two planes the gypsy said that he believed that to be so but he did not believe that by this act God had spoken to anyone. He said that he was not a superstitious man. The gypsies heard this out and then turned to Billy to see how he would respond. Billy said that it seemed to him that the freighters did not hold the identity of the airplane to be of any great consequence but the gitano only turned and studied him with those dark and troubled eyes. He said that it was indeed of consequence and that it was in fact the whole burden of their inquiry. From a certain perspective one might even hazard to say that the great trouble with the world was that that which survived was held in hard evidence as to past events. A false authority clung to what persisted, as if those artifacts of the past which had endured had done so by some act of their own will. Yet the witness could not survive the witnessing. In the world that came to be that which prevailed could never speak for that which perished but could only parade its own arrogance. It pretended symbol and summation of the vanished world but was neither. He said that in any case the past was little more than a dream and its force in the world greatly exaggerated. For the world was made new each day and it was only men's clinging to its vanished husks that could make of that world one husk more.

La cáscara no es la cosa, he said. It looked the same. But it was not.

Y la tercera historia? said Billy.

La tercera historia, said the gypsy, es ésta. Él existe en la historia de las historias. Es que ultimadamente la verdad no puede quedar en ningún otro lugar sino en el habla. He held his hands before him and looked at his palms. As if they may have been at some work not of his own doing. The past, he said, is always this argument between counterclaimants. Memories dim with age. There is no repository for our images. The loved ones who visit us in dreams are strangers. To even see aright is effort. We seek some witness but the world will not provide one. This is the third history. It is the history that each man makes alone out of what is left to him. Bits of wreckage. Some bones. The words of the dead. How make a world of this? How live in that world once made?

He looked toward the pail. The steam had ceased rising and he nodded and stood. Rafael rose and took up the musette bag and slung it over one shoulder and picked up the pail and all followed the gypsy up through the river woods to where the horse lay and there one of the men knelt and raised up the horse's head from the ground while Rafael took from the bag a leather funnel and a length of rubber hose and they gripped the horse's mouth and opened up its jaws while he greased the hose and ran it down the horse's gullet and twisted the funnel over the end and then they poured with no ceremony the contents of the pail into the horse.

When they had done the gypsy washed again the dried blood

from the horse's chest and examined the wound and then dredged up a double handful of the cooked leaves from the floor of the bucket and packed them against the wound in a poultice which he bound up with burlap sacking and tied with cord over the horse's neck and behind its forelegs. When he was done he rose and stepped back and stood looking down at the animal with long contemplation. The horse looked very strange indeed. It half raised its head and blinked at them and then wheezed and stretched its neck in the leaves and lay there. Bueno, said the gypsy. He looked at Billy and smiled.

They stood in the road and the gitano pulled the brim of his hat down level and slid the scrimshawed length of birdbone which he used for a drawtie up under his chin and looked at the oxen and at the float and the airplane. He looked out through the trees to where the rolled soogan that held Boyd's body was wedged in the low branches of the tascate tree. He looked at Billy.

Estoy regresándole a mi país, Billy said.

The gypsy smiled again and looked north along the road. Otros huesos, he said. Otros hermanos. He said that as a child he had traveled a good deal in the land of the gavacho. He said he'd followed his father through the streets of western cities and they collected odds of junk from the houses there and sold them. He said that sometimes in trunks and boxes they would come upon old photographs and tintypes. These likenesses had value only to the living who had known them and with the passage of years of such there were none. But his father was a gypsy and had a gypsy mind and he would hang these cracked and fading likenesses by clothespins from the crosswires above the cart. There they remained. No one ever asked about them. No one wished to buy them. After a while the boy took them for a cautionary tale and he would search those sepia faces for some secret thing they might divulge to him from the days of their mortality. The faces became very familiar to him. By their antique clothing they were long dead and he pondered them where they sat posed on porchsteps, seated in chairs in a yard. All past and all future and all stillborn dreams cauterized in that brief encapture of light within the camera's closet. He searched those faces. Looks of vague discontent. Looks of rue. Perhaps some burgeoning bitterness at things in fact not yet come to be which yet were now forever past.

His father said that the gorgios were an inscrutable lot and so he found them to be. In and out of all depicting. The photographs that hung from the wire became for him a form of query to the world. He sensed in them a certain power and he guessed that the gorgios considered them bad luck for they would scarcely look at them but the truth was darker yet as truth is wont to be.

What he came to see was that as the kinfolk in their fading stills could have no value save in another's heart so it was with that heart also in another's in a terrible and endless attrition and of any other value there was none. Every representation was an idol. Every likeness a heresy. In their images they had thought to find some small immortality but oblivion cannot be appeased. This was what his father meant to tell him and this was why they were men of the road. This was the why of the yellowing daguerreotypes swinging by their clothespegs from the cross-wire of his father's cart.

He said that journeys involving the company of the dead were notorious for their difficulty but that in truth every journey was so accompanied. He said that in his opinion it was imprudent to suppose that the dead have no power to act in the world, for their power is great and their influence often most weighty with just those who suspect it least. He said that what men do not understand is that what the dead have quit is itself no world but is also only the picture of the world in men's hearts. He said that the world cannot be quit for it is eternal in whatever form as are all things within it. In those faces that shall now be forever nameless among their outworn chattels there is writ a message that can never be spoken because time would always slay the messenger before he could ever arrive.

He smiled. Pensamos, he said, que somos las víctimas del tiempo. En realidad la vía del mundo no es fijada en ningún

lugar. Cómo sería posible? Nosotros mismos somos nuestra propia jornada. Y por eso somos el tiempo también. Somos lo
mismo. Fugitivo. Inescrutable. Desapíadado.

He turned and spoke in romany to the others and one of them
took a bullwhip from the keepers nailed to the sideboards of the
float and uncoiled it and sent it looping through the air where
the crack of it echoed like a gunshot in the woods and the caravan
lurched into motion. The gypsy turned and smiled. He said
that perhaps they would meet again upon some other road for
the world was not so wide as men imagined. When Billy asked
him how much he owed him for his services he dismissed the
debt with a wave of his hand. Para el camino, he said. Then he
turned and set off up the road after the others. Billy stood
holding the thin sheaf of bloodstained banknotes he'd taken from
his pocket. He called out to the gypsy and the gypsy turned.

Gracias, he called.

The gypsy raised one hand. Por nada.

Yo no soy un hombre del camino.

But the gypsy only smiled and waved one hand. He said that
the way of the road was the rule for all upon it. He said that on
the road there were no special cases. Then he turned and strode
on after the others.

IN THE EVENING the horse rose and stood on trembling legs.
He did not halter it but only walked alongside the animal out
to the river where it stepped very carefully into the water and
drank endlessly. In the evening while he was fixing his supper
from the tortillas and goatcheese the gypsies had left him a rider
came along the road. Solitary. Whistling. He stopped among
the trees. Then he came on more slowly.

Billy stood and walked out to the road and the rider halted
and sat his horse. He pushed his hat back slightly, the better to
see, the better to be seen. He looked at Billy and at the fire and
at the horse lying in the woods beyond.

Buenas tardes, said Billy.

The rider nodded. He was riding a good horse and he wore good boots and a good Stetson hat and he was smoking a small black puro. He took the puro out of his mouth and spat and put it back.

You speak american? he said.

Yessir. I do.

I thought you looked about halfway sensible. What the hell are you doin out here? What's wrong with that horse?

Well sir, I guess I'm mindin my own business. I reckon I could even say the same about the horse.

The man paid no attention. He aint dead is he?

No. He aint. He got cut by roadagents.

Cut by roadagents?

Yessir.

You mean they nutted him?

No. I mean they stabbed him in the chest with a pigsticker.

Whatever in the hell for?

You tell me.

I dont know.

Well I dont either.

The rider sat smoking contemplatively. He looked out across the landscape to the west of the river. I dont understand this country, he said. Not the first thing about it. You aint got any coffee anywheres about your person I dont reckon?

I got some perkin. You want to light I got some supper fixin. It aint much but you're welcome.

Well I'd take it as a kindness.

He stepped down wearily and passed the bridlereins behind his back and adjusted his hat again and came forward leading the horse. Not the first damn thing, he said. Did you see my airplane come through here?

They squatted by the fire as the woods darkened and they waited for the coffee to boil. I never would of thought about them gypsies stickin the way they done, the man said. I had my doubts about em. One thing about me, when I'm wrong I'll admit it.

Well. That's a good trait to have.

Yes it is.

They ate the beans rolled up in the tortillas together with the melted cheese. The cheese was rank and goaty. Billy lifted the lid from the coffeepot with a stick and looked in and put the lid back. He looked at the man. The man was seated tailorwise on the ground holding the soles of his boots together with one hand.

You look like you might of been down here a while, the man said.

I dont know. What does that look like?

Like you need to get back.

Well. You probably right about that. This is my third trip. It's the only time I was ever down here that I got what I come after. But it sure as hell wasnt what I wanted.

The man nodded. He didnt seem to need to know what that was. I'll tell you what, he said. It will be one cold day in hell when you catch me down here again. A frosty son of a bitch. I'll tell you that flat out.

Billy poured the coffee. They drank. The coffee was vilely hot in the tin cups but the man seemed not to notice. He drank and sat looking out through the dark woods toward the river and the silver panels of the river plaited over the gravel bars in the moonlight. Downriver the nacre bowl of the moon sat swaged into the reefs of cloud like a candled skull. He flipped the dregs of coffee into the darkness. I better get on, he said.

You welcome to stay.

I enjoy to ride of a night.

Well.

I believe a man can even cover more ground.

There's robbers all in this country, Billy said.

Robbers, the man said. He contemplated the fire. After a while he took one of the thin black cigars from his pocket and studied that. Then he bit the tip from it and spat it into the fire.

You smoke cigars?

I aint never took it up.

It aint against your religion?

Not that I know of.

The man leaned and pulled a burning billet from the fire and lit the cigar with it. It took some lighting to get it to burn. When he had it going he put the piece of wood back in the fire and blew a smoke ring and then blew a smaller one through the center of it.

What time did they leave out of here? he said.

I dont know. Noon maybe.

They wont make ten mile.

It might of been later.

Ever time I lay over somewheres they have a breakdown. They aint failed a time. My own fault. I keep gettin sidetracked by them señoritas. I liked them mamselles over yonder awful well too. I like it when they dont speak no english. Did you get over there?

No.

He reached into the fire and took out the stick he'd used to light his cigar and whipped away the flame and then turned and drew in the dark behind him with the red and smoldering end of it like a child. After a while he put it back in the fire again.

How bad's your horse? he said.

I dont know. He's been down two days.

You ought to of got that gypsy to see about him. They're supposed to know everthing there is about a horse.

Is that right?

I dont know. I know they're good at makin a sick one look well long enough to sell it.

I aint lookin to sell it.

I'll tell you what you better do.

What's that?

Keep this here fire built up.

Why is that.

Mountain lions is why. Horsemeat's their favorite kind.

Billy nodded. I always heard that, he said.

You know why you always heard it?

Why I always heard it?

Yeah.

No. Why?

Cause it's right is why.

You think most of what a man hears is right?

That's been my experience.

It aint been mine.

The man sat smoking and contemplating the fire. After a while he said: It aint been mine neither. I just said that. I wasnt over yonder like I said neither. I'm a four-F. Always was, always will be.

Did those gypsies bring that airplane out of the sierras and down the Papigochic River?

Is that what they said?

Yeah.

That airplane come out of a barn on the Taliafero Ranch out of Flores Magón. It couldnt even fly where you're talkin about. The ceiling on that plane aint but six thousand feet.

Was the man that flew it killed in it?

Not that I know of.

Was that why you come down here? To find that plane and take it back?

I come down here cause I'd knocked up a girl in McAllen Texas and her daddy wanted to shoot me.

Billy stared into the fire.

You talk about runnin into the arms of that which you have fled from, the man said. You ever been shot?

No.

I have twice. The last time was in downtown Cuauhtémoc broad daylight on a Saturday afternoon. Everbody run. There was two Mennonite women picked me up out of the street and loaded me into a wagon or I'd still be layin there.

Where'd they shoot you at?

Right here, he said. He turned and pushed the hair back above his right temple. See there? You can see it.

He leaned and spat into the fire and looked at the cigar and put it back in his mouth. He smoked. I aint crazy, he said.

I never said you was.

No. You might of thought it though.

You might of thought it about me.

Might.

Did that happen or did you just say it?

No. It happened.

My brother was shot and killed down here. I'd come down to take him home. He was shot and killed south of here. Town called San Lorenzo.

You can get killed down here about as quick as anything else you might decide to do.

My daddy was shot and killed in New Mexico. That's his horse layin over yonder.

It's a cruel world, the man said.

He come out of Texas in nineteen and nineteen. He was about the age I am now. He was not born there. He was born in Missouri.

I had a uncle was born in Missouri. His daddy fell off a wagon drunk in the mud one night goin through there and that's how it come about that he was born in Missouri.

My mama was from off a ranch up in De Baca County. Her mother was a fullblooded Mexican didnt speak no english. She lived with us up until she died. I had a younger sister died when I was seven but I remember her just as plain. I went to Fort Sumner to try and find her grave but I couldnt find it. Her name was Margaret. I always liked that name for a girl. If I ever had a girl that's what I'd name her.

I better get on.

Well.

Mind what I said about your fire.

Well.

You sound like you've had your share of troubles in this world.

I just got to jabberin. I been more fortunate than most. There aint but one life worth livin and I was born to it. That's worth all the rest. My bud was better at it than me. He was a born natural. He was smarter than me too. Not just about horses. About everthing. Daddy knew it too. He knew it and he knew I knew it and that's all there was to say about it.

I better get on.

You take care.

I will do it.

He rose, he adjusted his hat. The moon was high and the sky had cleared. The river where it lay behind the trees looked like poured metal.

This world will never be the same, the rider said. Did you know that?

I know it. It aint now.

Four days later he set out north along the river with the remains of his brother trestled up in a travois he'd made from sapling poles dragging behind the horse. They were three days reaching the border. He rode past the first of the white obelisks marking the international boundary line west of Dog Springs and he crossed the ancient dry reservoir there. The old earthworks were broken out in places and he rode across the cracked clay floor of the reservoir with the travois poles rasping behind him. There were prints in the clay of cattle and antelope and of coyotes that had crossed after some recent rain and he came upon a place that was runed over all about with the random trident of cranetracks where the birds had glided in and stalked about upon that barren mud. He slept that night in his own country and he had a dream wherein he saw God's pilgrims laboring upon a darkened verge in the last of the twilight of that day and they seemed to be returning from some deep enterprise that was not of war nor were they yet in flight but rather seemed coming from some labor to which perhaps these and all other things stood subjugate. A dark arroyo separated him from the place where they were going and he looked to see if he could tell by the nature of their implements what it was that they had been about but they carried none and they toiled on in silence against a sky that was darkening all around and then they were gone. When he woke in the round darkness about he thought that something had indeed passed in the desert night and he was awake a long time but he had no sense that it would ever return again.

The day following he rode through Hermanas and out along the dusty road west and that evening he sat the horse in the crossroads in front of the store in Hatchita and he looked away toward the southwest where the late sun was on the Animas Peaks and he knew that he would not be going there again. He crossed the Animas Valley slowly dragging the travois and he was all day in the doing of it. When he entered the town of Animas the morning of the following day it was Ash Wednesday by the calendar and the first folk he saw were Mexicans with sootmarks on their foreheads, five children and a woman walking singlefile along the dusty edge of the road out from the town. He wished them a good day but they only blessed themselves on seeing the body in the travois and passed on. He bought a spade at the hardware store and set out south from the town till he came to the little cemetery and he hobbled the horse and left it to graze outside the gates while he worked at digging the grave.

He was down to his waist in the dry dirt and caliche when the sheriff pulled up and got out and walked down through the gate.

I suspicioned it was you, he said.

Billy paused and leaned on the spade and squinted up at him. He'd taken off his rag of a shirt and he reached and picked it up off the ground and wiped the sweat from his forehead with it and stood waiting.

That's your brother layin yonder I take it, the sheriff said.

Yessir.

The sheriff shook his head. He looked off out over the country. As if there was something about it that you just couldnt quite lay your hand on. He looked down at Billy.

There aint much to say, is there?

No sir. Not much.

Well. You caint just travel around the country buryin people. Let me go see the judge and see if I can get him to issue a death certificate. I aint even sure whose property that is you're diggin in.

Yessir.

You come see me in Lordsburg tomorrow.

All right.

The sheriff pulled his hat down and shook his head again and turned and walked back out through the gate toward his car.

Days to come he rode north to Silver City and west to Duncan Arizona and north again through the mountains to Glenwood, to Reserve. He worked for the Carrizozos and for the GS's and he left for no reason he could name and in July of that year he drifted south again to Silver City and took the old road east past the Santa Rita mines and on through San Lorenzo and the Black Range. A wind was coming off the mountains to the north and the prairie before him had darkened under the moving clouds. The horse shuffled along with its head down and the rider rode very erect with his hat pulled low across his eyes. The country was all catclaw and creosote on a gravel plain and there were no fences and little grass. A few miles on and he struck the blacktop road and sat the horse. A truck whined past and drew away into the distance. Eighty miles away the raw rock ranges of the Organ Mountains shining under the clouds in the paneled light of the late sun. As he watched they faded into shadow. The wind coming off the desert had spits of rain in it. He crossed through the bar ditch and rode up onto the blacktop and slowed the horse and looked back. The panicgrass volunteered along the selvedge of the road heeled and twisted in the wind. He turned back along the highway toward some buildings he'd seen. The castoff tirecasings from the overland trucks lay coiled and corrugated by the highwayside like the sloughed and sunblacked hides of old dryland saurians shed along the tarmac roadway there. The wind blew down from the north and then the rain blew down and went gusting in sheets across the road before him.

They were three building of adobe set just off the road that had at one time been a waystation in that country and the roofs were all but gone and most of the vigas carried off. There was an old rusty orange gaspump out front with the glass broken out of the top of it. He led the horse into the largest of the buildings and unsaddled it and stood the saddle in the floor. In one corner was a pile of hay and he kicked at it to loosen it up or perhaps just to see what it might contain. It was dry and dusty and held a depression where something had been sleeping. He went out and walked around behind the building and came back with an old hubcap and poured water in it from the canvas waterbag and held it for the horse to drink. Out through the wrecked wood sash of the windowframe he could see the road shining blackly in the rain.

He got his blankets and spread them in the hay and he was sitting eating sardines out of a tin and watching the rain when a yellow dog rounded the side of the building and entered through the open door and stopped. It looked first at the horse. Then it swung its head and looked at him. It was an old dog gone gray about the muzzle and it was horribly crippled in its hindquarters and its head was askew someway on its body and it moved grotesquely. An arthritic and illjoined thing that crabbed sideways and sniffed at the floor to pick up the man's scent and then raised its head and nudged the air with its nose and tried to sort him from the shadows with its milky half blind eyes.

Billy set the sardines carefully beside him. He could smell the thing in the damp. It stood there inside the door with the rain falling in the weeds and gravel behind it and it was wet and wretched and so scarred and broken that it might have been patched up out of parts of dogs by demented vivisectionists. It

stood and then it shook itself in its grotesque fashion and hobbled moaning to the far corner of the room where it looked back
and then turned three times and lay down.

He wiped the blade of the knife on his breeches leg and laid
the knife across the tin and looked about. He pried a loose clod
of mud from the wall and threw it. The dog made a strange
moaning sound but it did not move.

Git, he shouted.

The dog moaned, it lay as before.

He swore softly and rose to his feet and cast about for a
weapon. The horse looked at him and it looked at the dog. He
crossed the room and went out in the rain and walked around
the side of the building. When he came back he had in his fist
a threefoot length of waterpipe and with it he advanced upon
the dog. Go on, he shouted. Git.

The dog rose moaning and slouched away down the wall and
limped out into the yard. When he turned to go back to his
blankets it slank past him into the building again. He turned
and ran at it with the pipe and it scrabbled away.

He followed it. Outside it had stopped at the edge of the road
and it stood in the rain looking back. It had perhaps once been
a hunting dog, perhaps left for dead in the mountains or by
some highwayside. Repository of ten thousand indignities and
the harbinger of God knew what. He bent and clawed up a
handful of small rocks from the gravel apron and slung them.
The dog raised its misshapen head and howled weirdly. He
advanced upon it and it set off up the road. He ran after it and
threw more rocks and shouted at it and he slung the length of
pipe. It went clanging and skittering up the road behind the dog
and the dog howled again and began to run, hobbling brokenly
on its twisted legs with the strange head agoggle on its neck. As
it went it raised its mouth sideways and howled again with a
terrible sound. Something not of this earth. As if some awful
composite of grief had broke through from the preterite world.
It tottered away up the road in the rain on its stricken legs and

as it went it howled again and again in its heart's despair until it was gone from all sight and all sound in the night's onset.

HE WOKE in the white light of the desert noon and sat up in the ranksmelling blankets. The shadow of the bare wood windowsash stenciled onto the opposite wall began to pale and fade as he watched. As if a cloud were passing over the sun. He kicked out of the blankets and pulled on his boots and his hat and rose and walked out. The road was a pale gray in the light and the light was drawing away along the edges of the world. Small birds had wakened in the roadside desert bracken and begun to chitter and to flit about and out on the blacktop bands of tarantulas that had been crossing the road in the dark like landcrabs stood frozen at their articulations, arch as marionettes, testing with their measured octave tread the sudden jointed shadows of themselves beneath them.

He looked out down the road and he looked toward the fading light. Darkening shapes of cloud all along the northern rim. It had ceased raining in the night and a broken rainbow or watergall stood out on the desert in a dim neon bow and he looked again at the road which lay as before yet more dark and darkening still where it ran on to the east and where there was no sun and there was no dawn and when he looked again toward the north the light was drawing away faster and that noon in which he'd woke was now become an alien dusk and now an alien dark and the birds that flew had lighted and all had hushed once again in the bracken by the road.

He walked out. A cold wind was coming down off the mountains. It was shearing off the western slopes of the continent where the summer snow lay above the timberline and it was crossing through the high fir forests and among the poles of the aspens and it was sweeping over the desert plain below. It had ceased raining in the night and he walked out on the road and called for the dog. He called and called. Standing in that inexplicable darkness. Where there was no sound anywhere save only the wind. After a while he sat in the road. He took off his hat and placed it on the tarmac before him and he bowed his head and held his face in his hands and wept. He sat there for a long time and after a while the east did gray and after a while the right and godmade sun did rise, once again, for all and without distinction.